FRAMED BY LOVE

"There's not a man on this ranch who believes you're guilty."

"They've all been wonderful, but there's not one of them who believes a pretty woman *can* commit a crime."

"An investigation would cost a lot of money. If you have it, why are you wasting your time with me? You ought to hire a professional."

"How do I know he wouldn't turn against me? No one seems able to stand up to that judge."

"How do you know I could?"

She looked directly into his eyes. "I just do."

Trinity hadn't expected that. It caused the knot which had been in his stomach for several days to tighten with a jerk.

"You don't know that. I could be a bounty hunter or a sheriff's deputy, or even a private investigator."

Her gaze didn't falter. "You could, but you're not."

LEIGH GREENWOOD

ARIZONA EMBRACE

ZEBRA BOOKS
KENSINGTON PUBLISHING CORP.

ZEBRA BOOKS

are published by

Kensington Publishing Corp.
475 Park Avenue South
New York, NY 10016

First Printing: May, 1993

Printed in the United States of America

Chapter One

Arizona, 1878.

"Just a few more weeks, and another murderer will hang."

Trinity lowered his field glasses. He spoke the words into the wind, something he did a lot more these days. Hangmen didn't have friends.

Not that Trinity Smith was a hangman . . . but he felt like one. It wasn't a feeling he liked, but he had become aware of it over the last few years. During the past month it had settled over him like a thick fog, obscuring his vision and making him wonder what lay ahead.

Never before in thirteen years of tracking down convicted killers and returning them to justice had he doubted the justice of what he did. Murderers had to be punished. They couldn't be allowed to flout the judgment of society, or decent men and women wouldn't be safe.

Still the uneasy feeling nagged at his conscience.

Trinity reminded himself that entire towns had turned out to thank him. They had tried to give him money, make him their sheriff, give him cows and land so he would settle nearby and continue to protect them, but he never accepted a reward. Knowing he had brought a murderer to justice had been all the reward he wanted.

Trinity raised his field glasses and surveyed the scene below him once again.

Mountain Valley ranch lay snuggled between two low ridges in Arizona's Verde River valley. Through the mountainside scattering of pines, fir and spruce, their top-knots waving in the breeze, he glimpsed several meadows covered in the pinkish purple of an abundant wildflower. Everywhere grass grew to a height and thickness that testified to a winter of heavy snow and a spring of generous rains.

The valley lay quiet below him. Something whispered this was a place where men lived together peacefully and in harmony with nature. It felt like a place where a man could spend his life the way he wanted, without the pressures of the outside world, without having to deal with the evil in people.

Yet, he knew his feelings betrayed him. Evil had brought him to this unspoiled valley. Evil clothed in innocence, beauty, and tranquility. He would hunt it down just as he had so many times before.

Still, the feeling wouldn't leave him, the presentiment that he, rather than the person he hunted, posed the greater danger. At first, unable to figure out what bothered him, he had shrugged it off. Now he could no longer ignore it. Nothing like this had ever happened to him before, but the feeling grew stronger every time he looked at the valley.

Why?

He couldn't doubt the justice of his mission. The killer had been caught virtually in the act. A jury sat in judgment and returned a verdict of guilty. The judge had pronounced the sentence of death by hanging. No one doubted the guilt of the killer or the justice of the verdict.

Then why did he feel so uneasy? All he had to do was do his job and move on.

But there was something different this time. The killer was a woman, and she had murdered her husband.

The muted footfall of an approaching horse caused Victoria Davidge to look up from the bed of yellow poppies she was transplanting. Visitors to her uncle's ranch were so rare she didn't stop to remember she was alone until a man riding a powerful dark bay gelding came into view.

A stranger!

A stab of fear caused her heart to skip a beat; a vein in her temple began to throb. She felt her body tense. She took a deep breath to help herself relax. It didn't work. Her fingers clenched into tight fists, breaking the delicate plant she held in her hand. Even as she discarded the ruined flower, she remained helplessly in the grip of suffocating anxiety.

Victoria hated to feel this way, but she had to be wary of strangers. Her life depended on it.

Would she ever be able to hear the sound of approaching hoofbeats without tensing with fear? Or look into the face of a stranger without caring if he knew her name? Would she ever be able to live her life without worrying that the next day, or the next visitor, might destroy everything?

Yet, for the first time she could remember, the familiar wave of nausea didn't rise in her throat. Neither did she feel the need to hide behind the trellis of a newly leafed climbing rose her uncle had given her two years earlier. She brushed the loose, moist soil from her fingers. Rather than allow her hands to clutch at the heavy material of her skirt, she clasped them in front of her.

Victoria took a step forward to get a better view. Instinctively she reached up to pull the wide brim of her straw hat farther down over her eyes. Her hand slowed, then paused, her fingers not yet touching the brim.

This man was different.

Don't be silly. You can't tell anything about a man just by watching him ride a horse.

But she could.

He approached with a lazy assurance that could have come only from years of matching his skills against all comers, a confidence as apparent in his posture as in his unhurried pace. Even though she'd been constantly warned her safety depended upon no one knowing the location of her hiding place, Victoria felt irresistibly drawn to this cool, self-confident man.

As she started forward, she detected the sound of a second horse. Turning toward a stand of pines which grew along the ridge behind the ranch, she saw Buc Stringer, her uncle's foreman, ride out of the trees and head toward the bunkhouse. He would ride between her and the stranger. He would talk to the man and see what he wanted. There would be no need for her to reveal her presence.

Buc would be angry if she did.

It had been such a long time since Victoria had talked with anyone from outside the ranch, but she reluctantly decided to stay in her garden. Buc and her uncle had risked their lives to bring her to Arizona. They had organized the ranch around her safety. She couldn't ignore all their precautions for nothing more than a brief chat with a passerby.

She stepped back into her garden. She still had a dozen wild iris to set out. Maybe he would be gone by the time she was done, and perhaps temptation would be gone, too.

But curiosity about this man overrode caution. Shielded by branches heavy with purple lilac, Victoria drew closer.

Trinity Smith rode with all his senses alert. He had no reason to expect trouble, but in the territories a man learned to be cautious.

Or he died.

He allowed his horse to pick its way through the shallows of the wide, meandering stream that ran though the center of the valley. Occasionally he would move into deeper water to avoid rock outcroppings or the overhanging limbs of trees which lined the banks, grew in clusters in the valley, and climbed the hillsides in thinning ranks.

The plop of his horse's hooves as they struck the water, the soft swish as they pulled free of the heavy gravel in the bottom of the stream, barely intruded on the sound of water rushing over rocks and swirling in eddies. Patches of unmelted snow on distant mountain peaks still fed this ice-cold stream, but he could feel the promise of summer's heat in the afternoon air.

Trinity pulled up when the ranch buildings came in sight.

He saw only two, a ranch house and a bunkhouse, each large and well-made, each built of unpainted wood turned grey with age. Their builder had positioned the buildings to allow the defenders to cover an attack from any direction. They had also leveled the ground and cleared all the rocks for a hundred yards around the enclave.

The occupants had come to stay.

He counted two corrals. The still-peeling wood of one indicated its recent construction, as did the pristine carpet of grass it enclosed. The older corral showed well-worn paths among the trees and bare spots around the feeding shed and water trough. Deep chewed spots in the smooth wood and a tangle of heavy-scented honeysuckle covering the poles gave additional testimony to its age.

A faint plume of smoke issued from the ranch house chimney. Someone was cooking. Trinity could almost smell the aroma of baking bread. His stomach growled in anticipation. Most likely just wishful thinking, he warned himself.

Of course he noticed the flowers. They were everywhere. Roses, lilacs, wisteria, mock orange, spirea, weigela, tulips, lupines, delphiniums, iris, and many other flowers he knew didn't grow naturally in Arizona. It must have taken a lot of planning and work to nurse them through the cold mountain winters — and a lot of love to coax them into such lavish bloom.

A feeling of tranquility gradually settled over Trinity, but bitter experience caused that illusion to fade. No world could be built on the rustle of leaves, the murmur of a stream, the tranquility of a lonely mountain setting, or his own weariness with the trail. People determined the character of their setting. He had never found any place where the character of the people matched the beauty, purity, or majesty so abundant in Nature.

Trinity saw a cowboy ride out of the pines and up to the bunkhouse.

Buc Stringer, foreman.

Trinity had spent hours watching Buc through the binoculars, watching him interact with each person on the ranch. He liked to know everything he could before he exposed himself to danger. He had discovered that sometimes watching people could be almost as good as talking to them.

He could tell Buc considered himself to have as much authority as the owner. And everyone else seemed to feel the same way. Buc slept in the bunkhouse, but the rest of the time he treated the ranch house as his own.

Buc towered over the hands. Trinity guessed he stood at least six feet three inches. Judging from the size of his biceps and the breadth of his shoulders, he would be at least twice as strong as the average range rider. A bull of a man. And handsome enough to turn any young woman's head.

He couldn't underestimate this young man. Sheriff Wylie Sprague believed he had been the one to engineer the woman's escape. It was well done. They were gone long before anyone knew.

Buc dismounted but didn't enter the bunkhouse. He turned and looked down the creek toward Trinity. And waited. With a gentle nudge of his heel, Trinity started his horse forward again.

Trinity could tell from his aggressive stance that Buc had taken a dislike to him. Leaning against the corral fence, Buc began to roll a cigarette. About the time he spread the tobacco over the cigarette paper, he got a good look at Trinity, and Buc's body stiffened like a starched shirt drying in a high wind. He stopped in the middle of moistening the cigarette paper, and his tongue stuck to the paper. It tore when he pulled his tongue away. With a gesture of disgust, he tossed the ruined cigarette away.

Trinity couldn't decide whether to curse or laugh. He shrugged instead.

"What do you want?" Buc asked when Trinity dismounted. Victoria continued to spy on the confrontation. *He was making no attempt to be polite; he wanted the stranger gone as fast as possible. She hoped he would at least stay for supper. His nonchalance intrigued her.*

"Just riding through," Trinity replied, keeping his voice

10

casual. It would be fatal to respond to Buc's dislike. He removed his hat and wiped his forehead with his sleeve. "It's a bit warm today. Thought I might drop in for a drink. The name's Trinity Smith."

Buc didn't introduce himself or take Trinity's extended hand. "Pump's next to the trough. Water's scarce out here, so don't waste it."

Trinity knew most Easterners thought of Arizona as a desert, but here in the snow- and tree-covered mountains, the range stayed green. In a good year, the streams would run all summer. There was no need for Buc to be stingy with water unless he wanted to get rid of the man with the thirst.

Trinity led his horse to a trough set half-in, half-out of the well-used corral. Buc followed. A little water remained in the bottom of the trough. Trinity scooped it out with his hat.

"I told you not to waste water," Buc said. "There was plenty for your horse."

"It was warm," Trinity said. "Spangler hates warm water." Trinity primed the pump and began to run fresh water into the trough.

Victoria couldn't help but smile to see this Mr. Smith twist Buc's tail so easily. *Buc shouldn't be so bossy.*

"Cold water's not good for a horse when it's hot. It'll give him colic."

"Spangler knows that," Trinity replied, still pumping. "He'll drink real slow, but he sure does like cold water." Trinity doubted his horse cared what kind of water he drank. He just wanted to nettle Buc, to see what he was made of.

"Get your water and get going," Buc said irritably. "I got things to do."

"You don't have to watch over me. I don't expect to come to any harm."

"I'm watching to make sure you don't *do* any harm," Buc replied. "I don't like strangers nosing about the place."

"Surely you can't be getting into a dither over one lone cowboy looking for a drink of water," Trinity said as inno-

11

cently as he could. He shook his head like he was feeling sorry for Buc. "It sure must make you feel awful skittish knowing there's Apaches in them hills."

Buc had no excuse to be so rude to a stranger, even on account of her safety. Victoria stepped forward to make her presence known. But just as she started to speak, Trinity's gaze turned toward the house.

An older man came out of the ranch house and started toward the two men. He was a nice-looking man, tall, thin, greying at the temples but in good physical shape.

Grant Davidge, the owner of Mountain Valley Ranch. He acted like a man in control of his destiny, not someone who needed to depend on Buc Stringer to do his work for him. But he did. Why?

"We don't have trouble with Apaches anymore," Grant said. "They know we can kill too many of their braves."

"I never noticed that stopping an Apache," Trinity replied. "Seems it only makes them more determined."

"That's something I never could understand," Grant said, his hand extended in welcome. "I'm Grant Davidge, and this surly young man is Buc Stringer, my foreman. I own Mountain Valley Ranch. You come far?"

"You might say that," Trinity answered, taking Grant's firm handshake. "My last stopping place was Texas. Don't have any particular place in mind for the next, but I got a hankering to see California."

A shadow of suspicion flitted across Buc's face at the mention of Texas, but it didn't impair Grant Davidge's good humor.

"You looking for work?"

"Nothing permanent. I figured on punching a few cows until I got a grubstake together. I'll probably move on after that. Can't seem to stay in one place too long."

Victoria felt a twinge of regret. She liked Trinity's sense of humor. It had been a long time since she had felt so much like laughing.

"You can move on now," Buc said. "We don't want your kind around here."

"Take it easy, Buc," Grant said. "You don't have to treat every stranger like a bounty hunter."

"It's not that," Buc replied. "I just don't like him."

"I don't blame you," Trinity volunteered. "No way to tell what I might be up to. As for bounty hunters, well, I never had much use for them myself. But I don't think you got any call to worry. I'm sure Mr. Davidge won't let no bounty hunter hurt you."

Victoria came perilously close to laughing aloud. It amused her to see Buc needled. He always took himself so seriously. But it was his look of affronted manhood which nearly caused her to betray herself.

Trinity turned back to Grant Davidge. "I wouldn't turn down a job if you was to offer me one."

"We don't need you," Buc repeated, very much like a man used to having his opinion obeyed. "Now get on your horse and ride."

Victoria decided she couldn't in good conscience listen any longer without making her presence known. There was no longer any question of her safety, not with Buc and her uncle present. Besides, if she didn't do something, Buc's rudeness might cause Trinity to leave.

"We could use an extra rider," Victoria said as she stepped out of her garden.

The sound of the feminine voice caused Trinity to twist to his left. The sight of the young woman coming toward him from between great clumps of white daisies and purple lupine caused his heart to leap into his throat.

Victoria Davidge! He had been told of her beauty, warned of its power. He had studied her in his binoculars, carefully accustoming himself to the perfection of her features, to the seductive curve of her breasts, the sinuous movement of her hips as she walked. But nothing had prepared him for Victoria Davidge up close.

Startlingly clear blue eyes, with only a hint of uneasiness in their depths, stared at him from under a wide-brimmed hat clearly chosen to protect her nearly pure white skin from the sun. Nearly, because Trinity could count at least

13

three freckles on the bridge of her nose. He felt certain he would find more if he looked closely.

Her expression showed curiosity mixed with amusement, excitement dulled by caution. She seemed open and friendly, intelligent, willing to be entertained — maybe hoping came closer to the mark. Anticipation shone in her eyes.

Several strands of dark red hair had escaped from under her sun hat to curl at her temples and dangle in disorder around her ears. An uncertain smile hovered on her lips. Lips which seemed too full and moist. Lips which seemed to be made expressly for kissing.

Trinity could see nothing wrong with the rest of her. Neither the long-sleeved shirt buttoned up to her throat nor the divided skirt which barely overlapped the tops of her boots hid the curves of her body. But they didn't accent them either. She had dressed for comfort, in the certain knowledge she didn't need to draw attention to herself.

Trinity knew his astonishment showed in his face, but he couldn't do anything about it. Only a dead man could have failed to respond pretty much as he had. In all his life, he'd only once seen a more beautiful woman.

Queenie.

Yet Victoria Davidge had murdered her husband. And he meant to take her back to Texas to the gallows.

Trinity pulled himself together. He saw amusement in Grant Davidge's eyes and knew it stemmed from his reaction to Victoria. He saw fury in Buc's eyes and knew it came from the same source. He wasn't sure what he saw in Victoria's eyes, but he hoped it wasn't amusement. He didn't relish being laughed at by a woman, especially a woman who had just rocked him off his feet.

"You any good with a gun?" Grant asked.

"I usually hit what I aim at," Trinity replied, wishing the brim of his hat covered his face, "but I don't suppose you'd call me a gunhand."

"That's all the better," Grant replied. "A man ought to know how to handle a gun, but he's got no call to like using it."

"But we still don't know anything about him," Buc said.

"Yes, we do," Victoria contradicted. "He's a man looking for a drink of water. I was in my garden when you rode up. I couldn't help overhearing." She flashed a friendly smile when Trinity sent her a questioning glance.

"You better on the trail or in a roundup?" Grant asked.

"I never had any need to decide."

"You like to work alone or in pairs?"

"Never had any complaint either way."

"Is there anything you do like to do?" Victoria asked.

"I like to move about, do different jobs, get to know new places."

"Sounds to me like you're trying to get the lay of the land so you can come back later," Buc said, suspicious.

"Just trying to keep from getting bored," Trinity explained. "I don't suppose I'm any smarter than the next man, but riding through canyons looking for cows don't keep a man's mind occupied."

"It better had if you want to stay alive," Buc shot back.

"It's about time you two stopped sparring," Grant Davidge said. "Buc, we need some more help right now, and he looks a likely type."

"You know I don't like taking on just anybody who rides in here."

"That's how I hired you," Grant reminded him, "and I've been thanking my lucky stars ever since."

"But—"

"I know what you're worried about," Victoria said, "but you can't run off every man who rides in here just because of me."

Victoria's expression softened so much when she looked at Buc, Trinity would have sworn they were lovers. She put her hand on his arm in the kind of intimate gesture two people use who are extremely close. The warmth in her eyes, the caress in her voice, the unconscious freedom with which her body drew near to him said she trusted Buc entirely.

Much to his surprise, Trinity found his body stiffening in

reaction to their intimacy. What was wrong with him for God's sake? Why should he be acting like an adolescent suffering from a case of puppy love? He didn't even know this woman. He had come to take her back to Texas to hang. How in heaven's name could he be feeling jealous?

He must have mistaken his reaction. It must be anger that anyone as honest as Buc Stringer could be taken in by a lovely face, a few soft words, a touch. That must have been how she lured her husband into marrying her. If the poor fool had been as susceptible as Buc, it wouldn't have taken her more than five minutes. He guessed Buc would do just about anything in the world for her.

Even murder.

Chapter Two

"Stow your gear in the bunkhouse," Grant Davidge said. "Buc will show you around."

"He just got out of the saddle," Victoria said. "Why don't you give him a chance to rest a little? In the meantime, you can all come up to the house, have some coffee, and get acquainted. Do you like pecan pie? I made one fresh this morning."

Trinity didn't care much for food, but desserts were his downfall. He would ride forty miles for a slice of good pecan pie.

"Ma'am, you done said the magic words."

"You don't know a thing about him, and you invited him in for pie," Buc complained.

"I was born in a cabin on the banks of the Trinity River," Trinity said. "That's how I got my name. My parents are dead, and I've been wandering over the West ever since. Ain't nothing else to know. Now if you'll give me a few minutes to unsaddle my horse and separate myself from a little of this trail dust, I'll see what I can do about getting on the outside of a piece of your pie."

"It'll be ready when you are," she said. "By the way, my name's Victoria Davidge. Grant is my uncle."

So she used her maiden name. But then he expected she would. No use announcing you're the widow of a murdered man. Even in the wilds of Arizona someone might put two and two together. And with a thousand dollar reward on her head, there'd be plenty willing to come after her.

17

He hadn't come because of the reward. He wouldn't take one cent of it, but he was no less determined than a paid assassin or a bounty hunter that Victoria Davidge, also known as Victoria Blazer, also known as Mrs. Jeb Blazer, would go back to Texas to pay for her crime.

"Come on, Spangler," Trinity called to his horse as he lowered the corral poles. "Looks like you're getting off work early today." Trinity didn't even glance over his shoulder, but his horse obediently withdrew his dripping muzzle from the cool water and followed him into the corral.

"I'll bring him up when he's ready," Buc said, irritated by Victoria's interest in Trinity. "No need for you to stand about waiting."

"I don't mind," Victoria replied. Her curiosity about Trinity had just intensified. She'd never known anyone who treated his horse like it was human, or a horse that responded so readily to its owner. "I've never seen such a beautiful stallion," she said to Buc. "How do you think he compares to your Appaloosa?"

While Buc and her uncle talked horses, Victoria watched Trinity. She liked what she saw, but she didn't understand why her reaction should be so intense, so visceral. It wasn't like her to be drawn to strangers. For five years she had made a practice of staying away from new hands until Buc and her uncle decided they could be trusted. She had avoided casual visitors altogether.

Yet she had been lured out of her garden in less than fifteen minutes by this man's physical presence. The situation both intrigued and frightened her. No man had affected her this strongly—not even her husband.

She couldn't tell if Trinity was as handsome as Jeb Blazer—the sun was in her eyes and she couldn't see under the brim of his hat—but that hardly seemed to matter. Neither did the fact he didn't stand as tall as Buc or have the same breadth of shoulders. Everything about him fitted together as though each part had been carefully chosen: long legs, powerful thighs, slim hips, flat stomach, broad shoulders, everything a man ought to be. Still she hadn't touched on the force which drew her from her hiding place.

A casual observer might not see it because of his calm and slightly bored demeanor, but Victoria sensed that within this man burned a driving force, a stinging sense of purpose that would pulverize anything that stood in his way. Buc and her uncle had always seemed so vital and determined, but when set against this man, it was like comparing lighted matches to a forest fire.

"Mighty neighborly of you to wait for me," Trinity said to Victoria as he replaced the corral poles.

"We don't get many visitors," she answered. "It'll be nice to catch up on all the latest news."

"I don't hear much news, ma'am. I keep pretty much to myself."

Victoria turned to him, her eyebrows arched in a look of mock surprise. "You do know who's president, don't you?"

Trinity smiled. "Yes, ma'am, I know that. I also know Reconstruction has ended in Texas. Outside that, nothing much else matters."

"How's the cattle market?" her uncle inquired.

"It's recovered somewhat, especially since the blizzard a few years back, but it won't ever be what it was."

"I was afraid of that," Grant said. "It's a good thing we sell to the Army."

"Closer, too," Buc said. "I don't like being gone on long drives." He looked at Victoria when he spoke, pride of possession sounding in his voice.

That same sound put Victoria's teeth on edge. She hadn't particularly minded it before, but today, with Trinity here, it annoyed her. She knew Trinity must hear it as well. She felt compelled to make sure he knew Buc had no claim on her.

"I should think you and the boys would be glad to get away as often as you could," she said. "There's nothing to do here. Nobody to see. Worst of all, no women."

Before Buc could protest, she changed the subject. "If you've never been to Arizona, Mr. Smith, you're in for quite a surprise. It's nothing like Texas."

"No, it's not," Trinity replied, managing to insinuate himself between Victoria and Buc. "It reminds me more of Colorado."

"You must have seen a lot of places." She couldn't keep a note of envy from her voice. "What's your business?" The words came out before she could stop them. "I know I shouldn't have asked," she apologized quickly. "Uncle Grant keeps telling me I'm not supposed to ask questions like that, but my mama grew up in Alabama. To her a person just wasn't a person until she knew where he came from, what he did, and who his kinfolk were."

Trinity smiled as he followed her into the kitchen and took a place at the long ranch table.

"I guess my ma felt the same, but she didn't give me any real home, and she left me without kinfolk."

"Sorry. I didn't mean to . . ."

"Don't worry about it none. Just cut me a slice of that pecan pie. Haven't been able to get my mind on anything else since you mentioned it."

Trinity had never been in such an enormous kitchen. A huge black monster of an iron stove dominated one end. Cupboards covered another wall. A fireplace dominated the third. Windows with a view of the distant mountain peaks took up the fourth. A table, made of hand-hewn oak and long enough to seat close to two dozen men, filled the room. A dull cream-colored tablecloth decorated with a border of poorly executed embroidery covered the center of the table.

But it was the flowers that overwhelmed him. They were everywhere, in large sprays or small bunches, in teacups or large jars on the table and the mantel, even hanging from baskets in front of the windows. And they were fresh from the garden. The pungent odor of newly cut greenery nearly overpowered the softer, more pleasant fragrance of the multitude of blossoms.

Trinity felt like he'd wandered into a daydream.

While Victoria took a still-warm pie out of the pie keep and set plates, forks, and cups before them, Grant Davidge plied Trinity with questions about everything from the condition of grass in the country he'd passed through to the whereabouts of various renegade Indian bands. Buc positioned himself by the door, close enough to hear everything being said, but far enough away to show his disapproval.

"I don't know anything about this kind of country," Trinity said when he got a chance. "Does it make good grazing?"

Victoria tried to tell herself Trinity paid close attention to her uncle, but his gaze hardly seemed to leave her. At first she felt flattered, but she soon found herself wishing he would look elsewhere. His attention disconcerted her. After five years in an all-male environment, she had grown used to being the center of attention, but something about his scrutiny made her feel uncomfortable.

It wasn't an appraising glance. She knew that kind well enough. It felt almost as if he disapproved of her. No, something stronger than that. It delved deeper, like he was trying to discover her secrets.

But that wasn't quite it either. There was something covertly harsh and accusing about his glance. He couldn't have appeared more respectful, but she felt his distaste. And she didn't like it.

She saw him glance over his shoulder at Buc before giving her a particularly penetrating glare. Did he think she was having an affair with Buc?

The idea made her furious at Trinity . . . and at Buc.

Trinity had no right to look at her that way. He didn't know anything about her. Did he just dislike her, or did he dislike women in general? No, not women. She remembered the way he looked at her when he first saw her. It was the look of a man who liked women and who fully appreciated what he saw.

Oh well, it hardly mattered what he thought. He wouldn't be here more than a few weeks. A few months at most.

Still she hated to give up on him so soon. She had been sure he would prove interesting to talk to and spend time with.

"Can I get you anything else?" she asked as she set the pie before Trinity.

The strange look deep in his eyes had disappeared; a glint signalled the return of his sense of humor. Maybe he did disapprove of her, but it would be nice to be around someone who could make her laugh.

Besides, she had to figure out why she felt so drawn to him. She felt like she'd known him for years, there had to be some explanation for this feeling. Victoria decided right then and there to find out what it might be.

"A second piece."

Victoria looked at him in surprise, then laughed. "You haven't eaten the first one. How do you know you'll like it?"

"You baked it?"

"I made it. Ramon baked it."

"Then I know I'll like it."

"You must be Irish."

"Or one of them Frenchies that came into Texas some time back," Buc said. "They'll lie as fast as their tongue can fly."

"Don't you like compliments?" Trinity asked.

"I guess so, but only when they're earned."

Trinity took a bite of the pie. He chewed slowly, savoring the rich taste.

"This one's earned," he said. "If I'd known what you could do with pecans, I'd have lugged me a sack all the way from Texas."

"It's a good thing I can cook. There's not much else anybody will let me do," Victoria said.

The words were out before she could stop them. The stifled anger, bitterness, and frustration were apparent for all three men to hear. She knew Buc and her uncle didn't understand. They never had. She tried to keep her feelings under control, to show only her gratitude and not her unhappiness, but once in a while it would leap out before she could hold it back. It irritated her it had done so before this stranger.

"There's so little a woman can do on a ranch like this," she explained, hoping Trinity wasn't as intelligent as his eyes seemed to indicate. "There are times when I'd like to do something really useful, something more than bake pies, grow flowers, or do terrible embroidery."

Trinity concentrated on his pie, resisting the natural inclination to let his glance stray toward the scorned needlework. He left it to Grant Davidge to respond to his niece.

"I suppose you do get tired of being cooped up in the house, but I wouldn't have a moment's peace knowing you were out there with Indians and goodness knows who else wandering through this valley."

"I don't know," Trinity mused, devils dancing in his eyes. "If I was a cow used to coming nose to nose with bobcats, bears, and the like, I'd be so happy to come upon this little lady I'd probably lie down and hold my feet together so she could tie me up. And being branded wouldn't be more than a bee sting compared to some cougar making fresh steaks out of me."

Victoria laughed, a delighted peal which reverberated about the room.

"Do give him a job, Uncle," she said. "He lies shamefully, but he does it with such charm."

"I assure you, ma'am —"

"Don't. Women delight in flattery. Maybe we should be more fond of the truth, but it's nice to hear ourselves described in more glowing terms than we deserve. However, flattery loses some of its appeal when you start swearing it's the truth."

"You're very wise to be so young."

A cloud passed over Victoria's spirits. "I'm older than you think."

"I knew you were no longer in your girlhood," Trinity said, recovering swiftly. "A girl, by definition being a woman still unformed, could never have attained such perfection."

Victoria laughed again, even more easily than before.

"Are you never without an answer? I wouldn't be surprised to find they ran you out of Texas."

"I'd like to run him out of Arizona," Buc said, making no effort to keep the animosity from his voice.

"I'm really quite harmless," Trinity said. "My old man used to say, 'Never worry about a man as long as he's talking, but look out when he stops.'"

"Then I guess we got nothing to worry about from you. You haven't stopped jawing since you rode in. Think you can stop long enough to get some work done?"

"If you give me the right kind of job."

"And what might that be?" Buc asked, sarcasm in his voice.

"Why a talking job, naturally."

Victoria and her uncle grinned. Buc didn't.

"We don't have any jobs like that."

"Sure you do. I could fetch and carry for Miss Davidge. She must need lots of wood and water for cooking. Then there's the slops to be thrown out and the sweeping up to be done. And of course a lady can't be allowed to go fetching eggs and feeding chickens. And all the while I would be talking steady so she wouldn't worry about whether those Indians have got you yet."

"When we want a housemaid, we'll hire a female," Buc said.

"I bet Miss Davidge would like it better if you hired a house fella. It would make things more interesting."

"Things are interesting enough around here," Buc sputtered. "And they'll be a whole lot more pleasant after you're gone."

"Maybe for you, but not for me. I'm not looking forward to the long ride through the desert. You want to go with me, ma'am? Sure would help to while away the hot afternoons. They say Los Angeles is making up into a right fair town. Of course it don't compare to San Francisco, but I'd take you there, too, if you wanted."

"Victoria doesn't want to go to California, and certainly not with the likes of you," Buc exploded before Victoria could respond.

"It's a good thing I don't take that as a personal insult,"

Trinity observed, sounding too amiable to get insulted about anything.

"I meant it personal. Now if you want this job, you'd better shake a leg. And forget you ever found your way into this kitchen. Hands don't eat up at the house."

"There's no one but you in the bunkhouse just now," Victoria objected, "and you eat with us. You can't expect him to eat alone."

"Somebody'll be back in a couple of days," Buc said.

"I won't mind," Trinity said, "as long I can come up for a piece of pie now and again."

"You'll eat with us," Grant Davidge said.

Buc didn't like it, but Grant's decision put an end to the discussion.

"I'm heading over to the bunkhouse," Buc said to Trinity. "I'll settle you in."

"No need to be in such a hurry," Grant said, "You can take him over after dinner. I want to talk to him." Buc seemed reluctant to leave. "He's got to know sooner or later."

"Can you trust him?" Buc asked, casting Trinity an angry glance.

"It's not much of a secret. Half of Texas knows already."

"Still, I don't think —"

"You can go on. I'll take care of it."

Buc leaned against the wall, his frown of disapproval deepening into a scowl. "I'll wait."

"Buc doesn't dislike you," Grant assured Trinity. "He's just worried every man who sets foot in this valley is after Victoria."

Trinity tried to look surprised and mystified in turn. Fortunately, Grant didn't seem much interested in his facial expression.

"Five years ago somebody killed Victoria's husband," Grant explained. "Nobody could find out who did it so they tried to put the blame on Victoria. By the time I got there, they had set the date for a trial and picked the jury. They had also made plans to hang her at the end of the week. The scaffold was already going up. Can you imagine any man meaning to hang a lovely, innocent young woman like Victoria?"

It took no special intuition to see Grant believed implicitly in his niece's innocence. The man actually vibrated with the fury inside him.

"The judge wouldn't listen to a word I said. He was Victoria's father-in-law, you see, and he was all eaten up with grief. Jeb was his only boy. I don't think he would have managed to hold up at all if it hadn't been for his wife. Victoria didn't much like her stepmother-in-law, but Myra Blazer is a remarkable woman. Quite handsome, too." Grant looked embarrassed to have ventured so far from the topic. He cleared his throat.

"I intended to appeal to the governor, but Judge Blazer held the trial early. The jury never even left the room."

"What did you do?"

"Buc came up with a plan to break her out of jail. Worked like a charm. Not a single shot fired and nobody hurt. We were halfway across Texas before they even knew Victoria was gone."

"Is she safe here? Maybe you ought to take her to California."

"As long as she's not in the states, they can't touch her. The territorial governor is a personal friend of mine. Besides, he wouldn't send Victoria back. He doesn't believe in hanging women."

"Not even the ones who're guilty?"

Trinity hadn't meant to say anything, but he couldn't restrain himself. Grant's words had scraped against old wounds. Even after all these years, just remembering what Queenie had done to him and his father made him burn with rage.

Now sitting here, listening to Grant Davidge talk about helping his niece escape, as if it were his right to decide when the criminal justice system did and didn't work, made him furious. Queenie had gotten away. She had disappeared without a trace. But by God, Victoria Davidge wouldn't, not if he had anything to say about it.

"Since Victoria's not guilty, I never considered it," Grant said, impatiently dismissing the idea.

"Did you have any trouble with people coming after her?" Trinity asked, changing the subject. "I mean, is there any kind of reward for taking her back?"

"You wouldn't be thinking about trying to collect it, would you?"

"No, but there's a lot of people who'd turn in their own ma for no more than fifty dollars."

"There's a thousand dollar reward, but Judge Blazer has offered several times that amount to any coyote who'd come after her."

Grant's eyes had turned steely cold, his features set in the cement of rock-hard determination. In that moment Trinity had no trouble seeing in this mild-mannered, fond uncle the man who had carved a ranch out of the Arizona wilderness and held it against Indians and rustlers.

"But he reckoned without Buc and me. If they couldn't be bought off, we . . ." Grant stopped himself. His gaze met Trinity's gaze and held steady, challenging. "Let's just say I was able to convince them they could earn easier money somewhere else."

Trinity wondered if there were any bodies buried in the remote reaches of Mountain Valley Ranch. It wasn't his job to check on Grant or his foreman, but it would be helpful to know. A wise man always takes careful inventory of the obstacles facing him before undertaking a task if he wants to be successful.

And Trinity Smith was always successful.

"Why're you telling me all this?" Trinity asked.

"Because part of your job will be to protect Victoria. In fact, it's the most important part. Every cowhand here knows what happened and has sworn not to let anyone take her out of this valley."

"I suppose it can get mighty tiresome being kept under lock and key," Trinity said, turning to Victoria.

"Yes, it can," Victoria agreed, glad to be able to turn the conversation, if only slightly, from her awful past. "This

27

may sound ungrateful, but there are times when I wish I weren't so much a prisoner and could go anywhere I liked. I especially wish I were a man."

"Lord almighty!" Trinity exploded. "Think of the waste."

Victoria laughed again. She couldn't remember ever having laughed so much in one day, and it felt good.

"I'm going to insist Uncle Grant keep you around for a long time," Victoria said. "You're wonderful for my ego."

"All the men think you're beautiful," Grant told her.

"I know, but they're afraid to say anything. Trinity just wades in and says what he thinks. I imagine there'll be times when I'll wish he hadn't, but on the whole I prefer it."

"I can't imagine saying anything against you, ma'am."

"You just did."

"Ma'am?"

"You did it again."

Trinity looked confused.

"My name's Victoria. I don't know anyone named *Ma'am*."

"But it ain't polite to call the boss lady by her first name."

"Then it's fortunate I'm not the boss lady," Victoria said when Trinity started to demur. "Uncle Grant is the boss and Buc is the foreman. I just live here. If you want any more pecan pie, you'll have to learn to call me Victoria."

"Ma'am, I'd learn to call you anything if you just keep on baking those pies."

"Call me *Ma'am* again, and you'll eat dinner in the bunkhouse."

Trinity hung his head and shuffled his feet a bit. Then he looked at Victoria, rather sheepishly. "I'll do my best, but you got to forgive me if I forget now and again. My pa was real strict, you see, and he used to cane me if I didn't call every female I saw 'Ma'am.' Didn't matter if they was so little they could hide behind their ma's skirts. It was 'Ma'am' or nothing. It got to be such a habit I don't know if I can break it."

The imps dancing in Trinity's eyes convinced Victoria she couldn't believe a word he said. "You'll just have to try. A few missed meals ought to help sharpen your memory."

"Is she always so cruel?" Trinity asked Grant.

"She's real determined," Grant said, an answering gleam in his eye. "I guess you'd better do like she orders."

"Do you think she might order me to keep an eye on her? It would be terrible if some Apache was to get hold of her."

"You said they were a couple hundred miles south of here," Buc interrupted.

"They might get tired of all that desert. It's much nicer up here in the mountains. Lots of cold water to drink."

Victoria turned away to hide her smile.

"It might not be such a bad idea for you to stick close to the house for the next couple days," Grant said. "We're too short of hands to pull anybody off the range, and Buc and I have to ride pretty far out the next few days."

"Victoria doesn't need the likes of him hanging about," Buc protested.

"I never do like leaving her," Grant explained to Trinity.

"She's got Ramon and Anita."

"They'd be no help if trouble came."

"We haven't had any trouble in three years. I don't see why we should expect it in the next two days."

"It'll also give him a chance to get familiar with the place, learn his way about," Grant continued, good-naturedly ignoring his foreman's repeated objections. "You wouldn't mind, would you, Victoria?"

"Not if he helps me with my survey," she answered.

"Have him do anything you want. That okay with you?" Grant asked Trinity.

"Looking at a pretty woman is always better than chasing after ornery cows that don't want to be found."

"Now you look here—" Buc started.

"He's just kidding you, Buc," Victoria interrupted. "Can't you see that?"

"All I see is a nameless cowboy who's wormed his way into this ranch in less than an hour."

"I told you my name was Trin—"

"That's what you say," Buc replied angrily. "It could be Billy the Kid for all we know."

29

"He's about six inches shorter than I am," Trinity pointed out. "Besides he's going to fat. And he's got this big ugly chin that—"

"You know what I mean!" Buc roared furiously.

"We all do," Grant said. He didn't raise his voice, but his expression clearly showed his impatience. "But I trust Trinity. I like the look of him. And I'd feel a lot safer knowing he was with Victoria."

The tension in the room was almost tangible. Trinity could see Grant had brought the discussion to an end, and he guessed Buc was barely able to keep a rein on his tongue. He didn't know what Victoria thought, but she didn't seem to mind the idea.

That was enough for now. He stood up.

"Thanks for the pie, Miss Victoria. I don't know when I've tasted any half as good."

"You still want a second piece?" Victoria asked, the tension gone from her eyes.

"I'll save it for tomorrow. That ought to make sure I don't get lost."

"If you didn't get lost from Texas to Arizona, I doubt you'll get lost between here and the bunkhouse."

Trinity grinned in response. "Not with Buc here to guide me."

"I wouldn't depend on that too much. The way he's looking at you right now he's liable to lead you right off the mountainside."

"Buc doesn't dislike you," Grant told Trinity for the second time. "He just doesn't trust you yet."

"I can understand that," Trinity said, "but surely he knows I'd do everything I could to protect Miss Victoria."

"We'll see," growled Buc, stymied for the moment. "Let's get you settled."

Trinity followed Buc to the bunkhouse. He could see the anger in the man's stride, the stiffness of his carriage, the hurry with which he expected Trinity to follow. Like he wanted to get him settled in the bunkhouse and then wash his hands of him.

30

Trinity didn't plan to be dismissed that easily. He had a job to do, and he didn't mean to let anyone stand in the way.

And that included Buc.

"You can take your pick of the bunks," Buc said when they reached the bunkhouse. He had *escorted* Trinity in silence. But for some reason, the bunkhouse loosened his tongue. "Let's get a few things straight. I don't trust you, and I don't like you either. I don't know why, I just don't. And I'm a man who always goes with his instincts."

"That's okay with me," Trinity said, as he tossed his gear on the bunk nearest him. "I tend to do the same thing myself."

"Well your instincts had better not cause you to start sniffing around Victoria. She's going to marry me, and I won't have any man nosing around my woman."

Trinity looked him in the face. "I can't imagine Victoria would be any man's *woman*, however much she might want to be his wife."

"I don't care what you imagine. You won't be here long enough for it to make any difference."

"What makes you say that? This looks like a good place to work."

Buc's expression turned grim. "You said you planned to move on as soon as you got a grubstake together."

"I did at first," Trinity said, lowering himself on his bed and stretching out his full length, a grin calculated to annoy Buc on his face. A soft mattress covering the boards made the bunk more comfortable than he'd expected, and Trinity let his body relax. After sleeping on the rocks and hard ground, this felt almost as good as a San Francisco hotel. "I never stayed too long in one place, but I think I'm going to like it here."

"Now look here—" Buc started.

He never finished. Trinity exploded off the bed. Before Buc knew what had happened, he found himself nose-to-nose with a very different kind of man from the easygoing stranger who had lain down on the bed just seconds before.

31

"You listen to me," Trinity said, his voice soft, his eyes dark, his body tensed for action. "I don't like being threatened. You're welcome to dislike me as much as you want—I don't much care for you either—but I won't be threatened. I'll do any job you give me, and I'll do it over if I don't get it right the first time, but you keep riding me, and I'm going to be all over you like a coyote on a jackrabbit. You hear?"

"Yeah, I hear," Buc said, as though he'd heard it all before and wasn't the least bit impressed. But he stepped back, a silent admission he had overstepped his limits. "You just keep in mind I oversee this outfit. Mr. Davidge might have given you the job, but you're going to have to work for me to keep it."

"Does that mean you're changing my work orders for tomorrow?" A challenge flashed in Trinity's eyes.

"Mr. Davidge is the boss. If he tells you to keep an eye on Victoria, then that's exactly what you're supposed to do. Though I would have supposed he would have picked someone he knew he could trust."

"You meaning to hire more hands?"

"Not if I can help it. I'd rather work everybody until they drop than bring in another man. Might be like a man we hired a few years back. Nearly didn't find out until it was too late."

"Didn't find out what?"

"He'd been sent to take Victoria back. He was the second one."

"What happened?"

"We got rid of him."

Trinity didn't have a chance to ask any more questions before Buc stormed out of the bunkhouse, but the question continued to burn in his mind. Would Grant or Buc, or both, kill a man rather than let Victoria go back to stand trial? He hoped not. He didn't much care for Buc, but he had taken a liking to Grant.

Besides, this valley didn't feel like a killer's hideout. Neither Victoria nor her uncle acted like they had anything to fear from strangers, but then they didn't need to. Buc was suspicious enough for both of them.

Trinity couldn't find it in himself to blame any man for doing whatever he had to do to protect Victoria. Men had robbed, cheated, and killed for less beautiful women. Scaring off strangers seemed almost harmless by comparison. He certainly wouldn't be too particular about what he did if Victoria were his woman.

The thought caught Trinity by surprise. After Queenie, he had sworn he'd never let another woman have any power over him. Despite the many beautiful women he'd known, and the several who would have been willing to forsake everything for him, he had kept his vow.

There could be do doubt Victoria killed her husband. The evidence said it couldn't have been anybody else. So there must be a good reason why she did it. Oddly enough, Trinity felt compelled to find out what it was.

Don't be a fool. Your job is to bring her back, not understand why she did what she did. That's what the jury was for, and they've already made their decision.

But Trinity couldn't rest. He turned over several times, trying to find a more comfortable position. He knew the fault didn't lay with the bed. The trouble lay in his head.

He didn't yet understand why, but he couldn't just take Victoria back to Texas and forget about her. Even though it couldn't make any difference, even though it wasn't part of his job, he had to know *why* she did it.

But how could he find out?

Trinity didn't get a chance to explore that question. Without warning the bunkhouse door flew open with a noisy crash. In a flash, Trinity dropped to the ground, his gun drawn.

Chapter Three

A Mexican, short, thick waisted, and fortyish, entered the bunkhouse. He leaned on a skinny, carrot-topped, freckle-faced boy for support. For a moment the three men stared at each other. Trinity spoke first.

"Sorry for the chilly welcome. You surprised me."

"Who're you?" the kid demanded. "And what are you doing here?" He didn't look more than eighteen, fresh-faced but wary.

"The name's Trinity Smith. I just hired on."

"Buc never hired you," the kid said, openly suspicious.

"Mr. Davidge hired me against Buc's advice."

"That I believe," said the Mexican. He hobbled to the nearest bunk and lowered himself carefully. His bronzed, leathery skin and permanently bowed legs branded him a man of the range. His skeptical black eyes and piercing gaze said he wouldn't be fooled easily. "He needs to hire new *vaqueros* to replace old men like me."

"You'll be as good as new in a couple of days," the boy said, his fondness for the old man easy to hear despite the gruffness in his voice. "Just make sure you stay off that leg."

"How will you manage? You have nobody to ride with you."

"Maybe Buc will let me ride with him," Trinity said to the Mexican. "I don't know the layout of the ranch, but I'm better than an empty saddle."

"I don't need no stranger making free behind my back," the boy said. He wasn't exactly hostile, but close enough to suit Trinity.

"Forgive our manners," the old man asked. "We worry every stranger is after the *senorita*."

"Now that I work for the Mountain Valley, she's my worry, too.

The old man responded with a cautious smile.

"I am Perez Calderon. My sister keeps house for *Senor* Grant. That is the only reason Buc keeps me. This young *gringo* is Michael O'Donavan." He tousled the boy's hair. "We call him Red."

"Would you like me to have a look at that leg?" Trinity asked.

"There is no need. My horse fell on me and pinned my leg under him. He would have broken it if Red had not got to me so fast. It would not happen if Buc would hire more men. We work so hard we get careless."

"Is that what you meant a minute ago?" Trinity asked.

"Si. Buc is not hiring anybody now. When he does, he will hire only old men, ugly *hombres* like me, or young *gringos* like Red." He winked and nodded his head in the direction of the house.

Trinity smiled in understanding. "Too young or too old."

"Buc means to marry *Senorita* Davidge."

"He already told me."

"Nothing wrong in that," Red piped up. "A man would have to be crazy out of his mind not to want to marry Miss Victoria."

Trinity's gaze appraised the young man. Earnest. Idealistic. Temper probably as hot as his hair. He might be able to get a few more answers if he prodded the boy a little.

"I got to admit Victoria's a fine-looking young woman, but I don't think I'd like to be married to her."

"She's *Miss Victoria* to the likes of you," Red snapped. "And you'd jump at the chance to marry her."

"Naw. I don't think I could lie comfortable in my bed married to a woman who killed her husband."

The words were hardly out of Trinity's mouth before Red had covered the space that separated their bunks, his drawn

35

gun inches from the bridge of Trinity's nose.

"Take that back, or I'll kill you where you sit," he said, his young voice no more than a harsh growl.

Trinity never expected anything like that. The boy was like lightning. Trinity doubted he was as fast.

"Easy, Red," Perez cautioned. "No call to get upset. He is an outsider. You cannot expect him to know the *senorita* like we do."

"He's got to take it back," Red said, too angry to be swayed by reason or caution. "Nobody's going to say Miss Victoria's a murderer. The boys will kill to protect her. You'll be expected to do the same thing."

"But if she killed that man . . ."

"She didn't kill nobody."

The words sounded like those of a youth in passionate defense of an idealized love.

"That pure, sweet girl could not kill her husband," Perez said. "Anybody can see that just looking at her. Judge Blazer paid the jury to convict her. He did not even let Mr. Davidge bring a lawyer or make an investigation."

"They had a trial."

"There was no *trial*," Perez told Trinity. "The judge already decide everything. He have to hang somebody, so he choose *Senorita* Davidge. He say they find her with a gun in her hand."

"But if she held the gun . . ."

"She didn't fire it," Red insisted. "Somebody else killed Jeb Blazer, and Miss Victoria got blamed for it."

Trinity let the old Mexican tell him every detail of the efforts Grant made to postpone the trial, of the people he contacted, the conflicting evidence he turned up about that night. But like everyone else, Perez ignored the fact that Victoria was found holding the gun with nobody else around. To him, Victoria was innocent. Period.

Just like with Red.

Trinity had to admit it was difficult for him to see Victoria in the role of a killer, but not for the same reason. He didn't see her as a weak, helpless woman afraid of her husband or of a gun. Killers were usually timid people who saw murder as the only way out of an unbearable situation, people so greedy for power or money they would do anything to get more, or cruel, heartless brutes who killed because of their contempt for human life.

Victoria didn't seem to fit into any of those categories, but Trinity reminded himself he knew nothing about her except she grew beautiful flowers and baked a marvelous pecan pie. No telling what she had been like five years ago. A girl could change a lot between seventeen and twenty-two. Still, it didn't fit.

"I didn't know all of that," Trinity said. "Her uncle said they had plans to hang her, had the scaffold all ready. I just figured the jury must have found her guilty."

"They paid them to lie," Red said, the gun barrel now pressed against the skin between Trinity's eyes. "Now take it back."

"You better," the old man advised.

"I was just repeating what I'd heard," Trinity said. "I didn't even know Miss Victoria until today. She doesn't look like a murderer to me."

"She isn't," Red said, slowly backing away from Trinity, his gun still leveled at him.

"It is better that you not say what you heard in front of the *vaqueros*," Perez advised. "They take it bad."

"You mean they're all as convinced as Red here she's innocent?"

"How can you have seen her and ask such a damned fool question?" Red demanded. "Could an angel kill anyone, even a drunken sot who didn't have the sense to know what he'd got?"

"I don't know as much about the situation as you."

"Then make sure you learn more before you go shooting off your mouth again," Red said, stepping back and holstering his gun. "We don't allow nobody to slight Miss Victoria. There's people who could vouch for that if they could talk."

"That's not likely, them being far away and understanding how we feel about the *senorita*," Perez added. He said nothing more, but Trinity couldn't mistake the warning directed to Red.

Trinity knew then that at least one man had died in his attempt to take Victoria back to Texas.

"What happened when they went to Texas?" Trinity asked. "Mr. Davidge told me Buc broke Victoria out of jail."

"We all go," Perez said. "We mean to burn town if we have to."

"Don't pull your gun on me for asking," Trinity said to Red, "but why were all of you ready to take such a risk?"

"You have to know *Senor* Grant and his brother, the *senorita's* papa," Perez said. "Some of us come from Texas with *Senor* Grant. Not Red. He is too young. I know *Senorita* Davidge as a girl. She can not kill anybody, not if she loves them."

"Are you certain she loved her husband?" Trinity asked.

"Are you saying she'd marry a man because of his money?" Red challenged.

"I'm just asking," Trinity said. "A man can't help being curious."

"Better to leave questions unasked than be dead," Red advised. "People around here don't take kindly to questions about Miss Victoria. *Any* kind of questions."

Apparently convinced that any threat to Victoria's safety had passed, and that any question about her reputation had been settled, Red launched into a paean of praise that bespoke of a young man in the throes of love with a woman he considered so far above him as to be completely out of his reach.

Perez didn't look nearly so certain. He didn't watch Trinity directly, but Trinity realized he was being closely observed.

Trinity soon managed to get Red's mind off Victoria. Later they swapped yarns. Perez proved to have an inexhaustible supply, but Trinity got the feeling the man's thoughts were never entirely off their earlier conversation.

He would do well to keep his eyes on the old man.

* * *

"I hope you don't mind going with me today," Victoria said when Trinity had finished his breakfast next morning. "Uncle Grant says following me about while I work on my survey is the perfect way to get to know the ranch."

Trinity didn't get a chance to answer before Buc burst out with an objection.

"I still don't trust him. How do we know he's not one of Judge Blazer's men?"

"It's been more than five years, Buc," Grant said. "Surely Blazer has given up by now."

"Are you afraid Trinity will overpower me?" Victoria asked.

"No, but —"

"Or do you suspect he'll talk me into something I don't want to do?"

"Good God, no, but —"

"Then what's your objection?" Grant asked.

"I don't like him, and I don't trust him," Buc stated bluntly. "He could be a bounty hunter."

A faint shadow passed across Victoria's face.

"Nonsense," Grant said. "Bounty hunters are known."

"Not all of them. There's one who uses a different name every time. Nobody knows much about him, but they say he's hanged more than a dozen men."

"Where's he from?" Trinity asked. He couldn't just stand there and let Buc accuse him of being a bounty hunter.

"Nobody knows that either. Seems he just shows up, gets himself deputized, and disappears. Next time anybody sees him he's bringing in the man he went after. Then he disappears again. He must know the West better than anybody alive."

"Then I can prove I'm not that man," Trinity said. "You can follow my trail all the way back to Texas. I must have asked a dozen people the way to California."

"If Trinity can't possibly be this bounty hunter, you've got nothing to worry about," Victoria said.

"I'm worried about everybody," Buc confessed. "I'm never

39

comfortable when you're out of my sight unless I know you're here at the ranch, inside, safe from any prying gaze."

"That's sweet, Buc," Victoria said, a softness and affection in her voice that caused Trinity's stomach muscles to knot, "but you can't keep me indoors for the rest of my life."

"I don't see why not," Buc said. "There's no reason for you to leave the house."

"Yes, there is," Victoria contradicted, with a sharpness Trinity hadn't expected. "I'd go crazy if I didn't get out of this house once in a while. And as much as I love being with you and Uncle Grant, I've got to *do something* or I'll die on the vine, like pods drying in the summer sun."

"Nonsense," said her uncle. "I don't agree with keeping you locked up, and I've told Buc, but I don't want to hear any more talk about your going crazy or drying up like a pea pod."

"Wouldn't you go crazy if you were kept locked up all the time?" Victoria asked, turning to Trinity for support.

"I don't know," Trinity confessed. "It's been more of a worry with me to find a place to lay my head for the night."

"That's always the way it is with men," Victoria said, her mouth twisted with disgust. "No matter what a man wants to do, no matter how foolish it might be, he's perfectly free to do it, and nobody thinks the worse of him for it. But let a woman try to do the same thing and she's hemmed in from all sides."

"Now, Victoria."

"Nobody's hemming you in."

Grant and Buc spoke at the same time. Victoria ignored them both and turned to Trinity.

"Do you mean to hem me in as well?"

"I expect I'll just do what I'm told," Trinity replied.

"Victoria may get a little impatient with her confinement," Grant said, "but she'd never do anything foolish."

"I'm not asking anybody to do anything foolish," Victoria said with a sigh, "but there are times when I wonder if it's all worth it."

"How can you say that?" Buc demanded. "The thought of

you in that filthy jail with the gallows just outside your window . . ."

"You know she doesn't mean it," Grant said. "She just gets out of humor once in a while. You go on with Trinity. You can start on the ridge you've been wanting to survey. Pack a lunch and stay all day if you like. I want you to work this restlessness out of your system, but no matter how fretful you become, you've got to remain on your guard."

"I know," Victoria assured him. "Even if I didn't do it for myself, I'd never risk your happiness, or forfeit the risk you took just getting me here. I love you just as much as you love me."

"Go along and enjoy yourself," her uncle said, a slight catch in his voice. "Trinity will take care of you."

"I'll check on you," Buc offered. "Trinity might get lost."

"I won't get lost," Victoria said, affronted. "I've been here five years. The shape of this valley is imprinted on my mind."

"Then why do you need to make so many of those peculiar maps? Nobody's ever going to look at them."

"Because I've got to have something to do besides cook and clean house," she replied, ignoring his insult to her work. "If I didn't get out once in a while, I think I would go crazy enough to kill somebody."

"Don't say that," Grant implored, "not even in jest."

"It's no jest," Victoria said.

Trinity quickly discovered that being alone with Victoria all day wasn't going to be as easy as he'd expected. She might be a murderess, but she was a very beautiful, sensuous, desirable woman. The kind that drove a man like him crazy.

There was nothing provocative about Victoria's dress. There couldn't be with her bundled up inside a deerskin jacket against the morning chill. But even though he had to wrestle with the willful packhorse bearing her precious surveying equipment, Trinity seldom took his eyes off her. With her riding directly before him, it would have been virtually impossible to ignore her.

And he didn't want to.

Riding astride, Victoria sat perfectly straight in the saddle. The gentle curve of her shoulders and her long, slim neck contributed to her delicate appearance. Despite the concealing bulk of her coat, she looked too fragile to handle the packhorse or her equipment.

She never turned around, thus denying him a glimpse of the outline of her breasts, but he had an uninterrupted view of the soft, white skin at the nape of her neck. Only a few moments of allowing himself to imagine how it would feel to kiss her neck, to tease the strands of hair that floated on the cool morning air, and he felt his body swell with desire.

He found it very uncomfortable to ride in a perpetually aroused state and cursed himself for responding like a randy youth. But even when he tried to concentrate on the scenes around him, the sound of her voice, soft and enveloping, like a warm blanket on a cold night, provided him with a constant reminder of her presence.

He must have been away from women too long. He couldn't think of any other explanation for the spiral of sensations rapidly destroying his ability to concentrate. He was going to have to do better than this, or every Apache between Colorado and Mexico could be on his trail and he'd never notice.

Besides, if the rest of the hands were like Red and Perez, he was going to need all his concentration to get her away without shooting anyone. He had never killed an innocent person. He had no intention of making this the first time.

"It feels wonderful to get away," Victoria said as they topped a rise. A panoramic view of the mountains lay before them.

Mist blanketed the valley below. Bright rays of morning sun struck countless tiny droplets turning them into a thick, billowing cloud of purest white. The pointed tops of Ponderosa pines pierced the edge of the mist like thousands of stakes holding a blanket tightly in place. A brisk wind rushed down on them from distant, snow-covered peaks.

"A few hours of freedom is worth hauling the equipment out, even if I don't get any work done."

Of course it is, as long as the horse and I are doing all the work, Trinity internally droned.

"Who usually comes with you?" Trinity asked. He couldn't see Buc or Grant letting her go this far from the ranch without someone with her.

"Anyone who's free," Victoria replied. She removed her hat and let her hair fall free.

Trinity couldn't imagine how he had forgotten her hair. In the soft light of the ranch house, it had seemed as dark as burnished copper. But this morning, in the full glare of sunlight, it looked like something alive. The rich mahogany hues retreated to make way for the flame of titian. Trinity had always preferred blond hair. Queenie had the longest, most luxuriant blond hair he had ever seen. Now he decided titian was just as beautiful.

"With us being so shorthanded, I haven't been out for a while," Victoria told him. "You can't imagine how relieved I was when you showed up."

"One look and you were certain I'd want to lug all this equipment around the mountains."

Victoria laughed. He was getting used to the sound . . . and he liked it.

"Nobody does, not even me, but I knew Uncle would send you with me."

"Why? I'd have thought he'd send one of the older hands."

"He wanted to, but I asked for you."

Trinity took a moment to digest that surprising piece of information. Getting involved with Victoria wasn't part of his plan, but he'd be a liar to say he wasn't tempted. He had withstood temptation before, though he couldn't remember when it had been quite this difficult.

"Buc doesn't trust me," he said.

"Buc doesn't trust anyone, but I trust you."

"Why?"

"Usually men who reach your age are either very dependable, or they take up easier work."

43

"What do you mean by *reach my age?*" Trinity demanded. He hoped he didn't sound vain, but no one had ever remarked on his age in quite that way.

Victoria laughed at his reaction.

"Don't tell me you're sensitive about your age." She looked at him more closely and burst into cascades of laughter.

"My God, you are. You are positively rigid with outraged pride."

"It's not my age," Trinity said with as much conviction as he could muster. He didn't like being off balance, and this unexpected turn in the conversation had caught him completely unawares. "I don't even mind telling you how old I am. I'm thirty-one, but I didn't think that made me an old man."

Victoria laughed again. Clearly it didn't occur to her that her amusement might hurt his feelings.

"I didn't mean it that way. Usually boys take to being cowhands because they think it's fun and they have lots of freedom to act like a man. You know, get drunk, shoot at anything that moves, and chase women. But by the time they reach their mid-twenties, they either decide they like being a cowhand and settle down to doing it properly, or they look for something easier. I have a great respect for anyone who can do the job. A cowhand who's reached thirty has to know what he's doing. Otherwise he'd have been dead or seriously wounded long ago."

Trinity hoped he didn't show his embarrassment. To have gotten upset when she meant to compliment him mortified him. Besides, he had just suffered another shock. Never in his entire life had he been around a woman who could laugh as Victoria just had: honestly, freely, unconsciously, with no ulterior motive.

The women he knew laughed only with their voices. Everything else about them seemed to be waiting and calculating, but it was a nervous expectation, one they didn't seem to enjoy. Everything about Victoria's laugh spoke of her pleasure, and the pleasure she would have if he joined her.

Even though he knew he was smiling at himself, he didn't mind this teasing. Her eyes sparkled, and mischief danced in and out of her pupils. She made it impossible for him not to smile back at her.

"I don't know why I reacted that way. You made it sound like I was aging rather than maturing. I'm no expert on women, but I don't imagine men like getting old any more than women."

"Then you'll hate it when you turn grey or start to lose your hair, or your waist starts to hang over your belt."

"I think I have a few good years left in me yet," Trinity declared. "And a bit of brown hair."

"Sandy," Victoria said.

"What?"

"Sandy. Your hair's not brown. It's sandy."

"It used to be brown."

"Maybe it faded. Hair does that to some people when they get older."

"I hope you plan to help me down from my saddle," Trinity said, more acid than amusement in his voice. "After riding this far, I doubt I'll be able to stand by myself."

Victoria's laughter trilled in the crisp, morning air. "Nonsense. You'll be riding just as straight in the saddle when you're seventy as you are now."

"To hear you tell it, that can't be more than a few weeks away."

Victoria laughed again then sobered. "I don't know why I'm picking on you. I'm nearly twenty-three and unmarried. That's the same as being a confirmed old maid. Not that I'm likely to ever be anything else."

She spoke the last sentence more to herself than Trinity.

"I didn't mean to start feeling sorry for myself. I suppose being an old maid is better than being hanged."

"Most people would say so."

"It's just that when I remember my wedding day, and what I thought my life would be like, well, it's hard to accept."

45

Chapter Four

She seemed to give herself a mental shake.

"I didn't mean to go on about myself. I'm afraid that's one of the results of being left to myself too much, of not seeing anyone new for months, or years, at a time. When you finally do meet someone, you chatter your head off."

"Chatter all you want," Trinity said. "I've got nothing to do but listen. By the time you get through playing with all your instruments, I hope you won't have a single thought you haven't dragged out, dusted off, and thoroughly aired."

"What do you mean, playing with my equipment?" Victoria asked, slipping from the saddle before Trinity could lift her down. "Surveying isn't a game to keep me busy."

"Then what are you doing?"

"I'm making an accurate map of my uncle's land."

"Surely he could hire someone to do it."

"He could if either he or Buc thought it was important enough."

"And you do?"

"Uncle Grant can't seem to understand people won't be able to use government land forever. The only way to keep land is to own it. And the only way to own it is to survey it so you'll know what you have, what you don't, and what you want."

"Does your uncle subscribe to this theory?" Victoria asked.

"Unfortunately, no. But he thinks it'll keep me busy, so he lets me do it."

"Where did you learn how to survey?"

"From my father. My mother died when I was a child. I used to beg my father to take me with him when he traveled. He wouldn't let me go until I learned to do something useful. So I learned to survey."

"I thought your father owned a ranch."

"He did, but he was a surveyor until he inherited the money to buy it. Unfortunately, he died before he could really enjoy it. I'm going to need you to help me set up."

Trinity helped Victoria set up a tripod and settle the telescope into place. He watched with growing respect as she anchored her equipment firmly and then spent several minutes of intense concentration getting it level. Next she laid out a set of charts, which Trinity admitted he didn't understand. Whatever she was about to do required knowledge that went beyond his experience.

"Now I need to measure the distance to that large pine," Victoria said. "After you call back the measurement, I want you to hold this pole as straight as you can. I have to get a sight on it."

Over the next several hours Victoria worked her way across and along the ridge, measuring a rectangular grid and taking sightings from each of the intersections. When they stopped for lunch, Trinity asked her to explain what she was doing.

"I'm laying out everything in blocks which can be claimed as homesteads. That's what the cabins are for."

"Buc told me they were so the men could stay out on the range and not have to ride so far each day."

"That's what he and Uncle Grant decided when I proposed the idea. It's really the only reason they let me do the survey."

"Does your uncle realize what a service you're doing for him?"

"Of course not," Victoria said, laughing easily. "My uncle loves me dearly, but he thinks women are helpless creatures who have to be cared for and protected. He's certain I know nothing about the ranch, that I'm merely playing at surveying, and that if I would only take a greater interest in cooking and cleaning, I'd be completely happy."

"But you wouldn't?"

"Would you?"

"Not the way I cook."

Victoria laughed again. "You know what I mean. It would be different if I had a family and the normal life a married woman expects. I'd probably be so busy having children, taking care of them, and planning their futures I wouldn't have any time or energy left to worry about claiming land, surveying homesteads, and planting a flower garden big enough for a whole village. My uncle has organized his whole life around my protection, but he won't let me do anything to pay him back."

Trinity saw sadness in her eyes. The kind that stays until it becomes a permanent part of one's thinking and one's life.

"But things didn't work out the way I expected, so I've had to think of something else to keep me busy." She appeared to take a deep breath and shrug her worries from her shoulders before she stood up. "I have to get back to work. I'll never get this ridge done if I sit around talking all day."

She worked him just as hard as if he'd been riding the trails. By the time he had hauled her equipment over several miles of mountainside, climbed over boulders bigger than the house he'd been born in, scrambled up and down ravines, even climbed a tree, Trinity was ready to head home. He had a much greater respect for the men who surveyed the seemingly trackless miles of the West.

He also had a much greater respect for Victoria.

He had better make his move soon. If today was any example, the more he learned about Victoria, the harder it would be to take her back to Texas. He had never gotten to know his victims before. There had been no need . . . and no desire.

This time things were different.

Whatever kind of woman lived inside that beautiful, desirable shell, it was a very different woman from the one

48

he'd expected when she stepped out of her flower garden. It didn't bother him that he was strongly attracted to her. He'd have been worried about himself if he hadn't been. By any standards, Victoria was a lovely woman, and he had always had a weakness for beautiful women.

But there was something more about Victoria, something about her character which had gotten in his craw and wouldn't let him go. She had been characterized as a cruel, selfish woman. Yet instead of complaining about the work she had to do, she looked for things to keep herself occupied. She chafed under the restrictions that were imposed upon her, a captivity nearly as confining as the one from which she had escaped; yet she tried to make sure her frustrations and irritations didn't worry her uncle and Buc. She denied having committed the killing that made it impossible for her to lead a normal life, yet she seemed reconciled to spending the rest of her life in this valley.

There were too many contradictions, but he did understand one thing. Whatever reasons she'd had to murder her husband, they weren't what he'd been led to believe.

A bountiful and delicious dinner awaited them when they returned.

"Now you know all this talk about my cooking and cleaning is just fiction," Victoria admitted when Trinity looked at her, a question in his eyes. "Ramon and Anita do it better than I ever would. And they like it."

Two diminutive Mexicans grinned at Trinity.

"You could try reading," Trinity suggested.

"I'm not much of a scholar. I like to read newspapers, and I'd love to have some magazines with pictures of the latest fashions or stories about what people are doing these days, but I'm easily bored and much too restless to sit still." She laughed. "I even tried embroidery. You only have to look at this tablecloth to understand why Uncle Grant was glad I gave it up."

"And quilt making," Buc added.

"Wouldn't you know I'd be terrible at the only practical things I know how to do. I like to sketch, but nobody can tell what I've drawn."

Grant Davidge looked uncomfortable. "I've told you over and over, I have no eye for art."

"But you're perfectly capable of telling when a tree doesn't look like a tree."

"You can ride out with me whenever you like," Buc said.

"And be treated like a fragile flower by every man on the place," Victoria said, her mouth compressed in annoyance. "No, thank you."

"You make sure nothing happens to her," Buc said to Trinity as they walked back to the bunkhouse later that evening. "I can't make her believe it's dangerous for her to be riding around in those mountains."

"She's working too hard on that survey to get into trouble."

"I don't know why she insists on doing it. I can't make her see it's not the kind of thing a lady ought to do."

"She's bored. She's an intelligent, active woman. She needs to be doing something."

"Don't you go putting notions into her head," Buc said, spinning around to face Trinity. "She ought to stay home. My mother did. So did every other woman in the town where I grew up. It's not normal for a woman to run about the way she does."

"There's nothing *normal* about Victoria's life. How many women in your neighborhood had been convicted of murder? Or lived on a remote ranch with absolutely nothing to do from dawn until dusk? How many were completely cut off from other women? How many had given up hope of having a husband and a family?"

"Victoria will have a family," Buc stated, the light of triumph in his eyes. "She's going to marry me."

Trinity fell instant victim to two emotions: Jealousy at the thought of Victoria becoming any man's wife, and scorn that Buc would expect Victoria to marry him without his showing the slightest concern for her thoughts and emotions, or anything that didn't have to do with the physical requirements of being a wife, mother, and manager of a household.

He would have bet his horse Victoria had no intention of marrying Buc. A woman didn't turn her back on the man she loved. Or completely forget his presence. Or treat him like a brother and talk to him like a child with limited understanding. Hell, since he'd arrived, she'd reacted more to him than she had to Buc.

"Have you talked with her about it?" Trinity asked, trying to sound offhand.

"Of course not. Not after the terrible time she had with Jeb Blazer. I talked to her uncle."

Just like a man of Buc's stamp to decide Victoria was going to marry him even though he'd never broached the subject with her. Did he think he owned her just because he saved her life?

Trinity felt something inside him knot.

"I think you'd better talk to her. She may have some different ideas."

"What do you know about Victoria's ideas?" Buc asked, his stance belligerent. "You spend one day following her over the mountainside and think you know more about her than I do after five years of living with her day to day."

"I didn't say a thing about knowing her better than you," Trinity said, hoping to neutralize some of Buc's anger. He didn't like the man, but he didn't see any point in unsettling him needlessly. "I just think you ought to talk to her. When a woman has as much time on her hands as Victoria, you never know what kind of things she'll get to thinking about."

"Ain't that the truth," Buc said, with an abrupt about-face. "There's no end to the number of excuses she can come up with for not staying inside the house. Not to mention going about on her own, no matter what I say to the contrary. At least when we're married, I can tell her to stay home."

"And you think Victoria will do it, just because you say so?"

"It's a woman's duty to obey her husband."

"I wouldn't be surprised if Victoria has a slightly different idea of duty."

"It don't matter what you think," Buc responded irritably. "She'll do what I tell her. And while I'm thinking of it, you stop calling her Victoria just like you been knowing her since the two of you were babies."

"She asked me to."

"She asks everybody to, but they all call her Miss Victoria. Only Mr. Davidge and I call her by her Christian name."

"And what am I supposed to do when she jumps all over me? She's already forbidden me to call her 'ma'am.' "

"Just tell her you don't think it's proper to call her by her first name until you're better acquainted."

"Suppose she says she wants to get better acquainted?"

Trinity said the words partly out of frustration with Buc's blindness, partly to needle him, and partly as a joke. He got more than he bargained for. Buc had his hand on the bunkhouse door, but he turned and came at Trinity like a wounded grizzly.

Trinity drew his gun and fired into the ground between Buc's feet. Buc stopped in his tracks.

"You make another disparaging remark about Victoria, and you'll have to use that gun to keep me from tearing you apart," Buc said.

"I didn't say anything disparaging about Victoria, and I didn't mean to get you upset," Trinity said, "but you've got some ideas that won't jump with Victoria's. There's no need to get out of frame with me," Trinity said when Buc showed signs of starting for him again. "If I'm wrong, you've got nothing to worry about. If I'm right, Victoria would have felt that way whether or not I came along, so you can take it up with her. Either way, I don't like to be crowded. I intend to speak my mind whether you like it or not."

Trinity saw Buc's eyes cut to something behind him. Trinity whirled around to find Perez leaning against the bunkhouse doorway, a rifle aimed directly at Trinity's heart.

"Put that away and get back inside," Buc called out. "This is between Trinity and me."

"Just making sure," Perez said as he pulled his rifle and his head back inside.

"You be careful what you say," Buc said to Trinity. "Perez and I aren't the only ones who'll take exception if you say anything against Victoria. And a couple of them are better with guns than you are."

"I've already run afoul of Red. You people have got to stop acting so jumpy every time a stranger rides up. You're going to shoot somebody one of these days, and then the territorial marshal will be on top of you."

"You threatening to notify him?"

"You don't listen to anybody, do you?" Trinity realized he'd never be able to explain anything that the big man didn't want to hear. "All I'm saying is you got to be careful not to give the law a reason to come nosing about. The best way I can think of to bring them down on you like a nest of hornets is to start shooting at people any time they say something you don't like."

"He's got a point there, Buc." Grant spoke from the shadows behind Buc. Neither man had heard him come up. "Gunshots don't go uninvestigated," he said, "even in the wilds of Arizona."

"Is anybody hurt?" Victoria asked.

"I told you to stay in the house," Grant said, turning. Impatience made his voice sharp. "You didn't know what might have been going on out here."

"Let me guess." It only took a glance to see Buc and Trinity were squared off against each other. "Trinity said something Buc didn't like, so Buc charged him, and Trinity fired over his head to prevent a fight."

"Close enough," said Trinity.

"He said things about Victoria," Buc explained.

"What kind of things?" Grant asked, firing up dangerously.

"I doubt he said anything to justify a fight," Victoria said, intervening to stem her uncle's anger. "I don't know Trinity yet, but I have a feeling he likes to bait people. I do know you, Buc. An outsider being around me for more than five minutes winds you up tighter than a clock. All you need is one ill-chosen remark and you explode like a wild man."

"And I provided the remark," Trinity confessed. "I wouldn't have if I'd known the kind of response I was going to get."

"Well, now you do," Victoria said, "so please be careful what you say. I'd hate to have to patch either of you up."

"Come on up to the house and cool off," Grant told Buc. "Perez, maybe you'd better take a bunk between these two." The old man had remained standing just inside the doorway.

"You've got to stop fighting with every man who comes on the place," Victoria said to Buc. "Pretty soon there won't be anybody here but you and Uncle Grant. And you've got to get some sleep," she said, turning back to Trinity. "I've got a whole ridge to survey tomorrow."

Trinity watched the trio walk back to the house together, and a flicker of loneliness flared in his heart. For the first time in years, he wanted to belong someplace. For the first time since his father's death, he didn't look forward to traveling the trails alone, spending the night by himself under the stars, cooking his own food over a solitary campfire.

And he understood for the first time that, even in the midst of a dozen men sworn to protect her, Victoria might be just as lonely as he. Victoria had looked at both men as she spoke, but Trinity knew she spoke only to him.

He knew it because of little things. She had looked for him the moment she emerged from the shadows. Her gaze lingered on him a moment too long. Did he detect a shade of warmth in her gaze which hadn't been there yesterday? He could hear a different nuance in her tone when she spoke to him and when she spoke to Buc. He could feel an invisible reaching out he could neither see nor explain.

He felt an answering response within himself. That didn't surprise him. He already knew he found Victoria attractive. What did surprise him was the strength of his response. If Grant and Buc hadn't been present, he would most certainly have taken her in his arms—damn the consequences.

He found himself being thankful for her quick departure. He didn't like feeling out of control. He never felt that way with men, no matter how dangerous the man or the situation.

"You better come in," Perez said from the bunkhouse doorway. "If Buc comes back and finds you standing there, he will have a fit. We had enough fireworks for tonight."

"I'm not looking for a fight. I just want to be by myself."

Victoria's departure left Trinity feeling abashed. He and Buc must have looked like two damned fool boys, standing in the middle of the yard, fighting over a girl who didn't care that much about either of them. Damn Buc anyway. And to hell with his obsessive jealousy.

Trinity didn't want to stick his nose in Buc's business. It went against the grain for him to offer advice to any man. He had wanted to help Victoria, but from now on she could handle her own affairs. Interfering only made him feel foolish.

Unfortunately, rushing pell-mell to Victoria's aid didn't seem to demoralize anyone else. Everybody on the place lived in constant readiness to do battle at the most trifling provocation. And they didn't think it the slightest bit unusual, the whole place was a tinderbox. He would have to be very careful, or he might inadvertently strike the spark that would cause the whole situation to explode.

Victoria needed time to think.

She liked Trinity Smith too much. She liked him more than anyone who'd ever come to Mountain Valley, and that upset her.

She enjoyed talking to him. He made her laugh and he made her forget. No female could help but be attracted to a man with Trinity's good looks and his teasing smile, but that didn't explain why the first thought to pop into her head when she heard the gunfire was Trinity might be hurt.

She hadn't stopped to ask herself if Trinity had caused the trouble or had been the victim of it. She hadn't thought of Buc or any of the hands. And that made her feel guilty. She owed her life to Buc. Why hadn't she thought of him?

She hardly knew Trinity. Actually, she didn't know him at all. She didn't know where he had come from, where he had been, or anything he'd done before he came riding up the creek yesterday.

Then how could she possibly have become so enamored of him?

Victoria rejected the most obvious answer. No matter how attractive and fascinating Trinity might be on the surface, she couldn't be falling in love with him in just one day. She had done that with Jeb, and she'd vowed she'd never again become involved with a man she didn't know thoroughly. One such mistake was enough for a lifetime.

But Trinity treated her differently from any man she'd ever met. She couldn't put it into words just yet. It seemed to be more in the way he thought of her than in his actions. She felt he saw her as a real person, someone with the same rights and privileges he had, someone capable of having opinions and feelings worthy of respect.

But even that couldn't entirely explain her reaction to him. Did she feel responsible for him?

If anything happened to him, especially if it involved Buc, it would be because of her. It didn't matter that she couldn't help it or didn't want it to happen. It would still be due to Buc's inordinate jealousy of every man who looked at her . . . and his distrust of strangers. She'd be doing Trinity a kindness if she told him to leave. Bue would never like him and would always be looking for some reason to start a fight.

But no sooner did she think of Trinity leaving than she knew she wanted him to stay. She had never met anyone who made her feel so anxious to taste the wine of life. She didn't know what the key to his secret might be, but he couldn't leave until she had discovered it for herself.

And if it should turn out that he liked her a little bit. . . . Well, she wasn't sure about that. A tremor of excitement ran through her. What woman wouldn't be excited to have such a man interested in her? She couldn't see anything wrong with a little harmless flirtation.

Just as long as neither of them took it seriously.

"What are you thinking about?" Victoria asked the next day. Trinity stood looking out over a remote canyon in the valley while she relaxed sitting under a giant oak.

"Not much," Trinity replied.

"You've hardly said a word all day."

"After Buc tried to make mincemeat out of me, I decided it might be best if I kept my mouth shut. And my opinions to myself."

"So you do have opinions?"

"Yes, Miss Victoria, I have opinions."

She threw a stone at him. He looked up in surprise. It was a large stone, and it hurt. He could tell from her look that she intended it.

"I'd rather you didn't talk to me at all if you're going to call me *Miss Victoria*. I've tried everything I know to convince you I hate it."

"Everyone else uses it, and you don't seem to mind."

"You're not everyone else, are you?"

"No."

"Then why should I treat you the same way? I knew you were different the moment I saw you. I *counted* on your being different. You can't let me down."

"I don't quite understand."

"You're the only person who treats me like a normal person instead of some precious doll to be protected from outsiders and from myself. If you're going to act this way, I might as well have asked Buc to come with me. He might suffocate me, but at least he talks to me."

Trinity dropped his reserve, and an irresistible smile

57

danced across his face. "I tell jokes. I tell stories. I even tell tales. Which would you like?"

"Nothing like that," Victoria said, an answering smile in her eyes. "I'd just like to be treated like a normal person."

Trinity picked up a small stone and threw it at Victoria. It hit her on the shoulder.

"What was that for?" she asked, startled.

"You wanted to be treated like a normal person. Well, if a normal person had thrown a rock at me, I'd have thrown one back. So I did."

"Just like when you were eight," Victoria said with a chuckle. She found a pinecone and tossed it at Trinity. He caught it, but the points stuck in him so badly he dropped it.

"More like six or seven," he said as he lobbed it back. "I matured early."

"I guess that makes you an old man by now."

"If you're going to start on my age again, I'm not going to talk at all," Trinity threatened. "Who knows, I might grow so old by nightfall I won't be able to make it home on my own."

"Since I'm in the bloom of youth, I'll help you."

"Not with broken bones you won't."

"How ungallant," Victoria responded with feigned shock.

"You don't think comparing me to Father Time is ungallant? A man's age is a sensitive thing. A woman's fate may depend on her beauty, but a man's fate often depends on his strength and quickness as well as his youth."

"You don't think brains count for much?"

Trinity helped her up. She brushed off her skirt.

"Yes, but unfortunately most young men don't put much store by brains. They haven't had enough experience to know better."

Victoria had started toward her horse, but the bitterness in his voice caused her to direct a sharp look at him.

"Do you have something particular in mind, or is that a general observation?"

"General," he said, deciding to turn the conversation to

something else. He didn't want to go into his past. He didn't want his foolishness exposed, but the buried vitriol pushed its way to the surface, and his anger and frustration poured out.

"You've been complaining about being looked after and cared for and worried about until it's about to drive you crazy. But men are taught to do that *by women*. By our mothers, grandmothers, sisters, aunts! Everybody keeps telling us how we have to honor a good woman, cherish her, protect her from harm, give up our lives for her, until we can't think any other way."

"It sounds like your education was a little excessive, but I don't see how—"

"Nobody ever tells us about the other women."

"Other women?"

"The ones who'll cut your throat, or lie to you, or take everything you've got as quick as a man. They don't teach you how to tell the good ones from the bad. All the women who hang out in saloons aren't bad, and all the women who go to church on Sunday aren't good. But nobody tells us that. They just keep telling us to worship at a woman's feet until we can't do anything else.

"Of course the day comes when you meet your first *other* woman. And she takes advantage of everything you've been taught. It's as easy as taking candy from a baby. Before you know it, you're in so deep you don't know which way is out. Half the time you wouldn't get out if you could. Until the morning you wake up and find it's all been a lie.

"And do those *good* women help you then? Not a bit. They push you down farther. They tell you she was a bad woman and it was your own fault for putting yourself in her way. You deserved what you got. You'll know better in the future. In fact, some of them are so helpful they want to keep you from having any contact with a good woman. Like that's going to solve anything."

Trinity stopped abruptly, then took a long, slow breath as if to regain control of his stampeding emotions.

"I wanted you to talk to me, but I didn't know you were

going to explode. I should have thrown a rock at you earlier."

"Sorry," Trinity replied more calmly. "You hit a sore spot."

"So I see."

Trinity helped her into the saddle.

"You want to tell me about it?"

"I don't know why I mentioned it. It happened fifteen years ago."

"People can get hurt just as much at sixteen as any other age. Probably more," Victoria added. "You have so little knowledge at that age. And no thick hide to dull the blows when they come."

"I certainly didn't have one, but I guess that was my own fault. You don't want to talk about my callow youth," Trinity said, mounting up. He didn't want to recall an incident which, after fifteen years, still had the power to make him feel stupid.

"Girls want things that can do them just as much harm as the things boys want. I thought I wanted a husband who was handsome and rich and rebellious, but I only had to be married to Jeb for one hour to realize I had made a mistake. Only problem is, there's no way for a girl to escape her mistakes. A boy can go West, but what can a girl do?"

Chapter Five

"Run away and become an actress," Trinity answered, his devil-may-care smile banishing the solemnity of their discussion. "With that glorious head of red hair and your wonderful skin, men would pay to see you even if you had a stammer and a squint."

Victoria nearly choked on a gurgle of laughter. It was just as well—it helped to disguise her extreme pleasure at Trinity's modest compliment. She felt herself grow warm about the face; something fluttered in her stomach; her nerve endings were suddenly alive and sending messages at a frantic rate.

"I could see a stammer. It might be thought affecting, but surely not a squint."

"A squint. They would all think you were winking at them."

"Are men so susceptible to a wink?"

"They are when a woman like you does the winking."

Victoria longed to have Trinity explain to her why her winks would be so entrancing, but she knew that would be indulging in pure vanity. With a considerable effort, she compelled herself to forego that pleasure, but the effort brought forth a sigh of regret.

"Unfortunately I didn't have your bold vision. I reached the conclusion I had no way out."

"What did you do?"

"I didn't do anything. It was done for me, though it nearly cost me my life."

"Do you know who murdered your husband?"

"No. Everybody was around, but nobody was *there*."

The sound of a rider coming toward them along the trail distracted Trinity's attention. He thought nothing of it until he saw Victoria tense and grow pale. She pulled her horse off the trail and into the shadow of a large boulder. Seconds later Buc rounded a bend up ahead, and Trinity watched Victoria visibly relax.

The men of Mountain Valley Ranch weren't the only ones wary of strangers.

"What are you doing over this way?" Victoria asked. "I thought you were at the other end of the valley."

"I came to ride home with you. We can't have Trinity hogging all your time. Pretty soon he'll start to think it's his right, and the rest of us won't get so much as a smile."

"I don't think Mr. Smith is particularly anxious to monopolize my company. I even had to take him to task for not talking to me. There were times when I thought he'd forgotten I was here."

"He'd have to be dead to do that," Buc said. "There's not a man who's ever set eyes on you who isn't counting the minutes until he'll see you again."

Trinity dropped back to allow them to ride abreast. After a few minutes he didn't even hear Buc's fulsome compliments. He had wanted to hear Victoria's version of what happened that night, and he cursed the jealous temperament that made Buc ride thirty miles across the valley for a thirty minute ride home with Victoria.

He was also extremely angry at himself for mentioning Queenie. He had told himself it didn't matter any more. He hadn't spoken of her to a living soul since his father's death.

Now, in one brief, unanticipated conversation, the bitterness and anger came spurting to the surface. But worse than that, he had been so weak as to tell it to someone else. *To another woman.*

In all the years since it happened, he'd never lost control.

What kind of hold did this woman have over him? He'd never manage to fulfill his mission if he didn't get his response to Victoria under control.

Or cut it off altogether.

"Tell me about the places you've been," Victoria asked.

They were on their way home after another long day and had stopped at one of Victoria's favorite spots, an outcropping of rock which afforded them a view up and down the length of the valley.

They stood side by side, next to their horses, not looking at each other—that would have been too dangerous—but at the distant mountains. In the pristine mountain air, Trinity could see with amazing clarity peaks nearly a hundred miles away.

The sun had burned away the mist, and everything below stood out in fine detail. The lighter green of maples and aspen against the darker shades of pine and fir were as vibrant as a magnificent painting. White fleabane, rose-colored asters, and the brilliant yellow of poppies, goldenrod, and sunflowers splashed colors across a landscape dominated by brown and green.

In such a spot, it was possible to feel like they were the only two people in the world.

Trinity knew they shouldn't linger. He had already proven he couldn't control his feelings when it came to Victoria. Just knowing he was alone with her, close to her, made his muscles ache with delicious tension. He could feel his fingers nervously flex at the thought of touching her.

Only her horse stood between them.

"There's not much to tell," Trinity replied, deciding to make the story of his life brief and his description of the places he'd been unglamorous. "All towns look pretty much alike. And people aren't much different no matter where you find them."

"I've never been anywhere. I grew up on my father's ranch, moved to my husband's, and then to my uncle's. I've never seen anything but cows, and I've never talked to anybody but cowboys."

"Most of what's out there isn't worth the trouble. It's certainly not worth exchanging for a place such as this."

Victoria looked at him across her saddle. "You can say that because you've seen it for yourself. I haven't *seen* anything. I don't *know* anybody. No matter what Uncle Grant tells me, I know there's more to this world than Mountain Valley Ranch."

"Most women live out their lives on some farm or ranch."

"But they know they can leave if they want," Victoria said. "I can't. Not ever. It makes me feel absolutely desperate sometimes."

"Not too desperate I hope."

Victoria laughed despite the gravity of the subject. "Not desperate enough to let somebody take me back to Texas, if that's what you mean. Missing something is quite different than being cut off from it altogether."

Trinity couldn't resist her laugh. He turned to Victoria, a quirky smile on his lips.

"I wouldn't recommend visiting friends in Texas just now, but I don't see why you have to stay here if you don't want to. There are lots of places you could go. I doubt anybody outside of Texas has heard of you. You could go to London or Paris. Even New York. There're so many people there nobody would find you, even if they were to come looking."

"I don't know why I didn't think of it before," Victoria said, excitement shining in her eyes. "You can defend me."

"No, I can't," Trinity stated flatly. "I'm not a lawyer."

Victoria laughed at him. "And you're not an ignorant cowpoke either, even if you do try to talk like one when you remember."

It was impossible for him to concentrate when she laughed. It simply engulfed him. Her smile teased and tempted him, but there was a timbre in her voice which invited him to share something intimate with her.

"Maybe not," he said, trying to push every sensation out

of his mind, "but that's a far cry from knowing the law and how to use it."

"I'm not asking you to do anything with the law. I want you to organize an investigation into Jeb's murder. You would hire detectives to collect the evidence and lawyers to present it in court."

"But . . ."

She came around her horse and stood in front of him, her eyes looking up at his. "Don't say no, at least not yet. Think about it."

Trinity forced himself to step back. If he stayed that close to her a minute longer, he wouldn't be able to think of anything but her eyes . . . or her lips. He might not even be able to think at all.

"Have you talked to your uncle about this?"

"Several times, but he doesn't think it would do any good. Neither does Buc. They think I ought to be content with things as they are."

"And you can't be?"

"How would you feel if everybody thought you were a murderer who was only alive because your uncle broke you out of jail?" Her glorious blue eyes entreated him to help her. How could any man resist such a look?

"There's not a man on this ranch who believes you're guilty."

"They've all been wonderful, but there's not one of them who believes a pretty woman *can* commit a crime."

"An investigation could cost a lot of money."

"My inheritance will cover the costs."

"If you've got plenty of money, why're you wasting time with me? You ought to hire a professional."

"How do I know he wouldn't turn against me? No one seems able to stand up to Judge Blazer."

"How do you know I could?"

She gazed directly into his eyes. "I just do."

Trinity hadn't expected that. It caused the knot which had been in his stomach for several days to tighten with a jerk.

"You don't know that. I could be a bounty hunter or a sheriff's deputy, or even a private investigator."

Her gaze didn't falter. "You could, but you're not."

"You can't be sure."

"I'm just as sure as I could be of anybody else."

Trinity felt desperate. He didn't want to refuse. But worse than that was the feeling he was somehow betraying her, that he had become a Judas rather than a Paul.

"What would your uncle and Buc say?"

"They wouldn't have to know. This would be between you and me."

The words were like an electric shock. He had scrupulously avoided any thoughts involving just the two of them. He couldn't do that any longer, the vision was too sweet.

"Why me?"

She came a step closer.

"I like you. There's a kind of kinship between us." Victoria looked a little uncomfortable about being so direct, but not embarrassed. "You're different from Buc and my uncle. I haven't figured out what it is just yet, but I tend to trust people I like. People I'm attracted to."

Trinity swallowed hard. For three days he had struggled to control his growing attraction to Victoria. She probably liked him for no other reason than he was someone new to talk to. Only reminding himself it would be insane to become involved with a woman who was about to be hanged for murder had enabled him to maintain his control. . . . A control her last words shattered.

Of all the futile things, he wanted to protect her: a woman surrounded by a small army sworn to defend her with their life's blood, and he wanted to protect her. But they only protected her body. Not one of them had taken the time to get to know the woman inside. That made him feel protective.

"Being attracted to me isn't the same thing as liking me."

He had to touch her. He couldn't stand here any longer and wonder what it would feel like to brush her cheek with his fingers.

"You mean I can't be attracted to you or like you in a general way?"

Her cheek felt soft. There was a firmness to her flesh, but it dimpled beneath his touch. He twisted his finger around one of the errant locks which clustered about her face. He barely resisted the impulse to run his fingers through her hair.

"Not when it's between a man and a woman."

Victoria leaned closer and tilted her face up to his. He couldn't concentrate on anything but her lips and her deep blue eyes. Victoria pressed ever so slightly against his hand. "Are you saying there's something sexual in my feeling for you?"

What was he doing? He couldn't afford to let an emotional bond develop between them. The scars would stay with him for the rest of his life.

Trinity snatched his hand back like it had been burned. He'd met several direct women before, but never one who would ask such a question. And the fact that it could be coming from this gorgeous redhead made it even more difficult to believe.

"Ma'am, I'd never say a thing like that."

"Don't call me ma'am, and don't avoid the question."

"Okay, if you insist, no. I don't think you can be attracted to me without it being sexual as well."

Boy, wouldn't Buc love to hear him say that! He'd probably blow a hole right through him.

"Why?"

"Because I can't be attracted to you without feeling hot as hell."

Damnation! He could have sworn he saw a gleam of satisfaction in her eyes. Why did women always feel they had to humble a man? Couldn't they just like him in an ordinary way?

Can you like her in an ordinary way? That was a foolish question. Only Buc could like Victoria in an ordinary way, like a stallion pursuing a mare because instinct told him to.

"Are you telling me I excite you?" Victoria asked, coming so close he could almost feel her body heat.

"Didn't you expect I would?"

"No."

She may have been around men most of her life, but she obviously didn't understand her effect on them. He had to get the conversation on another track, or he'd get himself thrown out before nightfall.

Trinity stepped back. "I think it's time we started back. This discussion is headed in the wrong direction." He took a good grip on the saddle and started to put his foot in the stirrup.

Victoria didn't move. "Why haven't you said something?"

The woman was determined to get him shot. Had she been so protected she didn't know how she affected boys like Red or men like himself?

"You're a beautiful, desirable woman, ma'am, and I wouldn't mind the opportunity to tell you how much I appreciate your kind of beauty. However, I'm nothing but a cowhand, and every man on this ranch is just waiting for me to make a wrong move. Reminds me of a week I spent in a small gold mining town in Colorado several years back. I didn't find any gold, but I did find out I could live without a woman better than I could live with holes in my hide."

"I don't believe you scare that easily." She took a step toward him. Trinity stood his ground.

"It's not a question of being scared. It's a question of common sense. And honor." Desperation made Trinity add, "A man doesn't jump another man's claim."

Victoria stepped back, her eyes flashing fire. "What a disgusting thing to say. I'm a woman, not a piece of property. Besides, I don't belong to Buc."

"You'd better tell him that. He and your uncle seem to think you're going to marry him any minute now."

"I like Buc, but I feel more strongly attracted to you than I do to him."

Hell! Why did she have to go and say that just when he'd gotten his gumption back. He had met half the famous "ladies" of the West. He'd loved a few, he'd left them all. Yet, he'd been brought to his knees by little more than a pair of lovely blue eyes, some unmanageable locks of titian hair, an irresistible laugh, and a relentless desire to turn him inside out. Not to mention the candor to tell him she liked him more than the man she was supposed to marry.

If it were possible, that admission seemed to shock Victoria more than Trinity.

"Why?" asked Trinity.

"I didn't mean that like it sounds." Victoria seemed to be searching for words to blunt the impact of what she had just said. "It's just that Buc wants to own me. That suffocates a woman. You seem more interested in discovering what I'm really like. I like that."

Trinity gripped the saddle as though it were his lifeline. He had to get himself in hand. He needed something to block her view of the swelling bulge in his jeans.

"Why?"

"Don't you know any other word?" Victoria asked, exasperated. "I don't know why. Maybe you don't have to understand why to be attracted to someone. Maybe it's just there the moment you set eyes on them."

"You're a beautiful woman," Trinity said, keeping his hold on the saddle. "A man would have to be unnatural not to feel attracted to you."

"I didn't mean like that," she said, annoyed. "I meant a special kind of attraction, the kind you have when you want to know more about a person. It's a desire to be with him, to share yourself with him as much as you want him to share himself with you. It causes thoughts of him to pop into your head all the time. It keeps you wondering what he's doing, what he's thinking. Surely it's happened to you before."

"You mean the way it happened with your husband?"

He couldn't have checked her intensity more if he'd thrown a bucket of water in her face. She turned away from him and looked out over the valley once more.

"No, I don't. I was sixteen years old, and my father was dying. Something had to be done about my future. Dad picked out a rich, handsome young man and asked me if I thought I'd like to marry him. He was twenty-one, charming, and devil-may-care. I thought he was wonderful, and I said yes. I knew I was supposed to. Only after I married Jeb did I realize the kind of hell I'd wandered into."

Trinity could visualize Victoria as a helpless young wife terrorized by her drunken husband, and a dangerous feeling of sympathy welled up inside him. Much too dangerous when they were standing this close.

"I don't think we ought to think too much on this attraction stuff," Trinity said. He wondered if he'd be able to take his own advice.

Victoria spun around to face him. "Why?"

"I thought you didn't like that word."

"It's precisely the one I want. Why?"

Trinity knew the best thing for him to do was mount up and head back to the ranch. He shouldn't even wait to see if she followed. Leaving her to find her own way home wouldn't get him into half the trouble answering that question would. He was a fool to have let things get this far. He was slipping. His nerve wasn't what it used to be.

"Let's suppose, for the sake of argument, I fell in love with you."

"Could you?"

"Ma'am, any man would find it hard not to fall in love with a woman who looks like you."

"I didn't say anything about my looks," Victoria corrected. "I said *me*."

Why couldn't she ask questions like "Do you like my hair this way?" or "Isn't this a pretty dress?" He could handle those without endangering his hide and his soul.

Trinity concentrated on keeping his hands on the saddle.

"I don't really know you, ma'am, but I don't imagine it would be too hard. Anyway, I've wandered away from my point. Suppose a cowpoke like myself was to come wandering in here and fall head over heels in love with you. Your uncle and Buc would put a stop to that before you could take a deep breath."

"Suppose I were to fall in love with the cowpoke?"

Any cowpoke worth his salt would move heaven and earth to make her his wife. That's what he'd do. It's what Red would do. But he couldn't tell her that.

"It wouldn't make any difference. They still wouldn't have any part of it."

"Even if I told them I loved him, that I'd never love anybody else?"

Her eyes had never looked as blue, as sincere. Trinity wondered if Jeb might not have been as thoroughly bewitched by his young wife.

"Especially if you said that."

"What if I were willing to run away with him?"

She was relentless.

"He wouldn't do that, not if he loved you."

"Why?"

"Growing fonder of that word all the time, aren't you?"

"Don't stall."

She came closer, but Trinity had managed to keep his horse between them. She looked at him across the saddle.

"Because a cowpoke wouldn't have anything to offer a woman like you."

"All I would want would be the cowpoke."

"He would want to give you the world. It would kill him not to. It would be worse than turning his back on you."

"How stupid." Her exasperation was unmistakable. "Only a man would think of leaving a woman just because he couldn't give her things she might not even want."

"Not *a* woman, Victoria. *You.*"

"It wouldn't matter. A woman wouldn't think like that. As long as she were with the man she loved, nothing else would matter."

Trinity found it difficult to doubt her. Yet he could never quite forget she had been found with the gun in her hand.

"Not all women are like that. Some of them want what a man can give them more than they want the man."

"But if a man *really* loved a woman, he could tell the difference."

He wondered if she had looked at Jeb like this. If so, the

71

poor man never had a chance. Not even alcohol could make him indifferent to such a woman.

"Not always. Love can do terrible things to a man's judgment."

"I don't imagine it could affect yours any longer."

"Not as much as it once did."

"But it can still affect it a little?"

"When it's combined with an aching physical need, yes, too much."

"Are you aching?"

Trinity felt his temperature rise about ten degrees.

"Ma'am, that's an unfair question. How can I be this close to you and not feel the need?"

"A man *needs* a woman, but he *aches* for a certain woman."

"How do you know that?"

"A woman feels the same way."

Trinity's grip on the saddle tightened until his knuckles turned white. If he didn't head this conversation in a different direction, she would pick his defenses apart. She was twisting him around her fingers, just like Queenie.

"One thing you don't do is throw yourself at a man. He might get the wrong idea," Trinity cautioned.

"Suppose he had the right idea."

"Another thing, you don't tease a man with what he can't have."

"How do you know you can't have anything? You haven't asked," Victoria parried.

"Ma'am, you got things in the wrong order. A woman like you had better know exactly what she's offering before she lets a man know she's interested. Once he knows she's available, he makes the decisions."

"That doesn't seem fair."

"Maybe not, but it's the way the game's played. Now you pull in your horns and stop teasing me. I know you're just trying to twist me around your finger so I'll set up this investigation for you, but another man might not. Let me help you mount up. It's time we were going."

Relinquishing his death-like grip on his saddle, he walked

around his horse and put his hands around Victoria's waist to lift her into the saddle. She didn't move. In fact, she planted herself more firmly in front of him.

"What makes you think that's all I'm interested in?"

Trinity paused. "That's all I got to offer."

"You're wrong, Trinity. I *do* want you to help me, and I *was* trying to coax you, but that's not all you have to offer. It's not even close to all I like about you."

"The sooner I get you back to the house, the sooner I can go stick my head in a bucket of cold water."

Once more he started to lift her into the saddle. Again she didn't move. He became terribly conscious of his hands on her waist. The intimate contact gave rise to all sorts of visions that further challenged his self-control.

"What would you do that for?" Victoria asked, caught between a gurgle of amusement and surprise.

"There's nothing like cold water to cool a man off so he can start thinking straight."

"You mean you really are attracted to me, not just my face or my hair?"

Trinity didn't know whether to move his hands or try once more to lift her into the saddle. He liked them where they were, so he left them.

"I never thought about you divided up into parts."

"I'll make you a deal," Victoria offered. She stood so close he could see his warmth reflected in her eyes. "If you'll stop playing the wandering cowboy and talking like you never saw the inside of a book, I'll not try to cajole you into taking my case."

"Are you going to try to cajole me into anything else?"

He wondered if she would interpret the quiver in his voice as fear or anticipation. He certainly wasn't going to tell her it was naked lust. He doubted she would understand. But more important, with that terrible admission out of the way, he didn't know if he could restrain himself any longer.

"Why would you ask such a question?"

"I learned long ago I had a weakness where pretty ladies

73

were concerned. I make it a practice to stay away from them."

"Like you're staying away from me?"

"Can't very well do that unless I quit the Mountain Valley Ranch."

If you don't let me help you into your saddle, my hands are going to grow to your sides. Then Buc and your uncle will have a good reason to shoot me, he observed.

"Are you going to quit and run away?"

Trinity gave up. He drew her to him until his lips brushed her hair. She didn't smell of perfume like Queenie. He detected the faint aroma of scented soap, but nothing he could identify. Just a good, clean smell. Her hair felt softer, thicker, looked more lustrous. He longed to bury his fingers deep in its abundance.

His hands shifted position. Instead of being around her waist, they held her in a loose embrace. Not quite against him, but so close he could hardly control his muscles. His whole body wanted her.

Victoria tilted her head until she looked into his eyes. Then, as though flustered by the intensity of the feeling she saw there, she lowered her lids. Trinity lowered his head until his lips brushed her left eyelid. He felt her quiver beneath his touch and then go still.

"You want me to stay a while?"

"Yes." The laugh wasn't so easy this time. "I'd like that."

"I'd like it, too," Trinity said.

He had become so mesmerized by Victoria's nearness, the feel of her in his arms, he didn't hear anyone come up behind him until a massive hand clamped on his shoulder in a paralyzing grip.

Chapter Six

At the first intimation of danger, Trinity whirled to face his attacker and ran into a punch that sent him staggering.

"Stop it, Buc!" Victoria shouted. "He was just helping me mount up."

"I saw what he was doing," Buc snarled as he jumped on Trinity before he could regain his balance. He struck him a vicious blow to the jaw and followed with another to the stomach which sent Trinity to the ground, groaning in pain. "He was kissing you."

"He was not," Victoria said. She tried to grab Buc's arm and hold him back, but he set her aside, hardly slowing down.

"I won't have any man putting his hands all over my woman," Buc said. "I'll break his neck first."

Victoria's interference had given Trinity time to regain his feet. Somehow he avoided Buc's first rush, but the rapid turn made him too dizzy to escape a second. Before his vision cleared, the two men were down on the ground pummeling each other with all their strength.

Buc outweighed Trinity by at least fifty pounds and stood three inches taller. His biceps were the size of Trinity's thighs, yet Trinity's experience, his methodical manner of fighting, and his excellent physical condition gradually turned the fight from a rout into an even match.

Victoria didn't wait to see which man would wear the other down. The moment they hit the ground, she unstrapped her tripod and removed one of the legs. Waiting until she got a good shot, she cracked Buc over the head.

She didn't knock him out, but he slumped to the ground.

"What do you mean, *your woman?*" she demanded, ignoring Trinity and her uncle, who had just ridden up. "How dare you say something like that. You never said a word about marriage to me."

"I talked to your uncle," Buc muttered, holding his head.

"I told you," Trinity said to her as he gingerly fingered a laceration on his face. His fingers came away bloody.

"You're not ever going to tell her anything again," Buc threatened, struggling to his feet. Not even a blow from an oak tripod leg could make him forget what he had started to do. "I take care of my own."

"I'm not anybody's woman to be taken care of. Listen to me," Victoria demanded, when Buc ignored her, "or I'll hit you again."

But Buc was too enraged to heed Victoria. He had gone beyond the reach of rational thought. He charged Trinity the minute he got to his feet.

"Stop acting like a fool," Grant Davidge ordered. "You know I can't have my foreman getting into fights with the men."

Buc backed away, but his gaze never left Trinity. "He was being familiar with Victoria," he said between gasps for breath. "I found him with his hands all over her. He was practically kissing her."

"He was just helping me into the saddle," Victoria said, raising her pole threateningly.

"You never wanted help before," Buc said.

"You never offered," Victoria shot back. "And what did you mean by telling Buc I'd marry him?" Victoria demanded, rounding on her uncle.

"Victoria, honey, you've got to marry somebody. And nobody loves you more than Buc."

"I don't love him."

"But you like him."

"I *like* Trinity, but you didn't promise I'd marry him."

76

"I'll kill him," Buc raged.

"You hit him once more, and I'll never speak to you again," Victoria said.

"You don't have much choice, honey. Stuck here in this valley, you're not likely to meet too many other men," Grant said.

"What you mean is a murderess ought to be grateful for any husband she can get."

"I don't mean any such thing. I don't say this trouble about Jeb hasn't messed things up a bit, but you won't find a better man than Buc no matter where you look. And he's a good cowman. I'd be content to leave the ranch in his hands."

"Then let him marry the ranch," Victoria stormed, "but I won't marry a man somebody else picks out for me. I did that once. I'm not fool enough to do it again."

"Your uncle didn't pick me out," Buc said, pleading with Victoria, completely forgetting Trinity. "I fell in love with you all by myself."

"If you love me so much, why don't you have some faith in me? If you think I'd stand around letting myself be kissed by a man I've known less than a week, you don't know me as well as you think."

With that, Victoria spun on her heel and started toward her horse.

"I ought to kill you," Buc said, turning on Trinity.

"Don't try it. You won't catch me from behind a second time."

"Knock it off, Buc," Grant ordered. "If you can't stay here without fighting, go for a ride until you cool down."

"But Victoria . . ."

Without waiting for anyone to help her, Victoria swung into the saddle and headed for the ranch at a gallop.

"I think you'd better leave her alone for the time being," Grant said. "It looks like we went about things the wrong way."

"It's all his fault," Buc said, advancing on Trinity once more.

Trinity braced himself for an attack, but Grant's next words halted Buc's advance.

"It's not his fault," Grant said. "It's ours, yours and mine. We got so used to thinking for Victoria when it came to her safety, we started doing it all the time."

"I want you out of here," Buc thundered at Trinity. "I want you off the place come sunup."

"No need to get mad at me just because you made a mistake," Trinity said.

He didn't want to get fired just now. It would ruin his plans.

"You heard me, sunup tomorrow or I won't be responsible for myself." He swung into the saddle and rode after Victoria.

"This is unfortunate," Grant said. "I didn't realize Buc's jealousy had gone so deep. I'm sorry to lose you. You're a good man, and we could use the help right now, but I think you'd better go. I can't have Buc rampaging about. It'll upset the rest of the men too much."

"Don't worry about me," Trinity said. "It just means I'll have to move out a little sooner than I expected."

"I'll bring your wages over to the bunkhouse. I'd rather you didn't come up to the house this evening."

"Don't you trust your niece?"

"It's not Victoria I'm worried about."

"It should be."

"What do you mean?"

"When a man has to fire a good hand because of his foreman, he's lost control of his ranch. If you're not careful, Buc's going to cause you to lose your niece as well."

"I can't believe you fired him just because Buc fell into a jealous rage," Victoria said to her uncle.

"What else could I do?"

"You could have told Buc to start acting like a grown man or find himself another job."

"Don't be ridiculous, Victoria. I wouldn't risk losing Buc

over a fight with a cowhand who probably won't stay the summer."

"I was thinking more about you than Buc."

"I don't understand."

"This is your ranch, Uncle Grant. You claimed the land, fought off the Indians, and brought in blooded cattle despite enormous difficulties. Yet Buc goes around giving orders, throwing fits, and acting like it's his."

"Trinity just said pretty much the same thing."

"You ought to listen. He's not the dumb cowboy he pretends to be."

"He also told me I was in danger of losing you."

Victoria went up to her uncle and put her arms around him. "He's wrong about that. There's nobody in the world I love more than you."

"I don't think he meant I'd lost your love. He meant I'd lose your respect."

An awkward silence fell.

"I was angry with you and Buc for talking about my marriage like it didn't concern me," Victoria said, making sure she looked her uncle full in the eyes, "but I know you were doing what you thought was best. It's just that you were wrong on that. And some other things, too."

"Such as?"

"They don't really matter. The important thing is for the first time in five years I'm thinking about what I want to do rather than worrying about what somebody else will do and what I'll have to do as a consequence."

"Maybe Buc was right to be worried about Trinity."

"Don't men ever give a woman credit for some sense?" Victoria asked, annoyed. "I can listen to Trinity, I can even believe what he says, without falling in love with him. He's traveled all over the world. He's seen things I'll never see. Felt things I'll never feel. Done things I've only dreamed about. He's made me realize I don't want a life dominated by fear."

"What are you meaning to do?"

"I don't know," Victoria confessed. "My feelings are all

turned upside down. I need time to sort them all out again."

"I'm glad that's all. Now if you'd just let Buc explain why he—"

"I am sure of one thing," Victoria said, interrupting her uncle. "I'll never marry Buc Stringer."

"But he's a wonderful young man. Nobody could love you more than he does."

"Marrying Buc would be the same as admitting I can only have what someone else is willing to give me. I can't accept that. Not any more."

"Buc was right. I never should have hired Trinity."

Later that evening, after a couple hours of fruitless reflection, Victoria came close to agreeing with her uncle. Trinity had had nothing but trouble since he arrived, and she felt responsible for it.

He would never have gotten into the fight if she hadn't been so determined to explore the nature of his feelings for her. She should have gotten on her horse *by herself* and ridden home.

Instead she let him stand there with his hands on her waist, his body nearly touching hers, his eyes drilling holes into her soul, and his lips brushing her hair and eyelids. But she liked it. She'd never felt that way before, in a kind of heedless wonder, like she was on the verge of discovering something marvelous.

Trinity had been right. There *was* something sexual in her attraction to him. She'd tried to tell herself it was purely intellectual, but his touch had destroyed that illusion. She could still feel his fingertips on her cheek. She could still remember her delight in their brief embrace.

Victoria's body grew uncomfortably warm. She had tingling feelings in her breasts, in her belly, in her groin. Feelings she had never had before, bone-melting feelings which continued to grow stronger the longer she thought about Trinity's touch. It was a strange but not uncomfortable feeling, one that made her long to increase its intensity tenfold.

But her worry wasn't all for Trinity. She didn't know what to do about herself. Trinity had stirred her up, made her unsatisfied with her life, but he refused to help her change it. Now, after a couple of hours of intense concentration, she still hadn't come up with any answers. Not any she liked.

She could try to lose herself in someplace like New York or London, but she would need to get control of her inheritance. She couldn't go on expecting her uncle to support her. Only thing was, she didn't want to leave the ranch. She loved the feeling of limitless space. Crowds of strangers would smother her.

She couldn't go back to her mother's home. Nobody. there wanted anything except her money. And of course she couldn't go back to Bandera. Not until she was proved innocent.

She had to convince Trinity to go to Texas. Buc wouldn't like it, but that was too bad. He had gotten what he wanted: Trinity was leaving. She deserved a chance to see if she could have what she wanted: freedom.

Trinity crouched in the shadows of the pines, which covered the hill behind the ranch house, and waited for everyone to leave. During the night he'd considered and tossed aside several plans for getting inside the house without anyone knowing. The one he'd chosen depended upon Victoria's being so angry and upset she wouldn't stay home.

He didn't have to wait long to see he had made the right choice. Fifteen minutes after Buc and Grant left the house, Victoria came out through the kitchen door. She nearly ran to the bunkhouse. She emerged a few seconds later, her mouth compressed in anger. Shortly after that she saddled her horse and took to the hills. Trinity had an idea she meant to follow Buc and have some rather sharp words with him.

He smiled at the thought.

Being careful to stay under cover, Trinity scrambled down the ridge. Ramon and Anita were still in the house. He didn't want anybody but Victoria to know he hadn't left Mountain Valley.

It took Trinity nearly an hour before he was able to get into the house without anyone seeing him. But he didn't care. He had all day.

First he went through Victoria's room, taking a few pieces of clothing from each drawer and chest and putting them into a leather bag he brought with him. After he satisfied himself he had taken enough, he placed a folded note in her hair brush where she couldn't miss it. He hoped Anita wouldn't discover it and destroy it.

Then he climbed out of a window and melted into the pines once again.

Victoria didn't reach home until after her uncle and Buc had returned. Despite a fight with Buc, the tenor of which should have banished any hope he had of marrying her, her mood hadn't improved. She had hoped Trinity would want to see her before he disappeared forever. She was upset he hadn't.

She had tried to finish surveying the ridge they had begun together, but every time she needed a second pair of hands, she thought of him. Every time she wanted to share a thought, she missed him. Every time she wanted to ask a question, she felt his absence.

Trinity had excited her more than any man she'd ever met. He had so much energy, vitality, a sense of humor, a confidence, an outlook on life which allowed him to laugh at himself and the things that happened to him.

After five years, during which even trivial occurrences were viewed with life-and-death importance, Victoria had exulted at the change.

It had been like a breath of fresh air, a rekindling of interest in living. For years she had believed her life continually hung in the balance, that any event or stranger could mean a return to Texas and the gallows. Somehow Trinity had made her feel it was possible to prove her innocence if she had the courage to ignore her fears and break the fetters placed on her by others.

Despite all that, she couldn't rationalize why his leaving

caused her to feel such a terrible loss. How did a cowboy she had known for just a few days become more than a passing interest?

She had wanted to thank him for his support, but Buc's temper and Uncle Grant's officiousness had driven him away.

She wondered if her uncle paid him. Three days' wages wasn't much of a grubstake. It certainly wouldn't get him to California. Where would he stop next? How long would he stay?

"Where've you been?" Buc demanded when Victoria walked into the house. Her uncle threw her a questioning glance but said nothing.

She had had a long day; she was tired, and she was angry. Buc's assumption that she owed him an accounting for her time made her furious. He was her uncle's employee, in a sense her employee as well. If any one of them owed the other an explanation, it was Buc.

"Riding."

"Where? I've told you time and time again you can't go wandering over the countryside alone. Who knows when another stranger will come wandering in?"

The possessive tone in Buc's voice, combined with the "another stranger will come wandering in" remark, was the last straw. She lost her temper.

"And will you drive him off like you did Trinity? Are you going to drive everybody off for the rest of my life?"

"He wasn't any good, Victoria, just a wandering cowpoke looking to have a little fun. You only noticed him because he made you laugh."

"Is there some law which says I can't have fun?"

"Aw, Victoria, you know what I mean."

"I'm afraid for the first time I do."

"What do you mean?"

"You've got me locked up in this valley and you mean to keep me here for the rest of my life."

"You've got to have someone to protect you."

"Have you decided on the wedding date? How many children will we have? Do I get to name them, or do I just get to have them?"

"Now Victoria—" Grant began.

"Don't 'Now Victoria' me," she nearly screamed. "I won't be kept in prison, and I won't have my entire life decided for me. You should have left me in Texas. I couldn't be any more imprisoned there than I am here."

"Stop it right now, before you say another word," Grant Davidge ordered, his own temper rising. "Buc risked his life to get you out of that jail. The very least you owe him is gratitude."

"I am grateful," Victoria said, "but I don't owe him the rest of my life."

"Buc would make you a fine husband."

"I'm sure you're right, but Buc never said a word about loving me before Trinity came along. How do I know it's not simple jealousy?"

"I loved you from the moment I saw you," Buc protested.

"Then you should have told me instead of my uncle. Did you ask him to walk in the moonlight, sit with him on the porch, or whisper secrets in his ear?"

Buc's face turned a dull red. "I wouldn't do that to anybody."

"That's right," said Victoria. "You just assumed I'd been bought and paid for."

"I thought you were still upset over your husband. What would I look like trying to talk love to a woman grieving over the death of her husband?"

"You'd look like a tortoise. Had there been a jackrabbit anywhere in sight, you'd have lost the race years ago. Only there was no jackrabbit. There wasn't even a coyote or a sidewinder. Just the tortoise. And after five years you've finally reached the finish line. I wonder if you'd have reached it at all if Trinity hadn't arrived."

"What the hell are you talking about?" her uncle demanded, his expression a mixture of impatience and confusion.

"This is all Trinity's fault," Buc exploded. "You never talked like this before he came."

"You're right. I'd forgotten what it was like to live without fear."

"All he did was put ideas into your head that can get you killed," Grant said. "You know you can't leave this valley."

"Like I know I ought to marry Buc," Victoria finished for him. "He's the only man you can trust."

"I've always had complete confidence in Buc," Grant said.

"I have, too, but that's not why a woman marries a man."

"Then what is?"

"I'm not certain, but I don't mean to marry anyone until I find out."

Victoria turned on her heel and stalked from the room.

"If I ever see that man again, I'll kill him," Buc stormed.

"She's been restless for some time now," Grant said. "If he hadn't come along to stir her up, someone else would have. You can't keep a woman locked up and not expect an explosion once in a while."

"What do you think I ought to do about it?"

"Hell, I don't know. I don't understand women. That's why I didn't get married."

"I don't understand them either, but I want to marry Victoria."

"Then let her alone. Things will be right uncomfortable for a while, but she'll settle down."

Victoria wasn't thinking about marriage when she stomped into her bedroom. Neither did she think vengefully of wringing Buc's neck and hanging her uncle up by his toes until he admitted she might have a mind of her own. Instead her thoughts were more concerned with a sandy-haired cowboy and his impish smile.

She would miss him . . . more than she dared admit.

It wasn't right for her to blame Buc and Uncle Grant for everything. Even if she hadn't said anything, she had tacitly accepted that someday she would marry Buc.

Now she couldn't imagine why. Buc had absolutely no understanding of her feelings. Trinity had learned more about her in five minutes than Buc had learned in five years.

She'd never again make the kind of mistake she'd made with Jeb. This time she intended to choose her husband because she liked being with him, because she couldn't think of living the rest of her life without him, because just being with him was the most exciting thing that could happen to her.

Odd how natural it all sounded, yet until a few days ago none of this had occurred to her. It made her feel stupid, and she didn't like that.

She sat down at her table and picked up her brush. A note fell to the floor.

Chapter Seven

Even before it fluttered to the floor, Victoria knew it had to be from Trinity. Her hands shook so she had difficulty picking it up. She unfolded it quickly.

> I wanted a chance to say goodbye. I'll wait for you at the base of the old pine you used as a marker. I'll understand if you don't come.
>
> Trinity

Victoria didn't understand the tangle of emotions which erupted within her. She shouldn't be having such a strong reaction to a man she would have trouble recognizing again. *Don't lie to yourself. You could pick him out in a crowd of thousands.* Even his profile remained etched in her mind. He was too muscled to be slim. Rather he was lean, the way a man is lean when he uses his body too hard and feeds it too seldom. A man of muscle and bone. He had none of Buc's size, but Victoria wouldn't have been surprised to find he was just as strong.

She was attracted to him in ways that confused her, ways that excited her, ways that had caused her to lie awake at least an hour each of the last two nights.

Victoria didn't know what she expected to get from this farewell, but she was sure if she didn't meet him she'd regret it for the rest of her life.

* * *

With a loud curse, Buc turned his horse and headed back toward the ranch. He didn't know what had gotten into Victoria, but something was wrong. Grant said it would be a long time before her sweet disposition returned, but when she sat down to dinner last night, she seemed like her old self. *Almost.* She talked and acted like she used to, but behind the smiles lay something he could sense but not see.

This morning her mood had seemed a little forced. At first he thought she was trying too hard to pretend her outburst had never happened. He wanted to think that. It answered everything in a tidy, satisfactory way. But his intuition, honed to needle-sharpness by jealousy, provided him with another answer.

Victoria acted like a woman about to meet her lover — she was going to meet Trinity.

"How can I do that, even if I wanted to?" Victoria asked when he taxed her with his suspicions. "Uncle Grant sent him away two days ago. He's probably out of the territory by now."

Her answer seemed more logical than his suspicions, but he couldn't get the idea out of his head. She *did* act like she was up to something. She *did* want to get them out of the house. Somehow, she intended to meet Trinity.

He would see about that. No flea-bitten cowpoke was going to make time with his girl. He was the one who rescued her out of that Texas jail. She belonged to him.

He would follow Victoria. He wanted another chance to break Trinity's neck. And this time Grant wouldn't be there to stop him.

Victoria made herself wait a full hour after Buc and her uncle left before she saddled her horse. She wanted to make certain no one followed her. Besides, she didn't know if Trinity would be at the tree this early. He might not be so anxious to see her he would get up before dawn.

She felt a little self-conscious, like a young girl sneaking off to meet a boy her parents didn't like. Not that she'd ever had a chance to sneak off to meet anyone. Jeb had been the only boy she'd ever known, and her father had wanted her to spend as much time with him as possible.

She'd never even seen a boy from *the other side of the tracks*. She wondered if Trinity qualified. Buc certainly seemed to think he was up to no good.

The less she thought about Buc, the better. If Trinity had done nothing else for her, at least he had jolted her out of accepting the notion of marrying Buc.

But what else could she do? Nothing until she found a way to get control of her inheritance. Maybe she could still talk Trinity into helping her. If not him, then lawyers. Judge Blazer couldn't keep her money from her. There was no law which said people convicted of murder couldn't be rich.

Victoria experienced an upsurge of hope. She felt happier than she had in years. Everything seemed possible once again. She only had to figure out how to accomplish what needed to be done.

But where did Trinity fit in?

Now that he was leaving, apparently nowhere.

But she couldn't let him leave just yet. He was her beacon to the future. Would she be able to stand against Buc and her uncle if she stood alone? Trinity was no ordinary man, and her response to him hadn't been ordinary. She believed they would never be able to forget each other.

As she drew near the ridge where the great pine grew, she had second thoughts. Wasn't it really a little strange for him to want to say goodbye? Couldn't he have put all he had to say in the note? Or, he could have left a message with her uncle, or have waited until morning and said goodbye in the natural way?

Victoria let her horse drop out of a trot into a fast walk. What did she expect from Trinity? It made her feel foolish to realize she didn't know.

She had allowed herself to become so excited over seeing him one more time she hadn't figured out what she hoped to get out of it. Well, yes, she had, but she'd thought more about what he represented than the man himself. And that mortified her. She'd just complained about Buc and her uncle treating her as only a body and here she was looking at Trinity only as an escape route. An attractive, exciting, exhilarating way out, but a way out nevertheless.

Seeing him meant more than trying to find someone to investigate Jeb's death. It meant more than thanking him for giving her the courage to fight against her mental and emotional imprisonment. It meant saying goodbye to someone who, in a very short time, had become terribly important to her.

But saying goodbye meant bringing something to an end. It came as a shock to her she didn't want things to end.

Victoria pulled her horse to a halt.

She would miss his humor, his sensitivity about his age. And of course she'd miss being with him. Despite the disturbing sexual tension that had started to develop between them, he had been a comfortable companion.

Maybe it would be better if she didn't see him after all. It would only create more memories, which might come to haunt her in the years ahead.

The sound of hoofbeats on the trail below scattered her reflections. It must be Trinity, but she didn't know what direction he might be coming from. He might have been watching to see that she came alone, to make sure Buc hadn't planned an ambush. But even as she turned around to wait for him, a shadow of fear skittered through her mind.

Victoria pushed the thought aside. She would soon be as bad as Buc, seeing bounty hunters in every shadow, suspecting every stranger she saw. She had to get over being frightened. She didn't want to spend her whole life jumping at shadows.

She recognized Buc's big Appaloosa as soon as it came into view. He had followed her.

Victoria felt anger heat her face until she felt certain her skin flamed as red as her hair. She didn't know which made her more angry, that Buc distrusted her enough to follow her or that she might not get to see Trinity. Either way, she was furious.

"Where is he?" Buc demanded, as soon as he came within shouting range.

"Who?" Victoria replied. Again, she wondered how she could have ever thought of marrying Buc.

"Trinity," Buc said, spitting out the name like it tasted bad. "I know you came to meet him."

"You know nothing of the sort," Victoria challenged. "You only think I'm going to meet Trinity because you're so jealous you can't think of anything else anymore."

"I knew something was wrong at dinner. Your uncle thought you'd cooled down, but I knew you were up to something. And this morning I figured it out."

"Then tell me where Trinity's been hiding for the last two days and how I'm supposed to find him."

"I don't know, but I know you're going to meet him. You can't do it, Victoria, not when you're about to become my wife."

"I like you, Buc, I always have. And I'll be eternally grateful to you for springing me from that jail, but I can't marry you because of gratitude."

"Why not?"

"Why not!" Victoria repeated, aghast. "Don't you want a wife who loves you, who will look at you with adoring eyes?"

"I'd be suited if she liked me pretty good. You do like me. You said so yourself."

"It's not enough for me. That's the way I felt about Jeb, and look what happened."

"But I'm not like Jeb. I don't drink."

"That's not the point. Jeb and I had nothing in common. We didn't even like the same people."

"We like the same things."

"How can you tell? In the five years I've been here, I haven't seen anybody or done anything. We never talk. You never ask me what I would like. *I* don't even know what I like. Sometimes I feel like I don't know myself."

"Damn Trinity. He had no right to get you all confused."

"Will you never understand? This has nothing to do with Trinity. I had already changed before he got here. I've been in a cocoon, only I didn't know it. He helped me realize it. Suppose I had married you and discovered I hated everything you loved. I'd have made your life miserable."

"There's nothing you could ever do that would make me miserable."

"Go home, Buc. I want to be alone. There are some things I have to sort out." Victoria was almost defeated by his blind loyalty.

"You're going to meet him, aren't you? Answer me, Victoria."

"I'm not answerable to you for my actions."

"You can't meet Trinity. I won't let you."

Victoria was speechless. Buc had been telling her what to do ever since she had known him, but he had never attempted to interfere in her personal life.

"Do you love Trinity?" Buc asked before Victoria could respond.

"How could I? I hardly know him."

She couldn't have fallen in love with him, could she? No, but she found him extremely attractive. Maybe that was the answer. She had heard of men who were so overcome with physical desire for a woman they lost all common sense. Some even drove themselves to ruin.

But women weren't like that. Were they?

"No, I don't love him, but I would have liked to talk to him before he left."

"I don't believe you."

"I beg your pardon!"

"He's got you besotted. You never acted crazy before."

"So I'm crazy, am I?"

Buc couldn't see the trap he had built for himself. He sensed that Victoria was taken with Trinity when she ought to be looking to him. He was jealous, and he was angry.

"You're about to let your infatuation with him cause you

to throw away five years of caution, you've stopped looking over your shoulder."

"But you've been looking over my shoulder for me, haven't you?" Victoria demanded, furious. "You've been looking over my shoulder, and around the corner, and under the bed, and behind the door for five years. You had me so thoroughly terrified I did it, too."

"Don't turn away from me, Victoria," Buc said, bringing his horse up to Victoria until their knees touched. "I haven't thought about anybody else for five years. I love you. I want you to be my wife."

"I'm sorry, Buc, but I've already told you I don't love you."

"But you'd marry that saddle bum—"

"Buc, be reasonable. I've just met Trinity. I don't love him, and he doesn't love me."

"He's got you hypnotized. He wants to marry you so he can get the ranch."

"You're crazy."

"I won't let him have you. I've looked after you all these years and I don't mean to stop now."

"This is absurd."

"Are you going to meet him? Tell me!" Buc shouted.

"Yes, I'm going to meet him. To say goodbye."

"I knew it," Buc shouted. "Where is he?"

"I don't know. He left a note asking me to meet him on the ridge, but he's not here."

Buc moved closer to Victoria and grabbed her horse's reins. "I'm taking you back to the ranch. I won't tell your uncle what you've done, but you've got to promise you won't do anything like this again."

"Take your hands off my reins," Victoria ordered. She was so furious her lower lip quivered uncontrollably. That just made her madder. "How *dare* you threaten to say anything to my uncle. You're the most presumptuous, egotistical hardhead I've ever met. I'm not going anywhere with you. And I won't be treated like I'm doing something wrong."

"I'm only doing it for your safety. You know I never think of anything except you."

"Then it's high time you started. First chance you find, get yourself into Flagstaff. Get drunk or whatever you want to do, but don't come back until you've gotten over this crazy idea I'm going to marry you."

Victoria tried to back her horse away from Buc, but he still held the reins, and his strength gradually forced her mount alongside his.

"Nobody's going to have you except me."

Buc tried to kiss Victoria, but between trying to control his own mount, keep his hold on her horse, and take an unwilling Victoria into his embrace, he couldn't manage.

"Hasn't anyone ever told you it's unwise to attempt to make love to a woman on horseback, particularly if you're riding separate horses?" Trinity's voice came from close behind them.

Victoria ceased to struggle. She didn't have to. Instinctively, she knew Trinity would make everything right.

"Damn you to hell," Buc cursed. Whirling about to face Trinity, he let Victoria go so suddenly she nearly fell out of the saddle. "I said I'd kill you if I ever saw you on Mountain Valley range again."

"So you did, but then some of us make a practice of promising more than we can deliver."

The two men swung down from their saddles.

Victoria was furious at Buc for forcing a fight and angry at Trinity for agreeing so quickly. Couldn't men find a less barbaric way to settle an argument?

"Stop it right this minute," she said as firmly as she could. "I won't be fought over. Neither of you has any claim on me."

Neither man paid her any attention, and that angered her even more. How dare they pretend they were fighting because of her when it was nothing more than stupid male vanity! They were no different from range bulls or wild stallions.

"I have a score to settle with you for attacking me from

behind," Trinity told Buc. "A man of courage makes his presence and his intent known. Only a coward attacks from behind."

"I don't waste time talking to rattlesnakes," Buc said. "I just crush them."

"I don't crush easily," Trinity responded, "especially not by coyotes."

"Stop it!" Victoria cried as she drove her horse between the two men. "This won't settle anything."

"Stay out of the way, Victoria," Trinity said, trying to shove her mount aside.

Buc came around the back of the horse, attempting to catch Trinity on the blind side once more. Victoria's horse sidestepped, causing Trinity to lose his balance. He dived under the horse's belly to escape Buc's deadly rush.

"Stand and fight like a man," Buc said.

"I will, when you stop trying to get me from behind."

Trinity, the smaller and faster man, slipped around Victoria's horse and drove his fist into Buc's jaw. He followed that by a powerful punch to Buc's midriff. Buc doubled up with a groan of agony.

"Stop it," Victoria said. "Can't you see you're acting like animals."

"I didn't start this fight," Trinity said, "but I won't back down."

"You're both crazy," Victoria cried, but Trinity didn't hear her. Buc had regained his feet, and he charged Trinity with all the fury of a wounded bull.

Once again Trinity spun out of Buc's reach, but not before he smashed the big man's face. The blood which gushed from Buc's nose seemed only to make him more determined to murder Trinity.

This fight had an entirely different character from the first one. Then Trinity had been taken by surprise and the fight stopped before he could recover. This time, Trinity set the tempo and style of the conflict. Buc fell to his knees in less than two minutes.

"Please don't hit him again," Victoria begged. "Can't you see he's too weak to continue?"

"The hell I am," Buc said, getting to his feet.

But two more powerful blows from Trinity's fists sent Buc to the ground again, unable to get up this time. Victoria slid out of her saddle and rushed to his side.

"You've nearly killed him. Why didn't you stop when I asked? I thought you were different, but you're just like all the rest."

"I didn't start this," Trinity protested, but Victoria seemed not to hear him.

"Get his horse. I've got to get him home." Victoria tried to help Buc rise. He stunned her by pushing her aside.

"I don't need your help."

"You're hurt. Your eye's so swollen you can hardly see."

"Leave me alone," Buc shouted. "I don't need a Jezebel to help me into the saddle."

His words shocked Victoria so badly she stepped back giving Buc a clear view of Trinity's back as he attempted to catch Buc's horse. Without warning, Buc pulled his gun.

"Watch out!" Victoria screamed.

Trinity threw himself aside just as the bullet smashed into the rocks close to his head. Victoria threw herself on Buc's arm. The next moment Trinity had wrestled the gun from Buc.

"I think it's time you went home," Trinity said. "I'll forget you tried to shoot me in the back, but if you ever pull a gun on me again, I'll kill you."

"You'd better kill me now," Buc said, savage fury in his voice. "If you don't, I'll be on your trail until you're dead."

"Go home, Buc," Victoria said. "Think up something to tell Uncle Grant. I don't want him to know what really happened."

"Are you coming?"

"No. I can't go with anybody who'd try to shoot a man in the back."

"You don't warn a poisonous snake before you shoot it," Buc spat.

"He's a man, Buc. And any man deserves to see his opponent face to face."

"You're in love with him, aren't you?"

"Buc, I've already told you—"

"Don't lie to me." Buc wiped some of the blood from his mouth. "I know you love him. I could feel you start to tremble the minute you heard his voice."

"What's the point in answering when you won't believe anything I say?"

"Go on then. Go away with him. Turn your back on everybody who's ever worried about you, tried to keep you safe, wanted to take care of you—"

"Stop it!" Victoria nearly screamed. "You've done everything you could to make me feel indebted to you, to feel guilty if I do anything you don't like, but it won't work any more. Say what you will, do what you must, but I'm going to start making my own decisions."

"You mean you're going away with him."

Victoria looked upward as though beseeching God to give her patience. "Buc, I'm going to ride a short way down the trail with Trinity. If you want me to go back to the ranch with you, I'll be back in a little while."

"I can make it on my own."

"Fine. We won't speak of it again."

"I'm not done yet," Buc said. "I've got plenty more to say."

"Not to me. Let's go," Victoria said, turning to Trinity.

Trinity helped Victoria mount up and then vaulted into his saddle. Victoria twisted around until she could see Buc. "I never wanted any of this. I wish things could have gone on between us as they always had."

"They couldn't," Buc said, "not once he came."

Victoria turned and headed down the trail.

"Why did you fight him?" Victoria asked after they had ridden in silence for some time.

"He didn't leave me much choice."

"You didn't have to hurt him so badly."

"Maybe you forgot he attacked me from my blind side two days ago."

97

"He was just angry," Victoria said. "He thinks you're taking me away from him."

"It doesn't matter what he thinks," Trinity said, his voice caustic. "A bullet kills no matter why it's fired."

"I know that."

"Then act like it. You're blaming me because I won. Would you have blamed me if he'd shot me? Not that hitting somebody in the mouth and being shot in the back are quite the same."

"Now you're being just as insufferable as Buc. You can't seem to think you're a man unless you shoot somebody else or beat them up."

"As a matter of fact, people say I'm usually quite even-tempered. I'm just not used to being cussed out for trying to defend myself."

"I'm not blaming you for defending yourself."

"It sounds like it to me."

"I guess I'm just feeling guilty. Buc fought you because of me. Somehow I feel responsible."

"Don't. Nothing you can say will change Buc's mind. I know. I listened to you for a little while before I spoke up."

Victoria turned to face Trinity. "You mean you eavesdropped on our conversation?"

Now it was Trinity's turn to roll his eyes heavenward.

"You don't have to eavesdrop when two people are shouting at each other in the middle of a mountain trail. You could be heard for miles. Besides, I wanted to make sure you weren't having a private conversation before I broke in on you."

"We were."

"I know."

"Then why did you break in?"

"He started to force himself on you."

"That wasn't any of your business."

"Probably not, but I felt partly responsible."

"Why is everybody determined to take responsibility for what I do?"

98

"I thought it might have been something I said. You seemed willing to marry him when I arrived."

Victoria sighed, much of her anger disappeared leaving her limp and downcast. "You know, there are times when I almost wish you hadn't stopped here."

Trinity let Victoria explain all the things that had gone through her mind in the last few days. A judicious question now and then kept her talking steadily as they rode farther and farther from the ranch. She became so caught up in what she was saying, she didn't notice the distance.

Neither did she notice that the farther they rode, the more rigid Trinity's expression became, his body more tense.

An enormous pressure had built up inside her over the last few years, and she had to get it out of her system. Once she vented all her frustration, she turned to trying to get Trinity to agree to investigate Jeb's murder. He kept insisting she ought to hire professionals, but he never actually refused. Victoria felt sure if she just kept talking, she could talk him into it.

She had been talking steadily for nearly two hours when she abruptly drew rein.

"Where are we?" she asked. "I don't recognize anything."

"We're still on your uncle's range," Trinity assured her. "This appears to be a game trail. I haven't seen any signs of hooves, so I guess it's not much used."

"I'd better turn around," Victoria said. "It'll take me hours to get back to the ranch. I want to see how Buc's getting along."

"Ride with me to the other side of the ridge," Trinity asked.

Victoria noticed his eyes didn't shine with their usual energy and good spirits. He seemed unusually tense, even upset. It made her feel a little less downhearted to think he was unhappy about leaving.

"I'd better turn back now," she said. "I shouldn't have come so far. I don't know why you let me talk so much."

"I like to hear you talk."

"Thanks, but I'm worried about Buc. You really hurt him."

"Are all your thoughts for him?"

"No." She decided to tell the truth. "I've wondered a great deal about you, but I've made up my mind not to ask any more questions. You'll be a lot easier to forget if I don't know so much about you."

"You're going to forget me?" Trinity asked.

The injured vanity in his voice made Victoria smile.

"I'm going to try very hard. I already have too many ghosts to live with. I don't need any more."

"Sure you won't ride to the crest of the ridge with me?"

"I can't."

Trinity shrugged, seeming to accept the necessity for doing something he didn't want to do. She wondered again if there were some way for him to stay but knew there wasn't. He had to go.

Trinity brought his horse alongside Victoria's, both mounts pointed in the direction of the ridge. "See that pink shelf just beyond the saddle on the left?"

Victoria followed the direction of Trinity's hand.

"Yes," she said, wondering what the ridge could have to do with his leaving.

"Make for that point."

Before Victoria could ask Trinity what he meant, he rent the air with an earsplitting yell. At the same time he brought his crop down on the rump of her horse. The animal sprang forward with a scream of surprise and fear.

Trinity's actions were so sudden and unexpected they threw Victoria into a panic. She raced toward the ridge with unquestioning faith, certain Trinity wouldn't drive her mount ahead of him unless there was some dire emergency.

When they reached the ridge, she tried to pull up, expecting Trinity to explain. He drove her on, whipping her horse across the rump until it raced along the mountainside at a mad gallop.

A sudden suspicion pierced Victoria's heart like the sharp, cold blade of a knife.

"What are you doing?" she demanded, her words ripped out of her mouth by the cold wind.

All traces of feelings had disappeared from Trinity's face — all compassion, all humanity. He stared at her out of a stranger's eyes.

"I've been deputized by the sheriff of Bandera to take you back to Texas to hang for the murder of your husband."

For a moment Victoria's brain refused to accept any of what Trinity had said. It couldn't be true. If it were, Trinity wasn't any better than the rest. In fact, he was worse. Much worse.

A moan of anguish tore from Victoria, and she threw herself from the saddle.

Chapter Eight

Victoria's unexpected action caused Trinity to cast aside his pretended detachment.

"You crazy fool!" he shouted. Throwing his gelding on its haunches, he galloped back to the spot where Victoria had pitched headlong from the saddle. The mountainside fell away in a tangle of intertwining vines over a carpet of pine needles. He hoped it was enough to break her fall. They were a long way from a doctor.

The sound of something running through the undergrowth told Trinity Victoria was alive and on her feet. Throwing himself from his saddle, he leapt over the side after her.

It seemed every bush hit him in the face. There must have been a lightning fire a few years back. Everything was about the same size, his eye level. He couldn't see Victoria, but he could hear her, scrambling down the mountainside just ahead of him.

"Slow down. You could kill yourself."

He received no answer except the sound of Victoria crashing through the brush. He redoubled his efforts.

"You're lost. You don't know where you are."

He crossed a trickle of a stream and scrambled up and over a small spur which angled off the main ridge.

"You can't stay here by yourself at night."

The sound of her flight grew dimmer, and Trinity started to wonder how long it would take to catch her. She could dive under the dense brush while his height forced him to break a path through the tangle. He could only follow by stopping periodically to listen for the direction of her flight. They entered a stand of aspen, and he caught sight of her through the slender tree trunks which shot up from the meadow floor like thousands of silver needles.

Calling on his greater strength and better conditioning, Trinity sprinted after her, determined to catch her before she could disappear in the undergrowth farther down the mountain. But his boots weren't made for running, and his stride resembled a halting stumble rather than a smooth lope. His only consolation was that Victoria struggled along in the same kind of boots.

Much to Trinity's surprise, Victoria was still well ahead when she plunged into the dense brush once more.

Cursing, Trinity pushed in after her.

A few moments later he realized he didn't hear any noise. He waited and still he heard nothing. What had happened? Had she found a place to hide? Was she waiting for him to go past so she could climb back up the slope to the horses?

A chill of apprehension knifed through him. Had she fallen? Was she hurt? He had to find her. She had no food, no warm clothing, no horse, and no shelter for the night. She'd left her rifle in its scabbard. He didn't think any wild animal would pose a threat to her, but going about unarmed wasn't a good way to find out.

Trinity searched the ground for some sign of her passing, but the tangle of undergrowth and the carpet of leaves and broken twigs was undisturbed. He had lost her trail.

"Hell and damnation!" He couldn't remember when he'd behaved so foolishly. He had let his fear for Victoria's safety cause him to run after her like a scared lover rather than an officer of the law. He had responded to her femininity rather than her criminality. He was beginning to wonder just which one of them was the captive.

Retracing his path, he found her tracks a hundred yards back. She had turned back up the mountain. Trinity guessed she intended to made a big swing and end up on the trail where she left her horse. Fear might have lent speed to her flight, but it hadn't hampered her ability to think.

He had no difficulty following her trail. He would have to teach her how to cover her tracks if she was going to spend much time in the woods.

It was easy to see where she fell. It wasn't as easy to guess whether she had been hurt. Her trail gave no blatant indication of a twisted ankle or a favored leg. Five minutes later her trail disappeared into a cleft between two upstanding boulders. Trinity paused. He didn't trust places he couldn't see into. He wouldn't put it past Victoria to hit him over the head with the biggest rock she could find . . . or blame her.

He tossed a pebble in before him. Nothing moved. He heard no sound.

"Come on out," Trinity called. "You'll never be able to find your way back to the ranch alone."

Still no sound. He rounded the corner and found himself facing the opening of a small cave. He looked around but could find nothing to use as a torch. He would have to enter in darkness.

He called into the cave. "I know you're in here. It would be easier if you would come on out."

Still no answer.

He stepped inside, being careful to keep his hand against the wall. He felt the small hairs along the back of his neck prickle. Only an idiot entered a cave without a light. Any kind of wild animal could be using it for a lair. If there were young in the cave . . . well, he didn't want to think about it.

There could also be a ledge, a hole, any number of dangers, which could kill him, injure him, or trap him permanently. Keeping his hand against the wall and his left foot before him, Trinity edged forward. After he had gone beyond the light from the entrance, he struck a match.

He jumped back in surprise.

Hundreds of bats hung mere inches from his face. Disturbed by the light, they dropped from their perches and left the cave with a great fluttering of wings. The noise of their flight almost masked the sound of a gasped intake of breath.

Turning halfway around, he saw Victoria, huddled against the opposite wall, just before the light of the match burned out. Without waiting, Trinity plunged across the space between them. He was rewarded by contact with Victoria's body . . . her kicking, scratching, gouging, kneeing, biting, screaming body. He could have captured a mountain lion about as easily. He felt trails of stinging pain as her nails raked furrows across his cheek.

"Stop. I don't want to hurt you."

"You can't expect me to believe that when you're taking me back to Texas to hang," Victoria shouted, as she twisted away from him long enough to punch him in the shoulder.

"It's nothing personal." Trinity struggled to get her hands and legs under control. "I'm just doing my job."

"I hope you don't take it personally if I object to your doing your job," Victoria said, breaking his grip long enough to hit him squarely in the jaw.

"You hit me again, and I'm going to take it very personally."

Victoria kneed him in the stomach.

Trinity bent over with an agonized moan, and Victoria broke toward the mouth of the cave. He let her go. It would be easier to deal with her in the light. He hadn't expected this from her. She had seemed like such a lady at the ranch, so dignified, so restrained. Now he realized two people lived inside her head, and one of them fought like a wild woman when she was cornered.

It took his eyes a minute to adjust to the light, but he had no trouble catching sight of Victoria as she fled up the mountain. He decided to keep after her but not get too close. She'd be easier to subdue after she exhausted herself. Also, if she didn't change direction, she'd be closer to the horses and his chosen camp for the night.

Quite frankly, he didn't want another brush with her nails. He put his fingers to his cheek. They came away covered with blood. Between her and Buc, he'd lost more blood than from a bullet wound.

"You might as well give up," he called as she struggled up a particularly steep part of the mountainside. "I'm going to catch you sooner or later."

"I prefer later."

"Be careful," Trinity called out when he saw her leap across a deep ravine. "You could fall and hurt yourself on those rocks."

"Why so much concern all of a sudden? Do you lose your bounty if you don't bring me back alive? Do they take off for bruises and open wounds, or do you get a bonus for bringing me back fighting mad and in bustling good health?"

He didn't understand why her needling got to him. The others had cursed, begged, offered him money and women, called him the worst things they could think of, threatened him with vengeance from relatives, children, and from beyond the grave.

He had remained unmoved, but Victoria's words stung.

He felt guilty about his deception. He never liked deceiving people, but he'd always been able to excuse it because the end justified the means.

He didn't feel that way now, and he knew why. He had violated one of his cardinal rules: Never become emotionally involved with the prisoner.

That made him vulnerable.

He found himself thinking of the way she smiled when she teased him, staring at the delicate arch of her brows, studying the color of her hair, or thinking how much he would like to just sit quietly with his arm around her.

He gave himself a mental kick in the pants. He couldn't keep dreaming up things he liked about her or he'd end up wanting to protect her. And that wasn't his job. His *duty* was to take her back to Bandera and turn her over to the sheriff. He wouldn't let himself think about what happened after that.

But he still had to guard against his weakness and her

tantalizing presence. And the best defense was a good offense.

"Like you had sympathy for your husband when you shot him?"

"I didn't kill Jeb."

"He wasn't even armed."

Trinity knew all the facts. He had memorized them before he agreed to go after Victoria. He would never have set one foot outside of Bandera if there'd been the smallest doubt in his mind.

"Did you tell him you were going to kill him, or did you just let him get close, maybe even try to kiss you before you shot him in the heart?"

Victoria paused in her climb up the mountain. "I didn't kill him," she insisted, a catch in her voice.

"Then who did? You were right beside him when he was shot. If you didn't kill him, you have to know who did."

"I don't know, but I didn't."

"At first, I thought your lover had helped you. I meant to bring in Buc, too, until I found out you hadn't known him when he rescued you. I also know you haven't seen any other men since."

"You have a sickeningly lurid imagination," Victoria called back. "Is this how you spend your time when you're on the trail, speculating about women and their lovers?"

"Not all women. Just the ones who kill their husbands."

"I didn't kill Jeb," Victoria turned around and shouted at him. "There were a couple of times when I wished he'd disappear forever, but I never thought of killing him."

"Pity the jury didn't agree with you."

"I never expected them to, not after they'd been handpicked by my father-in-law's attorney. I'm surprised they bothered to hold a trial."

Victoria was scrambling up the mountainside with the agility of a mountain goat. Trinity decided her boots must have been made from something other than the hard, inflexible leather which kept him slipping on the damp leaves.

He began to wonder if he was going to be able to last

long enough to catch her. He prided himself on staying fit, too often his life depended on it, but Victoria obviously didn't spend her time in a rocking chair. She had the endurance of a mustang. To judge from the stinging scratches which crisscrossed his face, she also had the claws of a mountain lion.

Trinity wondered if he would have caught her if she hadn't fallen a second time. This time she did hurt her ankle. She didn't get up quickly. When she did, she didn't climb as quickly as before. It took just a few minutes for Trinity to corner her.

But a bad ankle didn't stop her from fighting.

Trinity tied her hands behind her back with his belt. He tied her ankles together with her own belt.

"Don't," Victoria said, when he pulled the belt one notch tighter. "You're hurting my ankle."

"You should have thought of that before you tried to scratch my face to ribbons. Not to mention the bruises I got from your fists or your boots."

Still he let the belt out a notch.

"I wish I'd hit you a thousand times harder," Victoria swore. "If I get loose again, I'll scar your face so bad no one will ever recognize you."

"I'll keep that in mind," Trinity said, preparing to pick her up. "This will hurt a whole lot less if you relax."

He picked her up and tossed her over his shoulder.

Victoria had never felt such agony. "How am I supposed to relax when you're squeezing the life out of me?"

"I'll let you walk if you promise not to hit, kick, or scratch."

"I promise to do all three every chance I get."

"That's what I figured, but it's good to get this sort of thing cleared up," Trinity said as he started up the slope.

"Bastard," Victoria cried, tears of anger and frustration coming to her eyes.

"You shouldn't use such language. It'll ruin your reputation."

"I didn't know you thought I had a reputation worth pre-serving."

"I always try to think the best of people."

"The hell you do," Victoria said, borrowing further from her uncle's vocabulary. "You only do what's convenient."

"I keep as close to the truth as possible."

"It'll be a waste of time to try to convince me you've got scruples. I won't believe you."

"It's a purely practical consideration. The fewer lies I tell, the less I have to remember," Trinity espoused.

"You must have had a lot to remember lately," she coun-tered.

Victoria tried to butt him with her head, but with her body slung over Trinity's shoulder, she had all she could do to breathe.

Trinity paused. "Are you ready to behave?"

Victoria gasped for air. "I'll do anything to get off your shoulder."

Trinity let her slide from his arms. She hit the ground with a big *oomph*.

"Sorry. I'm not used to carrying women over my shoul-der," Trinity confessed as he knelt to untie her feet. "It wasn't as easy to get you down as I thought."

"I don't suppose it would do any good to point out you should have thought of that before you picked me up."

"It's too late now."

"Men rarely accept correction. It threatens their sense of superiority. Yet they expect females to do it all the time."

"I don't have that problem," Trinity said, moving to where he could untie her hands. "I don't have a wife, daughter, mother, or any female I see regularly."

"I can't imagine why," Victoria said, rubbing her chafed wrists to restore circulation. "Certainly no one can fault your gentlemanly approach."

"Some have."

"I imagine she was a shrew."

"Not all of them."

"That many? You really have been unfortunate in your choice of women."

"I didn't choose them," Trinity explained. "I just happened to be around." He put his fingers to his lips and gave an earsplitting whistle.

Victoria winced. "What was that for? There can't be a living soul within twenty miles."

"My horse. He's trained to come when I whistle."

"What if he's tied up or hobbled?"

"I never tie him when I'm on the trail."

"You think you're very clever, don't you?"

"No. Just careful. Not everybody wants to go with me."

"I can't imagine why. Hanging is a such a once-in-a-life-time experience."

"So is being shot by your wife."

"That's what I kept telling Jeb as I filled him full of lead. 'Darling,' I said—I always called him darling. I wanted him to know how much I loved him—'You don't know how lucky you are. Not many men are fortunate enough to be killed by their wives. Most of the time they're killed by somebody they don't even like.' "

"Did anybody ever tell you you have an unnatural sense of humor?"

"Did anybody ever tell you you have a grotesque job?" Victoria responded sweetly.

"A time or two."

A crashing in the underbrush caused Trinity to look away from Victoria. His horse had found him. Victoria's horse followed.

"At least we won't have to walk out of . . ." he said turning back.

But Victoria wasn't there. She had escaped.

"Damn!" Trinity said, unable to hear Victoria because of the unholy racket the horses were making in the undergrowth. Fortunately, just as he was about to dust off a seldom-used portion of his vocabulary, he caught a glimpse of her brown deerskin jacket.

Trinity mounted his horse before the animal had come to

a halt. Victoria's horse came up behind, momentarily blocking Trinity's way, but he soon got turned around and headed across the ridge. Victoria might be able to thread her way through the underbrush faster than he could, but she was no match for his horse.

Victoria's look of fury when she glanced over her shoulder almost made him laugh. She dashed around a large tree, but one look around must have made it plain she couldn't escape. Much to his surprise, she stopped and waited for him to reach her.

"I can't believe you gave up," Trinity said, dismounting.

"I didn't give up," Victoria said. "I'm just not stupid enough to try outrunning a horse."

"I'm glad to see you've come to your senses."

But the minute he reached out to help Victoria mount up, she turned into a scratching, hitting, kicking virago. New scratches appeared on his face.

"Stop it before I swat you."

"Why the warning?" Victoria asked as she aimed a kick at his crotch. "I would have thought slugging females was part of your bag of dirty tricks."

"I never tried to bring in a female before," Trinity said, covering his face as he rushed in to overpower Victoria with sheer body mass. "I'm sorry I decided to make an exception in your case."

The two of them went over in a heap; Trinity ending up on top of Victoria, nose to nose, toe to toe.

"Get off me," Victoria grunted. "You'll break my ribs."

"You promise to stop scratching."

"Never."

She tried to rake his face, but Trinity's body pinned her down. He buried his face in her bosom while he captured her hands.

Had the circumstances been almost anything other than they were, Trinity would have laughed, or succumbed to his lust for her body.

Here he was, alone with a beautiful woman, and instead of having to fight off the raging desire which coursed

111

through his body, he had to fight for his life. He might as well have embraced a catamount.

Yet, as he struggled to capture her hands, he was more aware of her nearness, the feel of her softness beneath him, than of the painful bruises and scratches.

He tried to concentrate on tying her ankles, but her ankles were attached to her legs, and her legs to her thighs. The struggle had exposed one thigh completely. The unguarded expanse of tender white flesh caused Trinity to forget what he was doing until a painful kick reminded him.

Trinity forgot her ankles. He would tie them once she was on horseback. He tied her hands and got to his feet, shaken to the core. He had practically been fighting for his life, yet contact with her body had caused his own body to swell with a desire so naked and so strong they both saw it.

He'd never been ashamed of his reaction to a woman, but he was ashamed that his lust for Victoria had almost made him forget his duty. He kept seeing her as a beautiful, spirited, desirable woman, rather than a cold, dangerous, calculating, murderess. He kept thinking of her beauty, of her charm and allure, instead of her cold heart and lethal fingernails.

If he couldn't force himself to think of her as just another prisoner, he might never get back to Texas.

"I'll ask you once again, do you promise not to try to run away?"

"I'll never stop trying to escape from you."

"I've got to give you credit for determination."

"I don't know about the rest of your victims, but I'm not fond of the idea of hanging."

"You're not my victim."

"Yes, I am," Victoria shot back at him. "You came strolling into our valley like a wandering troubadour, easygoing and carefree. You made me believe there was more to my life than I'd let myself see. You made me want to be part of the world again. The moment you saw the stars of stupidity in my eyes, you tricked me into meeting you. And I fell into your hands like a ripe plum." She spat out a particularly col-

112

orful Spanish curse. "I'm not just mad at you. I'm so furious with myself I can't see straight.

"From the first, Buc told me you were nothing but a common cowboy, a saddle bum, a con man out for what you could get. But I wouldn't believe him. No, I was fool enough to like you. You can't know how that hurts now. All of us misjudge people now and again, but I must be really stupid not to recognize a vulture."

Her words stung.

Trinity had always regarded his work as on par with a U.S. Marshal. He repeatedly risked his life to protect society from lawlessness. He volunteered to take on particularly unpleasant jobs because no one else would or could. And he refused all offers of reward. He didn't expect people to praise him, but he'd always had a feeling of personal satisfaction. Now he felt guilty that he had betrayed Victoria's trust and destroyed her hopes.

It had never occurred to him to consider how his work was viewed by those he captured. They were guilty of terrible crimes. They had escaped without paying their debt to society. He didn't decide their guilt or pronounce their sentence. A judge and jury had already done that.

Neither had it occurred to him to care what his prisoners thought of him. They didn't deserve consideration because they were murderers. He had gone after them and spared no effort to bring them to justice. Once that was done, he never thought about them again.

But he knew he would remember Victoria. He wanted her to understand that as much as he'd give anything to hold her in his arms rather than in chains, he couldn't. He acted from principles which never wavered, never changed.

They couldn't change because the past never changed.

But he wouldn't explain. There wasn't any point in it. She might be a soft, vulnerable, sexy woman, but she had killed her husband just as dead as if she'd been Queenie.

Trinity looked at Victoria lying in the leaves and pine needles. She looked so beautiful, so kind, so gentle until you looked into her clear blue eyes. That's where you saw the real Victoria Davidge: cold, angry, and utterly determined to escape.

"I'd have thought living off other people's misery would leave a bad taste in your mouth."

"That's where you're wrong," Trinity said, relieved to have his gloomy thoughts interrupted. He picked her up and settled her into the saddle. "I get a good feeling knowing I've helped to make the world safer."

Victoria fell out of the saddle on the other side of her horse and headed quickly into the brush.

Chapter Nine

"Goddamn it, woman," Trinity shouted as he plunged after her. That's what he got for going soft. If he'd tied her across the saddle like the last two men he'd brought in, this wouldn't have happened.

Victoria didn't respond. He should have known she wouldn't waste energy talking to him until he captured her. At least her hands were tied this time. She wouldn't be able to scratch his face to ribbons before he could get her under control.

He had to follow on foot. There was no way he could ride down that slope. He just hoped his horse could find a way down. After all this running and climbing and fighting, he didn't know if he had the strength to carry her out.

Trinity captured Victoria with a flying tackle. He made certain this time to hold tight to both legs until he could sit on them. She lay flat on her stomach. He didn't look at her face or touch any part of her body except her ankles.

"I tried to make it easy on you," Trinity said between gasps for breath, "but now we play by my rules."

Victoria said something, but the words got lost in leaves and pine needles.

"I'm going to tie you on your horse. You can throw yourself over if you like, but if you do, you'll ride under his belly until we reach camp. It's about fifteen miles, so I'd advise against it."

Victoria glared at him in response.

"How I treat you when we get to camp is up to you. I can leave you tied up the whole time, or you can have some freedom in return for reasonable cooperation."

Victoria spat a leaf out of her mouth. "Go to hell!"

"So much for reasonable cooperation," Trinity muttered.

He sat down. He was breathing hard. He'd once captured a brawny six-foot-three fighter with less effort.

"What's the matter?" Victoria demanded. "Are you lost?"

"I'm waiting for the horses to find us," Trinity said. "I don't want to carry you up that slope."

"Too weak?"

Yes, but not in the way you mean. "Too tired," he said aloud. "I'm not used to foot races."

"Can't keep up with a mere woman?"

"So it seems," Trinity confessed, "but I'd like a rematch when I'm not wearing my boots."

"I'll race you now, bad ankle and all."

"Not a chance. One more race, and I'd have to tie myself on my horse."

His admission of weakness seemed to cool some of Victoria's anger.

"You know my uncle will come after me. It would save everybody a lot of trouble if you'd let me go now. You'll only get hurt if you force a gun battle. You can tell the sheriff you tried and failed."

Trinity was touched that even now Victoria could be worried about him. All the emotions he had ruthlessly pushed aside during the day threatened to break out of their confinement. But now was the wrong time, and Victoria the wrong woman.

But her words injured his pride as much as they gladdened his heart. It was bad enough she thought he might fail—he never had—but it jolted his sense of honor to know she thought he would give up and say he had tried.

No threat of danger had ever turned him from his purpose. It never would.

Many times during the past fifteen years his pride in his success and his belief in the rightness of his task were all

116

that sustained him. Her words, and his own weakness, threatened to take that away. He wouldn't let her. He couldn't.

"You're going back to Bandera."

"Never," Victoria replied hotly.

The commotion of the horses clambering through the brush kept Trinity from making a reply. He untied the rope from one foot and lifted her into the saddle making certain to stay clear of her teeth. He didn't think she would bite him, but at this point he didn't put anything past her. Before she had time to grasp the pommel and push off, Trinity reached under the horse's belly, grasped the dangling rope, and tied it securely to the other foot.

He knew it hurt because she winced. But she didn't say anything.

"Hold on to the pommel and keep your knees tight against the horse's side. It'll relieve some of the pressure."

"I know how to ride," she said through clenched teeth.

He watched her squeeze her eyelids together.

She swallowed. "You've got the rope too tight."

He knew that admission hurt her pride.

"Tell me when it stops hurting," he said as he loosened the rope. Victoria didn't say anything, but he could tell when the pain stopped by the way her body sagged in relief.

Satisfied the rope was tight enough to hold her, Trinity took her horse's reins and tied them to his pommel. He then took a rope from his saddle, put it over the horse's head, and tied that to the saddle as well.

"I know married people who aren't as securely bound together," Victoria commented. "Aren't you afraid I'll shoot you if I get too close?"

"You'd never shoot me."

Trinity's own words surprised him. They didn't make sense. Anyone who had killed her husband would shoot him the first chance she got.

"Keep on thinking that. In fact, I want you to be so sure you'll leave your guns and rifle out just to prove you're right."

Trinity laughed. "That would be egging you on. It'd be the same as an insult, maybe even a challenge. Then, even if you didn't want to shoot me, you'd feel honor-bound to do it just to prove you had the courage."

"Is that really the way men think?" Victoria sounded stunned by what she'd heard.

"Pretty much."

"I don't even think Buc is that dumb."

Trinity felt anger spurt through him. He didn't mind Victoria's disagreeing with him. He expected that. It was the way she said "even Buc."

"Every self-respecting man feels that way, especially here in the West. If you don't have courage, you might as well go back East."

"You make it sound like the East is only for cowards and scalawags."

"I didn't mean that," Trinity said, irked she had goaded him into saying something he didn't mean. "Living in the West requires a certain kind of physical courage from a man, a willingness to put his life on the line to prove himself."

"And if he fails?"

"At least he knows he died like a man. With respect."

"And his wife. Does she know it, too?"

"Of course. A real woman wouldn't want to be married to a coward."

"Maybe I'd better let you hang me. I certainly don't belong here."

"What do you mean by that?"

But Victoria didn't answer. Trinity tried several times to resume their conversation, but she made no reply to his remarks. He finally gave up and rode in silence.

He tried to concentrate on his plans for getting Victoria away from Mountain Valley Ranch and out of Arizona, but he couldn't keep from thinking about Victoria's words. Why should she feel such contempt for a characteristic which was basic to most men no matter where they lived? Other women believed in it. He knew because he'd seem them egg their men on. He'd seen it happen in saloons, at mining claims, even on poor dirt farms. Sometimes he wondered if the women didn't believe in it more strongly than the men.

That same characteristic in Buc and her uncle had freed her from jail. Or did she think there had been no risk just because it had been successful?

Another thing puzzled him. Why would she fight so hard to get free, then give up? She hadn't even struggled. Just said she didn't belong, turned her head to the wall, and refused to speak.

He didn't understand Victoria, but then he'd never understood women. Well, maybe he understood Queenie now, but he hadn't then. She'd plucked him like a banjo, and he'd twanged loud and clear.

But he didn't believe Victoria was like Queenie. Both had killed their husbands, but the similarity stopped there.

It had to.

Victoria was sure she couldn't remain in the saddle another mile. They had traveled for hours without stopping. Trinity had picked up a packhorse shortly after he recaptured her, and he had kept to the trail without a single break. It made her absolutely livid to know he had planned her abduction down to the last detail and she had fallen right into his trap.

"You can have all the jerky you want," he said when she complained she was hungry, "but we can't stop long enough to cook. I want to get as far from Mountain Valley Ranch as I can."

"It won't make any difference. My uncle will find you. And when he does, he'll kill you."

"That possibility keeps me moving," Trinity replied, a mocking smile momentarily vanquishing his stern expression. "I don't relish the idea of holding off a dozen men and trying to keep my eye on you at the same time."

"Don't worry. It won't be a problem for long."

"You have a lot of confidence in Buc, don't you?"

"Why shouldn't I? He took me out of the Bandera jail without anybody knowing, and he protected me from five other men just like you."

"But I captured you."

"Only because we got careless. No," Victoria corrected herself, compelled to be honest, "*I* got careless. Even worse, I ignored Buc's warnings."

"If it makes you feel any better, I've never failed to bring in a man I went after."

"It doesn't," Victoria snapped, convinced Trinity possessed a sadistic streak. "But it does make me happy to know you'll go back empty-handed."

"I'm taking you back even if we have to travel all the way to Texas without stopping," Trinity declared.

"The sun went down an hour ago," Victoria said, changing the subject. "Can't we stop now?"

"We've only got a few more miles to go."

"It's so dark I can't see where I'm going. We could fall off this mountainside."

"I can see."

"Now you want me to believe you can see in the dark. What other superhuman talents do you possess? No, don't tell me. A catalog of your many skills would surely extinguish all hope of escape. And the way my bottom hurts now, I live for the hope of returning the pain full measure."

"I'll trade my scratches for your sore behind."

"I didn't think Western men felt pain. I thought you took bullets, fists, kicks, anything man or beast could throw at you without flinching."

"I don't know about Buc, but I flinch. And these scratches hurt like the devil."

"You'll soon have more to add to those."

"The next attempt to scratch or kick me might well earn you a good paddling."

"You wouldn't dare. No man would strike a lady."

"You women are fond of using that, aren't you?"

"Using what?"

"A double standard. You think you can kick and scratch

120

and cuss, do just about anything you want, and men will go on treating you like something sacred. And most of us do, fools that we are."

"How is that a double standard?"

"When did you allow a man the same latitude? If we make one mistake, even if we live a blameless life afterwards, you never allow us to live it down. And it's the women who perpetuate our guilt. You whisper it to each other, to your husbands and sons, even to strangers, all in the name of protecting the innocent." He made a derisive noise. "You're no more innocent than the devil himself. In fact, if the Devil ever decides to come to earth, I bet he'll come as a woman."

Maybe Satan already had. Maybe he came as Queenie.

"You have an extremely poor opinion of women, don't you?"

"I haven't found any reason to change it."

"I don't know which of my misdeeds has earned your greatest condemnation, but if you think I'd shrink from fighting for my freedom, you have a very poor understanding of women . . . ladies or otherwise."

"I don't think ladies are any different from women, except women are more honest."

"Why do I get the feeling you're talking about someone else?"

Victoria's question silenced Trinity. He realized he had let his carefully sealed emotions seep into his voice. He had to watch what he said. He didn't want Victoria to know about Queenie.

He had always prided himself on his self-control, but ever since he decided to come after Victoria, thoughts of Queenie had plagued him almost constantly. For years he'd tried to forget her. Several times he'd believed he had, but she never stayed away for long. He had to get her out of his mind if he hoped to make it back to Texas alive. He had to be constantly alert if he wanted to be ready for Buc and Victoria's uncle, and thinking about Queenie always ruined his concentration.

"I wasn't talking about anybody in particular," Trinity answered. "Just my general experience with women."

"If you treated them all the way you treated me, I'm not surprised. Even fallen women take it unkindly when a man tells nothing but lies."

"What makes you think I know only fallen women?"

"If you knew any decent women, you wouldn't feel this way."

"The only *decent* women I've ever met were whores. They may not measure up to your idea of a lady, but they didn't shoot their husbands in the back."

"It's pointless to talk to anybody with your warped judgment," Victoria said. "Let me know when we reach camp, that is if I'm still conscious. Until then I relieve you of the responsibility of talking to me."

Trinity took her at her word, but Victoria found herself wishing he hadn't. She couldn't imagine what had happened to make him think so badly of women. She wished he would tell her, but she knew he wouldn't. At least not now.

She doubted he would ever listen to anything she said until he unburdened himself of some of his venomous anger, but she didn't know how to help him do it.

As much as she hated to admit it, she still wanted Trinity to like her. She also wanted to help him. Maybe it was because she was a woman and felt compelled to nurture. Maybe it was because she had become so fascinated by him, she wanted to know everything about him. Maybe it was because she wanted to keep her mind off her own problems. Maybe it was because she wanted him to help her prove her innocence rather than take her back to a cruel punishment. Whatever the reason, she hated to see anyone suffer. And as much as Trinity tried to hide it, he did suffer.

Or maybe it was because she still liked him.

"We'll stop here for the night."

Trinity pulled up on a ledge of rock which projected about ten feet out from the face of the mountain. A thick canopy of pine and oak filtered out the fading light. A jum-

122

ble of boulders hid them from the trail. They couldn't even be seen from above. He couldn't have found a more perfect place to hide.

Victoria didn't care where they were. She felt like she had been in a saddle most of her life. The throbbing in her ankle had been joined by the aching in her bottom, wrists, and hands. At the moment, she didn't care where she slept or if she ever ate again. She just wanted to get out of the saddle.

Trinity dismounted. He climbed a short way up the slope to check their back trail. Satisfied no one followed, he returned to Victoria.

"It's no use trying to escape. We're so far from your uncle's place no one would ever find you. You wouldn't last the night in the woods. At the very least there are cougars and wolves. Bears, too, but I don't think any of them are grizzlies." Trinity knew grizzlies almost never came this far south, but maybe she wouldn't know.

She didn't speak. Trinity untied her feet and reached out to her. She didn't respond.

"Are you going to let me help you down, or should I just let you topple over?"

Victoria gave him a withering look, but she still refused to speak.

"Sure is going to be a long night," Trinity said. "I can do many things, but nobody ever said I was good at making conversation."

Victoria opened her mouth to make a reply, but closed it again. Trinity chuckled.

"Don't try so hard."

Trinity lifted Victoria down from the saddle. He laughed when she tried to kick him, but she refused to break her silence. Quite suddenly Trinity grew tired of baiting her.

"Sit down. If you think you could behave long enough to eat your dinner, I'll untie your hands. If you promise not to escape during the night, I won't tie you to a tree."

Victoria remained standing, so he sat her down.

"I don't like repeating myself. I've got a lot of things to

do, so I can't afford to pay much attention to your whims or sulks. We'll get along better if you remember that."

Only Trinity had trouble remembering it himself. She looked so tired. Though she glared at him in defiance, she looked lonely, like she had been abandoned by everyone she loved and depended on.

That made him want to protect her, to hold her tight and assure her everything would be all right. But how could he feel that way and take her back to jail?

He resolutely put the question out of his mind. There was no solution. Whether he liked it or not, he had a job to do. Thinking about it would only torture himself needlessly.

After Trinity tied her feet once more, he turned his attention to the horses. He had to take good care of them. They would have to carry them all the way to Texas. He didn't have any extra mounts, and he didn't want to have to stop and buy some. That would make his trail too easy to follow. After he had unsaddled the horses and rubbed them down, he staked out Victoria's grey in a pocket below where there was a little grass.

Victoria was still sitting where he left her when he got back.

"Would you like something to eat? I forgot," Trinity said when she didn't reply, "you're not talking to me. It doesn't matter much. I'm used to camping by myself. I enjoy the silence."

Only he didn't tonight. He built a fire like he always did. He made coffee like he always did. He heated water and put in some dried beef and a few chips of dried vegetables like he always did. He fried bacon and set a can of beans in the coals to heat. Usually he liked the time alone. He found the peace a restorative, especially after a long chase.

But tonight he felt tense and jumpy. He rubbed the muscles in his shoulders and the back of his neck, but they remained unyielding. He could feel the ache of tension throughout his limbs. A muscle above his eyebrow quivered involuntarily, an infallible sign of stress. Even his voice had a sharp edge on it.

"Time to eat. Do you want me to untie you?"

Victoria said nothing.

"I guess I can feed you. I've never done it before, but I suppose there's a first time for everything." Trinity took a spoonful of the soup and lifted it to Victoria's mouth. "It's not as good as Ramon's soup, but it'll keep meat on your bones."

She pulled back.

"I feel like I'm trying to feed a baby."

Victoria moved her head as far away as possible, but Trinity pushed the spoon into her mouth. Victoria spat the food on the ground.

Hot rage flew all over Trinity.

"It's going to be very cold tonight. You'll need this food to keep you warm and give you strength tomorrow. You are going to eat it."

Victoria's eyes defied him.

"Don't misunderstand me. You can either open your mouth and swallow, or I'll pry your mouth open and force it down your throat. I have no intention of letting you starve."

Anger caused Trinity's hand to shake so much he could hardly keep more than a few drops of liquid in the spoon. He saw Victoria's eyes grow wide with fear and realized she was afraid he might strike her.

"I'd rather starve than hang for a crime I didn't commit. But if I must eat, I'll feed myself," Victoria said. "Untie my hands."

Trinity started to ask her to promise to behave then thought better of it. That would sound like he didn't trust her. And while he didn't, he had learned Victoria disliked being mistrusted. Even when she deserved it.

Trinity untied the rope around her wrists.

"My feet, too. Since I have no desire to become food for bears, wolves, or cougars, I'll remain in camp. At least for tonight."

"You relieve my mind."

"Just give me the soup. I doubt you have the least interest in my comfort or well-being, except as it affects your reputation, but I don't believe you have any desire to poison me."

"You honor me."

"No. I did that before. I won't do it again."

Her words were like sharp-pointed barbs, finding their way to his sensitive flesh, where they lodged, quivered, and hurt.

He gave up the uneven battle. He handed her a cup of coffee. She ate and drank without further comment.

"You'd better get some sleep. I mean to be on the trail before dawn."

"Buc and my uncle will follow you. You know that, don't you?"

"I've planned on it."

"They'll kill you."

"I haven't planned on that."

"It's your funeral."

"I mean to do my best to see it's nobody's funeral."

"How?"

"I don't know yet."

Victoria stared at him, surprised and a little confused. "I'm going to sleep," she announced.

Trinity opened one of the leather saddlebags Victoria had seen on the packhorse. He took out a pillow and a blanket.

"This will make you a little more comfortable."

Victoria took the pillow without remark, but when she saw the blanket, her eyes grew wide.

"That's my blanket. From my bed."

"It's your pillow, too. I thought you might want them. I took them when I left the note."

Victoria charged him like a she-bear. She made another set of scratches before he wrestled her to the ground.

"I don't know what's wrong with you, but you're the craziest woman I ever met. If I ever had any doubts about your killing your husband, they're gone now."

"You're a fool," Victoria flung at him as he tied her securely once more. "I would never have killed Jeb. He was too weak and harmless. But I could kill you. Very easily."

Trinity believed her.

Victoria rolled from side to side in a fruitless attempt to find a more comfortable position. It was difficult to sleep on the ground, but it was almost impossible to fall asleep with her wrists and ankles tied.

Trinity had retied both knots before he went to sleep. He said he wanted to make sure she couldn't escape during the night, but they were looser than before. If she tried very hard, she could probably work free. She suspected he did it intentionally, so she could be more comfortable.

There was never a question of escape. She would perish in the mountains if she tried.

All day long she had cursed herself for being such a fool as to trust him. But there had been no reason not to, at least not the same kind of trust she would have given any other wandering cowboy looking for a job. The trouble started when she let her liking for him influence her judgment.

She had allowed herself to be bamboozled by a handsome face, a well-muscled body, and behavior that she mistook for a real interest in her as a person. Just like she had allowed Jeb's handsome face and rebelliousness to overwhelm her judgment. The two men weren't alike, neither were the situations, but the principle was the same. Would she ever learn to wait until she knew something about a man before she allowed her feelings to run away with her?

She had practically thrown herself at him. She had even fancied he'd help her win her freedom.

How ironic that seemed now.

Her hip came into sharp contact with a stone. The resulting flash of pain caused her to think of some particularly awful things she'd like to do to Trinity. Her pillow cushioned her head, but nothing protected her from the cold, stony ground.

She couldn't imagine how he could go to sleep with a saddle under his head. That would give her a crick in her neck.

She had already decided he was without feeling for other human beings. Now she decided he was devoid of feelings altogether. No human could sleep on the ground night after night unless his nervous system had been disconnected. He couldn't be human.

The cold night air caused her teeth to chatter, and she pulled the blanket more tightly around her. And that was something else. It was one thing to trade on her credulity, to dupe her and kidnap her, but just knowing he had gone through her room made her too furious to fall asleep.

She felt violated.

It was the one place on earth which was hers alone. She didn't even let Anita clean her room. It wasn't just a matter of privacy. When she closed her door, she felt no one and nothing from the outside world could touch her. Now she had lost that because of Trinity Smith. A bounty hunter.

Even now she had trouble identifying him with that despised life form. Judge Blazer had sent at least two bounty hunters after her. They seemed to have as little pride and respect for themselves as the rest of the world had for them. She noticed the cowhands kept their distance, and the bounty hunters accepted it.

Trinity wasn't like that. She couldn't remember any man with more pride and self-confidence. She couldn't be certain just yet, but she suspected he took pride in what he did. She didn't know how he could, but then she had failed to understand Trinity on any level.

Calling him a bounty hunter felt wrong somehow. As furious as she was with him, she still harbored a desire to explain away this hideous blotch on the character of a man she had so wanted to believe in.

She guessed that was the root of the whole problem. Trinity had given her hope and something to believe in. Now that he had proved to be a charlatan and a hypocrite, she feared his words would turn out to have no truth as well. She didn't want that for she very much needed hope. Especially now.

Oddly enough she also needed to believe in him, even the

integrity of his determination to take her back to Texas. She wanted to believe he did it because he believed in justice. Knowing he did it for money would destroy that possibility. It would make him a man without a conscience, without the basic human stirrings of decency. It would make him a man to whom life and death were meaningless.

Victoria turned over, tried to get comfortable, and failed. She had to get some sleep. Lying awake all night wasn't going to help her escape. She needed to be alert. Her chance would come.

She could wait until he became so exhausted he could no longer guard her properly. Then she would make her escape.

Victoria came awake with a start. She didn't know what woke her. The coals of the camp fire had long since turned to ashes and grown cold. Little, insignificant sounds filled the night.

She listened carefully. She couldn't hear Trinity breathing. Had he gone to sleep? She would bet everything she owned he had at least one eye open and one ear listening for her. She started to turn over and go back to sleep, but an idea popped into her head.

She tested the belts. They really were loose. It only took a few minutes to free her wrists. The belt around her ankles proved to be more difficult. She didn't want to make any sound or movement that might wake Trinity, so she lay on her side and pulled her legs up behind her. The muscles in her shoulders and the back of her legs ached before she got the belt off, but at last she was free.

Moving with great care, Victoria began to slide the blanket off her. The bite of the cold air made her want to pull it back up again, but she persisted. Taking care not to make the slightest sound, she slipped her feet into her boots. Then without bothering to look for food or ammunition, she got to her feet and started to the clearing where Trinity had left the horses.

Unfortunately Victoria wasn't used to traveling in the

dark, or in the woods, and she stumbled over a limb. She didn't fall, but she made enough noise to startle the horses. Her grey tried to run with his hobbles and nearly fell.

"Now look what you've done."

Trinity's voice coming from the direction of the horses scared a small scream out of her.

"You can't expect to escape if you go about stumbling over rocks and screaming at strange sounds."

"How did you get here?" Victoria couldn't understand how Trinity could have reached the horses without her seeing or hearing him.

"I heard you come awake."

"You can't hear a person wake up," Victoria protested. "Even animals can't hear that well."

"You make a sound when you wake up. It sounds like a cross between a sharp intake of breath and a shudder of fear."

"You're lying. You had to be watching me all night."

Trinity laughed softly.

"A man who sleeps soundly in the wild is a dead man. We'll meet any number of men on the trail only too willing to kill me for the horses. In a place like this, they're worth more than gold. Then there's the question of you. How many men do you guess would kill me just to have a woman like you to themselves?"

Victoria wasn't willing to discuss that possibility. She didn't even want to think about it.

"Well, you've gotten yourself out of bed for nothing," Victoria said, heading back toward camp. She clearly wasn't going to get away and her teeth were chattering with cold. She turned back to face him. "I merely wanted to stretch my legs."

Trinity's expression was so condescending that she wanted to slap him.

"You don't have to believe me."

"I don't."

"I'm going back to bed," Victoria announced in a huff. "I never knew it could be so cold."

She hadn't expected him to believe her, but she hadn't expected him to tell her so to her face. She also disliked the fact she had lied. She never lied. Yet since she met Trinity, she couldn't seem to tell the truth, to him, to Buc, even herself. It was disgusting.

"Remember that the next time you think about running away. You could die of exposure out there."

"I told you I merely wanted to stretch my legs," Victoria said and turned her back on him. She settled back in her bed. It had gotten cold. It would take her a while to warm up again.

"Are you still cold?"

"No."

"You could use one of my shirts if you like."

"No, thank you," Victoria said with all the dignity she could muster.

Trinity laughed again. Just two days ago she welcomed his laughter. It raised her spirits and made her confinement seem less onerous. Now the very sound grated on her nerves.

"We could share a blanket to keep warm."

Victoria sat bolt upright. "Let me make something absolutely clear."

Trinity laughed again. God, how she hated that sound.

"You don't have to. I said it just to rile you."

"That's not very considerate."

"I know, but I've got to do something to keep myself amused until you try your next escape."

Victoria ground her teeth. It was bad enough he seemed to know what she was going to do before she did it, but it was unforgivable of him to make fun of her, too. She snuggled down and pulled the blanket up under her chin, determined not to say another word.

And she didn't until he started to whistle.

Chapter Ten

She knew he did it to annoy her. What other reason could he have? She made up her mind to ignore him. He'd soon stop.

But he didn't. He finished one tune and started another. It was bad. He couldn't carry a tune, and his tone was breathy and unsteady. She didn't know how he could stand to listen to himself. He must have a tin ear.

She put her fingers in her ears and tried to go to sleep, but she found herself becoming more and more awake. Finally she couldn't stand it any longer. "Would you please stop whistling?" she asked irritably. "I'm trying to sleep."

"I'm protecting you."

"From what?"

"From wolves and cougars. They don't like whistling."

"I can't imagine they would. Not the way you do it. I'm sure you could walk from here to Canada and be perfectly safe."

"I'll make you a bargain."

"What?" Victoria asked, wary of any bargain he might offer.

"I won't whistle any more if you won't wake me up with any more false escapes."

"What do you mean false escapes?" Victoria asked.

"Your dislike of me might lead you to do something foolish, but you're not stupid. And trying to run away in the middle of the night is definitely stupid. I figure you wanted to make me stay awake all night, get me so tired I couldn't see straight. Then you'd take the first chance to get away. Only you'd do it in the daylight. You know nothing about traveling at night."

"You're free to think whatever you like," Victoria said. "Only don't be surprised when you wake up one morning and find you're the only one sleeping around the campfire."

Victoria knew she couldn't have been asleep more than five minutes when Trinity shook her awake. She tried to open her eyes, but she couldn't see a thing. She tried to move, but her body was too stiff. She couldn't even turn over.

"Time to get up," Trinity announced with inhuman cheerfulness. "We have to be on the trail before daybreak."

That's why she couldn't see anything. Her eyes were open, but it was pitch black.

"I can't move," she groaned. "My whole body feels like dried leather."

Trinity twitched the blanket off her. Victoria gasped from shock and cold.

"A few seconds on your feet, and you'll feel like new."

"I'll never feel like new again," Victoria said, reaching for the blanket. "I won't be able to ride for at least a week."

"You're going to be in the saddle inside half an hour if I have to put you there."

Trinity bent over, took her under the arms, and lifted her to her feet in one swift, fluid movement. Victoria couldn't move her legs. She fell against Trinity. She struggled to push away from him, but her arms felt dead. Her whole body felt like it had been carved from wood.

If anything could have brought her immediately awake, it would have been finding herself in Trinity's arms, her bosom smashed up against his chest, her cheek against the softness of his shirt. Only two nights ago she had lain awake shivering from the thought of him crushing her to his bare chest. While this wasn't exactly the way she had envisioned it, it came disconcertingly close.

"Walk," Trinity ordered. It became immediately clear that if

133

Victoria didn't want to be dragged along the ground, she had to move her legs.

"Slow down, you brute," she said. She held tightly to him while she tested her legs to see if they would bear some of her weight.

Holding on to Trinity was like putting her arms around a corral post. Victoria took pleasure in knowing her nearness unsettled him, but she was shocked to realize his touch still had the ability to reduce her willpower to a vapor trace.

She knew the rigidity of his body and the awkward way he held her were the results of her nearness. Knowing she made him uncomfortable relieved some of her own shame at still being attracted to a man who believed her a murderess.

She must be crazy! What sane woman would have such feelings for her jailer, even one as handsome as Trinity?

"Do you enjoy torturing your prisoners?"

"No woman ever made that complaint before."

"I suppose you've had a wide experience."

"Wide enough."

"You probably enjoyed watching them throw themselves at you. I can't believe I'm like all the rest. I used to think I was different."

"You are."

"I suppose you're trying to tell me all the other women prisoners were better riders than I am."

"I wasn't talking about women prisoners. I told you before there haven't been any."

"There must have been. You must have captured dozens of prisoners over the years."

"Eighteen. All men."

"Who're you trying to fool? You spent half of yesterday telling me how much you despised women, how they use men every chance they get. Every one of your victims must have been female. Nothing else would appeal to your perverted sense of justice."

Trinity released her and stepped back, only by luck did Victoria balance herself on her own legs and keep from falling. She looked up at him, a question in her glance, then wished she hadn't. The expression in his face confused her. For the first time since he captured her, he seemed human and vulnerable. For a second she actually felt sorry for him.

"You're the first woman I've attempted to take back," Trinity said. "If I had it to do over, I wouldn't do it."

"Are you trying to make me believe that a bounty hunter has a conscience?"

"I'm not a bounty hunter," Trinity snarled, his lips drawn so tightly away from his teeth they looked like fangs.

The force of his rage nearly took Victoria's breath away. She shrank from him, fearing he might hit her. There was also an element of hurt in his look, fleeting, immediately covered up, but unquestionably there.

Pinpricks of remorse made Victoria hesitate. She had lashed out at him because she hurt. She hadn't expected to hurt him. He had seemed invulnerable. She didn't mean to; she didn't want to.

She rallied quickly.

"I suppose you're going to tell me you do this for free, for the benefit of your fellow man."

"You wouldn't believe me if I did."

"Why should I? You didn't believe me when I told you I didn't kill my husband."

"A jury found you guilty."

"Aren't you being paid to take me back?"

He was a deputy. He had been offered a deputy's salary, but he refused. He wouldn't tell her that. As long as she was determined to believe the worst about him, she could believe what she liked.

Victoria took Trinity's silence as an admission of guilt.

"You're a professional bounty hunter."

"Why do you say that?"

"You've done this before. You've probably got every camp site between here and Texas picked out and stocked with supplies. You've left nothing to chance. It's not just a job. You do it because you like it."

"Whatever you say."

She could tell he only feigned indifference. She could hear

the tension in his voice, feel the fury in his eyes, see the rigidity of his body. She sensed the pain beneath his expression of unconcern. It surprised her, and it also upset her.

"Why do you do it?" Victoria asked. "Nobody likes a bounty hunter, not even those paying the bounty. You can't have a home or friends or any place to go. You're an outcast from society."

"I don't care too much for society."

"Just about any kind of job would be easier," she continued. "You have to travel all the time, sleeping in the cold and rain on the ground, running from people, hiding, doing everything in secret. Worst of all, people are always trying to kill you. Not just outlaws and Indians, but honest, everyday citizens."

Trinity just stared at her, his face a meaningless collection of features. Even their perfection lacked force. He seemed to have withdrawn to some place deep inside himself where her words couldn't penetrate, some place where the hurt couldn't reach, some place Victoria couldn't go.

"You're right, but not for the reason you think."

Victoria felt rewarded to have goaded him into response, but she was reproached by the hollowness of his voice.

"Your 'honest, everyday citizens' are nothing but lazy, spineless, cowardly people hiding in their safe towns, complaining to their sheriff when someone steals their money or complaining to the government when they fail at one venture after another.

"How many of them had the courage to face down any one of the gunmen I've brought in? None! How many of the men who sat in judgment of you had the courage to go after you when your uncle broke you out of jail? None! They all depend on me or someone like me to do the work they are too cowardly, inept, or just plain stupid to do for themselves. They look down on me because otherwise they wouldn't have the guts to look each other in the eye."

Victoria felt appalled by the loneliness of his life. His isolation from humanity and his hunger for a caring relationship struck her. She longed to tell him to disregard the past, but she couldn't let him go on thinking he had a right to act as judge and juror for the human race.

"You're almost as bad as the criminals you bring in," Victoria said. "You don't commit murder, but you rob men of their courage and their self-respect."

"They've done that all ready. That's why they need me."

"For what? To protect them from me?"

"You were convicted of murder."

"And you were convicted of being a blight on society. What gives you the right to decide which sentence shall be carried out and which shall be withheld?"

"You were convicted in a court of law."

"Are you saying criminal injustice is worse than social injustice?"

"You're twisting my words."

"And you're twisting principles. You're protecting people from me. Who's going to protect them from you?"

"Nobody needs protection from me."

"I do."

"You wouldn't if you'd do what I ask."

"Wonderful. You'll treat me like an ordinary person if I don't do anything to prevent you from carrying me back to be hanged."

"I always knew a woman could twist the truth until a man couldn't make head or tail of it, but I've never known anyone who could do it as well as you. It all comes down to you're a felon and I'm not. That's the end of it. If you want any breakfast, you'd better eat it now. Otherwise you're going to be mighty hungry by nightfall. You've got ten minutes."

Victoria bristled. He had dismissed her like a fly. He made no attempt to defend himself. He seemingly put it out of his mind. That made her furious. But getting furious wouldn't help her get ready in ten minutes.

"I can't be ready that soon. Nobody can dress, wash and eat in that space of time."

"Then don't try. If you feel the call of nature, you can use that rock."

"I need more privacy."

137

"Suit yourself, but you've only got eight minutes now."

"You're a savage!"

"I suppose it seems like that to you, but I'm interested in just two things, staying alive and delivering you to the sheriff in Bandera. I'll do what I must to get it done."

Trinity knelt and took a piece of bacon out of a small pan. He placed it on some bread and handed it to Victoria. "Here, this is the last of the bread. At least the coffee's hot."

Victoria ignored the food. "I'm going to change and clean up."

"You've got seven minutes. I'll get the horses."

"I won't be ready by the time you've saddled up."

But Victoria spoke to empty air. Trinity had gone.

Mumbling very unladylike words under her breath, Victoria picked out a change of clothes. She looked about for a place to change but could find no place more suitable than Trinity's rock. She was tempted to use any place *except* that rock, but her common sense told her it made no sense to fight Trinity when he was right. She had more than enough to confront when he was completely off base.

Victoria hadn't emerged from behind the rock when Trinity returned with the horses.

"Time to go," he called.

"I'm not ready yet."

"If you don't come out in thirty seconds, I'm coming after you."

She heard the fire hiss. He must have poured the coffee on the fire. She hadn't had anything to eat or drink. Did he mean to starve her? She finished dressing, grabbed up yesterday's clothes, and emerged from behind the rock.

"I hope that wasn't the coffee you poured on the fire."

"You can't drink coffee riding a horse. You'll have enough trouble eating."

Trinity rolled up her blanket. He took her clothes, threw them into the blanket, and rolled it up. Victoria knew she'd never be able to wear them again.

"You'll ruin my clothes if you ball them up like that."

"Next time make sure you get dressed in time to do it yourself," Trinity said, not pausing. He tied the blanket on the packhorse. "Do you want me to give you a leg up, or can you mount by yourself?"

"I've barely gotten my clothes on. I haven't brushed my teeth or washed my face."

"I won't tell anybody."

Victoria would have dearly loved to scratch the grin off his face. But even though she knew he richly deserved it, she felt guilty about the swollen red lines which crisscrossed his cheek. She'd never done anything like that before, and she couldn't get used to it. She was continually of two battling minds when it came to this exasperating man.

"I'm starved."

"You can eat while you ride."

Trinity lifted her into the saddle with one swing. Even though she would rather die than admit it to him, Victoria liked the feel of his powerful arms around her, his capable hands on her body. It reminded her of his arms around her that day on the trail when Buc found them. She'd dreamed about that twice already. In her dreams, he didn't stop with his hands on her waist. She found herself wishing Trinity would behave like he did in her dream.

For God's sake, woman, he's your jailer! How can you feel that way about him?

She didn't know, but she did.

"Aren't you afraid I'll try to escape if you don't tie my hands?"

"No. I'm tying your feet."

Victoria tried to kick at him and lift her feet out of the way at the same time. But it was too late. He already had a rope around one ankle. He held the other in an iron-like grip.

"Do you enjoy forcing females to suffer indignities?" she demanded, unable to repress her resentment.

"I don't know. I never had a female in custody before. Am I forcing you to accept indignities?"

"How can you ask such a question? You steal me away from my home, bind me hand and foot, haul me about like a bag of pecans, force me to go without a proper change of clothes,

139

refuse to allow me to wash or brush my teeth, force me to sleep in the open—"

"Would you prefer a cave?"

"—and then throw me into the saddle before I've had a swallow of coffee or a mouthful of food."

"I warned you we were short of time," Trinity said.

"There's no point in talking to you. You have no feelings, not for yourself or anybody else."

"Not in the least," Trinity replied with cheerful sarcasm. "I like being in the saddle all day and sleeping on rocks at night and eating over a campfire. I make myself go out on the trail at least once a year so I won't become too comfortable living at my ranch."

"You own a ranch?" Victoria asked, jolted out of her train of thought. "Bounty hunting must pay better than I thought."

Trinity jerked the rope around her ankle so tightly she winced in pain. He loosened it again, but she promised herself to think before she spoke next time. He looked like he wanted to break her neck and throw her body into a ravine.

"I paid for that ranch with money I earned working small claims up and down mountains of Colorado. It took me more than ten years. It doesn't owe one cent to bounty hunting."

"I'll believe that when you believe I had nothing to do with Jeb's murder," Victoria said, glad to find a blade she could twist in his guts.

"Let's get started," Trinity said abruptly. "It'll soon be daylight."

Victoria swayed in the saddle. She had drifted in and out of consciousness all afternoon. Trinity had driven her unmercifully in his determination to get beyond the reach of her uncle. She would have traded her soul for just five minutes out of the saddle, but he ignored her pleas. Every time she tried to bring her horse to a halt, he would give it a cut on the rump with his reins. Now, having given up, she sagged in the saddle, not caring where they were or how far they had to go. She was glad he had tied her feet otherwise she would surely have fallen out of the saddle.

He had given her water as often as she had asked. For that she was profoundly thankful, even though she had to drink from a canteen and the water had grown warm and stale-tasting as the day wore on. He had also given her some jerky to chew on as she rode. She didn't think she could ever be thankful for that. She pitied anybody who had to live on it for weeks at a time.

Her twisted ankle no longer hurt, but stabbing pains radiated from her seat. Mercifully, her body had become numb to the pain hours ago, or she would surely have passed out. Victoria had always considered herself strong enough to withstand as much physical hardship as any man, but in the future, if she had any future, she would have much greater respect for anyone who could stay in the saddle for two days straight and still ride in comfort.

"When are we going to stop?" She didn't have to open her eyes to know the sun had gone down. She could feel the air begin to cool.

"Another couple of hours ought to be enough."

"It was enough twelve hours ago," she mumbled. "I don't see how you can do it."

"You get used to it."

"I don't think I could. I never really understood what Perez and the men went through on a roundup."

"You don't know anything about rounding up cows until you've had to flush ornery mossy backs out of the Texas brush," Trinity said. "Riding through hell would be easier."

"I thought you said you worked in the mine fields."

"I did, but I grew up in south Texas between the Nueces and the Rio Grande. I helped my daddy chase longhorns every day."

Victoria's mind felt like it was full of cotton. "I don't understand. I thought you said you paid for your ranch by mining. Did you inherit it?"

She was too tired to see the dark rage which flashed in his eyes.

"I grew up on other people's ranches until my daddy headed to Colorado and struck it rich. Well, not rich, but he found

141

enough gold to buy his own spread. I couldn't figure why he would head back to Texas and ranching, not after all the times he swore he hated it. But I guess the day comes when every man wants to go home."

"Did you ever want to head back home?"

"I had a lot of reasons not to go back."

"Probably a woman," Victoria mumbled, hardly conscious of what she said.

"What makes you say that?"

Even through the waves of fatigue which threatened to engulf her, Victoria could feel Trinity tense up.

"Why else would you hate women so?" Victoria said. "I figure you ran into several bad ones. If you can't go back home, one of them must have been there."

"That's rather good thinking."

"It's common sense. A man is most vulnerable to three women: his mother, his first love, and his wife. You said you weren't married, and in spite of all the lies you've told, I believe you. No woman would stay with a man as unfeeling and selfish as you. Your mother died when you were young, maybe even at your birth. There's no softness in you, none of the gentleness which would come from the woman who gave you birth and who would forgive you everything.

"A man never forgets the first woman he falls in love with no matter how much he might love his wife. Especially if she hurt him. He never forgives her either. How am I doing so far?"

"Are you sure you aren't a gypsy?"

Victoria tried to laugh, but she didn't have the energy.

"Men think they're such mysterious creatures, but they're all alike. A few variations here and there."

"What makes you say that?"

"My mother died when I was born. My life was dominated by my father and my four uncles. When Daddy bought the Demon D, I was surrounded by more men. When I married Jeb, I was surrounded by still more. Then I came to Arizona. Still more men. You're all alike," she mumbled. "Every one of you. No feeling or understanding. Just a noisy show."

* * *

It was well after nightfall when Trinity drew up to his camp. It had been more than a week since he had cached supplies here. He hoped no one had found them. He couldn't afford the loss of time to go into town for more. Nor did he want to run the risk of someone recognizing Victoria. Quite a few men might be tempted to try to take Victoria from him for Judge Blazer's thousand dollar reward. He didn't want a fight if he could avoid it.

He looked down at Victoria, so exhausted she didn't know he rode next to her, his arm around her waist holding her in the saddle. It was just as well. She'd probably claw his face again. It didn't surprise him Jeb Blazer hadn't been able to handle her. It would take a very strong man to tame this woman. And an even stronger one to capture her heart without caging her spirit. She was such a vital, passionate creature, so full of life. It felt strange to look at her now, a spent force gathering energy for the next explosion. How could anyone have believed she would be happy married to Jeb Blazer?

From all he'd been able to learn, Jeb had been a completely selfish young man, too preoccupied with his own pleasure to realize his youthful wife might have needs of her own. Even now, as she leaned against Trinity, she created a bonfire in his loins.

She must have had a similar effect on Buc. Even though he was overprotective, Buc must have been aware of her underlying sensuality. Maybe he was so protective because in the course of five years, passion had overcome protectiveness.

At least once.

The thought of Buc and Victoria in a passionate embrace caused such a surge of anger to rush through Trinity he nearly pulled her from the saddle. The force of his reaction stunned him. Why should he feel such anger? She wasn't *his* woman.

But he wanted her to be. Riding next to her, holding her close, feeling the mound of her breast against his hand, inhaling the fragrance of her hair, he couldn't think of anything else. Neither her past nor her future.

He couldn't help but wonder if she would respond to his touch as passionately as she responded to life. Of course she couldn't feel anything but anger and rage for the man who had abducted her. She certainly couldn't believe he could feel anything for her except indifference. She would be certain everything else was a lie.

Would she have responded differently if he hadn't kidnapped her? Could her response to him on the mountain have been merely a prelude to the passion she would have been willing to share with him later?

How could any woman who had known the pleasures to be found in a man's arms deny herself for five years? He couldn't have starved his body for that long. He thought of the faceless women with whom he had shared a fleeting passion. He wouldn't know them again. He didn't want to know them. They came together because each had something the other needed. They got what they came for, and that was the end of it.

Was that the way Victoria felt? He didn't know, but he doubted it. Maybe she could sleep with Buc because she thought she loved him, but he didn't believe she could sleep with just anybody. She felt things too intensely. Not like him. He didn't feel anything at all. He hadn't for years.

Why are you lying to yourself? You're feeling something right now, something you've never felt for anybody, not even for Queenie. You felt it the first time you set eyes on Victoria. That's why you're holding her in the saddle. She could stay there alone. She has all day.

He started to pull his arm away, but her warmth, her nearness, made it impossible. But it wasn't merely the physical attraction which kept him at her side. He liked the feel of her in his arms, but he also liked the feel of his arm around her. It made him feel needed. After thirteen years of loneliness, he wanted to feel close to someone.

There was nothing wrong with letting down his resistance just a little bit.

Maybe he had let it down too much. Needs from deep inside him, needs he had denied for thirteen years, cried out to him. He didn't know if he could turn them off again. Looking

144

down at Victoria leaning into the curve of his arm, he didn't know if he wanted to.

Trinity dismounted. For a minute he wasn't sure his own legs would hold him, but years of training stood him in good stead. In a matter of seconds, he started to move as easily as always. He led the horses into camp. The first thing he did was untie Victoria's bedding from the packhorse and lay it out on the part of the ground where the pine needles and leaves were the thickest. Then he untied the ropes binding Victoria's wrists and ankles. The raw, inflamed flesh of her wrists reproached him. He never meant to do anything like that.

Carefully he eased her from the saddle and laid her on the blanket. She moaned when he stretched her legs out, but she didn't move. Going to his saddle bags, he untied his bedding gear and searched inside until he found a small tin of salve. He rubbed this into the inflamed skin of each wrist. He hated to tie her up each day, but he didn't know how else to protect her from herself. If she escaped, she'd probably die.

She looked so pitiful lying there with her legs twisted beneath her. Trinity tried to make her more comfortable, but she only groaned. Her legs were so stiff they wouldn't bend.

Trinity pulled off her boots and began to knead the muscles in her calf. They were as hard as corded wood. With gentle but firm pressure he began to work the muscles, pressing hard, pressing deep to loosen the tension. Victoria groaned and tried to move away from him, but Trinity continued his ministrations.

He shifted to the other calf. He could hardly believe anyone could become so tense just from riding. He had done it for years, and he never had more than a momentary stiffness.

But as he worked Victoria's muscles loose, he felt his own tighten. He became so aroused his pants got uncomfortably tight. Self-consciously, Trinity rearranged himself so he didn't feel like he was being cut in two. Reacting like a teenager on his first date made him feel a little foolish, but he hadn't been so aroused in years.

He had been with many women, but he'd always gone on his way immediately afterward. He'd never been with a woman for days at a time. He'd never had the chance to discover them as people. He had never had the time, or the desire, to explore their bodies, to run his hands over every part of them, to luxuriate in their closeness. Their meetings had been urgent and over quickly.

But something felt different this time. The feel of her skin — the curve of flesh over bone, the give of the soft spots, the hard places where her bones lay just beneath the skin — defined Victoria. Each part had its own fascination, its own allure.

This surprised Trinity. It added a whole new dimension to his appreciation of a woman's body.

He turned Victoria over on her back and slowly began to knead the muscles in her slim, delicate neck; a neck too fragile to withstand the jerk of the hangman's rope.

Forcing that thought from his mind, Trinity's hands moved to her shoulders. The muscles were hard as iron. Even with the insistent pressure of his fingers, it took several minutes before he could feel the tension begin to leave her shoulders.

As the minutes passed, Trinity experienced more than just desire racing from his fingertips to every part of his body. Again, a sensual appreciation rooted in feeling close to Victoria, a feeling of sharing, of being needed rather than the bare drive for sexual gratification, coursed through him.

He was so enthralled by this revelation he forgot what he was doing with his hands.

He touched Victoria's thigh.

Chapter Eleven

"Move your hand." Victoria sounded very much awake and very much aware of what Trinity was doing.

The unexpected command caused him to jerk his hand back faster than if he'd touched a hot stove. His reaction made him angry and guilty.

He hadn't done anything improper, but he knew his thoughts had gone much further than simply thinking about which muscles needed to be relaxed. He had begun to think of her as a very desirable woman; if she didn't know it, he did.

"Did you imagine I was going to take advantage of you?" he asked, hoping his puckish grin would cover his discomfort. "You're a very attractive woman, but I haven't been reduced to forcing myself on helpless females."

"I didn't think you had," Victoria answered, struggling to sit up. She leaned against the pillow he had put behind her and dragged herself into a sitting position. "If other women fall over themselves as fast as I did to believe every word you say, I would rather imagine you look upon this trip as something of a vacation."

"You forget I'm a bounty hunter, scorned by man and beast alike."

"Unfortunately I can't forget it for even a moment, but I've no doubt there are plenty of females who wouldn't let that dissuade them."

"What an odd woman you are. One minute you accuse me of being so vile the entire human race has turned its back on me. The next you're saying half the women in the world can't resist me. Do you consider your own sex to be so weak minded?"

"Yes. I used to think I was a very strong-minded, clear-headed thinker. I thought marrying Jeb and being convicted of something I didn't do had knocked all the idealistic nonsense out of me. I guess I'm more romantic than I thought. If, after all that, I can't separate what is from what I would like to be, I can't expect other women, who haven't gone through such harrowing experiences, to be any less credulous."

"Why do you continue to maintain your innocence?"

"Why do you keep trying to make me believe you're not taking me back for money?"

"Because it's true."

"That's my reason as well."

"But you were convicted by a jury."

"And you've been convicted by circumstantial evidence, the same kind of evidence, by the way, that convicted me."

"We won't get anywhere talking about this. They didn't ask me to decide whether or not you were guilty. They just wanted someone to bring you back."

"And you don't care that you may cause an innocent woman to hang."

Trinity's gaze locked with hers. "If I believed you were innocent, I'd try even harder to make sure you remained free."

Trinity's eyes remained hard and unyielding, but Victoria felt an upsurge of hope. She knew by now Trinity would stick with anything he believed in, even if he had to lie and cheat to do it. He had done that to capture her. She believed he would do it to defend her.

But was there any hope of convincing him of her innocence? Probably not. He had closed his mind to the idea. She would have to wait until Buc and her uncle showed up. It might be better if she changed her behavior. If he were just a little less vigilant, she might be able to escape while he fought them off.

"But you're not innocent," Trinity continued. "Jeb's step-brother Kirby and Judge Blazer saw you with the gun."

148

"Kirby saw me holding the gun *after* he ran out of the house *after* he heard the shot," Victoria said. "I noticed it on the ground after I realized Jeb was dead. I foolishly picked it up thinking it was Jeb's gun. I thought he must have shot himself."

"Where did it come from if not from you?"

"I don't know. The killer must have tossed it there after he shot Jeb."

"And you didn't hear it hit the ground?"

"I don't remember the gun being there when I knelt over Jeb, but it wouldn't have mattered when it was dropped. I wouldn't have heard it. They were having a party in the house — they always seemed to be having a party — and there was a lot of noise, music, people laughing and talking. Judge Blazer had had a dance floor set up outside. Their boots and shoes made a dreadful racket on the wood floor."

"You're trying to make me believe someone shot Jeb the moment you turned your back, tossed the gun to the ground while you bent over his body, and fled without you seeing or hearing anything?"

"I know it sounds preposterous, but I was extremely upset. I wasn't paying much attention. I had just had a terrible argument with the man I'd married only seven days earlier."

"What was it about?"

"The same thing we always argued about. All he wanted to do was get drunk and stay up all night with his friends. I could understand one or two nights, but Jeb always seemed to be going to a party, or giving one. He started having them every night after his father announced our wedding date.

"I used to think he'd settle down after we got married and pay some attention to the ranch. His father had been hurt a few years earlier when a steer gored his horse, and he needed Jeb's help. But when he continued to get drunk after our wedding, I realized he had never grown up. I had to try to do something, or our marriage would be over before it even started."

"So you killed him."

149

"I didn't kill him," Victoria nearly shouted. "There was no purpose. I still thought I could reason with him, but he shouted at me like some kind of servant. I was glad nobody heard the things he said."

"Somebody must have heard?"

"What do you mean?"

"The man who killed him. He must have been close enough to hear what you said."

"I suppose so. I never thought of that."

"No wonder the jury convicted you. That story's got more holes in it than a target after a turkey shoot. You say you were alone, but you didn't shoot your husband. You say you don't know where the gun came from, but you were holding it when they found you. You say no one overheard you, but you insist someone was close enough to kill your husband, throw the gun at his feet, and escape without you noticing. Would you believe that?"

"Not if you were on trial," Victoria snapped. But her temper soon evaporated. "I don't suppose I would. I know it sounds impossible, but it's true nonetheless."

Unaccountably Trinity found himself listening to what she said and evaluating it. If she were lying, wouldn't she have come up with a better explanation? Even though that story had convicted her, she kept repeating it. She hadn't changed so much as a word.

"They held the trial right away. Judge Blazer assigned me a lawyer who didn't want me to be found innocent. I begged them to wait until Uncle Grant could get there, but they refused. They said they sent him my letters, but Uncle Grant never received them. When he did arrive, they wouldn't let him or his lawyer see me. Judge Blazer wouldn't grant a motion for a new trial. He wouldn't even grant a stay of execution long enough for them to go over the transcripts. My own father-in-law was determined to see me hang."

"They could have appealed to Austin."

"Uncle Grant started to, but Judge Blazer swore he'd hang

150

me before they could get back. That's when Buc broke me out of jail."

The coffee had nearly boiled away. There was just enough for one cup. Trinity gave it to Victoria and put on a pot for himself. He stirred the broth and added a few dried vegetables. It would be ready in about fifteen minutes.

"How did he do it?"

"He just walked in, took the key from the jailer, and we rode off in the middle of the night. We took the jailer with us so he couldn't warn anyone."

"You mean he just walked in? Nobody stopped him?"

"Nobody was expecting a jailbreak," Victoria said. "Buc came in sometime after midnight. He told the jailer my uncle had been taken with a bad heart spell and the doctor thought he was going to die. Since I was his only relative, he had to ask me what to do. The minute the jailer turned his back, Buc knocked him out. Uncle Grant was waiting behind the jail with the horses. Not a soul knew I was gone until daybreak."

"What did the judge do?"

"He sent a posse after us, but we were out of Texas before they found our trail. They sent some other bounty hunters after me, but Uncle Grant and Buc managed to buy them off or run them off."

"I'm not a bounty hunter."

"And I'm not a felon."

"I guess this is what you call a stalemate."

"I don't see how you can call it a stalemate when you hold all the cards," Victoria replied. "You may not like being called a bounty hunter, but you could change that by letting me go. I don't like the thought of being hanged, but what I want isn't going to change anything."

"The broth is ready," Trinity said, unwilling to pursue that argument. The more he talked to Victoria, the more uneasy he became. Reason told him she was guilty, but instinct whispered she might not be.

He had always been a man to trust his instincts, but how could he trust them now? She had destroyed his objectivity.

151

He couldn't differentiate between what instinct told him was true and what he wanted the truth to be.

Don't think. Do your job. Get her to Bandera and forget her.

But that was impossible. Traveling at her side for hours had been torture enough, holding her in his arms, touching her, running his hands over her body had completely unraveled what was left of the iron restraint he habitually practiced around women.

In just two days on the trail, he had become intensely conscious of her presence. No, that had happened the first day he helped her with her survey. It intensified the afternoon he held her in his arms, but another element had been added, an emotion much more dangerous than mere physical attraction.

Sympathy.

He found himself wishing Victoria were innocent. He couldn't believe the foolish story she told, but he *wanted* to believe it. He didn't know a thing about the Judge or Jeb or Kirby, but he wanted to believe they had somehow been at fault instead of Victoria.

He had to stop this before he completely disregarded the jury's decision, the evidence, the sentence. The turmoil boiled inside him; this debilitating battle between desire and principle was tearing him apart.

Had he lost his absolute certainty of her guilt?

He knew he didn't *want* her to be guilty, but did he still *believe* she had killed her husband? That question was crucial. Without this certainty, his mission had no moral justification; without such a justification, he would never have taken her from Mountain Valley.

He didn't know what he believed any more. He had only to look at her and nothing else seemed important. What did right and duty and self-respect mean when set against her life? Or his own peace of mind?

He was caught. No matter which way he turned, he would never know peace of mind where she was concerned.

Every time he tried to ignore her, his every sense seemed to focus on her presence. If he talked to her, she made him question her guilt. Half the time she made him so angry he wished he could hand her over to the sheriff right now. The other half of the time he wished Texas were on the other side of the world.

He could no longer control his response to her, and that scared him.

The sooner he got away from her the better.

"What are you going to do when my uncle comes?" Victoria asked when she had finished eating. She still hadn't moved from where Trinity set her down.

"Maybe he won't catch up with us."

"He will."

"Maybe we'll be in Texas before that happens. I've been deputized by Sheriff Sprague, so it'll be against the law for him to interfere with me."

"It was against the law when he broke me out of jail. Do you think he's going to hesitate with you?"

"No."

"What do you plan to do?"

"Fight."

"I know that. I want to know if you're going to try to kill him."

"I don't want to kill anybody. My only purpose is to take you back to Bandera. If I could do it without firing a shot, I would."

"But if you can't?"

"Then I'll fight."

"Will you try to kill Uncle Grant?"

"I'll first shoot to drive them off. Next I'll shoot to wound. Only in the end would I shoot to kill. I may be a despised bounty hunter in your eyes, but I'm not a killer."

"Do you expect a *killer* like me to appreciate the difference?"

"Why do you insist upon clinging to this tale of innocence?"

"Because it's true!"

"Only two people in the world believe you."

"A few more than that, and they're all coming after you right now."

"Your uncle can bring every cowhand in the Arizona Territory, and I'll still get you back to Texas."

"Have you stopped to realize you might be the one who gets killed?"

"I knew that before I started."

"Is it so important that you take me back?"

"Not you specifically. In one sense, you're not important at all. But in another sense you represent all the people who've committed crimes and escaped punishment. That's why I took the others back. That's why I'm taking you back."

"She must have hurt you very deeply for you to hate so long and so fiercely."

"I don't hate anybody long and fiercely," Trinity snapped. "I'm certainly not doing this because of some woman. Some of us have deeply felt principles we live by. When people violate those principles, we feel compelled to bring them to justice. Not every man can do that. I can, so I do."

He couldn't tell her of his disgust with his mission or of the doubts he couldn't dismiss. She wouldn't believe the one and would only take advantage of the other.

"Lots of men could do what you do, and many have for some part of their lives, but sooner or later they give it up. You have chosen to give up your life, or what anybody else would consider a decent life, to pursue this goal. No one does it year after year at the expense of the normal kinds of fulfillment, unless some powerful emotion drives him on and makes it impossible for him to do anything else. You're driven by such an emotion, and a woman was the cause of it."

"Even if you're right, it's none of your business," Trinity said. "You'd better get to sleep. Tomorrow will be another long day in the saddle. You'll need all your strength."

"You're never going to get out from under this compulsion to do something you don't want to do until you do something about it," Victoria said. "Keeping it locked inside just allows it to grow stronger year by year."

154

"And just what do you propose I do?"

"Talk about it. Get out all the hatred and anger you've buried inside you all these years."

"There's nobody to talk to, so I guess I'll have to put your excellent advice aside for a while longer."

"You could talk to me."

"Talk to a murderer about a murderer? Wouldn't that be something akin to carrying coals to Newcastle?"

"I guess I should have expected that," Victoria said. "Funny, I never have been able to get used to that word."

Trinity cringed at his unplanned use of the word as much as Victoria. It made him feel lower than a worm. She looked so tired, so defeated. No, not quite defeated, just momentarily down. And instead of worrying about herself, she had tried to help him. And he had cut her off.

But he had to. He couldn't deal with her selfless, altruistic side while taking her back to her death. Just another example of the effect Victoria had on him: He hadn't thought so frequently about Queenie for years.

No, you haven't tried to solve the problem for years. You've simply refused to think about her. Whenever your feelings got too near the surface, you started another chase. The physical change, the concentration needed to bring those men in without getting yourself killed, enabled you to put Queenie in the corner for another several months before the process started all over again.

But was he fooling anybody? Victoria had known him only a few days, and she figured him out. True, he dropped a few hints, but she guessed half of what happened. Had other people been able to read him just as easily?

He cringed at the thought of having gone through thirteen years with people able to look into a past he thought he had hidden. They must have thought him a great fool. Some must have even pitied him.

Trinity disliked being thought a fool, but it positively enraged him to be pitied. He had carried his own weight all his life, sometimes against considerable odds. He took pride in it.

He took pride in it because he couldn't take pride in having brought Queenie to justice.

So that was it. He had spent thirteen years trying to escape Queenie's curse without even once guessing the true nature of the curse. Yet Victoria had led him to the answer in just a few days.

He hadn't seen it because of his stubborn pride. Maybe he wasn't so damned smart after all. He certainly wasn't as smart as he thought.

"Maybe you're right," he admitted, "but it's not something I want to talk about. Now get some sleep."

But Trinity couldn't sleep. He had proven vulnerable to her every attack so far. He even found himself again wishing she were innocent then he wouldn't be suffering these pangs of doubt.

If he didn't get himself under control, he'd soon find himself looking for ways to prove her innocence. If that happened, he might as well hand her over to somebody else.

No, by damn, he hadn't failed yet and he didn't mean to start now. What might prove more difficult was dealing with his buried anger over Queenie's getting away with murder. That ate at him like a canker. That's where he had to start, but he didn't know how to begin. He'd run so long he didn't know how to stop.

Maybe he should ask Victoria. He hadn't been able to solve anything having to do with Queenie in thirteen years. Why not give her a chance?

But he couldn't do that. It would be the same as admitting he was wrong. All his adult life he had depended on being right. Everything he had done, the reasons for his doing it, depended upon an unshakable conviction that he was right.

How could he have taken so many men to their death without being absolutely certain of their guilt?

But nothing felt right about Victoria. And he was ashamed to admit he didn't know whether it stemmed from a deeply felt conviction or naked desire.

* * *

Victoria was so tired, her body ached so much, yet physical exhaustion couldn't eradicate the excitement she had felt over the intimate nature of Trinity's touch.

She had been nearly unconscious when he began to massage her body, or she would never have let him touch her. She doubted he would have offered if she had been awake. Now she couldn't forget the feel of his hands on her legs, shoulders, and back. Even now the spot on her thigh tingled.

When Jeb had touched her, it had been purely incidental, a brushing against her or rolling over on her in bed when he was too drunk to know what he was doing. She had felt nothing but disgust.

Everything felt different with Trinity. The last hour or so before they reached camp, she had responded to the strength of his encircling arm, the nearness of his body, the comfort of his protective presence.

She wanted him to touch her again, but she vowed to keep him at a distance. She didn't want him to guess she did it because she was afraid to let him touch her. If he knew, she would be lost.

The way he felt about women, he'd probably assume she would be willing to sacrifice her virtue to save her neck. She didn't want to die, but she'd never do that.

But hadn't she wanted to be alone with him at the ranch? Wasn't that thought somewhere deep in her mind when she ignored Buc's advice and went to see him?

Not exactly. At least . . . not at first. She had found him attractive, but she also found him conversationally exciting and stimulating. Now, however, she found her view of him rapidly changing. He was so cold. He had no emotional response. He had defined their relationship in exclusively physical terms. She didn't think he even had an idea there might be anything else.

But she was beginning to see much more than a man who went after criminals for money. He had spent years trying to hide from his past. Maybe that past had forced him to become

157

an outcast and take up this reprehensible profession. Maybe, if his past could be laid to rest, he could put all that aside.

Victoria hardly dared let herself think about the Trinity of her imagination. If she were ever seduced by the vision of what he could be, she might lose sight of reality and let herself love him.

The thought shocked her. She had to be insane. Only demented women fell in love with their jailers!

But Victoria couldn't think of him as a jailer. True, he held her captive, but only because something held him in an even more unyielding captivity. She might break away; he never could . . . but he must.

She had to help him. There was a very different man trapped inside. She couldn't tell what that man would be like. She might be foolish to tamper with something she knew nothing about — it might be dangerous. She wouldn't know, though, until she prodded him into opening up to her. Or turned on her. Was that a chance she was willing to take?

Yes. Unless she were mistaken, there was something quite wonderful inside him. Something tragic had happened when he was a young man, at a time when he was most impressionable, but also at a time when he was most idealistic. He might say he had become the man he was because he wanted to, but Victoria didn't believe it. He had become that man because he *had* to.

She didn't know if she could change that. She didn't know if she should try. Her safety, the rest of her life, depended on her escaping from Trinity and never seeing him again. If he ever found her after Buc and her uncle rescued her, he would try to recapture her.

"We ought to stop now," Grant Davidge said. "We've lost the trail. I doubt we'll find it again in the dark."

"It doesn't matter if we find it or not," Buc insisted. "There's only one way to Bandera. We've got to keep going."

"We haven't stopped since we started out," Grant pointed

out. "The men are all in, and so are our horses. We'll all be better for a good night's rest."

"You can rest if you want," Buc said, "but I'm going on. I can't sleep knowing he's out there alone with her. No telling what he's done." Buc ground his teeth in impotent rage. "I'm going to kill that man with my bare hands if I have to."

"He won't hurt her," Grant said. "He only wants to take her back to Texas."

"How can we know? Maybe that's all he wanted to do when he came here, but Victoria's a beautiful woman. I don't know of any man who could be with her for more than a few minutes without having thoughts he wouldn't dare speak of. Smith is not above telling lies. He has no honor at all."

"I'm with Buc," Red said. "I didn't like him from the start. I aim to put a bullet between his eyes."

"Nobody touches Smith until I'm done with him," Buc said. "After that, you can do what you like. If you can find enough of him to do anything with."

Trinity didn't have the heart to wake her. She looked so tired. And so lovely. He wondered how she could look so defenseless, so harmless in her sleep. He had plenty of proof to the contrary, yet all he felt now was a desire to let her sleep so he could look at her.

She lay on her side, her head resting on her arms, her hair falling across her face, the blanket pulled tightly up under her chin. She made him think of a family he had helped long ago. They had a little black-haired girl who insisted that Trinity let her sleep in his lap. That little girl had been the only human in the world who had ever completely trusted him, who didn't feel the slightest trace of fear. For three nights he had felt more contented than at any time since his mother's death.

Not that there was anything little girlish about Victoria, but watching her gave him the same warm feeling he got when he put little Maria to bed. He wanted to stay close, keep her safe, hold her in his arms, keep her warm.

He smiled ruefully. Victoria wasn't at all like little Maria. Victoria would probably freeze before she let him keep her warm. He thought of the feel of her warm, soft skin under his hands. She wouldn't have let him do that either if she hadn't been so stiff she couldn't move. He wondered if she enjoyed it or if she simply endured it because she had no choice.

He wouldn't ask her. There was no point in inviting her to tell him how little she thought of him. She seemed only too anxious to do that without prompting.

Chapter Twelve

The warmth of the sun on her skin woke Victoria. She opened her eyes only to be forced to shield them from the glare. She rolled on her elbow and looked for Trinity. She saw the horses saddled and waiting, coffee and breakfast warming over the fire. Trinity sat on a boulder nearby, watching.

"What time is it?" she asked. Very tentatively, she stretched. When she found her muscles didn't ball into painful knots but instead ached rather pleasantly, she indulged in a luxurious stretch.

"About seven-thirty."

"I thought you wanted to leave before dawn."

"I decided you needed some extra sleep."

"That was kind of you," Victoria said, surprised.

"Not really. If yesterday is any example, I'd have to ride with my arm around you, which you won't like, or tie you in the saddle, which I can't do without irritating the skin on your wrists."

Victoria was disappointed by Trinity's rationale. She wasn't sure what she wanted him to say, but he could have started with basic humanity. She found his coldly analytical attention to her comfort irritating. "Aren't you afraid the delay will give my uncle time to catch up?"

"We got a good head start. Besides, I intend to drive you extra hard today. You've got about five minutes to get dressed. We have to be gone in fifteen."

Victoria cursed silently. Every time she thought he just might be human, he proved her wrong. She didn't know why she continued to keep hoping he wasn't as bad as he seemed.

She threw back the blanket and started to get up. Her legs collapsed under her.

Trinity had his arms around her before she could fall.

"I guess I'm not in as good a shape as I thought," she said. She tried to push him away, but she didn't try very hard. She liked his arms around her. They felt just as good as she remembered. Besides, she really couldn't stand by herself.

"I thought you were in remarkable shape when I had to chase you all over that mountain."

"I don't spend all my time arranging flowers," she said, trying a few unsteady steps on her own. "I ride every day, and I've climbed a lot of mountains doing my survey."

"You'd better sit down. Let me get you some breakfast."

"That's very thoughtful of you, but I have to wash up and get dressed."

"Not today. I've wasted too much time already. You have just enough time to eat." He handed her a plate and a cup of coffee. She set both down without tasting either.

"I can't go a whole day without at least washing my face, brushing my teeth, and changing clothes. I should have a bath. I feel positively filthy."

"You'll feel a lot worse before we reach Texas," Trinity said. "Now eat your breakfast or toss it away. I can't wait any longer."

So much for thoughtfulness, Victoria said to herself as she quickly swallowed coffee, which had grown bitter from sitting over the fire so long. The beans were better, not that she liked beans for breakfast, but any food was welcome on a cold morning when she had been riding for two days.

While she ate, Trinity broke open the fire and kicked dirt over the hot coals. He poured the last of the coffee on the coals to make sure they were out. When Victoria finished eating, he rinsed her plate with water from his canteen and then stowed everything in his gear.

"Can you mount by yourself, or do you want some help?"

Victoria got to her feet unassisted, but she knew she'd never mount her horse alone.

"It would be nice if you would lend me a hand," she said. She wouldn't ask for his help. She just couldn't.

"Watch your legs. They're not going to work like you expect."

Trinity lifted her effortlessly into the saddle. Victoria had never realized how nice it was to feel as light as a feather. It wasn't so bad to be treated like a precious possession once in a while.

"Where are we?" she asked. "This is beautiful country."

"Leaving the Tonto Basin. That's the Salt River below. The Mazatzal Mountains are behind us. We're headed toward the Apache Mountains."

"Do you have a pair of binoculars? I'd like to get a better look."

"You just can't forget the surveyor in you, can you?"

"I didn't get much chance to look about when I came to Arizona. It's such beautiful country. I'd hate to miss it a second time, especially since you're determined I won't be back."

She hadn't meant to say that. She'd managed to put it as far out of her mind as she could, but she had the satisfaction of seeing him look uncomfortable.

Below the river twisted along the basin floor, a silver ribbon reflecting the morning sunlight off its surface. Sand, loose gravel, and scattered trees marked its flood plain. Tree-covered ridges ran to the river's edge from all directions, their spiny ridges cut into irregular shapes by the rain and snow of a million seasons.

In the distance, mountain peaks shrouded in mist loomed huge and green against a backdrop of blue, cloudless sky. A waterfall appeared as a small white slash set deep in a green canvas. A single patch of bright yellow poppies provided the only touch of contrasting color.

Victoria swung the glasses to the north, and her body stiffened. Riders. Where these men following them? She knew nothing of the trails. Was it her uncle? She glanced over at Trinity to see if he'd noticed her sudden interest, but he was loading the packhorse. She couldn't tell anything about the riders because they stayed in the shadows of the trees. Then one rider rode out on a low ridge, and using his own glasses, surveyed the valley.

Buc. She would know his Appaloosa anywhere.

Without a second thought, Victoria kicked her horse into a gallop and raced in the direction of the riders. The curses which echoed off the mountain behind her only spurred her to ride faster. She didn't know where the trail she followed led, but it seemed to be taking her down to the basin floor, closer to Buc and her uncle. She dug her heels into her grey's side and slapped its flank with her open palm. She had to escape.

Victoria cursed the fact that she didn't have a gun or a rifle with her. She needed something to draw Buc's attention. Trinity would be at her heels any minute now. It was vital they see her before he caught her.

It seemed no time at all had passed when Victoria heard a horse on the trail behind her. She looked around, certain Trinity would close in on her any moment, but he was still some distance behind. In the clear, still air of the mountains, sound carried a long way. If she screamed loud enough, maybe they would heard her.

Victoria let out a scream which sounded like a cross between a scream of terror and a long, high-pitched wail. It hung in the air like a sword. She took a deep breath and screamed again. Trinity was practically on top of her. She opened her mouth to scream once more. Trinity's arm snaked out and encircled her waist, lifting her out of the saddle. She hung suspended five feet above the ground on a galloping horse, and the only thing which kept her from crashing to the ground was the strength in Trinity's arm.

"You seem determined to get as many people killed as possible," Trinity growled, as he slowed his horse. "If you really cared for your uncle, you'd have let him go on by."

"That's just what you want, isn't it?" Victoria managed to gasp. He was squeezing the breath out of her body, but she couldn't wish for him to loosen his hold. "Another easy capture so you can get on to the next one."

"No capture is easy," Trinity said as he brought his horse to a stop and turned him around on the narrow trail. The sound of gunfire drew his attention to the riders below. "But yours is turning out to be the hardest of all."

Then to her surprise, instead of settling her in front of him, or even throwing her across the saddle, he galloped back to camp. She dangled above the ground which passed beneath her with terrifying speed.

Her horse, frightened by the gunshots in front of him, turned around before he reached the basin floor and headed back up the trail.

"Are you trying to kill me?" Victoria cried after her leg struck a tree branch so hard it went numb.

"Surprisingly enough, I'm trying to keep you alive, though there are times I ask myself why."

She struggled just to go on breathing. His arm felt like the crushing coils of a boa constrictor. She would never have guessed Trinity had such strength. She doubted Buc could hold her suspended for more than a minute.

"You're crushing the life out of me."

"Then you won't have to worry about getting hanged."

"You're inhuman. You don't have a single Christian emotion in your body."

"I'm a little busy right now, but as soon as I brush through this gun battle without killing any more people than necessary, I'll see if I can't come up with at least one."

"What do you mean 'without killing any more people than necessary.' You wouldn't dare shoot my uncle."

"You get him to promise not to shoot at me, and I'll promise not to shoot at him."

"But he has to. You won't let me go otherwise."

"I won't let you go either way. The faster he figures that out, the fewer people will get hurt."

They had reached their camp. The packhorse stood where he had left it. Trinity dropped Victoria in a heap and leapt from the saddle. Before she had time to pull herself together, he turned her over, tied her hands and feet with a strip of soft leather, and leaned her up against a rock. He took both horses

165

around a bend, out of range of gunfire, then climbed to a lookout point.

What he saw caused him to curse violently.

"They're headed this way."

"Good."

"You won't think so for long."

"I'll be free before long. There must be a dozen men out there."

"Your uncle must have left his herd unguarded. He obviously values you more than his ranch."

Trinity took a few minutes to study the terrain around their camp.

"I'd better get you behind some rocks," he said. "One of those hotheaded young fools might start shooting at me without realizing he can hit you just as easily."

Victoria hadn't stopped to realize she could be a target. Her enthusiasm for the coming fight waned.

"What do you think Uncle Grant will do?"

"It will depend on whether your uncle or Buc directs the fight."

"Uncle Grant."

"Then we may brush through after all."

"I don't want to 'brush through.' I want to go back to Mountain Valley."

"No matter how many men your uncle hires, no matter how many times they come after me, you're going back to Texas. Get used to it."

"What makes you think you can outshoot and outsmart all those men?"

"I've got the one thing nobody else has. *You.* If need be, I'll use you for a shield."

"I never thought you would sink so low."

"Self-defense isn't a matter of etiquette. It comes down to doing what you have to. They won't shoot you no matter what they might want to do to me."

"Where's my uncle? What are they doing?"

"Why do you want to know?"

"I don't trust you not to shoot him on sight."

"Do you really think I'd do that?"

She didn't. Only anger caused her to make such an accusation. But she wouldn't take it back. "Anyone who would use a female as a shield would do anything."

"I wouldn't use you if I thought you would get hurt. Even bounty hunters have some standards."

"How am I supposed to guess that?"

"I don't know. I suppose I thought you'd see me pretty much as I see myself."

"And how's that?"

"An ordinary man doing his job as best he can."

There's nothing ordinary about you, Victoria thought. *And nothing ordinary has happened to me since the day you rode into Mountain Valley Ranch.* Her horse trotted into camp and immediately sought the familiar company of Trinity's gelding and the pack-horse.

"Even your horse doesn't feel safe around Buc," Trinity observed, grinning.

Victoria failed to see the humor in his remark.

"Trinity!"

The call came from below. It was Grant Davidge.

"I've come for Victoria. I know you're up there. I've got a dozen men down here. You can't get away. We'll surround you and pick you off."

"You're welcome to try," Trinity called back. "Just remind those hotheads to be careful. Any shot can ricochet and hit your niece."

"If you let her go, the boys and I will go back to the ranch and forget we ever heard of you."

"You speaking for Buc as well?"

"Buc works for me. He does what I say."

"That's a pretty decent offer. Could you give me some time to think about it?" Trinity asked.

Victoria's unbelieving glance flew to Trinity's face. She had thought he would hold out until the bitter end.

"I'll give you ten minutes. You let Victoria go before then, and my men will swear you never set foot in Mountain Valley."

"I'm glad you came to your senses," Victoria said as Trinity

167

approached her. "There was no way you could succeed."

Trinity whipped the handkerchief from around his neck and folded it over several times. "You don't know me very well yet. When you do, you'll know I never give up."

Without warning, he took Victoria's jaw in his hands and squeezed. Her mouth popped open, and before she could close it again, he stuffed the handkerchief in her mouth.

"I'm not going to ask you if you'll be quiet if I take the gag out, or if you'll try to escape if I untie you. I'm going to throw you across your horse and hopefully get over that ridge before they realize we're gone. When your uncle comes looking for us, he'll find the nest empty."

Trinity lifted Victoria over his shoulder. Her furious grunts only made him smile.

The breath left Victoria's body with a painful whoosh when Trinity draped her over the saddle. In the agonizing minutes which followed, she vowed to pay him back for every tortured minute.

In the meantime, it was all she could do to breathe. She wondered if anybody could be carried this way for more than a few minutes and live. She felt her grip on consciousness slipping.

They hadn't gone far when Victoria heard a shout behind them.

"They're gone." It was Buc's voice. "The bastard has run out on us."

"Damn!" Trinity said. "Looks like your uncle didn't keep his word any more than I kept mine. Now we're going to have to find a place to hole up and fight."

Trinity mounted his horse and headed down the trail at a fast trot.

Victoria thought she would die. She was certain every rib in her body would break. She wondered if it might not be easier to hang. Certainly it would be faster.

"This will have to do," Trinity said a few minutes later, and mercifully the bouncing stopped. Victoria didn't even mind being dropped roughly on the ground. After the agonizing ride, she didn't feel it. Trinity took out the handkerchief.

"You're going to need to talk, and I may not be in a position to get to you just when I need you."

"What are you going to do?" Victoria demanded.

"That depends on your uncle."

"Where is he?"

"Coming down the trail right behind us."

Trinity lifted his rifle and put a bullet into the ground in front of Grant's horse. He had the pleasure of seeing the men scatter among the brush and trees along the trail.

"That's far enough, Davidge. I don't want to put lead in anybody."

"Give up," Grant shouted back. "We'll surround you and pick you off."

"Victoria will be sitting in front of me."

"I never thought you would hide behind a woman," Grant called.

"I mean to take Victoria back to Texas. I'll get there any way I can. That first shot was a warning. I'm a properly sworn deputy in Texas. You'll be breaking the law if you try to stop me."

"We're coming after you, Smith. Let my niece go."

"If anybody comes after me, let him know I'll shoot to kill."

Trinity went over to Victoria and took the rope off her feet.

"What are you going to do?" She hoped fear didn't show in her eyes. She had known Trinity could be hard, but she had never seen him cornered. Now she understood why he had never failed.

"We're riding out. Anybody who follows takes his life in his hands."

"But they'll follow."

"They'll keep their distance."

"For how long?"

"That depends?"

"On what?"

"On how much of a chance they're willing to take with your life."

Trinity lifted Victoria into the saddle and tied her ankles beneath the horse. He tied her wrists to the pommel.

"You don't mean for me to get away."

"I don't mean for you to fall off. We may have to run for it."

This began the strangest day of Victoria's life. Trinity led the way just as if they had been traveling in the normal way. If she twisted around in the saddle, she could see the group of riders led by her uncle. Every now and then they fanned out looking for a second trail, but they inevitably returned to the main trail, following like a pack train.

There were no shots. Victoria realized there wouldn't be any, at least not as long as they kept to the narrow mountain trail. As long as her uncle's men were unable to leave the trail, they couldn't get a shot at Trinity. She was directly in their line of fire.

But that didn't discourage her.

She knew Buc and her uncle would manage to free her. She also knew they would probably kill Trinity. No sooner had she accepted Trinity's death as inevitable when she realized she didn't want it. Despite all he had done, despite all she had threatened to do to him, she didn't want to see him hurt. Maybe she felt there had been enough killing because of her. . . . Maybe she had gotten softer as she matured. . . . Maybe she had gotten to like him too much before he kidnapped her to hate him enough to want him dead.

But how could they free her without killing Trinity? Trinity wouldn't let her go, not as long as he was physically capable of doing anything to prevent it.

She studied his back as she rode behind him. His strength of character appealed to her. It must be wonderful to spoil a man who didn't need it, a man who could easily meet every demand you or anyone else made of him.

She could remember a time when she thought Jeb was all a man could ever be. She had dreamed of him holding her in his arms, kissing her, making love to her. It had excited her, but it had been the cool excitement of a young woman thinking of a coming event.

There was nothing cool about the way she felt about Trinity. Even now she was sweating despite the frosty mountain air. Nor was there the young girl's eagerness to rush forward to another new and interesting experience; rather there was the feeling that if she stayed close to Trinity for too long, she would be changed forever.

Yet, she identified another feeling which surprised her. She was *angry* for Trinity. He had been badly hurt by some woman. He probably would have been a normal, cheerful, happily married man if that woman hadn't broken him before he developed a character tough enough to withstand such hurt.

Because of what that unknown woman did, Trinity had passed a sentence on himself. One he didn't deserve. One he couldn't escape. Victoria understood and felt a bond of sympathy with him. Of course, Trinity wouldn't admit to this—a man like him never admitted to any kind of weakness—but that didn't make any difference. She knew it was there. In a strange way, his denial made her like him more. It made him seem . . . human. To the world, he was remorseless—without feeling for himself or his victims. Inside, he still hurt.

It seemed strange he could be hurt by anything. He had dropped into their valley and plucked her out against all odds. And now he kept her uncle and a dozen men at bay. He seemed not to care about her, her uncle, or himself. Only about doing a job.

Did pain do that to people? Could it turn her into a woman incapable of feeling love or joy? Or admitting she needed someone else?

The thought was chilling.

She understood now that Trinity must have a great capacity to care. Nothing else could have laid him open to such deep and long-lasting pain.

Unfortunately, his pain had twisted this caring into a need for revenge. Trinity might think he was performing a duty for society, but she knew he was revenging himself on other criminals because he couldn't revenge himself on the only one that mattered.

The sound of a rifle shot brought Victoria out of her reverie.

Chapter Thirteen

Trinity's shot into the air above Grant's head jerked Victoria back to reality.

"It's time to eat," he called back to her uncle. "Make sure your men stay in camp."

"I don't want anything," Victoria said as Trinity lifted her down from her horse. He set her up against a rock but didn't untie her. She didn't ask him to. It would be too much like begging.

"Suit yourself, but the horses are tired. And if you'll remember, I didn't get any breakfast."

"I don't care if you never eat again."

"What a wonderful attitude that would make in a wife," Trinity said, smiling in the way that made Victoria long to put a new set of scratches on his face. The others were beginning to heal and her conscience bothered her less. "Were you planning to refuse to feed your husband whenever he made you angry?"

"He wouldn't make me that angry."

"Who were you planning to marry, some meek bank clerk or a nervous accountant? I don't care much for Buc, but I give him credit for some guts."

"For the last time, I'm not going to marry Buc," Victoria said.

"You'd better tell him. I don't think he knows."

"It doesn't matter."

"I think it does. It's not right to let a man risk his life for the woman he means to marry when you know all the time you have no notion of marrying him."

"I didn't expect him to come after me."

"Do you mean you told him to stay home if anybody carried you off?"

"Of course not. Buc would never do that."

"Then you *did* expect him to come after you."

"Yes, but—"

"And he knew you expected him to come after you?"

"Of course. Buc wouldn't stay home if he knew I was in trouble."

"Then you *did* expect him to come after you."

"You've twisted my words around until I don't know what I'm saying," Victoria said.

"I'm just making you say what you should have said all along. You know you let Buc look after you all these years."

"My uncle *paid* Buc to look after me. He didn't do it because I asked him to or because I promised him I'd marry him. I told him years ago I didn't love him."

"But you didn't tell him you could *never* love him."

"Why would I say that?"

"So he wouldn't go on pining after you."

"How was I to know he wouldn't fall in love with the next girl he met?"

"Men have a way of falling in love with women they rescue, especially if the woman is as beautiful as you."

"So now you're blaming me for the way I look."

"Just for taking advantage of it."

"If I'd been taking advantage of it, I'd have tried my wiles on you."

"It wouldn't have worked."

"You're immune to women?"

"Not women. Just you."

Victoria opened her mouth to ask him about his body's response to her, but changed her mind. She didn't know whether she wanted to wring a confession of vulnerability from him. She didn't trust her own response if he admitted he was interested in her. Despite the fact she should hate him for

173

what he was doing to her, he upset her calculations on just about every score.

"No man is immune to women forever. One day you'll find a woman who can make you do things you don't want to do. I hope I'm around to see that day."

"You won't be."

"Do you care to explain that remark?"

He stared into the fire so long she thought he was going to ignore her. Dark emotions distorted his features and caused his fingers to grip his battered tin cup until it bent under the pressure.

"It's already happened . . . fifteen years ago." He threw the last of his coffee into the fire. "I swore then no woman would ever again have that kind of power over me."

The sheer magnitude of the rage which gripped his body stunned Victoria. She hadn't anticipated the violence of the emotions that swelled inside him.

"It's time to get started. We have a long way to go to reach my next camp."

"You really think you're going to reach Texas, don't you? You've got your camps laid out, and you know exactly how far you mean to travel each day. Don't you think my uncle and a dozen men on your heels is going to make any difference?"

"It'll make things more difficult."

"You're the most incredibly stubborn and arrogant man I've ever seen. They're going to kill you. It may take a little while, but it's just a matter of time."

"Then sit back and enjoy the show. But you'll have to do it on horseback."

He'd never met a woman like Victoria. The longer he was with her, the more his fascination grew. The more he knew about her, the more he wanted to know. The more she struggled to escape him, the more determined he became to keep her with him. She had become part of his thinking and feeling, part of his world, and he couldn't imagine it without her.

Some alarm went off in the back of Trinity's brain. He didn't know whether it was instinct or whether he had actually heard something.

174

He sprang to his feet, irritated at himself for letting Victoria make him forget to keep close watch on Grant's camp. He didn't think they would try any maneuvers until nightfall, but he hadn't earned a thirteen-year record of success by forgetting for as much as one minute that only his life stood between his captive and freedom. But he'd never had a female prisoner before.

Trinity counted the heads in Grant's camp. Then he counted them again.

"Damn," he exploded. "Buc's gone."

"I told you he wouldn't give up."

"I thought he had more sense than to try to take you in daylight. He ought to know he can't do it without a shot. And unless he can get close enough for a sure shot, every bullet is as much of a danger to you as to me."

Trinity picked Victoria up and carried her behind a large boulder, which seemed to have been turned on its side. He laid her flat on the ground.

"Sit me up. I don't want to die with my face in the dirt."

"I want you under cover. I don't know what that fool might do. I wish to hell your uncle had better control over his men."

"I'm sure Uncle Grant told him to try to get behind you."

"I give your uncle credit for more sense. It's Buc who lets his emotions rule his head. A dangerous combination out here."

Trinity noticed movement in Grant's camp. Several of the men had moved out of camp and were approaching through the trees. That could only mean Buc had circled the ridge to come up behind him. They meant to draw him out of position. Either Buc would get him from behind or the others would get him from below.

As Trinity picked his way through the rocks above his campsite, he cursed everyone: Buc and Grant for being determined to rescue Victoria, Judge Blazer for having his own daughter-in-law convicted of murder, Jeb Blazer for getting himself killed, and himself for ever agreeing to go after Victoria.

He didn't curse Queenie because he'd been doing that for

thirteen years. He didn't curse Victoria because he didn't want to. He never had.

After a quick glance to assure himself the others wouldn't come into firing range for several minutes, he turned his attention to the hillside above. Even though he couldn't see Buc, Trinity knew he had to be up there. A careful inspection of the mountainside showed no sign of Buc.

Trinity studied his campsite. Was it vulnerable from another direction?

He had chosen a promontory to make his stand. It offered an excellent view of the mountain above, below, and most of the trail. All except the last hundred feet. That was hidden by a large outcropping of rock, part of the very outcropping Victoria sat on at this moment. Buc could come over the ridge. But instead of dropping down from above, which anyone would expect him to do, he could drop down to the trail before reaching the camp.

And Trinity would never see him.

Trinity scrambled down the mountainside so quickly he slid the last several yards.

Victoria had not been able to lie still while Trinity searched the mountainside for Buc. She had to know what he intended to do. Her uncle was out there with eleven men who would willingly give their lives for her. She had to do something. Rolling on to her stomach and pulling herself forward by her elbows, she crawled from behind the rock. She saw Buc and Trinity before they saw each other.

It horrified her to know her first thought was for Trinity. How could she be so unnatural as to think first of the man responsible for all her grief? If he hadn't arrived with his lying tongue and soft assurances, she would still be in Mountain Valley, safe in her own bed, and her uncle and Buc would be out of the reach of his guns.

These thoughts barely flashed though her mind when she realized Buc had his gun drawn. Trinity's gun was still in his holster.

Before she knew what she did, she cried, "Look out!"

The two men saw each other as the two words hung in the

176

air. Faster than she believed any human could act, Trinity rolled to one side, drew his gun, and fired.

Buc's first shot buried itself harmlessly in the ground where Trinity had landed. His second tore through Trinity's shirt, grazing his arm.

Trinity's only shot hit Buc in the chest.

Buc sank to his knees, his gun sliding from his loosened grasp. Then he toppled over and lay still.

Trinity came to his feet with the agility of a cat. Two quick shots at the men converging on him from below brought them to a halt.

"I got Buc," he shouted at them. "Anybody else want to try, come on."

Stunned and shocked, Victoria crawled frantically on her hands and knees. She had to reach Buc. He couldn't die, not because of her. She wouldn't let him.

Trinity was right. She was responsible. She had expected him to come after her. She had expected him to try to rescue her. She had expected him to risk his life for her. She had known it and done nothing to stop it. She had also known she didn't want to marry him. She had known he expected to marry her anyway.

She had brought him up here. She might as well have shot him. If he died, she would be the murderer they believed her to be.

No matter what she had to do, she couldn't let Buc and the others die because of her.

His breathing was ragged but steady. She got up on her hands and knees and managed to sit up.

"Buc," she called, "can you hear me?"

"He's not dead," Trinity called from the rock.

"You don't know where the bullet struck him. It might have hit his heart."

"Just like he could have hit my heart if you hadn't warned me. Why did you do that?"

"I don't know," Victoria said, too dazed and upset to pretend. "He had his gun drawn. I was sure he'd kill you. You are hurt!" She noticed the blood on his shirt.

"It's only a scratch."

"How do you know?"

"I thought you wanted me dead."

"I don't want anybody dead," Victoria said. "I never did. None of this is my fault, but it seems to be getting worse with no way to stop it."

"If you go back . . ."

"So many have died already. Somebody killed three of our men. I'm afraid to ask what happened to the second bounty hunter. Now Buc's lying here dying."

"He's not dying. It's only a shoulder wound."

"How do you know?"

"Because I hit what I aim for, and I aimed for his shoulder."

"My God, you're heartless. He's nothing to you but something to be shoved aside."

"You can look at it that way."

A burst of gunfire ended their conversation. The wicked zing of a bullet ricocheting between the boulders turned Victoria's blood cold.

"Trinity, how's Buc?" It was Grant Davidge.

"He took a bullet in the shoulder, but another ricochet like the last one could kill him."

"We're coming after you."

"You can't take me in this position," Trinity called back.

"You're surrounded. We're closing from all sides."

A bullet smashed into the rocks above Victoria's head. The angry whine of a ricochet pierced her ears just as the flattened piece of metal sheared off a length of leather from the sole of her boot. It surprised a cry out of her.

"If you can't control your men, you're going to have a dead niece," Trinity shouted, fury giving his voice conviction. "That last bullet took off part of her boot. Make them hold their fire, or I'm going to kill the first one who lifts a rifle."

"Hold your fire," Grant ordered.

"He's lying." It was Red. "I say we charge him. He can't get all of us."

"The bounty is paid whether Victoria's dead or alive," Trinity called out. "Judge Blazer would be happy if one of your bullets killed her. It would save him trouble and preserve his reputation."

Another burst of rifle fire. Victoria saw Trinity's hat go flying through the air as she fell to the ground. A bullet had come within inches of killing him. Trinity rolled away from the low rock where he had been crouched and scrambled to a position higher on the mountainside. Taking careful aim, he put a bullet through the leg of a man too anxious to be the first to reach him.

"Hold your fire," Grant shouted.

"We can't just let her stay up there."

"We can't get him without endangering Victoria."

"I'll get behind him."

"He's already got Buc."

"He won't get me."

Victoria recognized Perez Calderon's voice before another burst of gunfire pinned them down.

"Give him cover."

Fire from a dozen guns echoed off the mountains. Victoria saw Trinity holster his gun and pick up his rifle. As he took careful aim, she realized he would shoot to kill. There would be no more talk, no more bluffing, no more jockeying to see who had the better position or who would back down first. From here on, everyone would be trying to kill him.

And he would be trying to kill everyone from the ranch.

Her uncle, the only relative she had in the world, at least the only one who cared about her except for her money. He ought to be home enjoying the comforts of his long years of work and sacrifice.

Perez Calderon, a man who loved her as much as his own sister.

Buc who only cared for two things in life: Victoria and the ranch.

Red, a lanky, rangy teenager on the threshold of life whose unquestioning loyalty was to the man who paid his wages.

And all the rest of the men who had taken oaths to defend her with their lives.

Victoria called out, but Trinity couldn't hear her over the

noise of the gunfire. She had to get to him, to stop him before he killed Uncle Grant. She pulled herself along on her elbows. She ignored the pain as the rocks cut deep into her skin. She had to reach him before he killed anyone.

"Trinity, stop. Don't shoot," she called desperately. "I'll go back with you."

Trinity spun around, disbelief in his eyes. "Do you know what you're saying?"

"I'm saying I'll go back to Bandera with you. I can't let you kill my uncle. Or anybody else. Not because of me. But I have one condition."

"You're not in a position to make conditions."

"You're not in a very good position yourself."

Trinity looked at the eleven men determined to fill him full of bullet holes. That was unarguable. "What is it?"

"Before you turn me over to Judge Blazer, you've got to try to prove I didn't kill Jeb."

"You don't expect me to believe—"

"You've got to find Chalk Gillet. He was a hired hand on the Judge's ranch. He was a loner, a journeying man, but he's my witness."

"What if I can't? What if I'm still convinced you killed your husband?"

"If you can't find any evidence in two weeks, you can turn me in."

Trinity didn't like her offer, but he liked the prospect of a gunfight even less. No matter who won, too many people would die.

"And you'll go?"

"Yes."

"What about your uncle? He'll try to stop you."

"He won't have to if you find Chalk Gillet."

A great weight lifted from Trinity's soul. Not until this moment did he realize how much he wanted the chance to prove Victoria's innocence. Until now he hadn't let himself think beyond the moment he would turn her over to Sheriff Sprague. Everything would end there. But if she weren't guilty, if she didn't hang. . . .

Trinity struggled to keep himself from useless speculation. First he would deal with Grant and then with finding Chalk Gillet. Then if she were innocent. . . .

He'd better not think about that just yet. There were still eleven men down there determined to kill him.

"You're going to have to convince your uncle."

Victoria almost collapsed with relief. "Untie me. I'll go talk to him."

"You'll have to talk from here."

"I can't."

"And you'll have to convince all those cowhands. Davidge," Trinity shouted, ignoring Victoria's objection, "tell your men to hold their fire. Your niece wants to say something to you."

"If this is some trick . . ."

"You'll see it's not in just a minute, but for God's sake, hold your fire. Victoria's not under cover. Tell your men to stand up. I'm not letting her close to the edge until I count eleven heads."

Grant gave the order, and the men reluctantly rose up from their hiding places. A chill ran down Trinity's spine. They were well scattered and close. They would have surrounded him soon.

"I don't see Red. Tell him to stand up or no dealing."

"Red, you heard the man."

"I don't trust him," Red called out.

Trinity spun about. Somehow the boy had gotten farther up the mountainside. It would have taken him only a few minutes to have found a position above him.

"Stand up," Grant ordered. "He can see now we're not fooling."

Red angrily kicked a rock loose as he stood up. The stone tumbled down the mountain taking a dozen larger stones with it. Several men were forced to take cover to avoid being struck by the tumbling rocks.

"You young fool," Grant called out. "You nearly killed me."

"Talk," Trinity ordered Victoria, "and make it good. If that young carrot-top is anything to judge by, they're in a rotten mood."

"I suppose you're proud of yourself."

"No. I'd much rather have gotten you back to Texas before anybody noticed you were missing."

Victoria stepped forward until she could see the men scattered below. In their upturned faces she saw many stripes of the rainbow: youth, lovers, wives, children, the hope of a nation. They were ready to die for her, and she had done nothing to deserve it. She had to stop it.

"Uncle Grant, I've made up my mind to go back to Texas with Trinity."

"You can't mean that," Grant shouted over a chorus of protests from the cowboys. "They'll hang you."

"Trinity has promised to find Chalk Gillet."

"It won't do any good. If you don't remember the jury they picked out, I do. There wasn't a single man who wasn't handpicked by Blazer. They'd have found you guilty if you'd been ten miles away."

"Trinity will find proof."

"You can't go back, honey. I admit I think a lot of Trinity's ability to do what he says, but I can't let you risk the chance he won't succeed."

"Then you go ahead of me. You said before you wanted to hire a good lawyer and some Pinkertons. You can do that now. But you've got to see Buc gets to a doctor. He looks bad to me."

"Victoria, I don't know what kind of tales Trinity's telling you, but if he's telling you he can prove you're innocent, he's lying. I'm not letting you do anything this crazy. Now get back down behind those rocks. We're coming in, and we're coming in fast."

"No," Victoria called. "I won't let you."

"You can't stop me."

"I'm not moving. I'll stand right here. I'll stand in front of Trinity if I have to."

"Victoria, what's wrong with you? You're not trying to tell me you've fallen in love with him?"

"No," Victoria replied. "I've just realized somebody's going to die if I don't go back — you, Buc, one of the men, even Trinity. If not this time, the next. I never thought about it like this before. It seemed so simple on the ranch."

"If you'd just stayed there, everything would have been okay. It will be again. After we kill Trinity."

"It'll never be simple again, especially not if you kill Trinity."

"I can protect you."

"What for? To live locked away for the rest of my life, afraid to set foot outside the house?"

"I'll hire more men."

"And who'll take care of me if they kill you?"

"Your husband."

"And who after that, my sons, my daughters' husbands? No, I can't condemn you to the kind of life I would have to lead. And I can't condemn my husband and children to a future of protecting someone who can't be protected, of hiding someone who can't be hidden. What kind of life would they have? How could they respect me? They might only wonder in the back of their minds if I killed Jeb, but they would know I chose not to face justice."

"We can move to another ranch, somewhere they won't know us."

"And who's to say somebody won't recognize me. Then it would start all over again. No. I've cost you enough already. I'll not cost you your ranch."

"We'll work something out."

"I've made up my mind. This has to stop, and it has to stop now. I knew that as soon as I saw Buc get hit."

"I won't let you do it."

"You can't stop me."

"We'll get Trinity. We'll take you back to the ranch."

"Then I'll go back on my own."

There was a pause.

"You really mean it, don't you?"

"Yes. I never realized until today what this kind of freedom could cost. Now that I know, I've decided it's too much. I don't know why I didn't see it years ago. I suppose you and Buc guarded me too well. Did you kill that bounty hunter?"

Grant didn't answer right away. "There are no bodies buried on my land," he finally said.

Victoria heaved a sigh of relief, but Trinity looked unconvinced.

"Send someone up to get Buc," Victoria said. "He's got to see a doctor."

"I'm not letting you go," Grant said. "If you must go back to Texas, I'll take you."

Victoria thought for only a moment. "No, the time for that has passed. I have to go with Trinity."

"I trust him, but not that much."

"I do. Now there's no point in arguing any more. Once you know Buc's going to be okay, you can head for Texas. I'm sure Trinity will leave messages along the way to let you know I'm still okay."

"I'm coming up," Grant called.

"I'm coming, too," Red called.

"Leave your guns," Trinity ordered.

Both men took exception to this condition, but they finally allowed Victoria to convince them it was the only way they could remove Buc without someone getting hurt.

The sight of Victoria tied up almost started a fight. Grant and Red refused to do anything until Trinity removed the belts. Victoria hid her wrists. She doubted her uncle would keep his word if he saw the chafed skin.

"If anything happens to Victoria, either now or back in Texas, I'm coming after you," Grant said. "She wouldn't be going back if you hadn't come busting in where you had no business, pointing guns at the only people she has in the world. You remember that when you start rattling on about your *duty*. From this minute on your duty is to see nothing happens to Victoria."

Buc got to his feet, but he couldn't walk. One of the men brought up a horse. It took all three men to hoist him into the saddle. As soon as Buc steadied himself with a grip on the pommel, he turned his pain-filled eyes to Victoria.

"Why did you warn him? I could have killed him easy."

"I didn't want you to kill him," Victoria said. "I don't want

184

anybody to kill anybody. That's why I'm going back. This killing will never stop as long as I keep running away. I didn't kill Jeb, but if you had killed Trinity, or he had killed you, your death would have been on my head."

Victoria paused and looked at Buc. He was such a nice, honest, decent man. He worshipped the ground she walked on. He would love and cherish her for the rest of her life. He would spoil her and treat her like a queen. Any woman in her right mind would die for a husband like that.

Why couldn't she love him?

Because he would never have been able to see the real Victoria. Buc loved the helpless girl he rescued from jail, not the woman who had grown tough enough to face being hanged. He wanted a wife he could care for and protect, not one who would argue with every other word he spoke.

Victoria wanted to be treated like a real woman. She didn't know exactly what that entailed, but she did know it was as far from Buc's ability to understand as it had been from Jeb's.

But more than that, she simply didn't love him. She never had.

"I can't marry you, Buc. Not now or when I come back from Texas. I've told you before, but I didn't try very hard to make you believe me. That's my fault, and I'm sorry, but I don't love you. I tried to, especially when I first came to Arizona, but it never happened. Now I know it never will."

"But you like me. Isn't that enough?"

"Not for me. And it shouldn't be for you. You're a fine man, Buc. You deserve someone who can love you just as much in return."

"I won't ask any more than you can give."

"But I want more. I can't settle for *like* when I might have *love*. I did that once, and I'll never do it again."

"Are you in love with him?" Buc said, indicating Trinity.

"No, but if he hadn't come along to shake me out of the cocoon I let you and Uncle Grant build around me, I might never have known I wasn't in love with you."

"What you mean is if he hadn't come along, you'd have married me and been happy about it. I don't know what kind

185

of lies he's told you, but I promise he'll pay for every one of them."

"Buc, you've got to promise me one thing. You, too, Uncle Grant."

"Anything," Buc said. Grant didn't appear equally eager to commit himself.

"Neither of you will come after Trinity."

"You *are* in love with him," Buc growled.

"This has nothing to do with Trinity. I'm asking because of me. If you got killed, I'd never forgive myself. You're the only people in the world who love me enough to risk your lives for me. Do you know how precious that makes you?" Her eyes filled with tears. "If I lost you two, I'd have nobody."

"But we can't just let you go back to Texas and forget about you."

"There must be a way to find out who killed Jeb. You can work on that while Trinity goes after Gillet. But make sure Buc's all right first. Promise?"

"Okay."

"I don't promise," Buc said angrily.

"Buc, you so much as lay one hand on Trinity, and I'll never speak to you again."

"I knew you were in love with him."

"To hell with Trinity," Victoria snapped angrily. "I'm talking about you. Trinity can get himself shot to ribbons or beaten to a pulp. That's no concern of mine, but you are. I don't want you hurt, and I don't want men like Trinity coming after you for the rest of your life. You've got to promise you'll leave him alone. Promise. If you don't, you'll have to leave the ranch."

Buc looked to Grant for support, but he didn't get it. "She's right. As much as I like you, as much as I hoped you two would marry, I can't have my foreman on the run from the law."

Buc looked cornered.

"Okay, but you haven't heard the last of me," Buc said, turning on Trinity in helpless rage. "I vow to see your kind wiped from the face of the earth."

"Be careful of vows," Trinity advised, no anger in his voice.

186

"I made one, not very different from yours, and it has consumed my life."

"I mean it. I swear it on my mother's grave."

"I swore on my father's."

"This is no time for vows, old or new," Victoria broke in. "Get him to a doctor, Uncle Grant. Make sure he's completely well before you let him out of your sight. See you in Texas."

"Trinity—" Grant started to say.

"I know. If anything happens to her, half the world will be on my tail."

"You can count on it. She's all I've got."

"You ought to choose your next victim more carefully," Buc said. "One without friends or relatives."

"There won't be another *victim*," Trinity practically snarled.

"There'll always be another one for men like you," Buc said, too full of wrath to listen to Trinity, or to believe him if he had. "And one more after that until somebody kills you. It's in your blood, like a dog turned killer. You can't give it up."

But Victoria heard the smothered emotion behind the snarl in Trinity's voice. Was it bitterness, exhaustion, frustration, or disgust? She couldn't tell. She turned to Trinity, her eyes full of questions, her nerves strained.

Did he really mean he would give up this hideous pursuit of death? If so, did it have anything to do with her?

187

Chapter Fourteen

Trinity saw the questions in her eyes. Victoria was certain he knew what she wanted to ask, but he turned away.

"We've got to be going if we're going to make my next camp," he said.

Victoria controlled the feeling of excitement growing inside her. Trinity *did* mean it, otherwise he wouldn't have looked away, but he wasn't willing to discuss it. Not now. Not in front of Buc and her uncle. But there would be time before they reached Bandera.

Plenty of time.

Neither Buc nor Grant would be the first to turn his back on Victoria, so she took the reins of Buc's horse and started it down the trail. "Make sure you do everything the doctor says. Wounds like this can easily become infected. I'll be expecting you in a few weeks. And don't worry about me. You can be sure Trinity will get me to Texas in one piece. He's already given you a good sample of what he can do."

"I suppose so," Grant said, but he looked unhappy.

"Go on," Victoria said as she slapped the horse's haunches. "Go find that doctor."

Victoria watched as a few minutes later her uncle gathered his men. Several of them were vociferous in their objections to leaving Victoria in Trinity's keeping. After a heated argument, Red saddled his horse and rode away at a gallop.

His departure took the life out of the crew's resistance. Dispirited, they mounted up and started back along the trail. Many of them turned back for a last look. Victoria waved to each one, smiling as though she were absolutely certain she'd done the best thing for everybody. Rather than the only thing she could do.

"I'm ready," Victoria said, turning to Trinity after the last of her uncle's men had passed from view. "You don't have to tie my hands and feet. I won't try to escape."

"Maybe, but I'd feel a little more comfortable with you tied."

"Okay." She held out her arms, wrists together, like it no longer mattered what he did.

"Would you like to mount up first?"

"Okay."

She climbed into the saddle and immediately held out her wrists again. After checking to make sure the abrasions were healing, he tied them with fresh strips of soft rawhide. But his interest seemed to be more in the expression on her face than the tightness of the knots.

"We're going to have to move fast to make up lost time."

"Okay."

"Let me know if you need to stop for anything."

"I will."

Trinity didn't trust this new tactic. He was afraid the change was merely another attempt to get him off balance so she could escape, and he didn't care for the monosyllables or the set, empty expression on her face. He had come to expect fiery anger, strong language, open opposition. He didn't know what to do with stony silence. When she kept glancing behind her, he was certain she had something up her sleeve.

They had been on the trail less than fifteen minutes when she cursed and snatched the reins from his slackened grip.

"Red is following us. I've got to stop him," she said and headed back the way they had come at a gallop.

Trinity was at her side in a half dozen strides, his hand on her horse's bridle.

"Let me go alone," Victoria asked. "I don't want any gun-play."

"You won't get any from me."

"Maybe, but I don't trust Red."

Trinity stayed slightly ahead of her.

"At least ride behind me."

"I don't hide behind women."

"You would have earlier."

"This is different."

"I don't see how," Victoria said, giving up once more trying to understand this man who had so completely overturned her life. "I just don't want Red hurt. He's too young to think before he acts. He still sees me as the enchanted princess and you as the evil knight."

"Not a very flattering picture."

"How would you feel in his shoes?"

Trinity didn't answer.

"I'm not going back," Red said when they drew up in front of him. "And you can't make me."

At any other time, his youthful belligerence would have amused Victoria. He looked so much like the protective younger brother she never had, but there was too much at stake now to trust to his volatile temper.

"Uncle Grant promised not to send anybody."

"He didn't. When he said I couldn't come, I quit."

"Why?"

"I don't trust him," Red said, indicating Trinity.

"I promised nothing would happen to her."

"You're taking her back to jail, aren't you?" the boy suddenly exploded. "I consider that something."

"Have you ever been to Texas?"

Red shook his head.

"How will you get there? I'm not taking you."

"I ain't asking you to. I ain't *asking* anything. I'm telling you I'm following you all the way, and you'd better keep your promise."

"Isn't there anything I can do to make you go back?" Victoria asked.

"Nothing. I got no job. I got nothing to do but follow you."

"Do you have any money?"

"I got enough."

Victoria knew he didn't. Her uncle wouldn't have paid off

on the trail.

"Come on," Trinity said to Victoria. "We're wasting time."

Victoria didn't turn away from Red.

"Don't worry about me none," the boy assured her. "I'll be right behind you."

It was hard not to smile at his earnestness, but not a muscle in Victoria's face moved. It would have crushed his pride.

"Let us know if you need help."

"I'll be the one giving the help," Red said, glaring at Trinity.

They left him then, Trinity riding along at a fast trot.

"Seems Arizona is full of men all raring to throw up everything for you," he said. "I used to think Queenie was the best I'd ever seen, but I think you got her beat."

"I have no idea who this Queenie is, but I gather from the way you say her name, the comparison isn't flattering."

"Depends," Trinity said. "Queenie was good. She never said so, at least not to me, but I'll bet she took pride in every sucker she reeled in."

"Am I supposed to be 'reeling in' Red?" Victoria asked, her voice tight with anger.

"I don't know. To tell you the truth, I don't know what the hell you're up to. You're the most confusing female I ever set eyes on. First you're the darling, spoiled daughter of a very rich man who dies and leaves you a fortune. Then you marry the only son of a richer man, only you shoot him. Then your uncle, another rich man who has no relative but you, rescues you from jail. Now you have every cowhand on his ranch, and everyone in Arizona for all I know, ready to lay down his life for you. You keep Buc panting after you for five years because you can't bear to tell him you don't love him. You let the whole shooting match come after you knowing there's bound to be killing, then you tell me you've decided to go to Texas because you can't stand to see anybody you love killed. Does that include that poor, deluded Irishman?"

"Of course it does."

"How many more men do you love?" Trinity was embarrassed with himself. He was acting like a jealous lover.

191

"Do you always twist people's words?"

"Not honest people's."

"As many lies as you tell, how can you tell the difference?"

"I only lie when I have to."

"A lie is a lie, no matter why you tell it."

"How about you?"

"I haven't told any lies, to you or anybody else. Nobody except myself." She smiled unexpectedly. "Funny, it was your lies which stopped me lying to myself."

"How's that?" Trinity asked. He didn't know what she was talking about.

"All that stuff you told me back at the ranch, about other people and places and having a future and hope. They were lies, but they woke me up to the lies I'd been telling myself. You see, I'd told myself since no one believed me it was all right to run away, that I didn't mind living with fear. I also told myself I was happy in Mountain Valley, that I would marry Buc and settle down to be a good wife and mother. I told myself it was all right to live with the charge of cowardice and murder hanging over my head. I told myself I didn't care what others thought of me, that I could be happy there the rest of my life."

"And what I said caused you to change your mind?"

"Oh, you didn't mean to do anything admirable. You only wanted to get me off guard so you could kidnap me. You succeeded. You can take pride in that."

But he couldn't. Nothing she did made any sense.

Unless she was telling the truth.

But if she were telling the truth about this, was she also telling the truth about the murder?

If she were telling the truth, everything made sense . . . *except the murder.*

Trinity shook his head to clear it of the speculation buzzing furiously in his brain. He couldn't be mistaken in her character. The whole basis for what he did, his choice of people to bring in, the way he handled each situation—everything depended on his evaluation of the criminal involved. Never before had he been mistaken. Never before had he had cause to

192

doubt his judgment. But he did now.

Suddenly the wall he had erected in his mind crumbled and the enormity of what he had been about to do struck him. He had been taking her back to die! It wasn't Sheriff Sprague, Judge Blazer, the jury, or the Texas system of jurisprudence. It was he, Trinity Smith. He might as well have placed the noose around her neck with his own hands. He shuddered in horror.

Involuntarily, Trinity glanced at Victoria. She might be an outlaw to society, but like the cougar and the grizzly bear, she was a thing of wild beauty. It seemed a shame to squander it.

Like a wildflower bursting open to greet the warmth of a spring morning, she seemed too perfect to last. The delicate hint of mauve in her cheeks, the deep rose of her lips, the titian of her hair, all must fade before the searing heat of summer. He wanted to sit and stare at her, to drink it all in, before it slipped away.

It seemed like every man who knew her agreed with him. They were falling over themselves to fight for her. He had no difficulty understanding that. Hadn't he already done the same?

Why? Because there was something good and honest and admirable about her which made him want to protect her.

"Do you think he'll keep his word?" he asked Victoria, desperate to forget the doubts that nagged him.

"Red? I hope so, but I don't know him very well. Buc keeps the men in the saddle most of the time. Anyway the young ones tend to keep their distance. Sometimes the ones who stay the farthest away are the ones most affected."

"Do you think any of the others will join him?"

"I don't know."

"For a woman's who's the center of attention for a dozen men, you know very little."

"What do you expect?" Victoria shot back. "You've never been an unmarried woman living in the midst of so many men—"

"I've known a few who were."

"—or you'd know they enjoy engaging in fantasies. Every-

193

body dreams of having his own ranch, of marrying a beautiful woman, especially when they could achieve both in a single stroke. Well they can't help but think about it."

"Modest young woman, aren't you?"

"Do you want answers to your questions or do you want polite, ladylike denials like, 'how could little old me possibly know what a great big man like you is talking about?' "

Her parody of an artful southern beauty brought a smile to his lips.

"Got it down pat, don't you?"

"Every southern girl does. Just like every man learns to act like a tough *hombre* before he's old enough to wear boots. If I didn't know better, I'd swear you imbibed it with your mother's milk."

"Mine disapproved."

"Then it's a good thing she's not around to see how you turned out. Men like you are worse than lepers. You feed off other people's misfortune, and you don't even have the heart to see what you're doing."

"You seem to have conveniently forgotten the misery of your husband's parents and brother. What about the son and brother they lost?"

"*You* seem to forget I was Jeb's wife. What about my sense of loss, my feelings, my hurt?"

"Since you coolly put a shot into his head in the middle of a party—"

"I did not kill Jeb!" Victoria said loud enough to cause her horse to throw up its head. "And for the record, Myra is Judge Blazer's second wife. Kirby is her son. But I don't expect you to believe anything I say."

They rode in silence for the rest of the afternoon.

"I'll cook if you'll untie my hands," Victoria said as Trinity helped her down from the horse.

"So you've finally decided to talk."

"I'm a better cook," Victoria said. "Besides, you've got the horses to tend to."

194

He hesitated.

"I promise I won't run away, and I won't throw hot grease on you. I'm too tired to run very far even if I wanted to. All I want is something decent to eat. Then I want to sleep as long as I can."

Trinity untied her wrists. He felt the reoccurring sense of shame when he saw the raw places on her skin.

"I've got some salve for that."

"I'll be okay unless you plan to tie me up again tomorrow."

"I don't think that'll be necessary. I'm going to take your word you won't try to run away."

"Why the sudden trust?"

"I don't know. I have an awful feeling I'm making a fool of myself, but I can't see why you'd send your uncle back if you intended to escape."

"I'm glad to see common sense can penetrate your brain after all."

"My common sense tells me you're lying," Trinity responded more roughly than he'd intended. "It tells me nobody would be willing to go back to jail. It's screaming at me right now that your uncle must be out there somewhere, that Red is a spy to keep us under surveillance, that sometime during the night they're going to come down on us and my body will be left for the wolves."

"Then why did you untie my hands?"

"Because I got the same lessons with my mother's milk as Red back there. My father drummed it into my head that I should respect every female, treat her as a lady, defend her with my life. I keep thinking about my mother. She wouldn't have hurt a fly unless it was about to hurt me or my father. Then I think she would have taken on the Mexican army by herself. Anyhow, I keep thinking how I would feel to see her riding with her wrists tied up, her skin all torn up by the rope.

"I also think about what you said to those men back there. I don't know if you meant what you said, but any woman who could do that deserves a little trust."

"Do you have a hard time trusting all women, or am I the only one?"

"I don't trust anybody. But I guess I have a harder time with women."

"What did Queenie do to you?"

"What makes you think Queenie did anything to me?"

"She's the only woman besides your mother you've ever mentioned. One of them is responsible for the way you feel, and it clearly isn't your mother."

"I don't want to talk about Queenie."

"Then go take care of the horses. I'll see about something to eat while you're gone."

Trinity took so long with the horses Victoria had dinner ready when he returned. They ate in an uneasy silence, unanswered questions hanging in the air.

"What happened?" Trinity asked.

"What do you mean?"

"The night Jeb was killed? What happened?"

"But I thought—"

"Forget everything I said. Just tell me what happened."

Victoria hardly knew what to say. She had relived that night so many times, and she still didn't have any answers.

"My father came to Texas from Alabama right after the war. I don't really know why, but I think it had something to do with the fact he wouldn't fight for the South. My mother died when I was born, so there was nothing to hold him. We were happy in Texas. Daddy loved the ranch, and I liked the freedom from all my aunts.

"Everything would have been fine except Daddy got sick. That's when he made up his mind I ought to marry Jeb Blazer. Judge Blazer was the richest man in the county, and Jeb was his only son. Judge Blazer and Daddy were drinking buddies. They liked the same kind of whiskey. Anyway, they made an agreement between them and I went along.

"We weren't supposed to be married until I turned eighteen, but Daddy died when I was seventeen. I went to live with the Judge. Daddy had arranged that, too. The Judge said it wasn't right for an unmarried girl to live in a house with three men who weren't related to her. Myra thought I should be allowed to wait until I was eighteen, but the Judge wouldn't hear of it. That was the only time I ever heard them argue.

"By this time I had had a chance to see Jeb up close. My enchantment with him was wearing off. He was never unkind to me, but he didn't seem interested in me or any of the things I enjoyed. I got along much better with Kirby."

"What's he like?"

"He's Myra's son by her first husband. He was extremely handsome, but he was just a kid. Anyway, the Judge set the date, and Jeb and I were married. If he thought marriage would settle Jeb, he was wrong. Jeb actually got worse. He spent our wedding night, and every night after that, with his friends. He would spend the next day sleeping it off and then go out again after supper.

"The night he was killed, he was having a party at the house. He didn't want me to be part of it, but I came down anyway. The more he drank, the ruder he became. When I wouldn't go back to my room, he said Myra always stayed in her room. Why couldn't I behave like a lady, too! He said that to me in front of his friends.

"Some of them tried to laugh it off. Others ignored it. I tried to reason with him, but he stalked off. I know now I shouldn't have followed him, but I was upset. I had been married only seven days and hadn't spent an hour alone with my husband. Instead of making him sympathize with me, it made him furious.

"He shouted at me and said he didn't love me. He said a lot more that I'd rather not remember," Victoria said, her voice unsteady. "Finally, I couldn't listen to any more, so I turned to go back to the house. I had gone about a dozen steps when Chalk Gillet came around the corner of the house.

"Just as our eyes met, I heard a gunshot. I turned back in time to see Jeb stagger and start to fall. I ran to him, tried to hold him up, but he was too heavy. He fell to the ground taking me with him. I tried to move him, to sit him up, but I couldn't. He must have been dead already.

"I looked around for Chalk, thinking he would help me, but he was gone. That's when I saw the gun lying on the ground next to me. I don't know how it got there or when. I can only assume the killer tossed it down while I was bending over Jeb. There was a lot of noise coming from the house, there was a band and a lot of fun and high jinks with the dancing so there could have been other things I didn't hear, like someone moving about in the bushes."

"There were bushes in the yard?"

"Lots of them. The Judge was born in Alabama, too. That's why he and Daddy were so close. He thought Texas was too brown, so he had trees and shrubs planted everywhere. It took a man hours every day during the summer to water them. Anyway, I foolishly picked up the gun. I don't know why. I suppose I picked it up because I couldn't understand what it was doing there. Unfortunately, the Judge and Kirby found me kneeling over Jeb's body with the gun in my hands."

"What about Chalk Gillet?

"Nobody ever saw him again. I don't know what happened, but if he's alive, he knows I didn't kill Jeb. I was looking straight into his eyes when the gun went off."

"Wasn't it strange for him to disappear like that?"

"Not particularly. Chalk wandered in just like you. Kirby said he'd asked for his pay that afternoon saying he'd been in one place too long."

"Why should Kirby know that?"

"Kirby adored the Judge. He followed him everywhere. He liked everything the Judge liked, did everything the Judge did. As young as he was, he sometimes acted as part foreman, part manager. Somebody had to since Jeb couldn't, or wouldn't, stay sober long enough to remember whether we were rounding up to count and brand calves or rounding up steers to sell."

"And you have no idea who might have killed Jeb?"

"No."

"Who stood to gain?"

"I guess Myra and Kirby, but they're the only ones who believed in my innocence. Besides, the Judge is a relatively young man. He could go on living for twenty or thirty more years. There's also no assurance he won't give his money to some relative."

"What about your money?"

"What do you mean?"

"Who gets your money?"

"Jeb if I died, but I didn't."

"Where is it now?"

"The Judge still controls it, I guess."

"And if you can't go back to Texas to claim it, the Judge gets to keep it. So Kirby stands to get two inheritances if he can wait long enough."

"It couldn't have been Kirby. He was inside the house when the shot was fired."

Trinity had been unaware of a small surge of hope until he felt it die away. He had to get a hold on himself. He wanted to believe Victoria's story so badly he was ready to blame anybody, even a boy.

"I'm not surprised the Judge didn't believe you. The only thing worse than being caught with the murder weapon in your hand is being seen when you actually fire the gun."

"I know, but if you could find Chalk, I could prove I didn't kill Jeb."

Victoria stood up and yawned. "I can see Red's fire from here. He's awfully young to be out here by himself. Maybe you ought to check on him in the morning. I'd hate for anything to happen to him."

"Un-huh," Trinity grunted, deep in his own thoughts. He had never heard a more flimsy story, but the fact it was so weak and full of holes made him tend to believe it. Anyone with half a brain would come up with a much better story than that. And Victoria was much more than half smart.

But it was her words from earlier in the day which kept ringing in his brain. If she meant what she said to her uncle, if her willingness to go to Texas wasn't a ruse to get him off guard, then she wasn't the kind of woman to kill her husband.

The problem was Trinity didn't know what kind of woman she was.

One thing he did know, though. He wouldn't take her back to Texas to die.

Chapter Fifteen

Victoria barely said a word for the next two days. Trinity wanted to know more about Jeb Blazer's death, but she wouldn't talk about it again. She wouldn't talk about anything.

He didn't tie her up any more. It had nothing to do with the healing abrasions on her wrists or the fact she did all the cooking and was always ready to break camp no matter how early he woke her. He didn't tie her up because he didn't want to.

He liked Victoria. He had finally admitted that to himself. It didn't do any good to keep telling himself he had no place for a woman in his life, or that it was stupid to become involved with anyone under these circumstances.

Actually his feelings were stronger than mere like. He hadn't fallen in love with her, though there were times when he told himself he was acting crazy enough to do just that. It probably came closer to a combination of lust and fascination, not the kind of thing you'd want to confess to a woman like Victoria.

He imagined she would respond nobly to a declaration of love. If she couldn't return his passion, she would probably attempt to spare his feelings. She had made it clear to Red she considered him a brother, and he still adored her. But an admission that he both lusted after her and was fascinated by the complexity of her character would probably earn him another set of scratches.

His fingertips touched the still-raised welts on his cheek.

He would probably bear the scars until his dying day.

He watched as she prepared to serve the food, and he felt his body tighten. It was becoming more and more difficult to remain in camp with her and not do or say something that would let her know he practically had to sit on his hands to keep from touching her.

Even when he had thought her a cold-blooded murderess, he had battled the strong pull of physical attraction. Now that his feelings had made a one hundred and eighty degree change, he found it nearly impossible to think of anything else.

But, how do you tell a woman you've changed your mind? How do you tell her you've gone from thinking her a murderess who deserves to be hanged to seeing her as a beautiful woman you want to make love to?

She'd tear him to ribbons if he said that. And he'd deserve it.

Then how could he apologize for the way he felt about her in the beginning? He had changed the way he treated her and she had greeted that with stony silence. He had started to believe in her innocence, but she wouldn't talk about the murder. He'd tried to talk about her father, the ranch, her home in Alabama, and a dozen other things over the last two days, and she had responded with monosyllables, grunts, or silence.

Telling her he believed her and would do everything in his power to prove her innocence hadn't breached the wall she had erected around herself. Now that she had decided to go back and had gotten his promise to look for Chalk Gillet, she seemed to have lost all interest in what was going to happen to her. She had retreated into some part of her mind where he couldn't follow.

Ironically, he finally believed she was innocent. She didn't act guilty. She never had, but it was her attitude which convinced him. Victoria was a fighter, not one to give up on life. She wouldn't be able to face her return to Bandera with such calm unless she knew she was innocent, unless she had complete confidence Trinity would be able to find Gillet.

Trinity didn't know if Gillet was still alive, but if he was,

Trinity swore he'd find him. Jury verdict or no jury verdict, Victoria wasn't going to hang.

"He shouldn't be out there by himself." They had finished dinner. Victoria sat staring at the small pinpoint of a distant campfire. "Anything could happen to him and we'd never know."

"He's all right as long as we can see his campfire each evening."

"I was sure he'd have given up and gone back to Mountain Valley by now." Victoria was sincerely worried.

"Boys like Red don't give up, not at his age. Right now following us is the most important thing in his life."

"Were you ever like that?"

Had he ever been like Red? So green and tender, so full of the juices of life? After years on the trail spent learning to trust no one, believe in nothing, letting no one get close, it seemed incredible he could ever have been so young, so full of enthusiasm, so ready to believe passionately, to act on faith alone, so willing to offer his life at the altar of love.

What lay inside him now? A desert of distrust, deceit, and destruction. No matter how he looked at it, he destroyed lives. He had appointed himself judge and jury, and he had allowed no appeals from his decisions.

Quite suddenly Trinity was disgusted with himself. He still believed in his motives, believed his job had to be done, but he didn't want to be the one to do it. It had cost him too much. It had burned out the inner core of his soul. He would give almost anything to be that young boy again, but it was too late.

"Once."

"Was it Queenie?"

Trinity sighed and felt the wall which guarded his past begin to give way.

"Yes."

"Was she very beautiful?"

"She was the most beautiful woman I've ever seen. And the most evil."

Trinity looked up, but Victoria wasn't watching him. She was studying a small tear in her blouse. The tension inside him relaxed. He couldn't stand sympathy. Interest, boredom, even anger, but if she had shown the slightest sign of sympathy he would have closed his mouth and never said another word.

"I was sixteen, just like you had been, but I had even less sense. I thought I was somebody special, that there had never been a young man like me. I had reached most of my height, but I wasn't as skinny as most sixteen year olds. I had some bone and muscle, and the young girls flocked around me like I was catnip.

"But I wasn't content to stick with what I knew. I had to set my eyes on a dance hall singer. She called herself Queenie. Nothing else. And she was the queen of San Antonio. Men flocked to see her every night, but she kept her distance. That just made them all the wilder. Soon they weren't talking about anything else but Queenie.

"Now you can imagine how I felt when Queenie walked up to me one night and asked me to buy her a drink. I'd have sold my soul on the spot to buy her anything she wanted. We sat and talked until it was time for her next number. I don't know what we talked about. I don't know if I made any sense. I rode back to the ranch floating on air.

"When she invited me to her table the next time I went to town, I was completely lost. I'd have done anything she asked. I was in love and didn't care who knew it. I started talking marriage. I even tried to give her a ring, but Queenie said I was too young. She didn't look a day over eighteen, and I was only one month from turning seventeen, so I didn't accept that. I saw her every night for two weeks until I wore her down. But she insisted I bring Pa to see her before we got to talking about anything serious."

Victoria couldn't help but wish she'd known Trinity then, before the bitterness chewed so deeply into his soul, before everything inside him turned to stone. She could imagine him swaggering about town, proud as a peacock, anxious to prove his manhood. Desperate to prove himself worthy of winning the most sought-after woman in San Antonio.

"What did your mother say?"

"Ma died when I was twelve. Pa nearbout went *loco*, drinking and fighting and getting in so much trouble Mr. Slocum fired him. He'd been foreman nearly four years when it happened, but I never blamed Slocum. Pa drunk would have made a saint cuss. We went to Colorado after that, and spent nearly two years working the mine fields. We didn't get rich, but Pa made one strike big enough for him to come back and buy a ranch even bigger than Mr. Slocum's."

"Which ranch did he buy?" She had visited most of the ranches in the area and wondered if it was one she remembered.

"The Demon D."

"But that was my father's ranch."

"I know. The sheriff told me when I went to see him. Even back when my Pa bought it, it had a reputation for being cursed, but he didn't care. He bought it because the owner had just died, and it was cheap. But Pa still couldn't settle down. He would go to town and get drunk. I used to follow him to bring him home. He would sit in the corner of the Hitching Post Saloon and drink until it closed. Everybody knew he was pining for Ma, so they just let him alone."

Victoria wondered if it had ever occurred to Trinity's father that the boy might also be hurting from his mother's death. It must have been terrible to watch his father destroy himself so soon after losing his mother. He must have been a very special youngster to care so much for his father that he willingly gave up his own pleasures to look after him, see that he got home, care for him until he could get back on his feet.

"I'd get bored waiting for Pa, so I'd go check out the other saloons. That's how I discovered Queenie. Anyway, I told Pa I wanted to get married. He tried to talk me out of it, but I wouldn't listen. He finally agreed to see Queenie with me.

"He was pretty hard on her at first, but Queenie had a way with men, and pretty soon she had Pa eating out of her hand. They sent me away so they could talk. It seemed like they talked forever, but when we rode home, Pa told me he would have to talk with her again.

"If I'd had any seasoning, I'd have seen the signs right then, but my head was so full of being the man who won Queenie I

204

couldn't have seen anything if you'd printed it in letters a foot high. Pa stopped drinking and cleaned himself up. When he went back to see Queenie, he took a bath and put on his best suit. The third time he went to see Queenie, he wouldn't let me go with him.

"Even then I didn't see that's what Queenie was after all the time. Pa didn't either. Somehow she'd found out he was a grieving widower with a real big ranch, and she'd set her mind on marrying him. She just used me to get to him.

"When Pa came home that last time, he told me he and Queenie were going to get married. He tried to tell me how neither of them had meant for anything to happen, that neither had foreseen any thing like this. He told me Queenie was actually twenty-two, too old for a boy like me.

"But I didn't understand anything except Pa had stolen the woman I loved. I don't know why I didn't pick up a gun and shoot him. It was in my mind to do it, but I attacked him with my fists. I might have been well filled out for sixteen, but my father was a bear of a man. He sent me flying with one blow.

"I said a lot of things, some I'll always be ashamed of, but in the end I ran away. I couldn't stand to see them married. I hated my father as much as I loved Queenie."

"Where did you go?"

"Back to the mine fields. It was the only thing I knew. A year later I got word Pa had died. I couldn't believe it. He had always been such a strong, healthy man. I couldn't understand how he could have died unless it had been some accident. I headed home right away, all the while thinking of the changes I was going to make on the ranch. You can't imagine how stunned I was when I found out Pa had left everything to Queenie. He hadn't even left me his watch.

"But I wasn't such a naive kid anymore. I'd had time to do some thinking while I was working claims all over Colorado and Nevada. I had figured out Queenie meant to get Pa all along. Now I realized she hadn't wanted Pa, just his ranch. Queenie wouldn't see me, so I started asking questions.

"I found out Pa had died while they were on a trip to Galveston. Seems he'd eaten some raw oysters and they'd poisoned him. I knew right then Queenie had killed Pa. He'd rather starve than eat a raw oyster.

"Nobody would listen to me. Pa had died in Galveston, so it didn't concern anybody in Bandera. Queenie was a grand lady now, and everyone said she was in mourning, that she had really loved my Pa. She started telling people I caused Pa's death. She said he was unhappy I couldn't love his new wife, that I broke his heart when I ran away.

"I guess I went crazy then. I tried to kill Queenie. I fronted her in the street and announced what I was going to do. They put me in jail for six months. By the time I got out, Queenie had sold the ranch and disappeared."

"Did you ever see her again?"

"No, but I kept hearing about a woman a lot like her who moved from one mining town to another, just the ones where they had big strikes, setting herself up as a respectable widow. I don't know all the scams she used, but she must have robbed dozens of miners. In a few years I didn't hear anything about her any more. I suppose she got so rich she could go back East, or maybe out to San Francisco."

"What happened to you?"

"When I got out of jail, I went back to the mine fields. I couldn't stay in Texas, and mining and cows was all I knew."

"When did you decide to become a bounty hunter?"

Trinity flinched at the word.

"A man tried to steal my claim. It wasn't much of a claim, but it was mine and I intended to keep it. I found out he was wanted for murder in Nebraska, so I waited until he came sneaking up to my cabin at night, hoping to catch me asleep. By the time he woke up he was bound and gagged and halfway to Ogallala."

"Bounty hunting must have paid better than panning for a few dollars a day."

"I never accepted a reward for bringing anybody in."

"But you said you—"

"I never accepted any money, not even in the form of a salary. I only agreed to swear in as a deputy this time because the sheriff insisted. I don't take money even to pay for my supplies. I don't do it for money. I do it because I can't *not* do it."

Victoria couldn't disbelieve him now. Not when she could look into his eyes and see all the way into his soul. She felt lower than a snake's belly.

"I guess I owe you an apology."

"No, you don't. I didn't believe you."

"Maybe not, but that's no excuse for the terrible things I said."

"They're not half as bad as seeing decent people turn their backs on you."

"Then why did you decide to keep it up?"

"I never thought to do it again, but then a gambler shot three miners in a card game one night. They caught him cheating, but they were too slow on the draw. One of them was a friend of mine. The gambler was wanted in Denver, so I took him in."

"And you just kept it up after that?"

"Sort of."

He stopped, clearly reluctant to go on. Victoria felt certain he had never told anybody what he'd just told her. He must have been carrying it locked inside him all these years.

"I could forget losing the ranch, but knowing Queenie had killed Pa and was living free ate at me all the time. If I hadn't been such a fool over her, Pa would still be alive. The guilt was so bad sometimes that it almost choked me. Every time I saw someone who had escaped from the law, I'd see Queenie all over again.

"I couldn't do anything about her, I didn't even know where she was, but I could see that someone else didn't go free. Each time I took a man in, the feeling would go away for a while, but it always came back again."

"And when it does, you find someone else to kidnap?"

"That's about it."

"Why did you pick me?"

"I hadn't been back to Bandera since they let me out of jail. I had just taken a man to San Antonio, and I couldn't resist going by the old place. It was up for sale again. It seems the man who bought it from your Pa didn't have much luck either.

He was gored by a cow, and one of his sons died from a rattlesnake bite. The daughter and the remaining son decided they'd had enough of the Demon D and left with instructions to sell to anybody who was fool enough to buy it."

Victoria could well understand his temptation to buy back the ranch which should have been his in the first place.

"I offered them a ridiculously low price and they accepted. It was while I was seeing to the paperwork I heard about Judge Blazer's son. It sounded so much like Queenie I couldn't help myself. The Judge and his family were away in Austin, but I went to the sheriff and offered to bring you in."

"How much was the Judge willing to pay?"

"I didn't ask." Trinity got to his feet. "It's getting late. We have a long ride tomorrow."

"We always have a long ride," Victoria said, accepting that his confidences were at an end. "I'm finding it hard to believe I wasn't born attached to a horse."

Victoria went to bed, but she didn't go to sleep. She couldn't put Trinity's story out of her mind. She still didn't appreciate being kidnapped, but now she could understand his commitment to his task. Lots of people had causes to which they dedicated their lives. She hated Trinity's cause, but his reasons were laudable. And since he accepted no money, it amounted to some kind of crusade for justice. How could she condemn a man for that?

Easily when he's taking you back to hang for a crime you didn't commit!

But even that no longer had its former power to whip up her anger against him. He wasn't responsible for her being embroiled in a miscarriage of justice. He merely did what the law said should be done.

Victoria felt disgusted with herself. She was stumbling blindly over herself to find excuses for a man who had carried her off from her home and was determined to do anything necessary to get her back to Bandera. And all because he was handsome and amusing and charming and fearless and capable of doing anything he made up his mind to do.

Not just that, Victoria said to herself, though she couldn't forget either his smile or his strength. His touch turned her bones to wet rawhide. She had avoided him for the last few days, but she still remembered the ease with which he lifted her into the saddle, the way he held her suspended in midair with one arm. His smile always drew an answering response from her. It was contagious. She couldn't help it even when she was angry at him.

But it was the moments when she caught him alone with his thoughts, the moments when his pain was so near the surface, which touched her heart and dissolved her anger at him. At that moment he was neither enemy or friend, just a man in need of someone to love and to trust, someone to believe in.

Though her soul might be damned for it, Victoria knew she wanted to be that someone.

"Here, you ought to have this."

Victoria was getting ready to mount up next morning when Trinity handed her a rifle. Shocked, her gaze sought his face, but he had turned to attach the scabbard to her saddle.

"What made you decide to give me a rifle?"

"I'll give you some ammunition, too. If you need to shoot, you won't have time to ask for shells."

"Are you sure you can trust me?"

"I'll give you a gun, if you like, but I thought you'd be more comfortable with a rifle."

"How do you know I won't use it on you?"

Trinity grinned at her question. "You'd never use it on me."

Much to her surprise, Victoria realized what he said was true. "What makes you say that?"

"You said you would go with me to Bandera. You won't break your word."

"That decision was forced on me."

"If you felt you had to shoot me, you'd warn me first, hoping I'd get out of the way."

"Why would I do that?"

"You like me. You're mad as hell at me right now," Trinity added when Victoria swelled with indignation, "but you don't want to see anybody you like hurt."

Victoria was at a loss for words. She'd never actually considered the question of shooting Trinity, but she had vaguely assumed she'd do what she must to escape. Now she realized she had tried to escape several times, but she'd never once tried to steal a gun. Each day she spent the long hours in the saddle mulling over various ideas for getting away from Trinity, but none of them had involved shooting him.

Because she didn't want to. She never had, not even when she was most angry at his betrayal or most frightened for her life. She had even felt sorry for the scratches.

"That's one reason I knew you weren't guilty." Trinity dropped two boxes of shells into her saddlebags. "If you didn't want to hurt me after all I'd done, you'd never have shot Jeb."

"You couldn't know that."

"Last night, when I came back from taking care of the horses, I noticed I'd left my rifle with my saddle."

"Careless."

"Unquestionably, but it told me two things. One, I trusted you enough to forget to take my rifle with me. Second, you wouldn't use it even when you had the opportunity."

"I'm ashamed to admit I didn't even notice it."

"You would have if you'd been willing to use it. Let me give you a leg up."

Trinity tossed her into the saddle with his usual ease, but Victoria's mind was too full of Trinity's faith in her to think of anything else. She wasn't a weak woman. They both knew that. Trinity had no guarantee his trust was warranted. There was no need for him to give her a rifle.

But he had.

Victoria had forgotten how hot the desert could be. For two days they had been traveling through the parched land of southeastern Arizona. The area had had none of the spring rain which made the grazing on her uncle's ranch so abundant. Not even the rivers carried much water, and the washes were dry. Ridges of jagged rock rose from the desert floor at irregular intervals. Occasional cottonwood, sycamore, ash, willow, walnut and cherry grew on the lower slopes or in thickets in the canyons, but more often the mountains were treeless as they met a desert floor sprinkled with acacias, yuccas, creosote bushes, mesquite, and cactus of every shape and description. Various grasses had sprouted and grown earlier in the season, but little remained now except brown stems and dry seedpods.

Trinity had hardly spoken a word since they left the coolness of the hills behind. One word, Apaches, hovered in the silence between them. Twice they had come upon the trail of unshod ponies. There had been no additional prints; no moccasin prints of women, barefoot prints of children, tracks of dogs, or scrapes of travois. This was not a tribal migration. It was a band of men, most likely braves and warriors, anxious to wipe out the white men who were stealing their land.

The first evening after seeing the tracks Trinity had ridden to Red's camp, told him about the Indians, and encouraged him to turn back. Red refused. The second evening he had invited Red to camp with them.

"Aren't you afraid I'll shoot you when your back's turned?"

Trinity looked him square in the eyes. "No. You may be impulsive, but you're not stupid. You know damned well if there are Apache out there, you can't get out of here without me. What they'd do to you is bad enough, but what they'd do to Victoria is unthinkable."

"How do you know I wouldn't get out?"

"You don't know anything about fighting Apache. They'll kill you the first day."

"And they wouldn't kill you?" the boy replied, his pride injured.

"They haven't so far, but I don't mean to give them the chance. And I don't want you leaving them a trail they can follow with their eyes closed."

Trinity's brutal observations angered Red, but he joined their campfire that evening. They stayed away from the obvious routes, traveling on rock when they could, in soft sand when they couldn't, but it was impossible to cover their tracks completely.

211

Late in the morning of the third day, Trinity stopped to look at their back trail. After studying the horizon for longer than usual, he asked Red, "How much ammunition do you have?"

"Close to fifty rounds. Why?"

"I'd say there's a dozen Indians on our trail. We're going to need every bullet. Let's head for those hills. If they catch us in the open, we'll be sitting ducks."

They headed off at a fast trot.

Victoria spurred her horse alongside Trinity's buckskin. "How do you know Indians are following us?" she asked.

"By the dust cloud."

Victoria didn't see any dust. "But how do you know how many there are?"

"By the amount of dust."

"Are they really going to attack us?"

"The Apache doesn't like anybody, least of all white men. He knows only one way to stop them. That's to kill as many of us as possible."

"Isn't there some other way we can go?" Red asked. "This isn't all Apache territory."

"Not all Indians are as ready to fight as the Apache, but they're losing land, too. They're only too happy to let the Apache know where to find the white men."

They didn't stop for lunch.

"I can see it now," Victoria said in midafternoon, barely able to make out the dust in the pristine air.

"That's because they're traveling faster. They know we're trying to make the mountains. They want to catch us before we do. They may even try to cut us off. Let's ride."

They kicked their horses into a canter, Trinity leading the way, Victoria in the middle, and Red close behind. Their horses were bigger than the Indian ponies and, being grain-fed, stronger. Still the dust cloud seemed to come inexorably closer. Trinity dropped back until he was next to Victoria.

"They're riding hard. I'm going to cut off to the right. Maybe it'll confuse them and give us a few minutes more. You and Red keep to the trail. No matter what you hear or see, don't stop until you reach the hills. Head for that nest of boul-

212

ders, the ones that seem to be standing on end. I'll be right behind you."

"What are you going to do?"

"I don't have time to explain," Trinity called back. "Just do as I say."

With that he swung off to the left. For a time Victoria was able to keep him in sight, but he finally dropped into a wash and out of sight. She and Red were left by themselves in the desert with a dozen Indians chasing them.

Chapter Sixteen

Victoria realized now how much she depended on Trinity, how safe she felt when he was with her. She knew Red wouldn't leave her, that he would give his life to protect her, but he was just a kid, probably more scared than she was. He probably had no idea what to do.

The fleeting realization that she was armed and alone with Red, that if the Indians followed Trinity there was nothing to stop her from abandoning him and going back to Mountain Valley, flashed through her mind. She rejected the thought while it was still barely formed. She couldn't leave Trinity any more than he could leave her.

A bullet whizzed overhead. Startled, Victoria looked behind her. Trinity's ruse hadn't worked. At least a half dozen Indians followed them at a hard gallop.

"They're still behind us," she called out to Red as she brought her crop down across her horse's rump.

The hills seemed to recede before her almost as fast as her horse galloped toward them. She kept looking over her shoulder. She could hear the Apache war cry; more bullets whizzed overhead. Would they make it to the hills before the Apache caught up? She bent low over her horse, trying to conserve his strength, encouraging him to keep going. Her life could depend upon his speed.

She thought she could hear gunfire off to the left where Trinity had gone. She desperately wanted to join him, but that would allow the Indians to trap them between their two groups.

She drove her horse up the mountain. Red was right behind her.

Another burst of gunfire. Having stronger horses, they pulled ahead. She was tempted to drop down behind the rocks along the trail, but she knew she had to get into a concealed position behind the rocks. She had to provide a covering fire for Trinity when he came into view.

Heedless of his exhaustion, Victoria drove her horse up the trail at a breakneck pace. They were only a few hundred yards away. They could almost make it on foot.

Another burst of gunfire prompted her to use her spurs. Just a few more minutes. Out of the corner of her eye she saw Red drop the reins and slump forward in his saddle. He was hit!

Slowing down, Victoria reached over and took hold of the reins. She looked back. There were six Indians. She could see them clearly now. They were about five hundred yards behind; far enough away to allow them to reach cover as long as Red could stay in the saddle. He had been badly wounded, but she thought he would be all right if they could get him to a doctor soon.

She wouldn't allow herself to think of any other possibility.

Red slumped over his horse's neck, his body swaying from one side to the other. Victoria prayed he could hold on for just a little longer.

After what seemed like an eternity, they reached the rocks. Victoria slid from her horse. She ground-hitched Red's horse, wrenched her rifle from its holder, and rushed to a position atop a flat boulder. A half dozen quick shots prevented the Indians from coming up the mountain after her.

As the Indians scrambled for cover, Victoria turned her attention to Red. Unhooking his feet from the stirrups, she pulled him from the saddle. Both of them went to the ground. He nearly crushed her under his weight when he fell. Fortunately he was skinny. She tore open his shirt to reach the wound. The bullet had entered his back but hadn't come out the front. It was still inside. Maybe that would help slow the bleeding and keep him alive, until they could find a doctor.

She hurried back to her rifle. She didn't see any Indians or their horses, but she fired at the rocks where they had disappeared. She wanted them to know she was still there.

Victoria turned back to Red. He had passed out. She had to look after him, but she also had to watch the Indians. She couldn't do both from where he lay. Taking hold of his feet, she pulled him over next to the rock. Now she only had to look up to see the Indians or look down to check on Red.

The wound started to bleed heavily. She had to stop it. She had to find something she could use to make a bandage, but Trinity had taken the packhorse with him. She had nothing but the clothes on her back.

Without hesitation, Victoria took off her shirt and removed her camisole top. She ripped it to pieces. She made a pad from one of the pieces and put it over the wound. She needed something to hold it tight, but there wasn't enough material to make a bandage that would go around his chest.

Donning her shirt again, she looked up in time to see an Indian run from one rock to another. She snatched up her rifle and fired at him. She waited a few precious seconds. No one moved. But just as she looked back to Red, she saw another Indian start from behind a rock. A quick shot kicked up dust only inches from his feet, and the Indian dived back behind the rock. Maybe that would make them more careful. But they were getting closer. She couldn't afford to look away.

Blood had turned Red's pad bright crimson. She had to do something or he would bleed to death, but she couldn't ignore the Indians either. They would be up the mountain in minutes.

Keeping her eye on the rocks below, she folded a second piece of her camisole into a pad. She exchanged it for the blood-soaked pad. Then seizing a stone about five inches in diameter, Victoria placed it directly on the wound.

Turning back to the rock, Victoria picked up her rifle and aimed it at the rock the first Indian had disappeared behind. She only had to wait a few seconds. She saw his head appear as he started to make a dash to a clump of mesquite about ten yards closer. Victoria put a bullet into the ground in front of him.

The Indian dived back behind his rock.

Now they knew she was watching. They would be more careful. She glanced at Red. The bandage was still white. The weight of the rock had stopped the bleeding.

Now if Trinity would just come.

Trinity burst into view from a nearby wash as though he'd popped up out of the ground. Five Indians followed no more than a couple hundred yards behind.

Victoria raised her rifle to lay down covering fire, but Trinity was between her and the Indians. She considered herself a good shot. It was one of the things she'd occupied herself with during her years of enforced captivity, but she didn't trust herself to shoot that close to Trinity.

She shot wide, but the unexpected gunfire caused the Indians to pull up. Trinity used the chance to reduce the odds. Shooting from the saddle, he sent one Indian to the ground.

"Red's hurt," Victoria said when Trinity threw himself down on the ground next to her. She didn't take her eyes off the ground below. The Indians occupied two positions now.

"How bad?"

"I don't know, but he's bleeding a lot. He needs a doctor."

Trinity checked the wound.

"He'll be all right once we get the bullet out. Do you know how?"

"No."

They both looked down the mountainside to where the Indians had disappeared.

"Do you think they're gone?" Victoria asked, scanning the apparently empty desert.

"No. They're out there," Trinity said. "But you won't see them again until they try to kill you. You might not even see them then."

"What happened to their horses?"

217

"One of them took the horses into the wash. We have to make sure they don't get ours."

"What are we going to do?"

"We're going to wait. The game's in their hands now."

The afternoon passed with agonizing slowness. Trinity fired occasionally, as much to let the Indians know he was still there as anything else, but they seemed to have lost interest.

"I've already hit three," Trinity explained as they ate a dinner of jerky washed down with water. There was no wood for a fire. And no coffee. "They don't want to lose any more men, so they'll try to outwait us. They know there's no water up here. We might last several days, but the horses won't. They expect us to make a break. When we do, they'll be waiting."

Trinity didn't talk like a man who was desperate or afraid. He stated the cold facts and considered the options. He wasn't giving up.

"What do you have in mind?"

Trinity smiled, a silent acknowledgement that she had come to know him well.

"I'm going to get behind them. Sometime before dawn I'll move in. I want you to lay down as much fire from here as you can. Shoot from more than one position. We've got to make them think they're being attacked on two sides by a larger force. It might panic them into running away. It'll take me several hours to get into position, so why don't you get some sleep?"

"I couldn't sleep knowing you're out there."

Victoria hadn't meant to say that. She didn't want anyone, especially Trinity, to know the confused state of her feelings, but this didn't seem like a time for dissembling. He could die. She might never see him again. She didn't want her last words with him to be some meaningless lie.

"One of my aunts once told me a woman has two jobs in life. To help and wait. Tonight I get to do both."

"That seems like an awfully harsh thing to say to a young girl."

"I'd been acting frivolously. She didn't approve of frivolity."

"I've never known you to be frivolous."

"I'm not the girl I was at fourteen."

Trinity doubted she had ever had a chance to be a girl, to be frivolous, to worry about clothes, flirt with boys, to spend whole weeks pondering such weighty decisions as who would take her to the dance and what dress to wear. Instead she'd been running a household, taking care of a dying father, married as a teen, and driven into hiding. She had never known the little freedoms and innocent joys of being young, of being protected and cared for.

"I'm sure you'll get the chance again. Soon."

"I hope so, but first you've got to scare the pants off those Indians. How long will it take you to get into position?"

"No more than a couple of hours, but I've got a few surprises to set up that will take me most of the night. I intend to attack just before dawn."

"What are you going to do?"

"Watch. Be ready the moment the first beams of sunlight streak the sky."

Trinity spent the thirty minutes going through his saddlebags, his bedding, and every bag on the packhorse in search of ammunition. He took all he found.

"Is there enough left?" she asked.

"Red has plenty. Remember, just before dawn. Now get some sleep. It'll be a long night."

But Victoria couldn't sleep. Not with eight or nine savages out there waiting to kill her. Not with Red bleeding to death at her side. Not with Trinity out there risking his life to save hers. It was strange. She had wished him dead, threatened to kill him, had done everything she could to hurt him, but now his life was infinitely precious. Now all the things he had done for her seemed so much more important than anything he had done against her.

And it wasn't just because she needed him to stay alive. She thought of him in a completely different way. He was her companion, her ally, her friend. She might be facing death, but she wasn't facing it alone.

She had faced the possibility before, but she'd never been surrounded by it, and there was nothing imaginary or phantasmagoric about this night. It was real. When compared to death by torture and degradation, hanging seemed almost a boon.

Yet this Indian attack was just another in a chain of crises which had happened to her during her short life. As odd as it seemed, it wasn't as momentous as Trinity's arrival.

His arrival had caused her to reevaluate everything she'd believed for most of her life. It caused her to reject the protection her uncle had provided and the rationale he'd given her for it.

It resulted in her falling in love with a wandering cowboy, so much in love she couldn't completely turn away from him even when she thought he was a bounty hunter. Now that he had willingly risked his life for her, she had fallen even more deeply under his spell.

She didn't comprehend why this was love. She'd never felt anything so wild, so untameable. She wanted to be with him all the time, to follow him for the rest of her life. She knew she would risk her safety and the respect of those she loved to remain at his side. It was irrational. She had never felt like this about Jeb.

She had to be losing her mind.

Even when she thought she hated him, when she thought him cruel and unfeeling, she hadn't had a single thought that didn't include him. Most of them had him at the center.

Still she could have continued to hold him at a distance if he hadn't told her about Queenie. It would have been hard since his physical presence was so overpowering, but after Queenie, she saw him as a man who suffered a pain he didn't know how to escape. All her resistance seemed to wither away. By the time he finished that story, she felt so sorry for him she could have cried.

Victoria leaned her forehead against the rock, letting it cool her fevered brain. She had had the same argument with herself day after day. Now there seemed to be only one possible resolution. As incredible as it seemed, she had fallen in love with Trinity Smith the minute she set eyes on him. And nothing he had done since seemed able to change that.

Now that she knew he was the honorable man she thought from the first, she wanted nothing more than to be with him for the rest of her life.

She sighed and let her body relax further against the rock. She knew what Buc and her uncle would think. Her uncle wouldn't abandon her, at least she didn't think he would, but it would be impossible to return to Mountain Valley. Neither Buc nor the crew would accept their marriage. And Trinity wasn't one to endure the dislike and distrust from others. He'd already told her that.

But she was getting ahead of herself. She didn't know if Trinity wanted to get married to her or anybody else. She knew he felt strongly attracted to her. She could tell that by the tension between them, by the way his eyes devoured her, by the heat that burned between them. But she couldn't be sure he felt anything more than lust.

Victoria's body sagged against the rock.

Stupid woman. You'd think Jeb would have taught you to use your head rather than your heart. What kind of life can you have with a bounty hunter? And he is a bounty hunter, even if he doesn't take money. He goes after dangerous men who wouldn't hesitate to kill him.

What are you going to do? Go along with him to keep him safe? Sit at home with the children praying this won't be the time they send you a letter saying he's buried in an unmarked grave far from home?

No, that she couldn't endure. She had lived with death hanging over her head long enough to know she couldn't endure it for the rest of her life.

Of course, if he didn't find Chalk Gillet, she would still be under a sentence of death. She might never have the chance to marry Trinity or anyone else. And she couldn't help him find Chalk. She knew nothing about the man. She had no idea where he could be. She didn't even know if he was still alive.

Victoria's head hurt. She had never wrestled with so many unanswerable questions in her life, and each of them seemed to be inextricably intertwined with an equally unsolvable problem. She readjusted her body to be more comfortable. A

221

little longer and she wouldn't feel out of place on the trail.

Another change Trinity had brought about.

She pushed her tangled thoughts aside. She'd go back to them later. Right now she was worried about Trinity being out there alone. And there was nothing she could do but spend the long hours waiting.

Victoria woke with a start. The inky-blue of the sky above told her dawn wasn't far away.

She had fallen asleep sometime during the night. For a panic-filled moment she feared something terrible might have happened while she slept. But a quick glance at the hillside below told her the Indians hadn't yet begun their attack. The night was silent and still.

Red hadn't moved. That frightened her. She had helped nurse many men, several of them quite sick, and the biggest problem had always been how to keep them still. Red's breathing seemed slow, his heartbeat weak. She feared either or both might stop at any minute. At least the stone remained in place. He hadn't bled any more. She wondered how long before they could start for the doctor. Would he be able to stand the long trip? Would the doctor be able to help him?

Questions! She seemed to be surrounded by them. Why couldn't some of them have answers?

A splinter of light pierced the sky.

In retrospect it seemed to Victoria that with the first light of dawn, the desert simultaneously exploded into crashing, thundering violence. Rifle fire came from at least a dozen different locations. Coming to her senses, Victoria snatched up her rifle and peppered the rock below. She might not hit anybody, but at least the Indians would know they were being attacked on two fronts. Before her astonished eyes, the Indians rose out of the ground like prairie dogs out of their holes. They raced for their hidden horses. Almost immediately two of them fell.

In less than two minutes the Indians had disappeared. Victoria had the infinite pleasure of listening to the thunder of

222

hoofbeats fade away in the distance. She slumped against a rock. They were safe. Trinity's scheme had worked.

Trinity reached her only a few minutes later.

"Where did you find so many people to help you?" Victoria asked. "I thought you were going to have to attack them alone."

"I did."

"But I heard all that gunfire. It came from a dozen different places."

"It did come from different places, but it wasn't gunfire."

"What are you talking about?"

"Firecrackers."

"Firecrackers?"

"Yes. Special ones I had made to sound exactly like rifle fire."

"I don't understand?"

"I've used it before when I had to stand off a posse or a gang. Your advantage is very brief, but usually that's all you need."

Victoria looked at him with total bewilderment.

"I'll explain later. Right now we have to get out of here," he said. "The Indians will come back for their dead and wounded. When that happens I want to be as far away as possible."

"How are we going to carry Red?" Victoria asked, forgetting her curiosity about Trinity's firecrackers in the face of her real worry.

"We'll have to tie him to his horse."

"He might bleed to death. We need a wagon."

"Believe it or not, riding on horseback will be easier on him than a wagon. If his condition gets worse, we'll improvise a litter. The most important thing is to get out of here before the Indians return."

Trinity tied Red in his saddle and they left. They didn't eat. She wasn't hungry. She didn't wash or change clothes. She didn't care.

It only mattered that they were safe.

"He's going to be a mighty sick young man for a while, but

223

he'll pull through."

Doctor Urban Mills had been called away from his lunch to take the bullet out of Red. A ruddy-complexioned, obese, cheerful man, he didn't seem too concerned.

"I see a lot of bullet wounds," he had commented, "though not as many as in the War. I've gotten a little out of practice since then, but this is a good place to keep your hand in. Lots of fools who don't know what to do with a gun except point it at somebody else."

"We can't just leave him," Victoria said to Trinity. "He'll need somebody to take care of him until he's well."

"You and the missus in a hurry?" Mills asked Trinity.

"You might say that," Trinity replied before Victoria could speak. "We've got to give evidence in a murder trial in Texas. Do you know anybody we can hire to take care of him?"

"You can hire me," the doctor said, then laughed good-naturedly when he saw he had taken them by surprise. "I'm a lot better than any nurse. Besides, I'd like having the boy around. Had two of my own. Hardheaded, troublesome rascals they were, too, but I miss them now they're gone. One of them got gold fever. The other decided San Francisco was more fun than the Arizona desert. Can't say I blame him."

"How much do I owe you?" Trinity asked.

"Five dollars ought to do it."

"You sure?"

"I don't need to charge much. I'm the only doctor within a hundred miles. I get more business than I want. Now you be on your way. I'll send the boy after you soon as he's able to ride."

That taken care of, Trinity turned his mind to their situation. He asked Victoria if she'd like to spend the night at the Sunbonnet Hotel, the only hotel in the town of Gabel's Stop. As it boasted the town's only dining room, they'd eat there as well. Victoria nearly whooped with joy.

The first thing she did was take a bath. As she lay submerged in the water, she could almost feel the layers of dirt fall off, along with the fatigue and tension of the journey. By the time she stepped out of the tub, she felt almost like an ordinary human being again.

Going to dinner would make her feel like a young woman on a date. She'd never really had a date, and she fairly tingled with anticipation. This would be the first time Trinity saw her as anything other than a prisoner or a travel-worn companion.

What should she wear? She had never had a chance to dress for Trinity. Now that she did, she didn't have anything to wear. The man was depressingly practical. He must have rifled through her entire wardrobe, but he hadn't chosen to bring a single dress.

She settled on a cream shirt with a tan skirt and boots. She couldn't put her hair up. The only pins she'd brought with her were the ones she was wearing the morning he kidnapped her.

She'd lost every one of them on the trail.

She had no jewelry. Who would have worn jewelry on a dawn ride into the mountains? Naturally Trinity didn't bring any. If you couldn't shoot it, eat it, or ride it, it was no use — clearly a man's thinking.

Victoria combed her hair with her fingers. She'd have to go shopping for some essentials before they left town. She couldn't arrive in Bandera looking like a vagabond. She'd have to buy at least one dress. She hoped they had something in her size. She didn't know how to sew, and she didn't imagine Trinity would wait around for her to find a seamstress.

Victoria smiled at herself. It had been years since she'd been so excited about dressing for dinner. Jeb had never cared what she wore even when she had dozens of gowns to choose from. Myra paid more attention to Victoria's clothes than Jeb did, but then beautiful women always notice another woman's clothes. Judge Blazer's wife was the most beautiful woman Victoria had ever seen.

Buc and Uncle Grant never seemed to notice what she wore, either. They tended to take her for granted. She wondered if Trinity would be the same. But Trinity noticed. It was like they were seeing each other for the first time. No murder verdict hanging over her head, no kidnapping, no miserable trip across the desert. Just a man and a woman who liked each

225

other very much having dinner.

Victoria felt oddly self-conscious. Even though a brief glance at the other occupants of the room told her her subdued dress was best, she would have felt much more confident if she had been able to fix her hair and wear her best gown and her double rope of pearls. She felt very plain.

Trinity's plain clothes created just the opposite effect. He wore all black: black hat, black shirt, and black pants. Even the buttons and belt buckle were black. He probably didn't have any idea how his appearance affected Victoria, but there wasn't a woman in the room who could take her eyes off him.

He looked mysterious. Victoria was not used to men wearing hats indoors, but every other man in the room wore one, too. Trinity had pulled his low over his eyes. His jaw and lips were set. No smile of greeting. His eyes found her; his gaze swept the room, then locked on her once more. Possessive and protective.

He looked powerful. His clothes fit him like a glove. He tolerated no loose folds that snagged or billowed in the breeze. The cloth stretched tightly over his lean, hard, muscled shoulders and arms.

He looked seductive. His pants hugged his powerful thighs in a way which made Victoria's breath catch in her throat. She swallowed once. The ripple of muscle and tightly encased flesh as he walked toward her caused an uncomfortable feeling to well up in her middle. She swallowed again.

She wouldn't allow her thoughts to settle on the bulge in his pants. She'd never had this problem with Jeb or Buc. She hadn't had this peculiar feeling in her belly either.

"Feel better after your bath?" Trinity asked as he reached her side. She noted one difference in the way he looked at her. His eyes always smoldered when she caught him off guard, but now they smoldered despite the fact she was overtly watching him.

"Much better. I never knew I could miss a bath so much. Now if I just had some decent clothes."

Trinity guided her to a table nearly in the center of the

226

room. All the others were taken. He seated her facing the outside door. He sat down facing a huge mirror over the bar.

"Judging by the reaction of the men in this room, they consider your clothes much more than decent. So do I."

Victoria struggled to retain her composure. She hadn't counted on him saying anything quite so personal. She was having enough trouble just keeping her reaction to him under control. She didn't think she could handle his reaction to her at all.

"At least you've seen me looking better."

"No, I haven't."

"Of course you have. I wore clean clothes every day until you kidnapped me. I had hair pins, too."

"I still never saw you look better."

Victoria felt herself turn pink. With her nearly white complexion, she knew everyone could tell she was blushing. She hated that. They had no right to know she was uncomfortable, or so dazed by this man that his glance had the power to cause her heart to beat double time.

"It's too late to start flattering me now. We've seen each other at our worst. There's nothing new to learn about each other."

"I feel like I know nothing about you," Trinity said. "I might as well have been traveling with a stranger."

"It's hunger," Victoria said, smiling flippantly, looking for a way to release the pressure. The tension between them was too great for such a public place. People could practically read their thoughts on their faces. "It's caused you to feel lightheaded."

Trinity smiled. He nearly laughed. She liked it when he did that. He seemed more approachable. At times like this she could believe he had once been young. Usually he looked more unbending than vice, more knowing than evil itself. At those times she questioned whether he could ever feel such a human emotion as love.

Tonight she was sure he could.

"I'm keeping you from your dinner and giving all these men a chance to stare at you," Trinity said.

227

The food was delivered hot and plentiful.

"They have only one thing on the menu," he explained. "That way you don't have to wait."

Victoria had looked forward to dinner all afternoon. After dozens of meals cooked over a six-inch fire, or eaten cold, or not eaten at all, she practically salivated at the thought of decently prepared food. Now she had no appetite at all. She had to force herself to eat.

"What will we do next?" she asked Trinity, in an effort to get her mind off his physical presence. Maybe if she weren't so intensely conscious of his body, she would feel more comfortable. And her appetite would return.

"I thought we might stay here a day or two, long enough to talk to Red. I don't like leaving him without a word. Besides, it's settled in to rain. Looks like it'll rain all night." Trinity continued to outline his plans for the rest of the journey. Victoria was relieved to find it now included stops at several towns rather than a continuous series of wilderness camps, but she noticed he seemed a little preoccupied. He seemed to be watching the occupants of one table out of the corner of his eye.

Victoria glanced in the direction of his gaze and found herself returning the stare of four men she would have instantly characterized as hard cases. They wore dirty clothes, apparently had no concept of personal hygiene, and leered at her openly. Furthermore, they didn't think it necessary to make their remarks in a quiet voice. Victoria blushed at the publicly stated wish of a man with a rust-red beard.

She tried to concentrate on Trinity, on what he was saying, but the man's voice continued to get louder.

"We shouldn't have stopped," Trinity said, laying down his fork. "A town like this is no place for a woman. Especially a beautiful woman."

"He's just crude," Victoria said. "I'm sure he doesn't mean anything."

"They're miners. They always mean something."

Chapter Seventeen

The man in the red beard stood up and started toward their table. The others followed.

"Don't respond to anything they say," Trinity said under his breath. "No matter what happens, keep eating like you don't see them."

"Stop where you are," Trinity commanded when the red beard was about six feet away. "That includes the rest of you," he said when Red Beard's companions started to drift to either side. "I can put a bullet through your earlobe," Trinity warned an eyesore of a man who kept moving. "Don't force me to prove it."

Trinity held his gun above the table, aimed directly at Red Beard. The message was unmistakable.

"We don't want no trouble," Red Beard said. "We just want to talk to the little lady. We ain't seen nothing like her in some time."

"We ain't *never* seen nothing like her," his young, blond companion corrected. "I never knew a woman could be that beautiful."

"My wife and I would prefer not to be interrupted while we eat our dinner," Trinity said. "Now if you would go back to your own table. . . ."

"She ain't your wife," Red Beard contradicted.

"What makes you say that?" Trinity asked.

Victoria didn't have to look up to know Trinity's whole demeanor had changed. He was prepared to defend his woman. It rang in his voice like the clarion call of a wild stallion.

"She ain't wearing no wedding ring. A woman like that don't get hitched without a ring."

"Besides she wouldn't hook up with a dude like you," said the eyesore. "She'd go for somebody with money."

"I saw the way you looked at each other when you came in here," the blond said, "like you could eat each other up. Ain't no man looks at his wife like that."

"She's your fancy piece," Red Beard continued. "We don't mind that. We just want a little of the action."

The eyesore made the mistake of taking a step toward Victoria. The deafening report of a pistol rocked the room. The man screamed and his hand flew to his ear. It came away covered with blood.

"God Almighty!" he yelled. "You shot half my ear off."

"You moved too fast," Trinity said nonchalantly. "It threw my aim off a little."

"You can't go shooting people's ears off just like that," the blond said. "This is a civilized country."

"Then you can't go around ordering a man to turn over his wife so you can have a little fun for the evening," Trinity replied. "Now go back to your table and I'll try to forget the way you insulted my wife. If not, I have eleven bullets left. And I ought to warn you I can shoot equally well with either hand."

"She ain't your wife," Red Beard insisted. "Why don't you ask her what she would like? We got gold dust."

"Then I suggest you send it home to *your* wife. I'm sure the children need new shoes."

Red Beard flushed, a tacit admission that Trinity had correctly gauged his marital status, but the blond wasn't so easily silenced.

"I ain't got no wife, and I got the most dust." He took a heavy pouch from his pocket. "You can have the whole sack if you'll take me to your room for just an hour."

"Shit. I'm going to kill him," the eyesore swore as he

dabbed ineffectually at his ear with a discolored handkerchief. "Him and his whore. He done shot off my ear."

Trinity suddenly whirled and fired behind him. He spun back around and fired again. A man seated near the outside door sank back in his chair. His drawn gun slipped from his hand and fell to the floor with a clatter. The eyesore sank to the floor as well, his drawn gun still clutched in his hand.

"Anybody else who feels like trying his luck, go right ahead," Trinity announced. "I can see the whole room with the aid of this mirror."

No one moved; no one said a word.

"Get up and leave as quickly as you can," Trinity spoke to Victoria in a quiet, controlled voice. "Go to your room and lock the door. I'll be along in a minute."

Victoria didn't want to leave Trinity, but she knew an unarmed woman would be more of a liability than a help. No one stirred when she got up from the table and walked quickly from the room.

"I don't want anybody following me," Trinity said, rising to his feet. "I'd take it as downright unfriendly."

"You ain't leaving here," Red Beard shouted, "not after killing Hobie."

"Burns, too," someone called from close to the other man.

"I'm calling the sheriff," the blond said.

"Go right ahead if you think you can reach the door alive," Trinity said. "I suggest you see to your friends. Unless my aim is really off today, they're still alive."

"They'll follow you out of town," the man nearest the door hissed under his breath to Trinity as he passed. "And they'll kill you. They've done it before."

Victoria paced the floor of her room, the seconds since she left Trinity downstairs turning into an eternity. Never in her life had she been threatened by strangers. She had always been surrounded by a dozen ranch hands. She had been so well protected, she hadn't really been aware of the danger.

231

She was acutely aware of it now.

She was just as acutely aware that only Trinity stood between her and a nightmarish fate. No one had tried to help Trinity. One man had even drawn against him. She couldn't look to anyone in this town for help.

She stood perfectly still, listening intently, praying she would hear nothing more than the tread of Trinity's feet on the carpeted steps, petrified she would hear the explosion of gunfire.

After the last several days, her nerves were frayed. Nothing in her life had prepared her for the possibility she would be carried off to a cabin in the mountains to satisfy the lusts of three men.

Her brain was so tired she couldn't think, but she had to do something. She couldn't just wait, not with the whole town either ready to help the miners or willing to stand by and see what they would do. Trinity had risked his life to protect her. She couldn't leave him alone now.

The sound of footsteps coming up the stairs galvanized her into action. She snatched up a rifle standing in the corner and pointed it at the door. The hammer clicked when the door opened, and her finger tightened on the trigger.

Trinity stepped into the room.

"Thank God you're safe," she said. Sobbing with relief, she tossed the rifle on the bed and threw herself into his arms.

Trinity had been prepared for almost any reaction except this. He had never embraced a woman except in the throes of passion. While he was quick to crush Victoria to his chest, he didn't know what to do to make her stop crying. Except for little Maria, no one had wanted to nestle in the sanctuary of his arms. No woman had ever depended on him for comfort or protection.

Not since his mother rescued him from a brown bear had anyone put their arms around him and cried with happiness because he was safe. He simply hadn't been important to anyone . . . even his father. Yet this beautiful woman who had half the Arizona territory at her feet cared so much she was prepared to go back downstairs to fight for him. If she had pointed a gun at him, he'd have known what to do in an instant. One sob and he was completely at sea.

Victoria put her arms around him and buried her face in his chest. Trinity did all he could to accommodate her. He didn't care if she cried down the front of his shirt or ruined his coat. He knew how to stand still and get wet. And he didn't mind it a bit.

"I can't think why I'm acting like this," Victoria said, lifting her head up so she could look at Trinity, but making no attempt to leave his embrace. "I never cry, and I never go to pieces. I used to think I was so strong. I guess I'm not very strong after all."

Trinity felt as low-down as a bounty hunter ought to feel. What gently bred woman was strong enough to go through what he had put her through in the last week without breaking down at least once? He had sworn he would take her back to Texas one way or the other, but what kind of low-down skunk was he to expose her to marauding Indians and lust-crazed miners along the way? If he couldn't do any better, he should have left her alone.

"No reason why you can't cry a little now and then if you like," he said. "Nobody but me will see you."

"But I don't care about the rest of them," Victoria said, making a detailed examination of his vest button. "I'd bawl my head off if it would put those horrible men in jail."

"I should be shot for bringing you here. I should have known what would happen the minute men like that set eyes on you."

"You didn't have any choice. We had to get Red to a doctor."

"I should have gotten rid of him way back," Trinity said. "I had no call to get that boy into trouble."

"He brought it on himself."

"I had no call to go risking your life at every turn, either."

"But you saved my life," Victoria insisted. "I could never

233

have escaped those Indians alone. And not even Buc could have held off those men. I never saw anybody who could shoot like you."

"I wouldn't need to be saving you from Indians and holding off miners if I'd done things right," Trinity said. "I ought to turn you over to somebody else." — He tightened his hold on her — "You'd have every right to refuse to go with me any farther."

Victoria didn't seem to find anything unusual with that statement. In fact, she liked it so much, she put her arms around Trinity's neck.

"I wouldn't feel safe with anybody but you." Her eyes seemed to reflect her complete trust.

Trinity knew he wasn't worthy of her trust, but neither was he of a mind to give her a more correct impression, at least not just yet. "I promise I'll get you to Texas without any more danger."

"How are we going to get away from those men? Do you think they'll leave? It's raining awfully hard."

A soft knock on the door brought a gasp of fear from Victoria. Her grip on Trinity became gratifyingly firm. He was sorely tempted not to answer the knock. He knew he had no business letting Victoria's nearness influence his judgment, but he didn't care. The minute she threw herself into his arms, his common sense went out the window.

But the repeated knocking brought him back to a sense of time and place . . . and danger. He gently pried Victoria's fingers loose from his arms, drew his gun, and opened the door a crack.

"I got the horses away," a voice said.

"Did they see you?"

"No. They're still arguing."

"Take them to Dr. Mills's house. Leave them in the willow grove down by the creek. We'll be there in fifteen minutes."

The door closed. Victoria couldn't hear the receding footsteps.

"Get packed as quickly as you can," Trinity said as soon

as he closed the door. "We're leaving now."

"In the rain? It could turn into a bad storm."

"Those men intend to kill me. If they do, nobody's going to stop them from doing what they want with you."

"How do you know?"

"One of the men downstairs told me."

"But why?"

"They want you."

"That's the only reason? They *want* me?"

"They're probably watching the front of the hotel. They'll have someone at the livery stable in a minute. If we leave now, I'm hoping we can slip away in the rain. At the least it will wash out our tracks."

Victoria asked no more questions. Trinity had proven he wasn't afraid to face Red Beard and his friends. If he thought they needed to escape in the middle of a rainstorm, she believed him.

Ten minutes later they left the hotel by the back stairs. Keeping in the shadows of the half dozen false-fronted buildings that lined the only street of Gabel's Stop, they made their way to Dr. Mills's house. Twice lightning flashes turned the night to day. Victoria prayed the miners were still inside. She and Trinity had no cover and nowhere to run.

"It's not completely dark yet," Dr. Mills said when Trinity told him what they meant to do. "They might see you."

"We can't wait. If they discover we're gone, they'll start searching the town. It'll be bad for everybody if they find us."

"Don't worry about the kid," Mills told Victoria. "I'll make sure he's safe. You just make sure you get her out of Arizona," he told Trinity. "I won't be able to fix what they'll do to either one of you."

Victoria had thought she would look forward to the rain. After the scorching heat of the desert during the daylight hours, she expected to enjoy its coolness. Instead, she hated it. It continued hour after hour in a steady downpour, the kind she remembered from Texas in the spring.

Trinity had provided her with a rain slick and a hat large enough to keep the rain off her face, but the cold and the wet got in nonetheless.

The rain even managed to run down the back of her neck. She couldn't talk to Trinity because of the steady drumming of raindrops on leaves, the plunk of drops in puddles, and the noisy squishing and sucking of the horses' feet in the soft mud. Trinity rode slightly ahead, constantly on the lookout.

"They'll follow us," Trinity said when they stopped several hours later. "The only question is how to throw them off our trail."

"We must have a good head start. They don't know where we're going."

"There's only one trail in or out of Gabel's Stop."

"What are you going to do?"

"Double back."

"Are you crazy?"

It was so dark Victoria could barely see Trinity's teasing smile.

"We're going to use that creek," Trinity said referring to a shallow stream which only that morning had been a dry wash. "If we can get behind them, they'll never be able to follow us, even if the rain doesn't wash out our tracks."

By now Victoria had complete faith in Trinity's abilities and decisions, but every step in the direction of Gabel's Stop caused the muscles at the back of her neck to tighten. She was certain her heartbeat could be heard above the rain. As for her breath, she didn't know how she managed to get enough air in her lungs to remain conscious.

As the rain came down harder and harder, the stream grew in size and swiftness. Victoria knew a sudden downpour could turn it into a raging, death-dealing wall of muddy water. She couldn't help but cast anxious looks over her shoulder. Lightning illuminated the sky from time to time showing her trees and large boulders which could hide them from Red Beard or kill them in a merciless flood.

After what seemed like hours, Trinity signaled her to pull up. They drew the horses into the midst of a particularly thick grove of trees. A tangle of mesquite, Palo Verde, and creosote bushes effectively screened them from the trail.

"We'll wait here until they pass," Trinity said.

"How long do you think that will be?"

"I don't know, but I doubt more than a couple of hours."

If Victoria thought she had been miserable before, she was mistaken. The trees sheltered them from the rainfall, but fatter drops of water fell from their drooping leaves. There was nowhere to sit. Her feet quickly became wet and cold. They couldn't talk. It was essential not only that they hear the men first, but that their horses remained absolutely quiet when the others passed by.

They came by in less than an hour, but Victoria would have sworn she'd waited at least six. There seemed to be an unlimited number of hours in this cold, wet, endless night.

The rain continued to come down harder. The stream had overflowed its banks and was flooding the area beneath the trees. At this rate they would soon be knee-deep in water.

Victoria sneezed.

"Quiet," Trinity hissed.

"I didn't do it intentionally," Victoria hissed back, "but I'm cold and wet through. I wouldn't be surprised if I came down with a cold by morning."

"You're welcome to have pneumonia as long as you don't sneeze again."

"What am I supposed to do? Stop up my nose?"

"Think of something. Remember it's you they're really after."

Coldhearted brute—she really needed to be reminded of that.

She sneezed again a few minutes later. The horses moved about restlessly, stamping their feet.

Without a word, Trinity opened one of the saddlebags

and took out one of his shirts. "Here. If you have to sneeze again, bury your face in this."

She felt guilty about sneezing. She realized it could jeopardize their lives. "You act like I'm doing it on purpose."

"I know you can't help it, but it's just as dangerous no matter the reason."

Still, she was irritated Trinity had no sympathy for her. She didn't suppose he'd ever sneezed at such a moment, or coughed, or cleared his throat, or had to relieve himself. His body probably obeyed his orders just like he expected other people to do.

Well, she didn't work like that. She was cold and wet and probably going to come down with bronchitis. She'd been in the saddle all night. She was so tired she could hardly stand up, and all he could do was tell her to bury her face in his shirt.

Buc wouldn't have said that. Would he? He said he loved her and would do anything for her, but he'd been giving her orders ever since he'd known her. Even her uncle. They all tended to dictate to her. At least Trinity had a reason. If those men found her. . . .

She felt a sneeze coming on. Unable to stop it, she buried her face in Trinity's shirt. She felt like her head had exploded. She couldn't do that again. She'd blow out her ears.

"Someone's coming," Trinity whispered. "Get to your horse's head. Don't let him make a sound."

Victoria put her hand on her mount's nose. She had to keep him from nickering.

It was so long before Victoria saw anyone she started to wonder if Trinity had been mistaken. Then she saw them, too, dim shapes coming through the grey veil of slanting rain. At first, she couldn't recognize anyone, but she felt her body tense. She *knew* it was Red Beard and his companions.

There were just three of them, riding hunched over in the saddle, their heads lowered against the rain. They were bundled up against the cold and wet, but Victoria recognized Red Beard in the lead.

The horses, smelling the presence of strange horses, became restless. The packhorse swelled up to nicker, but Trinity stopped him. The horse stamped his foot in frustration. It sounded like part of the bank caving in on the rising creek.

Victoria's horse stood quietly, but she could feel a sneeze coming. She pressed the back of her hand against her nose, but that didn't help. She buried her face in Trinity's shirt, but that didn't help either. The closer they came, the more powerful her impulse to sneeze became.

Victoria rubbed her nose vigorously. She forced herself to take deep, slow breaths. She even turned her face up to the sky and swallowed a few drops of rainwater.

Nothing helped. She had to sneeze.

"We ain't never going to find them in this rain," one spoke. Victoria didn't recognize his voice. He must be the man who never spoke in the hotel. "Ain't no sense in us getting pneumonia for nothing."

"We'll find them," Red Beard said. "There's only one way to get to Texas from Gabel's Stop. Besides, you can still see the track of their horses. The rain hasn't washed it all away yet."

"It will soon. It keeps getting heavier."

"We ain't giving up," Red Beard reiterated. "I'm going to kill me that stranger. Ain't nobody kills my brother and gets away with it."

"I don't give a damn about Hobie," the blond said. "I want that woman. Hot damn! Have you ever dreamed of anything like her? It'll feel better than heaven to sink into her. I'll stay there all night just pumping her full until I plumb wear myself out."

"Can't you never think of nothing but women? That was your cousin that man killed."

"He told Hobie to stand still. Hobie never could do anything anybody told him. Wouldn't do a lick of work either, not if he could get out of it. Good riddance, I say."

"You son of a bitch," Red Beard exploded as he turned on the blond.

"Ain't no use in you killing each other over Hobie," said the other man. "He wouldn't care nothing about it."

"You just shut up about Hobie, you hear!" Red Beard told the blond.

"Sure. I'll just think about that woman. I think we ought to keep her. Take her back to the cabin. She's bound to be able to cook better'n Buster. And after she's done filling us with dinner, I'll fill her full of something even better." He laughed.

"Can't you ever think of anything except your dong?"

"I think it's a good idea," the one Victoria assumed was Buster said. "If we ever find them."

"You set that female up in our camp, and we'd never get nothing done. You two would be fighting over her from see to can't see."

"We could take her in shifts."

They passed on down the trail, arguing over how they would divide up the day so they could make the best use of Victoria.

Victoria didn't sneeze. Listening to what they said had scared it completely out of her.

She and Trinity remained perfectly quiet until a flash of lightning showed the trail to be empty.

"We'll stay here about fifteen minutes more," Trinity said.

"Then what do we do?"

"We follow them."

"Follow them!" Victoria squeaked. "You must be crazy." She sneezed. Twice.

"I've got to get you out of the rain before you get sick. I have a friend who has a ranch near here. We'll follow them until we have to leave the trail. We'll lose our tracks in theirs."

"But won't they be able to see where we turned off?"

"They won't have any idea we got behind them. There were no tracks there when they came by. If they do turn back, which I doubt, they'll think it's just somebody else coming along the same road after them."

Victoria wasn't about to argue. The notion of some place dry had taken hold of her imagination. It was all she could think about.

But her relief was some time in coming.

Morning came, grey and full of rain. And colder than ever. They soon left the trail, but it was past noon before they came in sight of a solitary cabin.

"Doesn't seem to be anybody home," Trinity said. "No smoke."

Victoria's spirits fell. She didn't think she could go on any longer. Only the prospect of getting warm and dry had kept her going this long. She'd been awake and in the saddle for the better part of three days now. She was so exhausted she didn't care if she had to find a cave. She had to get off this horse and out of the rain.

Trinity continued on toward the house. Victoria was surprised but didn't argue. If Trinity intended to break into the place, she'd be right behind him.

"Can't figure where Ben got to," Trinity said when they halted out of the rain under a broad overhang. "But he won't mind us putting up here for the night."

Trinity lifted Victoria out of the saddle. She couldn't have dismounted by herself.

The small cabin was only one room. Victoria gave silent thanks it had a wooden floor. After twelve hours of rain, a dirt floor would have been under several inches of water. A handmade table and two slat-bottom chairs stood in the center of the room. A small iron stove with a flue through the ceiling stood out from the far wall. To the left of the stove, the absent Ben had built shelves into the wall where he could keep all his supplies within reach. On the right, a small alcove formed by an open closet on one side and some deep shelves on the other contained the single bed. Even though the bed had been carefully made up, it hadn't been designed for comfort.

Victoria thought it looked heavenly.

Pegs along the inside and outside walls held saddles,

bridles, hats, and anything else the owner wanted to hang up.

Despite the long and heavy rain, only two places in the roof leaked seriously enough for Victoria to consider putting a bucket under them. A little light filtered in from three windows, all of which stood in need of a good cleaning.

"I'll start a fire and put some water on for coffee," Trinity said, coming in behind her with the saddlebags. "You get out of those wet clothes." Long years of practice enabled Trinity to have a fire going in less than a minute. Rainwater, even more quickly procured from a barrel outside, would serve to make coffee.

"Come on, get out of your clothes," Trinity said, when he turned around and Victoria still stood, dripping water on the floor.

"I can't. Not with you here."

"Don't be ridiculous. You'll catch your death."

"I can't," Victoria repeated.

"I've got to take care of the horses. By the time I unsaddle them, rub them down, and feed them, you ought to have had all the time you need."

"I hate for you to have to go back outside, but there's only one room."

"Don't worry," Trinity said. "I'd have had to take care of the horses even if this place was bigger than any house in Texas."

Chapter Eighteen

The minute the door closed behind Trinity, Victoria dug into her saddlebags for a complete change of clothing. She pulled off her boots and then began striping off her wet clothes. Even with the rain slick, she was wet through to the skin and chilled to the bone.

Standing as close to the small fire as she dared, she stripped down to bare skin. Shivering, her teeth chattering uncontrollably, Victoria hurried into her dry clothes. They felt damp and cold. She stood as close as she dared to the fire to dry her clothes and warm her bones.

That didn't warm her enough. She took a thick Indian blanket from the bed and wrapped it around her shoulders. She pulled one of the chairs up close to the fire and sank into it. For a few minutes, her body remained cold and stiff, her muscles taut. But as the fire began to warm the cabin, and the heavy blanket began to trap the warmth of her body, Victoria started to relax.

She couldn't believe how tired she was. Even in the flight from Texas, she'd never been in the saddle so long, never endured such physical exhaustion, never had to escape such a potpourri of evil pursuers.

But it was all over now. She was out of the saddle, warm and dry, with enough food to last for days. And she was safe. Trinity would see to that. For the first time in uncountable hours, she could relax.

She was getting too warm. She moved her chair back a little. The water was beginning to boil. She ought to look for the coffee, but she was too tired to bother. She was too tired to sit up. Her eyelids began to droop. All she wanted was to go to sleep, but she had to stay awake. She couldn't go to sleep before Trinity got back.

But he would be gone for a long time. It would take him more than half an hour to take care of three horses.

There was no point in her just sitting here all the time. She probably should see about fixing something to eat, but she wasn't hungry. Besides, she didn't like the idea of rummaging about in somebody else's house. *Let Trinity do it. The place belonged to his friend.*

Victoria got up, went over and sat down on the bed. It wasn't as comfortable as her bed back home, but it would do for a short nap. She lay down and pulled the blanket up over her shoulders.

She wouldn't sleep, just doze for ten or fifteen minutes. Then she'd get up and fix something to eat. Trinity probably left the supplies in the pile with the saddlebags. She'd look in a minute. No point in getting up now when she was finally warm.

Victoria gratefully relaxed into the bed. There were times when this journey with Trinity seemed like a nightmare from which she would awaken to find Anita shaking her and saying she'd never get anything done if she slept her life away.

Victoria closed her eyes and smiled. Anita was such a dear. She and Ramon had spoiled her. But so had her father and her uncle . . . and Buc. Everyone had spoiled her until Trinity came along. Only Trinity had decided she wouldn't break, that she was as tough as any man. She appreciated that, but she had to admit she liked being spoiled.

Maybe Trinity wasn't always like that. Maybe, when he was at his ranch, he could relax. He might even say something nice to her without spoiling it a minute later by saying something rude.

She wondered what his ranch was like. What would it reveal about him that she didn't know? Could she get past his distrust of women? She could try. Surely, if she went about it the right way. . . .

"It's getting worse out there," Trinity said as he entered the cabin. The wind sucked the door shut behind him. "I wouldn't be surprised if this turns into a. . . ."

Victoria was sound asleep. Not even his noisy entrance disturbed her. A strong odor of something burning pervaded the room. Trinity hurried to the stove. The water had burned out of the pan. Taking another pot from the shelf, Trinity hurried outside, dipped it into the rain barrel, and poured the contents into the pan upon returning. A loud hissing, a cloud of steam, and the water would soon be ready for coffee.

He walked over to the bed. He wanted to replace the blanket. It was heavy and coarse, made out of horsehair, but Victoria's fingers gripped it tightly. He wished he had a soft pillow instead of the hard, cotton-filled pillow Ben used, but she seemed to be sleeping soundly, despite the packed cotton and the coarse blanket.

He wanted to do something to make her more comfortable. It wasn't very satisfying knowing the best thing he could do was leave her alone. He wasn't doing a very good job of taking care of her. Grant Davidge certainly wouldn't have allowed her to go if he'd known she would be attacked by Indians, pursued by randy miners, and end up sleeping in a dirty cabin on a remote ranch across the New Mexico border.

Trinity certainly wouldn't have let any woman he cared for go under the circumstances.

That's why you feel so guilty. The undeniable realization nearly took his breath away. *You care for her. You care for her in a way you haven't cared for any woman since Queenie, in a way you swore never to care again.*

245

Panic rose in his throat. It was the same feeling he had for the first few months after Queenie married his father. That feeling of helplessness and hopelessness, of being sucked into a dark pit to be tortured with the promise of everything he ever wanted and couldn't have. For years it had pursued him like a wolf pursues a deer during a famine; it shadowed him relentlessly, remorselessly, unceasingly. It used to wake him up in the middle of the night in a cold sweat.

Falling in love was akin to losing control of his life, to yielding himself up to destruction, of letting someone suck the life out of his soul until nothing remained but a hard shell. He had fought it. And he'd spent fifteen years hardening his soul so he would never feel that way again.

Yet, much to his surprise, the panic passed almost as quickly as it came. It wouldn't be the same way with Victoria. But what did he want from her? What did he want *with* her? He hadn't stopped to consider that. He had often considered the fact that he desired her, but he wanted something much more meaningful, more long-lasting.

Don't be stupid. Women like Victoria only consider marriage. And they don't consider it with a thirty-dollar-a-month cowhand.

What was he? An ex-miner. A cowboy of some kind. He certainly couldn't call himself a rancher, even though he had owned a ranch. He hadn't had time to buy any cows. All he had were a few horses. Women like Victoria didn't marry impoverished miners turned ranchers; not when they had an inheritance in the bank, one of the richest men in Texas for a father-in-law, and an uncle who owned the biggest ranch in Arizona.

She might flirt with him, especially if she needed him to prove she was innocent of murder, but she wouldn't seriously consider marrying him. There were too many respectable men available for her to consider marrying a burned-out bounty hunter.

Trinity forced himself to consider the situation at hand. Victoria was asleep and likely to sleep through the afternoon, evening, and night. If he wanted any dinner, he'd have to cook it himself. And eat it alone.

He wouldn't wake her.

He set about the familiar task of preparing his own meal. He'd done it so often he didn't have to think about it any more. He didn't much care what he ate. Many times he ate nothing rather than go to the trouble of cooking. It was one of the many things he did in his life because he knew he ought to, not because he cared.

But it didn't take him long to realize that something felt different this time. And it had nothing to do with being inside Ben's cabin. It was a strange feeling, like he had enjoyed something quite pleasant but couldn't quite remember what it was. But the feeling didn't go away. In fact, it grew stronger as he fixed his dinner, ate it, and cleaned up after himself.

By the time he was ready for bed, he was practically purring with contentment. Why? What could have generated this feeling in him?

His gaze fell on Victoria, and he realized she was the difference.

It felt strange being in a cabin with a woman sleeping nearby. Sort of like being married, at least what he thought it would be like to be married. He'd never really considered it. He'd refused to let any such thoughts enter his mind. He didn't want his life controlled by anyone else, especially a woman. They never seemed to want the same things as men. They were always trying to get men to change or do something they didn't want to do.

But it wouldn't be too bad if it were always like this. There was an ease about Victoria which made her as comfortable to be around as most men. This cabin was very simple, even crude, but it had a homey feeling. There were none of the feminine touches he associated with women. On the whole he felt more comfortable that way. But he wouldn't mind a flower garden, as long as he didn't have to work in it. Flowers inside the house were nice, too.

Trinity leaned back in his chair and stared into the fire.

Having a woman around made a man see things differently. It was real different from being around a woman. When a man was around a woman, he was sniffing her out, acting like a tomcat, thinking of what he could get, thinking of his own pleasure and not much else.

But having a woman around was something else entirely. It didn't mean a man couldn't let his mind contemplate pleasure now and then. No man could look at Victoria and not think about sinking blissfully into her embrace. Whether she knew it or not, she was made for love. And if he had his way, he'd prove it to her before they said *adieu*.

But he thought of other things, things Trinity had never thought about before. He thought of building something solid, of making a home. He couldn't do that when he behaved like a one-man crusade. He never made any money. Funding his work took most of the gold he could dig out of the ground. Chasing criminals was expensive. He wasn't home long enough to put up a house or build up a ranch or a business.

He thought of permanence, of staying in one place for years, of building a network of friends, of having a family, of being tied to people by unbreakable bonds. That meant more than buying someone's favors by the hour . . . or by the evening.

It meant changing the whole way he lived, the way he thought, everything he wanted from life. It meant facing himself.

Trinity knew he wasn't ready to do that.

They were sitting at the table in front of the fire. Trinity had fixed dinner and cleared away the dishes. Victoria had awakened about dusk.

Now it was time to go to bed, but neither of them seemed willing to make the first move.

"The rain's letting up," Trinity said. "We ought to be able to leave first thing in the morning."

"We won't run into those men?"

"They ought to be about a hundred miles west of here."

Silence filled the room.

"How long do you think it will take us to reach Bandera?"

"That depends on how hard you want to ride."

"Not as hard as we rode to get here."

"Then it'll take longer."

More silence permeated the air.

"Don't you want to wait for your friend?"

"No. He might be away for weeks. I didn't see any signs of cows about. Maybe he took his herd off to sell. He didn't have many cows, but they were good breeding stock."

"As good as Uncle's?"

"Better."

"Do you think Uncle Grant will be in Bandera when we get there?"

"I doubt it, but I'm certain he'll have hired someone to meet us."

"How are you going to find Chalk Gillet?"

"I don't know. I was hoping Ben could give me a line. He knows practically every cowboy between here and Galveston."

"How, running this ranch?"

"Those cows belonged to the last man I took in. He murdered a man for them. I had nothing to do with them, so I gave them to Ben. Before that he spent all his time riding the trails north."

Silence.

"What happens if you can't find Gillet?"

"I'll find him." Trinity stood up and stretched. "It's time for bed. I'll check the horses."

Victoria was in bed with the light out when Trinity returned. He put a few more pieces of wood on the fire. The sky had cleared, but a cold wind blew down from the north. They were about three thousand feet above the desert floor, and the night would be cold.

Trinity spread his bedding on the floor and undressed. He consciously made himself keep his back to Victoria. She was sound asleep, but he didn't trust himself. Ever since that day on the mountain when he kissed her, he had been finding it harder and harder to keep his hands off her.

He told himself at the time it was okay to kiss her because it was part of his plan to lure her into trusting him. Since then he'd kept his distance, partly because she would have nothing to do with him after he kidnapped her, and partly because neither one of them could figure out how to reestablish their easy relationship.

The fact that he was taking her back to Bandera still stood between them. It didn't matter that she was going willingly. He was still endangering her life. He had dragged her into one dangerous situation after another. He had also been prepared to shoot her uncle. That wasn't a very good basis for establishing a relationship of love and trust.

Yet he did want her to trust him. He knew she depended on him, and he thought she respected his position. What he wanted most, though, was for her to like him.

Don't be a fool, he told himself. *No woman could feel about you the way you want her to, not after what you've done, not even if you were to let her go. The only way you can make up for what you've done is to prove her innocent.*

But he didn't want to wait that long. He was here now. So was she. His body ached to touch her, to feel the softness of her skin just once more. He moved next to her bed.

He could see her in the firelight. Her hair looked nearly brown, subdued, the way she looked in sleep. She lay still, quiet, but she had a funny way of tucking her lower lip under her teeth. It made her look like she was having a nightmare.

He felt a pang of guilt. If she were having a bad dream, he was the cause of it. She had been safe and content in her mountain valley, but he couldn't wish that he'd never gone to Mountain Valley Ranch. No matter what happened to him, he would never forget Victoria, and he would never regret finding her.

He wondered if she was warm enough. While she slept, he had found a lighter blanket, one made of soft cotton, dyed with native dyes, and woven into intricate geometric designs. Ironically, she would probably need the horsehair blanket tonight.

The flickering flames caused tiny shadows to dance across her cheeks. Her thick eyelashes appeared black in the dim light. It felt odd to look at her with closed eyes. It was almost like looking at somebody who wasn't there. It gave her the look of a demure maiden, a young woman shy of the world, one who had retreated within herself rather than face the danger of her emotions.

Her lip slipped from under her teeth, and her mouth slowly curled up in the hint of a smile.

She still looked demure and shy, but now she looked like a young woman who merely showed a modest, timid face to the world. Inwardly she was smiling to herself, pleased with the power she exerted over men, quite content to continue wreaking havoc in the hearts of her swains.

Trinity could restrain himself no longer. Moving still closer to the bed, he reached out to touch her cheek. He let his fingers savor the downy softness of her skin. His fingertips traced the outline of her jaw, the smoothness of her lips. He liked the warmth of her. It felt soothing.

He also liked the stillness which surrounded her in sleep. It made him feel peaceful, too, something he could never remember experiencing for more than isolated moments in his life. Being next to her could make his blood boil with heat, his muscles ache with tension, his body swell with desire. At the same time he could feel a tranquility that penetrated all the way to the core of his being. Odd, how being around her could strike up such conflicting emotions, which seemed to fit perfectly together.

She seemed too soft and fragile, so delicate he was sure she would break. Yet awake, she could stay in the saddle for three days and fight off Indians as well as he could.

He touched her hair—heavy and thick, yet soft and pliable. He longed to run his fingers through it, wind it around his fingers, cord it, knot it, but he didn't dare. It would wake her.

He touched every part of her face. Like a blind man memorizing the face of the woman he loved, Trinity absorbed the shape and texture.

Then he kissed her. He shouldn't have, but he did. It was a gentle kiss, no more than a touch on her lips. So much, and so little. Not enough.

He kissed her again, less gently this time.

She moved.

He drew back, certain that she would awake, but she didn't. He couldn't go back to his bed. He had experienced the intoxicating taste of her mouth, and he had to have more.

Trinity's body was so tense he trembled. His pants cut him uncomfortably, but he made no attempt to adjust himself. Only Victoria could provide the relief he needed. He kissed her eyelids. He had wanted to do that from the first time he watched her fall asleep. It was like kissing her to sleep, knowing she could fall asleep because he was watching, because he was protecting her. It was a wonderful feeling, one that made him feel like bursting his britches with pride.

It was also a disconcerting feeling: Such trust was an awesome responsibility, one he felt he had done little to deserve.

He brushed some errant locks back from her face. He kissed her forehead, the tip of her nose, the side of her neck. Each kiss grew in intensity. She stirred, but Trinity was too thoroughly under the sway of his desire to back away now. When her lips quivered under his, his kiss became more full, more greedy.

Victoria kissed him back. And Trinity lost all restraint. Taking her face in his hands, he covered it with hungry kisses. There was no pretense from either one of them now. No doubt either.

Trinity threw the quilt back and pulled Victoria into his arms. The warmth of her body was like an invitation to bury his face in the curve of her neck. He couldn't get enough of her. He couldn't hold her close enough. No woman he'd been with had ever made him feel like this. It was as though he'd done this many times before but was experiencing it for the very first time.

Trinity wanted to say something, but how do you tell a woman you're taking back to face a hanging you're mad about her and want to make love to her? He'd be well-served if she treated him like Red Beard.

But she wasn't. Victoria was holding him just as tightly as he held her. She had thrown her head back so he could kiss her throat. She covered his face with hot kisses. She pressed her body close to his, like she never wanted to let go. Trinity decided their bodies were saying all that was important just now. He would try to sort out the words later

Trinity's lips caressed her neck, lingered in the hollow of her shoulder while he pushed away the strap of her camisole. He planted a row of kisses down her arm. A moan of pleasure from Victoria encouraged him to slip the strap down to her elbow. The expanse of exposed breast nearly caused Trinity to lose control.

He ached to slip her gown down to her waist and feast upon her breasts, but he was afraid of moving too fast. Victoria wanted him as much as he wanted her, but he could not forget the obstacles that stood between them.

Taking a deep breath, he forced himself to center his attention on her other shoulder. But when he slipped the second strap over her shoulder, the second breast became exposed. That proved too much for his self-control.

Trinity took Victoria's mouth in a deep, lingering kiss. At the same time he covered her breasts, one with each hand. Victoria gasped from shock, but she didn't pull away. Trinity's tongue forced its way between her teeth and plunged deep into her mouth. At the same time, he traced circles around her nipples with his fingertips.

Victoria's body arched against him, and she broke the kiss. Her breath came fast and shallow. She didn't pull away. She lay still before Trinity's assault, waiting.

Deserting Victoria's lips, Trinity laid a trail of kisses down her neck. As his lips reached the mound of her breast, he felt her body stiffen. He slowed his advance while his fingers continued to create circles of fire around her nipples.

Then ever so gently, he touched the tip of one puckered, swollen nipple with the tip of his tongue. Victoria nearly rose off the bed. When he let his tongue caress its hot surface, she gasped for air. When he took it in his mouth and sucked it, he thought she would faint. Her body became as rigid as a corral fence.

Fearing he had upset her, Trinity pulled away, but Victoria took his head and pressed it tightly against her breast.

Before Trinity surrendered completely to her invitation, a feeling of danger fought its way through the tide of his inflamed senses. Even as he tried to push away this detested intrusion, instincts, honed by years of practice, scaled the walls erected by unleashed desire. The desire to consume her fought with the desire to shield and protect her.

Protection won.

Trinity broke his embrace. Only his understanding of the necessity for swift action enabled him to force his brain to ignore the objections of his enraged body. Their lives were in danger.

He listened intently.

"Wha—" Victoria started to say, but one hissed syllable cut her short.

"Shh! Somebody's outside," Trinity whispered.

Chapter Nineteen

In the single second that he recognized danger, Trinity transformed from an enraptured lover to a trained hunter. In a series of swift movements, he took a pair of guns from his saddlebags and handed them to Victoria. "Here. Shoot anybody who tries to get in. And shoot to kill. They will."

Trinity picked up his rifle then closed the door to the stove, casting the room into total darkness. Only gradually could his eyes make out the barely lighter squares that represented the cabin windows.

"Keep down. I'm going outside," he whispered.

Victoria fought to understand what was happening around her. She felt her body plummet from the heights of fiery passion to the depths of icy fear, but she lacked Trinity's experience. Her mind had none of his lucidity or elasticity. The quick descent left her shaking, the blood thundering in her ears, her brain a useless whirl of confused thoughts and sensations.

Red Beard.

Her numbed brain shouted that message over and over again. She told herself it could be anyone out there, but she didn't believe that. She was certain it was Red Beard and his friends. Maybe he had had time to get others to join him. Maybe there were too many for Trinity.

Why had he gone outside? Didn't he know it was much easier for them to kill him? And why had he left her alone? Her hands shook so badly she didn't know if she could hit anything she aimed at. Besides, she'd never shot at anyone except the Indians. She didn't know if she could shoot at a man now.

Get out of that bed. Trinity's risking his life for you. You can't let him go out there alone. That thought steadied her nerves. She was scared for herself, but she felt different about Trinity. The fact that anybody would follow her to kill him, just because he'd tried to protect her, made her furious. She wasn't about to let Trinity die while some miserable, lecherous miners lived.

Victoria got off the bed. Oblivious to the feel of her bare feet on the cold floor, she walked to the window. She couldn't see anything. There was no moon. She moved to the door. Trinity had left it slightly ajar. Opening it a few inches, she looked out. Nothing. Silence.

But she expected that. Red Beard wouldn't advertise his presence. He'd want to sneak up behind Trinity and shoot him in the back. Or they'd surround him and shoot him down from all sides. There were no mirrors to help him this time, but she would. She'd be his second set of eyes and ears.

Victoria eased the door open. Even in the dark night, she hesitated to step outside. Her white nightgown would make her an easy target. She rifled through Trinity's gear until she found a black shirt. Dropping her gown to the floor, she slipped the shirt on and stepped out into the night.

The cold snapped at her legs, whistled up the shirt to chill her inflamed body, but she hardly noticed. Trinity was outside, and so were the killers.

She slipped along the wall under the overhang. She noticed movement across the yard and froze. It was a man, but it wasn't Trinity. It didn't move like him. The man moved again, and Victoria raised her gun, drew back the hammer, and took careful aim.

"Ben! You goddamned son of a bitch. You scared the hell out of me."

Trinity's booming voice, breaking the tense silence like

the crack of falling timber, nearly caused her to fire the gun accidentally.

"You ain't been scared by anything since you popped out of your mother's belly," a strange voice replied. "What do you mean moving into my place behind my back? Next thing you'll be telling me you done drunk up all the coffee."

"Why didn't you come to the door instead of sneaking around like some lobo wolf?"

"Because there are too many lobo wolves about to suit me. Seeing tracks of three horses sorta made me careful. Knowed it was you the minute I saw that buckskin. But why do you need so many horses? I thought you were through chasing after gunslinging galoots."

"I decided to go out one more time."

"You got him tied up in the cabin?"

"Her."

"You got a woman in there?"

"Yes."

"Just the two of you?"

"Sure."

"This I got to see," Ben said, starting for the cabin. "She must be ugly as a sow. I ain't never seen you within fifty feet of anything but a whore."

Victoria scampered into the cabin, frantic to exchange the shirt for her gown. She didn't have enough time to get properly dressed, so she put the shirt on over her gown, for warmth and decency. She lit the lantern before the men reached the door.

"I may be ugly as a sow," she said as Ben stepped into the cabin, "but I'm not a whore."

Ben stopped in his tracks, unable to move. His eyes grew as big as hawk eggs, his jaw swung loose on its hinges.

"This is Victoria Davidge," Trinity said. "She was convicted of killing her husband."

"Involuntary manslaughter," Ben mumbled. "The little lady couldn't help it if he died on his wedding night. His heart was probably too weak to stand the shock."

257

His eyes twinkled. Definitely, they twinkled.

"He was shot with a small caliber gun. They'd only been married a week."

"For a week with her, I'd let you shoot me," Ben said. "Might as well. I wouldn't be any good for the rest of my life."

"I'm taking her back to be executed."

Victoria could tell Trinity was teasing his friend.

"If you're going to hang her, couldn't we just keep her here for a little bit? Somebody put in a lot of work on her. I'd hate to see it go to waste. Why don't you marry me?" he said to Victoria. "I could overpower him in his sleep, and we could escape to Colorado."

"Aren't you afraid I'd kill you?" Victoria asked, struggling to keep a straight face.

"You're not a killer, ma'am. I don't know what happened, but you never killed your husband."

"How can you know that?" Victoria asked, surprised out of any desire to joke.

"Trinity left you in this cabin with two guns and not tied up. I've known him for more than a dozen years. He'd never turn his back on anybody he didn't trust completely."

"Why don't you come inside your own house?" Victoria asked. "We didn't drink up all the coffee, but I'm afraid we did make pretty heavy inroads into your bacon."

"There wasn't much left. I only stopped off here to change horses before I went for supplies. Now I'm going outside to take care of my horse. When I get back, I want some hot coffee and some answers. I got a feeling this is going to turn out to be more than just a friendly visit."

"So what do you want me to do?" Ben asked Trinity. Victoria had fixed more than coffee. While Ben ate his supper, Trinity told him the story from the day he returned to Bandera until now.

"I'm not expecting anything."

258

"Oh, yes you are. There are dozens of places you could have gone to on earth, most of them a sight prettier than this place. Come on, tell me. What is it?"

"I want you to help me find Chalk Gillet."

"What makes you think I can? He may be dead. Five years is a long time for some people."

"I know, but if he's anywhere near Texas, you've heard of him. I never saw anybody like Ben for remembering everything he ever heard," Trinity said to Victoria. "He can quote conversations word for word more than ten years later."

"Suppose we do find this Gillet, how do you propose to get him to go back to Bandera? If he's stayed away this long, he's probably got a good reason for staying away a while longer."

"You let me worry about that. I just want you to help me find him. Can you?"

"I did hear something about him a couple of years back."

Trinity turned to Victoria, a grin of triumph on his face. "I told you Ben could find him if he were still alive."

"Now hold on there a minute. I didn't say I knew where he was. I just said I heard something about him. You'd have to go looking for him. And I don't think you'd find him, not with your reputation. Not even if you changed your name again."

"Changed his name!" Victoria hadn't said a word, but the shock of learning Trinity wasn't Trinity after all surprised her out of her silence.

"He goes through at least a couple of names a year," Ben said. "I never know when people are talking about him or somebody I never heard of before."

"You could find him for me," Trinity said. "He wouldn't hide from you."

"You want me to go chasing back and forth along the Mexican border for some guy you mean to shanghai back to Bandera? Somebody may be waiting to kill him."

"Why would you change your name so often?" Victoria asked point-blank.

"Can't use the same name all the time when you're catching criminals," Ben explained. "It warns them off."

"I'll see nobody kills him," Trinity said, "but I've got to talk to him. He's the only person who can prove Victoria didn't kill her husband."

"Except the real killer."

"If he hasn't come forward by now, I don't expect he means to," Trinity snapped.

"Probably right," Ben said, looking thoughtful. "I guess I could go. It'll cost you though. I can't go traipsing over half of the Rio Grande valley on a hope and a prayer."

"I'll pay you."

"I knew you would," Ben said with a grin. "I just wanted to hear you say it. I never knew anybody so tight with money," he said to Victoria. "You could have knocked me over with a calf's ear when he bought that ranch. Now I know what he's been doing with all that gold he dug up."

"Stop gossiping," Trinity admonished. "We've got to leave tomorrow. When can you get away?"

"I can leave with you. I'm not busy right now."

"That reminds me," Trinity said, "I didn't see any cows. You have trouble with rustlers?"

"Might have if I'd kept that herd long, but I got rid of it. Didn't want to be tied down."

Trinity opened his mouth to make an astonished reply.

"What's his real name?" Victoria asked.

"You'll have to ask him that, ma'am. Now if I'm to be in the saddle come dawn—I know it'll be dawn because he doesn't know how to break camp any other time of day—I've got to get my beauty sleep. I'll bunk outside."

"I'll bunk with you."

"No need."

"You don't think I'm going to stay inside with you outside with your ear to the door to hear what's going on."

Ben grinned unashamedly. "If we both sleep inside, I won't have to peep."

"If you both sleep inside I won't get a wink of sleep," Victoria said. "You'll talk all night."

"Found out already," Ben said with a chuckle. "You got a sharp one there, son. Just might have overreached yourself this time."

"And just what do you mean by that?" Trinity demanded.

"Exactly what you think I mean," Ben shot back. "You been looking at her like you was a bear and she was a honeycomb without a bee in sight. Never knowed you to come within fifty feet of a decent woman unless you was on a horse headed out of town. You been practically leg-shackled to this one for nigh unto a week. Got that much and more to go. Either something's gone wrong with you since I saw you last, or she's got you over a barrel. And if she ain't got you over a barrel, something *has* gone wrong."

"Your jaws flap more than a coyote thinking about a lamb chop dinner," Trinity said good-naturedly. "Get your bed gear and get outside before you spill everything you know."

"Did I say something I shouldn't?"

"Just about everything you said."

"You should have warned me."

"I'd have more success warning a deaf mute. Now outside before she knows more about me than I know myself."

"I'll go, but I'm counting to ten. If you haven't come out by then, I'll come back and rescue you."

"I constantly ask myself why I ever liked him," Trinity said to Victoria as Ben walked toward the door, a genuinely happy smile on his face.

"Because he seems like the best friend a man could ever have."

"Just about. You won't be upset about sleeping in here by yourself?"

"With two such men to protect me? Just make sure you don't spend the night swapping tales. You'll be too sleepy to see Red Beard if he does turn up."

Ben stopped in the doorway. "Red Beard?"

"I'll tell you later," Trinity said, pushing his friend out the door.

He looked back before he closed the door after himself, and Victoria thought she saw her need of him reflected in his eyes. It made it all the harder to face the prospect of being alone.

Victoria did mind sleeping by herself, but not because she was frightened. She liked Ben, but she wished he hadn't come back, at least not just now. The wall that seemed too thin when she was worried about bullets coming through it seemed much too thick when it separated her from Trinity.

Until this evening, she hadn't been certain what she wanted from Trinity. Now she knew. She wanted everything he had to give. She didn't know how such a revelation would affect him.

Naturally he didn't know she was still a virgin.

He had no way of knowing Jeb had been uninterested in sleeping with his wife and had been too drunk to have done anything about it if he had. Even his kisses had been half-hearted. She knew that, now that she had Trinity's kisses as a gauge. Before she had just assumed that was the way well brought up people kissed. It might be the way they kissed, but it wasn't the way she wanted to kiss or be kissed.

Not any more.

She had always assumed the fault was hers. She hadn't felt an overwhelming need of Jeb. She wanted to consummate their marriage. His nearness always caused her to become sensually aroused, but it wasn't anything she couldn't go to sleep and forget. It certainly wasn't the powerful force that Trinity had lighted inside her.

Now that she had some idea of the powerful feelings which drove a man to desire a woman, she wondered if there might be something wrong with her. Jeb never touched her and Buc never even hinted at a desire to sleep with her. Trinity had, but he had recovered quickly after Ben arrived.

Did he feel the frustration she felt, the aching body, the

heat, the still-surging desire? Was it so easy to turn away from her?

She remembered the need in his eyes and felt reassured. He wanted her as much as she wanted him.

She didn't know how she was going to get back to sleep. Earlier she had just slipped over the edge of sleep when Trinity touched her cheek. She hadn't moved because she'd been afraid he would stop. She had wanted him to kiss her. She had wanted him to arouse those hot, insistent feelings in her again.

Only she had miscalculated.

She never expected the explosion that happened when he took her in his arms. But even that had been nothing compared to the sensations he unleashed when he touched her nipples. Just the memory made her blush. She had wanted him to touch her. She had begged him to touch her more.

Not aloud, though. She couldn't do that, not yet. But her body had begged. It had responded to his every movement. Her body had acted on knowledge well beyond her experience. She supposed it was instinct, the need which had driven man to seek out woman for millions of years. Apparently woman had the same drive to seek out man. At least she did.

Despite the interlude of danger, her body still strained toward the fulfillment it had been denied. She could hardly lie still. She felt as though she would go crazy if she didn't get up and do something. She once had a rash which had driven her crazy for three days. This was worse. Her entire body felt as if it were being tortured. She knew Trinity was the answer to her distress. And that answer was denied.

At least for tonight.

But ultimately the sensations which threatened to drive her mad began to weaken. At last she lay still in her bed.

So this was what the need of a man did to a woman.

The second part of the trip was as uneventful as the first

had been dangerous. Ben traveled with them. The banter between him and Trinity kept Victoria on the edge of laughter for whole days at a time. It was the honest laughter of friends. Trinity was more relaxed, more open, more likeable than ever before. He was also more thoughtful. It often made her laugh to see Ben egg him on by telling him the things a true gentleman ought to do. If Victoria hadn't put her foot down, Trinity would have started carrying her across mud puddles.

"Sir Walter Raleigh did it for Queen Elizabeth," Ben had said. "I haven't been an ignorant cowhand all my life," he informed them when they looked at him like he'd lost his mind. "I went to school. I learned to read. And I learned about a lot of people nobody's ever heard of before. That's two of them. I know a whole lot more."

"Spare me the rest," Trinity had asked. "I know too many people who are queer in the head as it is."

They stayed at hotels and even rode in stagecoaches. Trinity insisted she have the best room everywhere they went. He also made sure she could have a bath every day and dinner every evening. He even forced her to buy a new traveling outfit.

"I know women hate to wear the same clothes too often. I must have seen everything you got at least three times."

"He means my clothes," she explained to a puzzled and suspicious Ben. "See if you can convince him the next time he kidnaps a woman he ought to give her time to pack her own clothes. He doesn't have any idea what to bring."

"He doesn't know too much about females," Ben said. "Leastwise not nice ones. Now there's one dance hall gal by the name of Betty Dean I've seen him with now and again. I imagine if you was to ask her, she could tell you a thing or two."

At that point Trinity had attacked his friend, gotten his neck in a firm hold, and threatened to break it if he said another word. Victoria had seen enough cowhands wrestle to know they weren't going to do each other any harm, so she'd left them. She'd gone off and bought herself a new hat, the most expensive one she could find, with the money Trinity had given her.

She felt like she had lost Trinity, and she didn't know how to get him back.

At first she thought Ben had come between them and, to a limited extent, he had. But it wasn't long before she realized Trinity was putting Ben between them, to keep them from being alone, to prevent a situation like that evening in the cabin from happening again.

Did he stay away for the same reason Jeb had stayed away? She had always wanted to know why Jeb didn't make love to her, she had *needed* to know, but she hadn't had the courage to ask him. With no woman to tell her what to expect or how to handle the problems which were bound to crop up between newly married people, she had fallen back on ignorance. If there was nothing there, maybe there wasn't supposed to be anything there.

But the last five years had taught her there was a great deal more to marriage. Jeb simply wasn't interested in building that kind of relationship with her.

It couldn't be because she was unattractive. She wasn't a vain woman, but she did know she was very pretty. Jeb may not have made love to her, but there were plenty of others who had wanted to. But they never touched her. They never even tried to kiss her.

Even Buc. He had told her he loved her, told her he was going to marry her no matter what, hated Trinity on sight because of his overwhelming jealousy, but he had never even tried to put his arm around her.

Trinity was attracted to her. She had known it within five minutes of stepping out of her flower garden. He had been so attracted to her he had been unable to keep his hands off her on several occasions. That night in the cabin he had finally lost control completely. He had shown her some of the passion she always felt should be in a relationship between a man and a woman.

But Trinity had taken himself in hand after Ben arrived, so well in hand Victoria could hardly believe he had been sincere before. Why had he done that? Why had he wanted to? Could a man who said he couldn't sleep for wanting her turn his back and not come close to her for nearly two weeks?

Not unless there was something wrong with her.

She would have to ask him. She didn't know how she would work up the courage, but she had to know.

He had caused her to feel things she'd never felt before, things she'd never anticipated, never even guessed were there. She hadn't been wrong about the relationship between a man and a woman, but she also knew the desire, the fiery passion, wasn't all on the man's side. She had felt as hot as an iron stove in winter.

She couldn't go through the rest of her life being admired and desired because of her beauty but held at a distance.

Being admired was wonderful; being held in Trinity's arms was heavenly.

Trinity dreaded the moment when it came time to say goodbye to Ben. He also looked forward to it with barely contained anticipation. Once again he would be alone with Victoria, and once again he would have a chance to expose his heart and hopes to disappointment.

He didn't doubt she liked him. She had proved that the last night in the cabin. He still could remember every second. He could remember the taste of her lips, the scent of her hair, the way her skin quivered when he kissed her, the way her body yearned for his touch, the firm hard peaks her nipples made when he teased them with his teeth.

He also remembered his own reaction. His body was so stiff he hurt. He could still feel that way. Every time he let himself think about Victoria and that night. Like right now. Trinity squirmed in the saddle. It was very difficult to readjust himself without being terribly obvious. He was willing to confess to Victoria's effect on him, but he wasn't ready to admit it caused him to act like a randy teen every time he thought of kissing her breasts.

But the physical effect didn't worry him. Not really. Had it been any other woman, he would have laughed with Ben about it, maybe even joked with the woman. They would have enjoyed their time together and let it come to an end naturally.

But he didn't want his time with Victoria to come to an end, and that's what scared him.

He found himself thinking of the years ahead, of many years of waking up with her face on the pillow next to his, of seeing her across the table each morning at breakfast, of coming home to her at the end of a long day in the saddle, of enjoying the warmth and comfort of her body. Worst of all, he found himself thinking of her daughters, each of them a perfect image of their mother, adorable because they were so small. And because they were his.

The appeal was incredibly strong. It was partly the appeal of the home he had been without so long. It was partly the appeal of a stability he had never known. It was partly a response to the instinct in nearly every man to put down roots, to build something he can be proud of, to father children through whom his name and his blood will live on afterwards.

But it scared him half to death.

Whenever he imagined himself ten years from now surrounded by a family, a prosperous ranch, and the responsibility for all the men who worked for him, he felt suffocated. He felt the freedom he had known his whole life vanish, leaving him in a vacuum with no place to go and no air to breathe.

It was like a man who panics when he gets in tight places. He'd known some miners like that. They couldn't work in any place they couldn't stand up.

Yet, no sooner did he decide he couldn't stand that kind of life when it became the one thing he wanted above all else.

What did he get from life on the trail? Eating by a campfire. Traveling in searing heat, bitter cold, rain, sleet, or snow. Sleeping on the ground. Risking his life without anything to show for it. Eating cold food, dodging bullets, being an outcast?

Yet, old habits were hard to let go, and new habits made him uneasy. But he had to decide between the two. He had to decide for or against Victoria.

Ben pulled up. "I think I'll leave you here."

"You can't leave now," Trinity protested. "We're only about ten miles from the ranch. You'll want to get cleaned up and rest up a few days."

"Naw. I don't exactly know where to find Chalk. I'll have to ask around. Hope to find him at Eagle Pass, but I may have to go into Mexico, possibly as far as Monterrey. Can you meet me at Uvalde in three days?"

"You'll need a fresh horse. I don't have any cows, but I've got some of the best horses in Texas."

"I don't need a fresh horse. My old nag wouldn't forgive me if I throw a leg across another bag of bones."

"Is there anything else you need?"

"Naw. Just meet me in Uvalde. If I can't be there, I'll leave a message at Blackpool's Livery. Ask for Jude. He's old, ugly, and mean, but you can trust him."

"Don't take any chances. Just find Chalk. I'll do the rest."

"After all these years of riding with you, don't you think I know what to do?"

"I guess so. See you in three days."

"You take care of the little lady. If I come back and find you've let the Judge chew her about the edges, I'm going to be right put out."

"After all these years, don't you think I can take care of a prisoner?"

"A man, yes, even if he's mean as a sidewinder and has a dozen relatives on your trail. But I don't think you have the slightest idea what to do with a woman. You've been out of practice too long."

"Get out of here before I decide to take you in for something."

"What?"

"Being a public nuisance."

"You may get a conviction, but it ain't a hanging offense. I'd be out within the hour."

He waved a cheerful goodbye and cantered away. Victoria couldn't see so much as a hint of a trail.

"How does he know where to go?"

"Instinct. You could drop that man down in the Black Hills and he'd get to Texas without so much as a wrong turn."

The country had changed completely from the mountains of Arizona and the desert which had seemed to stretch from southern Arizona through New Mexico past the Big Bend country. They were entering the cattle country of south Texas, the country Victoria remembered so well from her childhood.

She began to see a lot more mesquite, chaparral, prickly pear and a dozen other varieties of low-growing trees, shrubs and vines, all bearing sweet-scented flowers and succulent berries, and nearly all armed with vicious thorns.

She also saw white-faced cattle; first one, then another. The closer they came to the ranch the more frequently they spotted them.

"Something's wrong," Trinity said. "There wasn't a cow on the place when I left."

Chapter Twenty

"Maybe you've got rustlers."

"Rustlers take cows away, they don't bring them in," Trinity replied, "certainly not cows like this." Trinity looked like some new thought had just occurred to him. He looked harder at the cow. Then he rode off to get a better look. The animal ran away before he could get close enough to put a rope on it, but not before he read the brand.

"That's one of the cows I gave Ben," he said when he rejoined Victoria. "Now I know why he was away when we reached his cabin. I also know why he wouldn't come up to the house."

"He brought his cows here?" Victoria couldn't see why Ben should do that, but she didn't understand why Trinity couldn't decide whether to cuss or laugh.

"He gave them back to me. I now have a herd. And a damned fine one at that."

He kicked his horse into a slow gallop.

Victoria remembered the house like it was yesterday. It wasn't a pretty house. Now that it stood unpainted, its boards weathered grey, it looked more forlorn than ever. Its only attractive aspects were the veranda which ran around two sides and the spreading arms of elms and poplars which offered sorely needed shade from the blazing afternoon sun.

The yard was barren of any living thing except the trees. The fence, which had once enclosed the small yard and protected her flowers and a small piece of lawn from hungry cows, had disappeared completely. Only one corral seemed to have been repaired enough to be used. A single barn seemed to be the only thing which had received much attention for many years.

"It's a little run-down," Trinity said, but his mind seemed to be on something else. "The house had been empty for two years when I bought it."

"Do you intend to keep it?"

"I don't know. I bought it on a whim. Unfortunately I didn't check to see how much it would cost to put everything back in working order. I'm afraid the only way I could support the ranch for the length of time it would take to build up a herd would be to go back to prospecting."

"What about the cows we saw on the way in?' "

"I don't know. I mean to ask Ward about that as soon as I can."

They pulled up in front of the barn, and a thin, whipcord of a man ambled out of its shady depths. He wore his ill-fitting clothes with complete unconcern, but Victoria noticed they were clean and the man freshly shaved. Near-white hair showed from under his hat. He hooked calloused hands, the color of old leather, in his belt. A single glance at his face, and Victoria could tell he didn't know what to think of his boss showing up with a woman in tow.

"What are Ben's cows doing here?" Trinity asked without preamble.

"And a good morning to you," Ward said, a hint of a smile about his lips. "It's been right quiet around here. Too much work to do to go catting around. I trust you had a good journey."

"Okay, so I've got bad manners," Trinity said. The hint of a smile returned. "You knew that when you signed on, so don't go looking for any sudden improvement now."

"The house isn't in very good shape, ma'am, but it sure will get you out of the sun. I'd be mighty pleased to help you down."

"And I'd be mighty pleased to accept," Victoria replied, delighted to see that all of Trinity's friends seemed to treat him with complete disregard of his fearsome reputation. She would give a lot to see Buc's face if he could have seen Trinity wrestling with Ben just like they were fourteen-year-olds.

Trinity coaxed his horse between Victoria and Ward. "Nobody's going any place until you answer my question."

"I might as well tell him what he wants to know, ma'am, or he'll keep us out here until one of us gets a heatstroke. Seems he could ride through the frying pans of hell and not break a sweat, but I come all over dizzy if I stand in the sun too long."

"I must have come all over dizzy to have ever thought you'd make a foreman," Trinity said. "You're as bad as Ben. The pair of you could talk the ears off a donkey. What are his cows doing here?"

"Said he brung you them cows because you had no business saddling him with that much trouble. In the first place, he didn't want them. Too much work keeping them out of ravines, finding water, and running off rustlers and cougars."

"He should have sold them."

"Said that was too much trouble, too."

"So he walked them a few hundred miles across some of the worst desert in the country."

"Ben don't mind desert. Says he likes it right fine as long as it don't rain."

Trinity looked ready to wring his foreman's neck.

"I'll give him half the money when I sell them."

"He thought you might say that. Told me to tell you he'd open up a bank account in your name."

"I'll give it to him in cash."

"Said he'd bury it under your front steps."

Trinity broke out in laughter.

"I guess I have a herd. Now if I can just find the money to fix up the buildings."

"While you're looking for it, mind if I take the little lady in out of the sun?"

Trinity jumped down and helped Victoria dismount. "The little lady has a name. She's Victoria Davidge. And yes, she's the killer I went to bring back to Bandera to hang," he added when he saw the confusion in Ward's eyes, despite the amiable smile which remained in place. "I made a mistake. She's not guilty."

"So you brought her back here anyway?"

"She insisted."

Trinity laughed at Ward's incredulous look.

"Miss Davidge decided it was time to put an end to this unfortunate mess once and for all. She'll stay here while I look for a man who can prove she didn't kill her husband. Ben has already gone looking for him."

"Where'd he go?"

"Uvalde. I'm to meet him there in three days. He's looking for Chalk Gillet. Ever heard of him?"

"No, but then I wouldn't, not being curious as a female about every drifter between here and California."

"How's Diablo doing?"

"Mean as ever," Ward said. "See for yourself."

Trinity led Victoria inside the barn toward a stall at the back. The dark cool of the barn welcomed her. The familiar smell of hay and manure didn't offend her nostrils.

"Why do you keep your horses inside the barn? My father never did."

"We just keep Diablo inside. He's a stallion and insists on fighting every male horse he sees, stallion or gelding. He nearly killed a couple of cow ponies before I got him here."

A loud whistle made Victoria's ears hurt. A magnificent black stallion stood in the stall, angrily stamping his feet.

"Is he wild?"

"No, just angry. I won him from a gambler who had won him from some Eastern breeder. He nearly beat him to death before I got him. He'll let me put a saddle on him, but he goes crazy when anyone gets on his back."

"What are you going to do with him?"

"Tame him, I hope."

"If you can't?"

"Use him for stud. I could make a fortune selling his colts. Don't get too close. He bites."

"You wouldn't bite me, would you?" Victoria crooned to the horse. "I used to have a horse a lot like you. Only he loved for me to ride him. I rode him every day."

Trinity stood poised, ready to pull Victoria beyond reach of Diablo's teeth. Much to his surprise, Victoria's voice seemed to have a calming effect on him. She even put her hand through the bars. Diablo backed away, but he didn't attempt to savage her.

"You seem to have a way with horses," Trinity said. "He won't let anybody but me come that close without attacking."

"He's not mean," Victoria said as she stepped back from the stall. "He's just been badly treated. If you bring him along slowly, he ought to learn to trust you."

"That's what I'm doing," Trinity said, ushering her outside again, "but he responds to you better than anyone else. Maybe you can help me. It'll be something to keep you busy while I'm gone."

They hadn't discussed his leaving. His departure affected her in several ways which they hadn't discussed either. In fact, Victoria realized, they hadn't discussed anything at all. Except for the death sentence hanging over Victoria's head, they had talked only of things which meant little to either of them.

That would have to change. As long as he had been a cowboy drifting through, as long as he had been a bounty hunter taking her back to Bandera, what he was doing didn't really mean much to her. But all that changed along the way.

She knew she loved him. She knew she wanted to spend the rest of her life with him. She didn't know how he felt about her. She didn't know what he felt about marriage. He had never mentioned Queenie after that night. She didn't know if he could forget Queenie, and all the other emotions tied up with her, long enough to fall in love. She was afraid it might keep him from being able to settle down with any woman.

If only she knew how to fight Queenie's ghost.

She wasn't even sure Queenie's being dead would be enough. Trinity felt he had failed because he hadn't been able to punish her for her crime. If she were dead, she would still have escaped his vengeance. His load of guilt was so enormous and bitter, it had forced him to take up a profession he hated, to accept the reputation of a bounty hunter though he wasn't one, all in an attempt to exorcise the guilt that still rode him.

Victoria swore she would help him.

The house looked so much the same Victoria felt she had stepped back into the past.

"This is our furniture," she exclaimed upon entering the north parlor, known as the ladies' parlor. *Her* parlor. "I remember sitting here every Sunday waiting for Daddy to come down so we could go to church. The bank sold it with everything in it except the few things I took to the Tumbling T."

"The Daltons sold it the same way just to get rid of it."

"It wasn't lucky for your father either. Why did you really buy it?"

Trinity thought for a moment. "I suppose because it was the only place from our past my father could call his own. Bob Slocum still owns the Triple S. Our homestead on the Trinity got washed away by a spring flood, and there was no place in Colorado I wanted to call home."

"And now you don't know if you can keep it."

"Those cows will make a big difference, but I'm not worried about that now. First thing I have to do is find Chalk Gillet."

Victoria walked over to one of the windows. It looked north in the direction of San Antonio. "What are you going to do with me in the meantime?"

"You can stay here."

Victoria's heartbeat increased instantly. It was the one thing she wanted, and the one thing she'd been afraid to ask for.

"I figured you'd feel more easy in your mind if you were some place familiar. And of course I don't want Judge Blazer or the sheriff to know we're back. Not until I've found Gillet."

"Can I see the rest of the house?" she asked.

"Sure. I've got a few things to check on, but I imagine you'd rather see it by yourself anyway."

He was right. She felt like this was her home rather than his. It would take her a little while to accustom herself to the fact that all the familiar objects weren't hers any longer.

Yet, despite the weight of sadness, she felt like a young girl coming home after a long journey. She'd never missed the house until now, but now she wondered how she could have ever been content to live anywhere else.

The formal parlor, dining room, her father's office, and the kitchen looked like they always had. It was almost like she had never left.

The stair runner was more frayed and worn than she remembered. Maybe it was her imagination, but even the stair rail seemed to have been worn a little thinner. It wasn't her imagination that all the windows were in desperate need of a good cleaning. It was surprising any light got in at all. She doubted they had been touched since her father died.

Her father's room looked just the same as it always had, except that Trinity's things could be seen decorating the room. He was just as neat at home as he was on the trail. Everything appeared to have a precise place and to be in that place. Since she doubted Ward had ever straightened anything except a harness in his whole life, she assumed Trinity had done it.

Apparently he never left anything to chance. He had probably never lost anything in his life. No wonder he had been able to come up with the money to buy this ranch. There wasn't any gold in the world smart enough to hide from a man this organized.

She looked in the other bedrooms. A curtain here or there had been changed. Blankets, quilts, and bedspreads were new, but the furniture was the same.

She stepped into her old sitting room. It had been a luxury for a sixteen-year-old girl to have her own sitting room, but there had been so many rooms that her father had insisted. She had spent many happy hours here, planning her future, planning her wedding, looking forward to the fruitful years as a wife, mother, and lover.

She opened the door to her old room. It was empty, as empty as her dreams. All her furniture had gone with her to Blazer's Tumbling T. The Judge had wanted her to be surrounded by familiar things. He had wanted her to be happy.

He had wanted her to look forward to her marriage.

Now he wanted her dead.

Victoria closed the door. She would sleep in one of the guest rooms. It didn't matter which. The less she was reminded of the loss of her dreams, the better.

Trinity brought up the saddlebags containing her clothes. "Where do you want these?"

"Is anyone using the bedroom above the north parlor?"

"No."

"Then I'll take that room."

"The empty bedroom was yours?"

"Yes."

"What happened to your furniture?"

"I took it with me when I got married."

"Did you take the china and silverware, too?"

"No. Daddy sold it. He liked the Judge's much better."

She didn't even get to choose her own china and silverware, Trinity thought. They probably hadn't let her choose her linens either.

"I'm afraid there's not much here to make you comfortable. I wasn't here long before . . ."

"Before you went after me."

Trinity nodded.

"It's just as well. A person ought to live in a house for a while before he tries to furnish it. He needs to have time to discover its character."

"I thought the house was supposed to take its character from the owner."

"Most houses do, but not this one."

"This place has brought ruin to a lot of people."

"I think all men who suffer ruin have the seed within them long before it comes to flower. If a man doesn't want to be ruined, he won't be."

"Why do you say that?"

"Because of you."

Trinity looked nonplussed.

"Who had more reason to fail than you did? Who tried harder than you to fail? Yet it wasn't in you. You wanted to quit. You just didn't know how. You even tried to give away a herd of prize cattle and couldn't do it. You'll make something of this ranch just as you'll gentle that stallion."

Trinity didn't know what to say. He'd never had anyone show much faith in him. Most of the time, people said he was the luckiest man in the world to still be alive. Otherwise how would he have brought in eighteen wanted men and not gotten himself killed. Of course, they said the same thing when he found gold, though he'd never made anything but modest strikes. He only had enough gold to buy the ranch because he never drank it up, gambled it away, or spent it on women.

But in all these years, Victoria was the first person to see his success as anything but an accident.

"You may think differently when you take a look in the kitchen. There's hardly anything fit to eat, and it's too far to go to town."

"We have our supplies left."

"They're not fit to serve at a table."

"Maybe not, but I'd rather eat bacon and beans than go without supper."

"I think we can do a little better than that if you can figure out how to handle that stove."

"Is that big blue stove still here?" Victoria asked, remembering the many times she had helped their Spanish cook prepare meals.

"It's the biggest monster I've ever seen."

"Take everything to the kitchen. While Ward catches you up on what's been going on while you were away, I'll see about fixing dinner. Then I want a bath. Can I get someone to put a tub on the stove and fill it with water? It can heat while I cook. There used to be a copper bath upstairs. Do you know what happened to it?"

"No, but I'll find out."

Victoria had happy memories of this kitchen. Blue and white dominated the room, from the everyday china to the enameled finish of the stove to the oil cloth that covered the work table to the cloth which lined the shelves. There was even blue and white in the coarse rugs which covered the wooden floor. The sun had long ago bleached the irises from the curtains, but she could still see traces of the blue floral pattern. But the best part about the kitchen was the four huge windows which let in the outside world. Even in winter, they made her feel like a part of the vast open spaces.

By the time Victoria had gotten the fire going and started frying the bacon, Trinity had returned with a large tub which covered most of the stove top. Using the pump at the back steps, he proceeded to bring in bucket after bucket of water until it was full to the brim.

"Ward found the bathtub. Somebody has been using it as a water trough. He's washing it now."

Victoria quelled a shiver of disgust.

"Make sure he scrubs it out real good."

Trinity grinned. "He will."

"I hope he means to eat with us."

"He won't be here. I'm sending him to town. We need supplies if you're to stay here. The trip takes two days even with a couple of packhorses. You'll have to wait until tomorrow night to impress him with your cooking."

Victoria didn't have any thoughts to spare for her cooking. All she could think of was she and Trinity were going to be in the house alone for a whole night.

Dinner was tense, but it had nothing to do with the food or its preparation. The tension between them was even greater when Trinity helped her wash up. Now, as they sat in the stuffy, formal parlor, waiting to go to bed, it was worse than ever.

He sat across from her, uncomfortable on one of her mother's family's high backed sofas. He seemed very ill-at-ease in this setting of polished wood, velvet and candlelight. Even his clothes seemed slightly out of place.

Victoria's entire being concentrated on Trinity. Her skin felt so hypersensitive she was aware of each piece of her clothing, the texture of the material, how it swathed her body, the points of contact. Her nerves were strung tightly.

"I'll have to leave for Uvalde as soon as Ward gets back if I'm to meet Ben on time," Trinity said.

"When will you be back?" Why did he want to get away from her? He had spent the entire afternoon with Ward. He didn't come in until supper was on the table. Now he couldn't wait to leave for Uvalde.

"In a couple of days, I hope. It'll depend on how long it takes me to find Gillet. You don't have to be afraid the sheriff will find you. Ward can take care of you just as well as I can. As long as you don't go into town, nobody will ever know you're here. And if anything should happen, go to town and make the sheriff put you in jail. You'll be safe there until I get back."

"I'm not worried about that." She wanted to ask him why he found it so difficult to be close to her. She had tried during dinner. She had tried again as they washed dishes. She was trying now, but she couldn't get the words to pass her lips.

"If he's alive, I'll bring him back. I promise."

She wasn't even worried about Chalk. She had come to take it for granted Trinity would find him. She hadn't been afraid of hanging for some time now, probably not since that night in Ben's cabin. Something more important consumed her thoughts. What petrified her, what made her feel absolutely terrified, was the fear Trinity would disappear as soon as the threat to her life was lifted and she would never see him again.

She knew in her heart she could never love anyone else. No one else could ignite a fire in her merely by coming into the room. If he left her, she would always be alone no matter where she might be.

Knowing she would soon be free to go anywhere she liked should have made her happy. She should have been filled with plans and dreams for the future. Yet here she sat dreading the day she would be free. Then there would be no reason for Trinity to keep her with him, to protect her, to think of her all the time.

She didn't think she could stand that. For years she had lived in limbo, not knowing what life had to offer but knowing she couldn't take advantage of it if she had. Now she knew, and she had tasted just enough to know she couldn't live without it.

She had to know what kept Trinity away from her. She had to do everything in her power to change it.

"I know you'll bring Chalk back. I guess I've been taking that for granted."

"Even if I can't, your uncle is sure to find enough evidence to make the governor ask for a new trial."

"I know. For the first time in five years, I'm not afraid any more."

Not afraid of hanging, that is. If he left, she wouldn't have much to live for anyway.

"What are you going to do? Go back to Arizona?"

"What do you mean?" His question caught her off balance.

"Once you're free. You don't have any relatives here. I just assumed you'd go back to Arizona to live with your uncle."

"I wouldn't feel comfortable there, not with Buc."

"I guess you should go back to Alabama. You'd have a better chance of finding a husband there. You certainly can't stay here."

Victoria's gaze flew to Trinity's face. Was he making it plain he wanted her out of his house as soon as possible? He looked as nervous and uncomfortable as she felt. Was she so terrible he couldn't even spend one evening alone with her? Could a man be physically attracted to her and yet be repulsed at the same time?

"Why not?"

"I don't mean this house. I mean you can't live in Bandera, stay there as an unmarried woman. I suppose you could live with Judge Blazer, after all you are his daughter-in-law—"

"He'd never let me inside his house, not unless you find out who murdered Jeb. Besides, I don't want to go back there. It would remind me too much of the mistake I made."

She had given him a perfect opening. *Why didn't he say something? If he likes me at all, why can't he say so?*

"Don't plan the rest of your life just to avoid thinking of the mistakes you made."

"Is that what you would do?"

"It doesn't matter what I do."

"Why does it matter for me then?"

"You're a woman. You can't stay here without protection. There's always somebody like Red Beard around."

"I'll hire men to guard me."

"I forgot you were rich," Trinity said. He made it sound like something bad. "You can do anything you want."

He avoided her eyes. He squirmed in his seat. She was clearly making him miserable. She ought to let him make his escape, but she couldn't. She had to try once more.

"What do you think I ought to do?"

She couldn't understand his look. He looked like he wanted her so bad he could jump out of his skin, yet he seemed to be moving farther and farther away from her. She wouldn't be surprised to find he had actually backed his chair several feet across the room since they sat down.

"I think you ought to go back to Arizona. Or Alabama. You can't stay in Bandera."

Why? Because I'll be only a day's ride from you?

He stood up. "It's time I went to bed. It's a long way to Uvalde."

Suddenly she couldn't stand it any longer. Her pride didn't matter, not if she were going to lose the only thing she wanted. She had to know.

"What's wrong with me?"

Chapter Twenty-one

"What's wrong with you?" he repeated, perplexed. "I don't understand."

"Ever since that night in Ben's cabin you've stayed as far away from me as you can. Now you can't wait to leave for Uvalde. I know you want me. I can see it in your eyes."

Trinity didn't answer her. He just stared at her.

"It was the same with Jeb. He thought I was beautiful, too, but he never touched me." She stifled the sob which threatened to cut off her voice, but she couldn't stop the tears from welling up in her eyes.

"You mean . . ." Trinity couldn't find the words to finish the sentence.

"My husband never made love to me," Victoria finished for him. The tears flowed freely. "Just like you. What's wrong with me?"

Trinity covered the distance between them in the blink of an eye. He pulled Victoria out of her chair and into his arms.

"There's nothing wrong with you. You're the most beautiful woman I've ever seen. Jeb must have been crazy."

"Buc wouldn't touch me either. And you've been stumbling over yourself to keep as far away from me as you can."

"I've been practically sitting on my hands to keep from devouring you."

"No you haven't. You kept Ben between you and me as long as you could. This afternoon it was Ward and that horse. Now you want to go to bed. Tomorrow you're leaving for Uvalde.

Why are you always running away from me?"

"Running away?" Trinity looked dumbfounded by her interpretation of his behavior. "It's been all I could do to keep from telling Ben to go to hell and making love to you at least once every hour."

"Then why haven't you?"

"Because I love you. I love you so much it's driving me crazy, but I didn't think you could ever forgive me for what I've done to you. I can't expect a woman to love her jailer."

"Is that all?" Victoria asked, afraid she couldn't stand the swelling happiness inside her.

"Is that all?" Trinity repeated incredulously.

"I don't think of you as my jailer," Victoria assured him through tears of happiness. "You were always my protector. Even in the beginning, I always felt like your prize rather than your prisoner. I knew you wouldn't desert me once we reached Bandera."

"You don't hate me for what I did?"

Victoria shook her head.

"You forgive me for wanting to shoot your uncle?"

She nodded her head.

"Why?"

"Because I love you. And a woman will forgive the man she loves just about anything."

"You love me?" Trinity looked stunned, helpless. If Red Beard could have found him just then, he'd have been a goner. *"You* love *me?"*

"Yes. I don't know when it happened, I suppose it started the moment I saw you, but I don't think I'll ever forgive Ben for coming back that night."

"You *wanted* me to make love to you?"

"Yes."

"Even though you knew I still had to turn you over to the sheriff?"

"Yes."

"Do you know what you're saying?"

"I've known what I wanted to say for days now. I was just afraid to say it. I love you, Trinity Smith. I know why you came to Mountain Valley Ranch, and it doesn't matter. I can't regret that you came after me, not when I know otherwise I'd never have been able to fall in love with you."

"But you wouldn't want to marry me."

"Why not?"

"I don't have anything but this broken-down ranch and a terrible reputation."

"I married a man because he was rich and well-liked. I'll never make that mistake again. I'd marry you if you had nothing but Ben's cabin. I'd marry you even if you didn't have that much."

"But you're a wealthy woman."

"At the moment I'm poorer than you are. I'd be marrying above myself."

"You really mean it?" Trinity asked.

"Yes, but I do have one question."

She felt Trinity stiffen.

"Can you forget Queenie long enough for me to prove all women aren't like her?"

Some of the excitement seemed to leave Trinity. "I don't suppose I'll ever forget her, but it's not just Queenie that's bothering me. It's what I did. Do you think you can love a man with a ghost in his past?"

"A whole flock of ghosts, as long as I'm the only woman in your future."

He still seemed unable to believe her. "What will your uncle say?"

"All my life other people have made decisions for me: where I would live, who I could see, who I would marry. Most of them have been wrong. I'm going to do the deciding from now on, and my first decision is that I love you and I want to be your wife. Will you marry me?"

She couldn't believe she said that. Women didn't say such things. Men didn't expect it. They didn't like it either. Victoria held her breath, afraid Trinity would back away.

Trinity's happy grin relieved her mind almost immediately. "Yes," he said, picking her up and swinging her around in a circle. "Just as soon as I find Gillet."

"You're sure?"

"I've never been more sure of anything in my life."

"Then prove it."

Trinity just looked at her.

"You said you loved me, that there was nothing wrong with me, that you'd been trying to keep your hands off me for days. Prove it."

For an instant, he looked like he might refuse, and Victoria's heart sank. But before she could take a deep breath, Trinity swept her up in his arms and headed for the stairs at a run.

"Watch out, you'll fall," she warned, a laugh in her voice, when he caught his foot on the hall runner.

"I'm not giving you a chance to change your mind," he said, taking the steps two at a time.

But he did pause after he set her down on the bed. Victoria's heart beat faster as he sat down next to her, gathered her in his arms, and rested his cheek against her hair.

"I've thought of making love to you for weeks," he said. "You've had me so distracted I wasn't sure I could keep my mind on business long enough to get you here in one piece. If Ben hadn't been with us, I might not have."

"When did you know you loved me?" Victoria asked. She didn't care about Ben, and she didn't care about business. She just wanted the reassurance he loved her. She wanted to hear him say the words over and over again.

"That night in Ben's cabin."

"Why didn't you say anything?"

Trinity held her away from him so he could look into her eyes.

"I was the man who had taken you from the safety of your uncle's ranch and was returning you to Texas to be hanged. I had shot the man who rescued you. I was a bounty hunter. What could I expect you to do but spit in my face?"

"You could have told me how you felt."

"I might have if Ben hadn't come home. I don't think I would have been able to stop myself after you kissed me back, but I had myself under control by the next morning."

"Were you going to say anything the next day?"

"No, you acted like nothing had happened. I figured you'd been too sleepy to know what was happening. And too ashamed if you did."

Victoria took Trinity's face in her hands and pulled him to her until they were nearly nose to nose. "I remember every second of that night. I've relived it time and time again. I've prayed it wouldn't be the only time you wanted to make love to me."

"I'll always want to make love to you," Trinity whispered, "even if I grow too old to stand up or too blind to see."

He kissed her gently, but Victoria's kiss was hard and insistent. She wanted no gentle wooing. She wanted Trinity to convince her he loved her and wanted her with a desperation equal to her own. He could woo her tomorrow. Tonight she wanted to be swept away on a wave of passion.

Victoria put her arms around Trinity's neck and drew him to her. She didn't want to let him go. She wanted to be part of him. She wanted to feel the pressure of his lips on hers, feel her breasts pressed against his chest, feel the length of his body intertwined with hers. After so many years of wondering about love, she wanted to *know* he wanted her. She wanted to be so convinced she could never doubt it again.

Victoria fell back on the bed, pulling Trinity over with her. He tried to kiss her nose, to brush her eyelids, to nibble her ears. She wanted him to make love to her breasts. Even now she burned with the memory of his lips on her nipples. She pressed herself against him, trying to satisfy her urgent need of him.

"Make love to me," she whispered. "Now."

Trinity didn't need to be asked twice. Within seconds he had unbuttoned her gown and slipped it from under her. Her camisole took even less time. Soon Victoria lay bared to his vision. For a sliver of a moment, she felt uncertain. If she allowed him to make love to her tonight, she couldn't undo it tomorrow.

Then she felt his tongue touch the aching nipple, his lips bathe it in their warmth, suck it gently, and her body exploded with a symphony of sensations unlike anything she had ever anticipated. Her hands gripped the bed on either side of her as her body rose in an arch. When he began to massage her second breast with his fingertips, she collapsed on the bed and pulled his head against her as hard as she could.

She writhed beneath his touch, gasping for breath, groaning before each new assault on her sensibilities, welcoming each new salvo of sensations as a confirmation that Trinity did indeed love her.

Trinity's attention to her breast soon brought them to the point of painful sensitivity. He changed to a gentle brushing with his lips and the end of his tongue while his fingers searched out the mound between her thighs.

Victoria had never anticipated anything of such magnitude. As Trinity probed the moisture of her heat, she cried out, her body out of control. She drove herself upon his hand, wanting his touch, aching for it, needing it deeper and deeper inside her. She was beyond being aware of what he did, only of its effect on her.

She cried out a second time when he withdrew his hand even though he continued to torture her breasts with his lips and tongue. She craved his touch between her thighs. It was there the fire burned out of control. The center of her need lay there.

As he moved above her, Victoria felt Trinity's fingers invade her once again. She felt him open her wide, felt him stretch her still wider as he entered her. Then he stopped. She urged him on, but he remained poised above her. Without hesitation, Victoria threw herself against him. The stab of pain shocked her, but it faded almost immediately as Trinity sank deep into her welcoming warmth.

Victoria moaned and rose to meet him, hoping to drive him deeper until he reached the core of her need. She felt deserted when he withdrew and ecstatic when he drove into her again. Trinity covered her mouth, face, neck, and shoulders with kisses as he drove into her with increasing speed.

Sensations rose in waves, each one more powerful, each one pulling her deeper into its current. She clung to him, matching him stroke for stroke, gasping breath for gasping breath.

Just as she thought she could stand no more, she felt Trinity go rigid, felt his rhythm become uneven. Then as the last wave burst over her, she felt him explode inside her.

Trinity took a deep breath and allowed his racing heart to slow down. He wanted to kick himself. He hadn't meant to consume Victoria like a prairie fire. He had had too many women for no other reason than to slake the animal need in his loins. He had wanted it to be different with her. How could she believe he loved her when he couldn't take the time to make love to her? All he could think of was his own galloping obsession. The weeks of wanting her, the days of riding at her side, the nights of laying awake knowing she slept only a few feet away had all proved too much. Once he let the barriers down just a little bit, the backlog of passion swept him away in a flood of desire.

"Is it always like that?" Victoria asked.

"I don't know," Trinity replied. "I've never been with anyone I wanted to please. I always thought just of myself."

"Didn't you think of me then?"

"Yes, but not like I wanted to. I thought about you so long, I couldn't hold back. I'm sorry."

"You mean it can be better?"

"Yes."

"How much?"

"A lot."

Victoria was silent for a moment. "I don't think I could stand it."

"I know it hurt, but it won't next time."

"I don't mean that. I mean I don't think I could stand for it to be any better. I thought I was going to die."

Trinity rolled up on his elbow. "You mean it?"

"I mean it."

Trinity kissed her. "It was the best for me, too."

"Better than all those other women?"

"Do you remember the night I massaged your muscles?" Trinity asked. Victoria nodded. "I found out then just being near you, touching you, being able to do something for you was better than anything I'd ever experienced before. It was the best because I was with you. It'll only get better because next time I'll try to find out what pleases you."

Victoria wanted to cry with happiness. She put her arms around his neck and pulled him to her. "You can't know what it's like to spend five years wondering why your husband never touched you. Why Buc insisted he loved me but didn't try to kiss me. Why you wanted me but seemed relieved to have Ben travel with us. I was so afraid there was something wrong with me."

A horrible fear assailed Trinity. "You weren't using me just to prove there was nothing wrong with you, were you?"

Victoria looked puzzled at first but laughed in understanding.

"If you mean am I going to throw you over now that I know everything about me works right, the answer is definitely no. I've spent a great deal of time during the last weeks convincing you I was innocent. Now that I have, I don't intend to waste any of this newfound faith in me. I intend to make you marry me and protect me from the Red Beards of this world for the rest of my life."

Trinity sobered. "You realize I have more enemies than you do. The families of some of the men I've taken in would love to see me dead."

"Then I guess I'll have to protect you," Victoria said. "But you've got to promise to love me first."

"I'll love you for the rest of my life. I never thought I could love anyone like I love you."

Victoria's eyes filled with tears.

"I guess I can't ask for any more than that. Just love me the best you can, and I'll be satisfied."

Trinity made love to Victoria again. Only now he took all the time he wanted to explore her body, to search out the places which affected her the most, to find the little touches which deepened her pleasure. He ignored her protests that he was torturing her beyond the limits of the human body. He turned a deaf ear to her pleas that he put out the fire that raged inside before it consumed her.

In the process of seeking to bring Victoria to her most exquisite fulfillment, he discovered that despite his experience, he had never known a thing about love until this moment.

Victoria leaned against the corral fence as she watched Diablo stretch his legs in the confined space. Since Trinity left, she had spent every minute of her time with the horse, talking to him, feeding him, currying him, anything to forget Trinity's absence.

He had made love to her once more when they awoke, and her body still hummed with contentment. She was a happy woman. No longer did she worry that no one would ever make love to her. Trinity had convinced her that whatever the reason Buc and Jeb had kept their distance, it hadn't been her fault.

She tried not to remember too many details. It made her blush, especially when she remembered how she had begged him to make love to her. She knew nothing about what other women did, but she did know a man expected to take the lead. Yet Trinity hadn't seemed to mind. He had responded to her entreaty with satisfying vigor.

"Satisfying vigor" described a lot of things about him, as a man and as a lover. In fact, the more she learned about him, the more satisfying he became in her eyes. The faults which she once saw in him were now attributable to a determination to do a distasteful job, a task taken on for an even more laudable reason.

The reason was good enough for Victoria to forgive him for having catapulted her into this mess in the first place. But it would all be over as soon as he returned with Chalk Gillet. They might never be able to find out who killed Jeb, but at least she would be able to prove she didn't.

As certain as Victoria was that Trinity would be successful, she couldn't ignore the possibility that Chalk was dead. There had to be a reason no one had seen him since that night. He might even have seen the killer. Either someone paid him to leave, he left because he was afraid of the killer, or the killer decided letting Chalk live was a risk he couldn't take.

As certain as Victoria was that Trinity could do anything he set his mind to, she knew he couldn't bring Chalk back from the grave. Without his testimony, she would still be a condemned criminal awaiting execution.

Even if Trinity refused to let her face her sentence, she would always be a fugitive from justice. She would have to go back to living like she did in Arizona, looking over her shoulder for the rest of her life.

Victoria didn't think she could stand that, not after envisioning her life as Trinity's wife. Though he'd accepted her proposal, he hadn't *asked* her to marry him. There were too many things in his own mind he hadn't faced yet, but he would either by himself or with her help. She still didn't know how to help him erase feeling responsible for his father's death, but she'd figure that out, too. If only she could live!

She could recall thinking life a burden, of wishing it could somehow be over. But now nothing was more precious to her than the chance to spend her life with Trinity, to bear his children, to share his happiness and success, to comfort him when he hurt inside and didn't want anybody else to know. Everything she ever wanted from life was tied up in that man.

Such a priceless gift, an opportunity which should have been hers by right, and this monstrous miscarriage of justice stood between them.

"He's a lot like you," she said to Diablo as he approached the fence hesitantly, one step at a time, to take the sugar in her hand. "You're mad because someone hurt you, and you're determined to take it out on everybody. He's mad at himself and can't forgive himself. Both of you have got to realize it was something you couldn't help. You couldn't have done anything to prevent it. You've got to forget it, or it'll ruin the rest of your life."

"You always talk to horses, ma'am?" Ward asked. Victoria hadn't heard him come up. He had brought the bridle and saddle she wanted.

"Lots of times it's easier to say what you mean to an animal than a person."

"It's always easier if you're talking about Trinity, and I know you are."

"You ever try to tell him anything?"

"All the time. I told him not to come back to Texas. I told him not to buy this place. I told him to get rid of that horse."

"No wonder he doesn't listen to you," Victoria said. "You give terrible advice."

"I should have known you'd think that way."

"Why?"

"You agreed to come back to Texas knowing Blazer wanted to hang you."

Victoria laughed in spite of herself. "It does sound a little crazy. But even though it was the right thing to do, I didn't really have much choice. So I can't take credit for that decision."

"Well you think this devil can be gentled, and that makes you crazy in my book."

"We'll see. Trinity believes he just needs to know he's not going to be hurt anymore. Will you help me saddle him?"

"Not if you mean to ride him. Trinity would have my neck."

"I'm not going to ride him. I just want to see how he takes the saddle."

"He takes it all right, but his eyes turn white all around the edges. It gets so there's almost no color at all. When you hop in the saddle, he tries to kill you."

"I promised Trinity I wouldn't try to ride him, but I am going to try to convince him I'm not going to hurt him."

"You're wasting your time. I don't know what happened to him, but it's one lesson he's never going to forget."

"Is that how you feel about Trinity?"

Ward looked her square in the eye. "Yes, ma'am, it is. Something inside him got all tore up. I don't say it ain't possible for you to fix it up a little, but I don't see how you're going to do it from the end of a rope."

The unpleasant reminder of what awaited her in Bandera dampened Victoria's enthusiasm.

"Take down the bars. Trinity is going to find Chalk and prove I didn't kill Jeb."

"I hope so, but if I was you, I'd be looking about for another line of defense."

"Like what?"

"Like who did kill him."

"You don't think I did?"

"Trinity has gone after nineteen people. He took eighteen of them in. He wouldn't have brought you here, even if he was so nutty on you he couldn't think straight, unless he knew you didn't do it. Whatever Trinity thinks is good enough for me."

Victoria stepped across the lowered bars to cover her misty-eyed response to Ward's vote of confidence. "Hand me the bridle."

"You be real careful. Just because that Devil's always let Trinity saddle him don't mean he can't change his mind."

Speaking softly and in a steady, singsong rhythm, Victoria held out her hand with more sugar in the palm. Diablo took the sugar and stood calmly while she pulled the bridle over his ears. He didn't even seem to mind the bit.

"Somebody trained him very well."

"You only have to look at the scars to see why he forgot his lessons."

Victoria couldn't stand to look at the unsightly swath of scar tissue on Diablo's flanks. It was inconceivable to her that anyone could use spurs on a horse until his sides were torn and bleeding. As she spread the blanket over his broad back, she could feel his muscle begin to quiver. She stepped back far enough to look into his eyes. Sure enough, the pupils had begun to shrink in size. He stood perfectly still, but his eyes were the eyes of a dangerous animal.

"You'll have to put the saddle on him. I can't lift it," Victoria said. "For years I tried to figure out who might have killed Jeb, but everybody who had a reason was somewhere else. He must have gotten into trouble with somebody I didn't know about."

Ward dropped the saddle on Diablo's back. Victoria reached for the cinch.

"I wouldn't cinch him too tight if I were you," Ward warned. "It makes him kick."

"Okay. I just want him to wear the saddle for a couple of hours. If nobody rides him, maybe he'll begin to forget what happened."

After a look at his eyes, Victoria wondered if Diablo would ever forget. He watched her now with nearly white eyes; his pupils were tiny pinpoints. It gave her the shivers.

"If I was you, I'd forget about him. You got enough things on your mind without worrying about this crazy horse," Ward grumbled.

But for the next two days Victoria continued to worry about the horse. It did no good to worry about the other things on her mind. She couldn't do anything about them—not until Trinity got back.

Victoria watched Diablo from the shade of three huge pecan trees planted so they would shade one side of the barn and the corner of the corral from the blazing afternoon sun.

This was the third day she had put the saddle on him, and this morning his eyes hardly changed at all. In fact, after about half an hour, they seemed to have gone back to normal.

She sat on a bench built around the trunk of one of the trees. She ought to go up to the house and fix supper (she'd already learned she couldn't eat a thing if Ward did the cooking), but she wanted to be alone. She knew she shouldn't be. The minute she was alone, she started thinking about Trinity, and there was no point in that. Everything had to wait until he returned.

It did no good to feel love, anger, impatience, anxiety . . . anything . . . until he returned. She had spent the days since he left trying to turn off her emotions. She hadn't been very successful, especially at night.

Maybe she would be more successful tonight. Ward had promised to take her out to see the horses Trinity was so proud of. He kept them in a canyon not far from the ranch. As much as on cows, the future of the Demon D depended on those horses.

And Diablo.

She leaned back against the tree. After being awake most of the night, she felt sleepy. The warmth of the sun only made it worse. There was no reason to stay awake. Sleep would make the long hours pass more quickly.

Victoria tossed restlessly in the bed. Trinity had been away for three nights and she hadn't been able to sleep yet. She wished she hadn't taken that nap under the pecan trees, but she had been so tired she couldn't keep her eyes open. Now she couldn't get them to close.

She got out of bed. She had decided to sleep in Trinity's room tonight in hopes it would make her sleep better. It hadn't. It only made her think of the times he had made love to her. After a few minutes of remembering the wonderful things he had done to her body, she started to tremble with a need only Trinity could satisfy. She wouldn't get anywhere staying in bed; it would only get worse.

It didn't matter if she didn't get dressed before going downstairs. Ward slept in the barn. She had the house to herself. She didn't light a lamp. She didn't need one. She remembered every foot of the house. Besides, a full moon made it almost as bright as daylight outside.

She looked across the plain to the north, toward Bandera. It was just a little backward town, yet it held the key to the rest of her life. Most of the people who came to Jeb's parties lived in Bandera. She had never liked those people or that town at all.

She ambled down the steps. The hall was sunk in deep shadow, but Victoria reached the kitchen without bumping into anything. She didn't want anything to eat. She didn't want any coffee, but she did want some cool water. She would use the pump on the back porch. The water in the kitchen jug would be tepid after the day's heat.

Victoria's hand had closed over the doorknob when the sight of three men, running across the moonlit expanse of yard between the house and the barn, made her freeze. Through the open window she could just barely hear the scrape of their boots on the hard-packed ground.

She stood, frozen with fear. Who could know she was here?

Nobody, you fool, she told herself, trying to calm her fears. *They're probably after Trinity. It's got nothing to do with you.* But it didn't work. Suppose they were after her? She was all alone. If they took her away, no one would even know what happened to her. She tried to tell herself they couldn't possibly know she wasn't still in Arizona, but the fear wouldn't go away. She had lived with it so long it seemed a constant companion . . . except when Trinity was with her.

Just before they reached the shadows cast by the trees which shaded the kitchen, one of the men veered. He was headed for the front of the house. She was cut off.

Victoria drew back from the window as the two other men paused at the kitchen steps.

"We got to wait a minute so Johnny can reach the front door," one of them whispered. "We'll go in the back the same time he goes in the front." He very carefully tried the door-knob. "It's unlocked. Good. I wasn't looking forward to crawling in the window."

"Suppose he's in there," the other man whispered. "He can shoot a man through the heart before he can touch his gun."

"He's gone. I've been watching the house practically every minute since he got here. There's nobody else here but the old man. She's in there by herself most likely sleeping like a baby. It'll be real easy to slip in and carry her off without anybody knowing."

"The old man in the barn will know."

"He's not going to know who we are or where we've taken her, not with him being out cold."

"I still don't like it."

"Then stay here. Johnny and I will go inside and get her."

"Hell, no! I ain't giving you any excuse to tell your ma I didn't do my part. I'm scared to death of her."

Something about the voice sounded familiar, but it was impossible to identify the whispered sound. Besides, they sounded like boys. What would boys be doing coming after her? Was this some sort of prank? Something they were doing on a dare?

No. They had knocked Ward out so he couldn't interfere. This was no prank. They meant to kidnap her.

As she searched frantically for a way to escape, Victoria wondered what it was about her that seemed to invite kidnapping. Whatever it was, she didn't mean for it to happen again. She had had enough of being forcibly carried off.

"You ready?" the voice asked.

Victoria froze. The boy had forgotten to whisper. It was Kirby Blazer. He'd grown up and his voice had deepened, but she'd recognize that peculiar accent anywhere. A German family had kept him as a child, and he'd learned to speak German before he learned English.

What could Kirby want with her? How did he know she was here? What did Myra want with her? Myra always maintained her belief in Victoria's innocence, but Myra's support hadn't done her any good, not with the Judge wanting her dead.

But Victoria didn't have time to ask herself a lot of questions. She could hear someone, Johnny she presumed, turning the front doorknob. She heard Kirby order his companion to keep close behind him and be careful not to bump into anything.

They were nearly in the house!

Chapter Twenty-two

She had to get out of the house before they caught her. She dashed into the hall, but just as she turned toward the stairs, Johnny came through the front door. He would see her; she was trapped.

Victoria dashed for the only open door in the dim hall, her old sitting room. Her bare feet made no sound on the thick carpet. She pressed herself against the wall just behind the door. She held her breath for fear they could hear her. Her heart pounded in her ears.

How could they possibly know she was at the Demon D? They hadn't met anyone coming in. She knew Ward wouldn't have said anything when he went into town. It was almost like there was a network of spies surrounding her.

She had to think. There was no way to tell why they were here, but it couldn't be in her favor. If it were, they would have waited for Trinity to take her to town, or brought a lawyer with them, or brought the sheriff. They wouldn't have decided to break into the house.

She was in danger. It didn't matter that she didn't know what kind, she just needed to know what to do.

She couldn't find Trinity. He was too far away. She couldn't depend on Ward. There was nobody else who could help her. She could hide, but where? There was no place in the house. The barn! Maybe they wouldn't go there again.

The three men met in the hall, their footsteps muffled by the carpet.

"I don't like this," one said, his voice young and peevish. "It ain't right to go breaking into people's houses when they ain't home."

"We don't want anything except Victoria. I'll leave him the money Ma gave me. He ought to be glad to get rid of her. Save him the trouble of going all the way to Bandera."

This wasn't a bounty. It had to be a bribe, to keep him quiet. Even if it hadn't been coming from Myra, Trinity wouldn't accept a bounty. He wouldn't accept a bribe, either.

"I still don't like it."

"Then stay here. It doesn't make any difference to me."

But he didn't hang back. They climbed the steps one after the other. Victoria dashed back into the hall and to the kitchen. Not wanting to take a chance the hinges would squeak and alert the boys upstairs, she climbed through the open window and dropped to the ground outside. She had only a few seconds before they searched all the bedrooms and realized she wasn't there.

Could she make it to the barn without being seen? Not if one of them happened to look out the window. There was no cover, no gully or ravine she could drop into, only the flat hard ground flooded with bright moonlight.

Victoria headed toward the barn at a dead run. She was glad she was barefoot, but the night breeze cutting through her nightgown reminded her that she was practically naked. She made it halfway across the yard much faster than she'd ever thought possible. If she could just make it to the barn before anybody saw her. She was so close . . . only a few more seconds.

"Hey, Kirby, there's some gal heading toward the barn at a gallop," one of the boys yelled from the upstairs window.

If she ever saw that boy again, she'd give him a set of scratches that would make Trinity's pale by comparison.

She dashed inside the barn, but she knew they'd be after her in seconds. She found Ward lying just inside the door to the tack room. He'd put up a fight, but there had been too many of them. She took precious seconds to stoop down and untie his hands, but he was out cold. She was on her own. There was no one to help her. There was no place to hide. What could she do?

Diablo! He was her only chance—if he would only let her ride him. She didn't have time for a saddle or bridle. She opened the stall door, led him out, and took a firm hold on his mane.

"If you're ever going to forgive and forget, please do it now," Victoria pleaded. "You're my only hope."

Using the open stall door, Victoria vaulted on to his back.

She would never have stayed on his back if Diablo hadn't been more interested in the sound of the approaching footsteps than he was in this harmless woman he'd seen for hours each day. She had hardly gotten her balance when she felt Diablo's muscles gather. He would explode any minute.

"There she is," Kirby hollered as the boys reached the open barn door. "Don't let that horse get out."

Apparently the sight of three men running toward him, shouting at him, changed Diablo's mind about bucking. With a scream of fury, he bore down on the boys with bared teeth.

They flew out of his way like released springs.

Victoria had ridden all her life, but she had never ridden a crazy wild horse bareback without even a bridle to guide him. She didn't know what he might do or where he might go.

Diablo had hardly gone twenty yards before she felt him veer to the left. He was going back. He was going to attack the boys again. If he did, she'd never be able to stay on his back. If he did, they might shoot him.

"No!" Victoria screamed as she brought her open palm down on his withers. Diablo spun around so fast Victoria nearly fell off. He half reared. She only stayed on because of her death grip on his mane.

"After her before she gets away," Kirby yelled as the three scattered for their horses.

Diablo continued to twist and buck, caught between a desire to get rid of the human clinging to his back and the desire to run down the men on foot. Victoria was helpless.

301

Someone fired over their heads. Victoria never knew who it was, but the sound of gunfire cleared away Diablo's confusion. Whirling about, he headed for the nearest horse at a gallop.

He intended to attack both horse and rider.

Once more Victoria screamed and brought her open palm down on his withers. With a scream of rage, Diablo shot past the horse and straight toward the corral fence. Victoria had never jumped before. She held on and prayed.

Diablo took the fence with the ease of an antelope, and headed for the far side of the corral.

"Cut them off," Kirby yelled. "She's getting away."

They were closing in on her from two sides, and a second fence separated her and Diablo from freedom, but no one suspected Diablo's speed. He jumped the second fence as easily as the first and headed toward the open prairie. Even though the other horses had a shorter distance to run, he shot out of the trap like an unleashed thunderbolt. In seconds he doubled the distance between Victoria and her pursuers. A few more seconds, and it had doubled again. In a minute he was beyond the range of their guns.

Victoria's relief was short-lived. She had gotten away, but what could she do now? Where could she go? There wasn't anybody who would protect her. Her uncle couldn't possibly have arrived yet.

What would Trinity do? He gets out of trouble all the time. Think of what he would do.

He had told her to go to the sheriff and ask him to put her in jail. They couldn't hang her right away, not when she told them Trinity was bringing proof she hadn't killed Jeb. No matter what Judge Blazer said, they'd have to wait until Trinity got back.

She pulled on Diablo's mane. They had a long ride ahead, and she wanted to conserve his energy. She was confident Kirby and his friends wouldn't catch up. Not only had their horses already made the long trip, they weren't nearly as fast as Diablo. But if Kirby knew she was at the ranch, someone else might also know. She might have to make another run for it, and she didn't want Diablo to exhaust himself now.

Diablo resisted at first, but he gradually slowed down until he reached a canter. He was blowing a little at first, and that worried Victoria until she realized it was temper. After a little while longer, he relaxed into an easy canter. Keeping him locked up in the corral hadn't helped his condition, but he was fully rested. They ought to have no trouble reaching Bandera ahead of any pursuers.

Victoria entered through the back of the jail. Even though it was four o'clock in the morning, she hadn't dared ride down the main street in her nightgown. Sheriff Wylie Sprague came out of his bed with a flying leap when he saw her. His jaw dropped when he realized who she was. Victoria didn't give him a chance to say a word.

"I'm Victoria Davidge, and I've come back to prove I didn't kill Jeb Blazer. I've got a man coming with the proof in a couple of days. I've also got a lawyer coming to handle the retrial and a detective to find out who did kill Jeb.".

"What the hell are you doing here in your nightgown?" Sprague demanded, too staggered at the sight of a nearly naked woman in his jail. "If the Judge finds out you're here, he'll order a hanging before sundown."

"Then I suggest you don't tell him I'm here. My uncle has a stay of execution from the governor. If I'm not alive when he gets here, the Judge will hang for murder. And you'll hang right beside him."

Victoria hoped she had lied convincingly. That threat might be the only thing that would keep Judge Blazer from hanging her.

The sheriff swallowed. She could tell the whole situation had taken him by surprise. He wasn't ready to deal with such a complicated and delicate problem, but he knew something didn't smell quite right.

"Don't tell me you came here to sit quietly and wait for all these people to get here. You've been hiding somewhere. Why aren't you still there?"

"I was supposed to stay at the Demon D until everybody got here, but somehow Myra Blazer found out where I was. She sent Kirby and two other men to kidnap me."

"What did they want with you?"

"I don't know."

"But Myra and Kirby never believed you did it. They said so."

"I know that, but Trinity said I wasn't to go anywhere with anyone. They were going to take me away. I heard Kirby say so. They're probably behind me right now."

"What do you want me to do?"

"Keep me here in the jail until Trinity and my uncle get back."

"But if Blazer orders me to hang you—"

"The Judge can't hang me. Just you."

"But if Trinity doesn't have proof."

"He has it already. It's just going to take him a day or two to get here. If you don't believe me, go out to the Demon D and ask Ward Baldwin."

That name seemed to clinch it for the sheriff.

"You're lucky. The Judge is away in Austin. I'll keep you here until he gets back, but they'd all better be here by then. Otherwise I'm washing my hands of the whole business."

"You can't," Victoria said, so relieved she could hardly keep up the pressure on the sheriff. "From now on, you're responsible for everything that happens to me."

"Well the first thing I'm going to do is get you some clothes. If the ladies of this town ever find out I had a woman in my jail dressed like you, I'd be out of a job in ten minutes."

A few minutes later, dressed in a shirt and a pair of pants much too large for her, Victoria stretched out on the cot on the same cell where she had stayed five years earlier and watched the scaffold go up outside her window. She never thought she'd be glad to be inside a jail again, but she felt safe. Either Ward or Trinity would find out where she was, she needn't worry about sending a note. With Diablo guarding the rear of the jail, Ward would soon know where she was.

"You fool!" Myra glared at her son out of red, catlike eyes. "Three of you, and you can't even capture one girl. I can't trust you to do even the simplest thing."

Even in her son's eyes, Myra Winslow Blazer was a great beauty. Her features were classically perfect, but Myra's strong personality kept her beauty from being merely insipid. Though into her late thirties, her hair was the color of ebony silk. It grew in such profusion and to such a length it took her maid nearly thirty minutes each day to dress it atop her head. She had flawless skin, a generous mouth, and eyes which seemed to turn every color in the rainbow depending on her mood.

There was a timelessness about Myra's beauty and a forcefulness about her personality which never failed to subdue even the strongest male resistance. Over the years she had become accustomed to getting what she wanted, exactly what she wanted.

A woman of considerable property in her own right, she had achieved great wealth when she married Judge Blazer seven years earlier.

She kept a San Antonio seamstress and two assistants busy around the clock making gowns fashioned after the latest Paris designs. She wore enough jewels at her throat, in her hair, on her arms, and across her bosom to ransom a king. The house the Judge had built for her was spectacular even by Texas standards, but her bedroom was worthy of a Vanderbilt. A Louis the Sixteenth bed with a silk canopy dominated the enormous room. Gilt and velvet-upholstered furniture, red silk hangings, and an Aubusson carpet completed a room completely at variance with the rough and ready spirit of Texas.

"I keep telling you, I never saw a horse run like that," Kirby replied. "We might as well have been riding jackasses."

"At least you would have been appropriately mounted," she

305

snapped. Even in anger, Myra looked like a goddess. "Why did you let her reach the horse? Can she run faster than you?"

"I couldn't just bust into that house. He could have been inside. He'd have been within his rights to shoot me. She must have seen us coming and run out the back just as we went in the front. We thought we had her, but that horse jumped the fence like it had wings."

"Enough of this miraculous horse. You have bungled a perfectly simple job. Now I shall have to think of something else."

"Why is it so important for you to see Victoria?" Kirby asked. "You never liked her much."

"Because, you idiot, if Victoria has come back, it's only to prove she didn't kill Jeb."

"But you never thought she did."

"I know that, but as long as the Judge was convinced she did it, it didn't matter what I said. Now it will."

"I don't understand. If she can prove she didn't do it, you ought to be happy."

"If she didn't kill Jeb, you innocent fool, that means somebody else did."

"So?"

"So you and I have the most to gain by Jeb's death. We have the best motives. Even if they can't find any evidence, the Judge can't help but wonder. He might even decide to divorce me. I can't allow that."

"But we have alibis."

"We could have hired someone else."

"But we didn't kill Jeb."

"Apparently neither did Victoria, but they convicted her anyway."

"You mean they could convict us without evidence?"

"That's exactly what I mean."

"But what good would it do to bring Victoria here?"

"If she never tells her story, everything will stay just the way it is now."

"But why would she agree to keep quiet?"

"I don't imagine she will. Otherwise, why would she have left Arizona?"

"Then what are you going to do?"

"We've got to fix it so this can never happen again."

"But you can't mean to—"

"That's exactly what I mean to do."

It was a seedy hotel in a seedy town, but then Trinity expected that. It was nearly noon, not yet time for an afternoon *siesta*, but nothing moved. Not even in the American part of town.

The heat was stifling. It hovered over the town like a giant dome, drawing in the sunlight, shutting out the breeze from the river, turning the few raindrops, which dared fall, into steam. A horse stood at a hitching rail, too listless to fight off the flies that buzzed around its head. A skinny dog dozed in the strip of shade provided by a rickety bench.

Trinity had seen many such towns, towns that were dying because the reason for their birth no longer existed. The few unpainted buildings sagged a little more each year. Its population grew older and slower because the young moved on to more promising places. Trinity hated towns like this, but he didn't expect to stay long. He had come to find Chalk Gillet.

There was nobody at the hotel desk when he entered. The place exuded an atmosphere of death. An exceedingly plain woman with wispy grey hair and a faded dress came in answer to his kick on the desk with his dusty boot.

"Don't do that," she complained. "It leaves scars."

"I'm looking for Chalk Gillet," Trinity told her. "They said you'd know where to find him."

"Maybe I do. What's in it for me?"

Greed and cunning shone brightly in her eyes.

"A dollar."

She spat out a particularly foul curse. "I wouldn't talk to the Devil for no more'n a dollar."

"How about ten dollars?"

"You want him bad?"

"Enough to pay to find him." She held out a bony hand for the money. "But not enough to pay more than five now and five later."

She eyed him hatefully. "How's I to know you'll come back?"

"What proof do I have you know where he is?"

"Everybody knows. He's been living here for years."

"In that case I'll ask someone a little less expensive."

The woman dashed from behind the desk to stop him leaving the hotel. "Give me the five, and I'll tell you." Trinity handed her a coin which she inspected carefully. "You promise to give me the rest before you leave town?"

"If you'll tell me if he has an escape route."

The old woman eyed him suspiciously and then started to snicker.

"You're a crafty one, you are. He lives in a house just outside of town. A cabin really, but he insists it's a house. It backs up to a dry creek all covered in willows and mesquite thickets. If he sees somebody he don't trust coming up the front, he drops down in that creek and is up in those hills in a minute. Keeps a horse back there."

Trinity looked at the coin in his hand, then handed it to the woman.

"Anything else I ought to know?"

"He's got the place stashed with guns. If he's dressed, he's got one up his sleeve. A knife in his boot, too."

"How do you know all this?"

"He likes female company. Dora's up there right now."

Trinity stepped a little closer and said in a soft, deliberate voice, "If you've told me a single lie, I'll come back for my money. Then I'll burn down this rubbish heap with you in it."

Looking a little less sure of herself, the old woman watched Trinity leave. "Come evening, Dora's going to be looking for another job," she muttered to herself.

Trinity relaxed in the shade of a cottonwood and willow grove. Close by a short, powerful paint pony munched oats

308

from an open sack next to a tub one-third full of tepid water. Chalk hadn't skimped on his security precautions.

Neither had Trinity. He had loosened the cinch on the saddle. It just sat on the pony's back. And he had hobbled him. If Chalk was to get away, he would have to do it on foot. He looked at his watch. Ben ought to be approaching the front door in a couple of minutes. The hunt would soon come to an end.

It had taken more time than Trinity expected. When he reached Uvalde, he had found a message from Ben telling him to come to Santa Lucinda. That had taken another day's ride. He intended to be on his way back tonight, but it would be two days before he could reach the Demon D. He hoped Victoria was all right.

The sound of footsteps along the rocky path up to the house brought Trinity to his feet. Ben was going to pretend to be a sheriff from Texas. He was wearing Trinity's deputy sheriff badge. Trinity expected Chalk to reach the ravine about thirty seconds after Ben knocked on the front door.

He made it in twenty.

"I cut the cinch," Trinity said when Chalk and the saddle ended up in a heap on the sandy floor of the ravine. "I hobbled him, too."

"Who the hell are you?" Chalk demanded.

He was an ugly man, two inches shorter than Trinity, gone to fat, unshaven and unbathed. He eyed Trinity fearfully, but also with a crazy kind of courage, the courage of a man blessed with too much luck, a man who doesn't believe anything really bad can happen to him.

He wore nothing but his pants and boots. At least he had no hidden gun.

"My name's Trinity Smith. I've come to take you back to Bandera so you can testify that Victoria Blazer didn't kill her husband."

Chalk made a dash up the ravine, but Trinity intercepted him. Chalk's muscles had all gone to fat, too. Trinity had no difficulty overpowering him.

"You're crazy," Chalk gasped, as Trinity hauled him up out of the sand. "I'll be killed if I ever go near that place again."

"I'll guarantee your safety. And I'll see you get anywhere you want to go afterwards."

"You can't guarantee my safety from that devil."

"You know who killed Jeb?"

"No, but I know the man he hired."

"Tell me his name, or I'll beat it out of you."

"I don't know it. I've only seen him twice. Even if I knew it, you could beat me to death, and I wouldn't tell you."

"Then I guess I'll have to take you back to Bandera."

"I'll swear Victoria did it."

"And I'll produce Dora who'll swear you told her Victoria didn't do it."

It was a bow drawn at venture, but Trinity couldn't imagine a lazy swine like Chalk not having boasted of the truth to his mistress. Chalk's response convinced him he'd guessed correctly.

Chalk's hand flashed to his boot and came up holding a knife with a six-inch blade. He caught Trinity off balance and the two of them fell into the sand. Only Trinity's superior strength prevented the knife from entering his throat.

He bashed Chalk's wrist against a rock three times. The knife flew out of his grasp.

"Jesus God," Chalk screamed in anguish, "you broke my wrist."

"If I didn't need your testimony, I'd have killed you," Trinity said.

"I'll never testify."

"Then I guess we'll have to wait here until you change your mind."

"But I've got to have a doctor for my wrist. You must have crushed the bone."

Trinity made a quick assessment of Chalk's character. The man couldn't be depended upon to tell the truth. He'd do whatever he thought was in his own best interest. If Trinity tried to take him back to Bandera, even if he took him to a doctor first, he'd be twice as long on the trail. Clearly Chalk was a man who liked his creature comforts. He also guessed Chalk would find a way to make serious trouble along the way, trouble it might take him days to explain.

He couldn't afford to take that much time.

"I'll make a deal with you," Trinity said. "I sympathize with your not wanting to go back. I don't want to be bothered with taking you. So if you'll agree to swear before a judge that you saw Victoria walking away from Jeb Blazer when he was killed, I'll take you to a doctor."

"I'm not talking to any damned judge. I want a doctor." He rolled in the sand, his wrist hanging at a peculiar angle.

"I want something. You want something. I think an even exchange is called for."

"To hell with you!" Chalk shouted.

"Doesn't sound very cooperative to me," Ben said, coming up the ravine.

"He says he won't go back to Texas, and he won't testify in court. I offered to let him make a statement before a judge here, but he refused. Looks like there's nothing to do but to take him back just like he is. Maybe he'll change his mind after a while."

Ben looked thoughtful. "You'll probably have to tie him to his horse. Tie his wrists, too. Can't have him grabbing for a gun." Ben inspected Chalk's wrist. "Might be a good thing. Hold that wrist straight. It looks a mite crooked to me."

Chalk held his wrist and groaned.

"If you'll saddle up his pony, Ben, I'll get him to his feet. I want to get started right away. We've got a long ride."

"I'm not going," Chalk screamed. "My wrist needs to be set now."

"Don't let that worry you," Ben advised. "If it sets wrong, it's easy enough to break it again."

Chalk screamed when they lifted him into the saddle.

"Well it's your own fault," Ben said unsympathetically. "I told you it would be a lot harder if we had to lift you. I don't like holding on to hairy guys. It feels kinda queer."

Chalk screamed again when Trinity tied his wrists.

"You have a choice: talk to the judge here and get your wrist set today, or ride back to Bandera and talk to the Judge there. You got about five minutes to decide."

"You . . . sucking, mother . . . son of a bitch," Chalk swore. "I'll kill you for this."

"Not if you don't get that wrist set," Ben pointed out. "Probably can't even hold a gun, much less fire it."

"How am I going to make a living with this thing?" Chalk demanded. "If I talk, I won't get any more money."

Chapter Twenty-three

Trinity wanted to choke the life out of him on the spot. So he had been getting hush money all the time. He had been blackmailing the murderer. Victoria had been condemned to death so this spineless piece of slime could sit back on his ass for the rest of his life.

"Who killed Jeb?" Trinity demanded.

"I told you I don't know."

"I think we ought to break the other wrist," Ben said. "Shame to have them mismatched. It offends the eye, not being symmetrical."

"You're not scaring me."

"Tell me who killed Jeb, and we won't try."

"I wouldn't tell you if I knew."

"We could peel the skin off his stomach," Ben suggested. "He's got too much fat there. He'd look a whole lot better if you trimmed off a little bit."

"You're crazy," Chalk groaned.

"Just keep that in mind if you take it in your noggin to change your story," Ben said. "I always did want to know what it was like to peel a man. The Apache do it all the time. They seem to set great store by it."

"Could be, but I don't think it smells too good," Trinity observed. "I'm told human flesh doesn't cook up well."

"Guess that explains why there aren't too many cannibals about."

"Jesus God, you two mother . . . crazy bastards come near me and I'll scream my head off."

"I don't think your friends are too anxious to help out. You been screaming right regular and ain't nobody showed up yet."

They mounted up and started down the ravine. The pony's first steps caused Chalk to lurch in the saddle, which pulled the ropes taut around his wrists. He screamed again.

"Tell me who killed Jeb, and I'll untie your wrists."

"I don't know."

"You can't expect us to believe somebody's been paying you money all these years to keep quiet about a murder and you don't even know who it is."

"But it's true. I never saw who it was. They spoke to me from the shrubbery."

"Was it anything like Moses and the burning bush?"

"Be quiet, Ben," Trinity admonished, fighting back a grin.

"They told me to get out and never come back if I wanted to stay alive."

"Was it a man or a woman's voice?"

"I couldn't tell. They spoke in a hissing whisper."

"How'd you get the money?" Ben asked.

"It just started coming."

"How'd they know where you were?"

"Same way you did, I guess."

They had emerged from the ravine.

"How much?"

"No particular amount, but about five hundred a year."

"Why didn't they kill you instead of paying you off?"

"They couldn't. Not then. That place was crawling with people within seconds."

"Later then."

"I don't know. Maybe they figured if I was found dead, they might believe Victoria's story."

"Why didn't the sheriff look for you? Victoria said you were there."

"I had already drawn my pay and left. Several of them saw me ride out. I just came back to get something I forgot.

Maybe they figured she named me because they wouldn't be able to find me to disprove what she said."

"That's the most stupid story I ever heard," Ben said.

"But stupid enough to be true," Trinity said. "The closest judge is thirty miles from here. You swear to tell him everything you've just told me, and I'll see you get to a doctor."

"But not before you see that judge," Ben added.

"Suppose they come after me?"

"Head for the Arizona desert," Ben suggested. "I hear it's the perfect place for people with a weight problem. Sweat the pounds right off you."

"I didn't know you meant to get a stay of execution," Ben said as they left the judge's house.

"Neither did I. But when he offered, I realized I might need it. Judge Blazer will be mad as hell."

"You leaving now?"

"Yes. I'm riding through the night. You coming with me?"

"Not this time. I think I'll take it a little slow. Been going at a pretty fast pace for me."

"You thinking about California, too?"

Ben chuckled. "Naw, but I'm thinking about selling up and working for somebody else. I'm tired of having to rustle my own grub. Let the boss pay for it."

"You know there's a place for you at the Demon D. Just say the word."

"How much you paying?"

"Nothing but grub and a place to sleep until I get the place going."

"Sounds like my kind of pay."

"If I'm not there, tell Ward to fix you up." Trinity reached out and grabbed his hand. "Thanks, Ben. I owe you one."

"You owe me two or three, but I'll settle for having one of the kids named after me."

Trinity looked so surprised Ben burst out laughing.

"It's been all over your face ever since I busted in on you two in my cabin. You're crazy about that woman, and you won't

315

be right in your head until you marry her. Now get going. I'm sure she don't like being stuck away at the ranch. A gal that pretty ought to be out and about so ugly fish like me will have something to gawk at."

"If I'm not at the ranch, I'll be in Bandera," Trinity called out as he disappeared into the twilight.

"Now let's see about getting you to a doctor," Ben said to Chalk. "And let's hope he ain't no animal doctor. It'd be a shame if your wrist came out looking like a cow's hind leg."

"Victoria!"

The harsh whisper woke Victoria from her sleep.

"Victoria!"

It was coming from the window. Victoria looked up, but it was not yet daybreak. No light came through the window. She sat up and waited a moment until her wits cleared. Then she pulled the bed over to the window and climbed up on it. She looked down into Ward's upturned face.

"Thank God you're okay," the old man said. "I was afraid I'd never see you again."

"How did you find me?"

"I can follow Diablo's hoofprints anywhere, even in the moonlight. He's the only horse around here that isn't shod. I was untied when I came to. You do that?"

Victoria nodded.

"I thought so. Trinity said you were smart."

Victoria blushed, gratified at the compliment.

"What are you doing here? Who knocked me out?"

"Kirby Blazer."

"You just hold on. I'll have you out of there in five minutes."

"Kirby didn't bring me here," Victoria explained. "He and some of his friends tried to kidnap me. I came here myself. Trinity told me to. He said I'd be safe here if anybody found me."

"He's going to kill me when he learns what happened."

"He'd be angry at you for being overpowered by three men?"

316

"Three boys, more like. Besides, where you're concerned, he'd be in a rage if I was overpowered by a whole army. Nobody ever overpowered him, and he can't see how it could happen to anybody unless they was careless. And I was careless. I should have been sleeping in the house."

"You slept in the barn because you're a gentleman, and I'll tell him so."

"I would appreciate it if you would. I don't think I want to be the one to break the news to him. I've lived a good long life, but there're a few things I don't want to have to explain to St. Peter just yet."

"I'll be sure to tell him you found me and Diablo within a couple of hours."

"How'd you get here? I thought for a while you might have tried to ride that crazy horse. I was some relieved when I got here and found he had no saddle. How did he get out? I know I put him in his stall."

"I rode him bareback. And he goes like the wind. Kirby and his friends had me in a pocket, but Diablo blew right past them."

"You rode that broomtailed stick of dynamite bareback!" Ward exclaimed in disbelief.

"It was my only chance. One of them saw me run out of the house."

"He *will* kill me now, and I'll deserve it."

"No, he won't. I'm safe, and I found out Myra is up to something. I don't know what, but I don't trust her. And we know Diablo is the fastest horse in Texas."

"Trinity will claim to know a dozen ways to have found all that out while keeping you safe at the ranch the whole time."

"Maybe, but after all the trouble he got me into, he has no room to talk about anybody else."

"I hope you mean to tell him that."

"I do. Now you get Diablo home. I wouldn't put it past somebody to try to steal him."

"Not if they want to live."

"I really did ride him, and he really is as fast as the wind."

"I'll take your word for it," Ward replied, still skeptical. "But

317

I don't mean to ride him home to find out for myself. I'd rather be shot by Trinity than chewed to bits by that black devil."

Victoria woke to the sound of voices raised in anger.

"Open this door immediately. I can't believe you would keep her in this loathsome, squalid hole without informing me first."

Victoria could hardly believe her eyes when she saw Myra Blazer sweep into the jail. It was barely sunup, and Myra rarely left her bedroom before ten o'clock. The hapless sheriff followed behind in his undershirt and trousers, his face half covered with shaving cream, mumbling his apologies and insisting none of this was his fault.

"I'd like to know whose fault it could be when a Blazer is wrongfully incarcerated in your jail? Open this door immediately! You poor child. I came the minute I heard you were here."

The moment the sheriff unlocked the door, Myra pushed him aside and strode majestically into the cell. She enfolded Victoria in her embrace.

Victoria felt awkward. Myra's slim body and porcelain perfection always made her feel large and ungainly. Myra weighed barely more than a hundred pounds. The Judge said it came from drinking too much coffee and eating too little food. It didn't matter what it came from; she always made Victoria feel like a clumsy cow.

Victoria smiled to herself at Myra's insistence she had come as soon as she heard. Myra's face was perfectly made-up and her hair flawlessly dressed, a process that never took less than an hour.

Victoria fought down a twinge of envy. Trinity might say she was beautiful, but she never felt beautiful when Myra was around. No one else in the world could look that stunning.

And no one dressed like Myra. Who else would wear a rose silk dress fashioned after a Worth original to the Bandera jail? It must have taken her fifteen minutes to get into it. As for the

318

jewels, they staggered the mind. Robbers would do better to kidnap Myra for her diamonds than rob the Bandera bank for its gold.

Myra released Victoria and stepped back so she could look at her.

"I trust you have an explanation for your abominable attire. It is scandalous for a female. It is appalling for a Blazer."

Victoria felt thoroughly abashed. Myra could always make her feel like the silly little girl her Alabama aunts accused her of being.

"Three boys tried to kidnap me in the middle of the night."

Myra looked stunned. "Merciful heavens! Not again. Did you see who they were?"

"It was Kirby."

Myra's face cleared magically. "The naughty boy. I sent him to bring you to the Tumbling T," Myra explained. "I couldn't bear to think of you staying in that run-down place with only an old man for a chaperon."

"Then why didn't they come during the daytime?" Victoria demanded. "And why did they knock Ward out and tie him up?"

"Just a foolish boy's desire to play at being the hero," Myra said soothingly, "you know, rescue the beautiful princess from danger. All the young men still talk about your abduction from the jail five years ago. They admire this Buc of yours very much."

Her explanation seemed reasonable. Kirby was still only seventeen or eighteen. "Why were you going to give Trinity money?"

"It couldn't have been an easy thing to bring you all the way from Arizona. A man should be paid for his work."

"Trinity would never accept money for me. He's not a bounty hunter."

"You must forgive me. I was away when he came. I didn't know. I would never insult him. I naturally thought he would want to be paid."

Victoria's fears being laid to rest, her anger evaporated as well.

"Well, Kirby shouldn't have done it. He scared me half to death. I doubt Ward is thinking very kindly of him either."

"I shall speak to him," Myra said. "He should not have made you uncomfortable." She sighed. "It is so difficult to bring up a boy without a father. He always seems to have something to prove."

Victoria felt reproved for even mentioning Kirby's stunt. How was it that even when Myra was laying the blame elsewhere she managed to make Victoria feel it was her fault? She had always felt sorry for the boy. His hero worship of the Judge, his trying to do everything he could to please his stepfather, used to make Victoria feel sorry for him. But it wasn't her fault, and she resented Myra implying it was.

"Now that we've got that little misunderstanding cleared away, let me look at you," Myra said, apparently putting the attempt to abduct Victoria out of her mind just like it never existed. She subjected Victoria to a thorough inspection. "You haven't wasted these five years," she said, a trace of jealousy in her tone. "You have grown into an extraordinarily beautiful woman."

"Never as beautiful as you," Victoria said. "You've got to be the most beautiful woman in the world." The tribute obviously pleased Myra. The sharp look left her eyes.

"I couldn't believe you had come back to Bandera, not after the abominable way they treated you, but I was horrified you should have to spend the night in this cesspool."

"I—"

"I can't imagine what charge this fool has placed against you, but I'm certain it can be explained in no time."

"You don't have to—"

"You should have seen my face when Kirby told me you were in the Bandera jail."

Kirby had just entered the jail. He stood behind his mother. Now that Victoria could get a good look at him, she saw he had grown into an extremely handsome young man, almost as handsome as his mother was beautiful. But he looked shocked, colorless, like he didn't know what to say or do. He just stood there, staring at Victoria like his mind was para-

320

lyzed. She hoped Myra had given him a piece of her mind for his dangerous prank. If Trinity had been home, he could have gotten himself killed.

"You must leave this horrid place at once," Myra said. "I shudder when I think of you staying here, and your room at home empty all these years."

"I couldn't possibly go to the ranch," Victoria insisted, finding her tongue. "The Judge wouldn't allow it."

"He won't know. I left him in Austin to spend several days hunting with his friends." Myra shuddered artistically. "I hate blood sports. It's embarrassing to have to admit, but I faint at the sight of blood. Tell her she must come with us, Kirby," Myra said, turning to her son. "Maybe you can convince her."

Victoria saw horror in the boy's eyes. *He's mortified to have to look me in the eye after what he's done* she thought. *He doesn't want to be anywhere near me. He also knows it would be crazy to go back to the Tumbling T. The Judge would go berserk.*

"I've got to stay here," Victoria said. "Trinity's gone to find Chalk Gillet. He said that once I prove I didn't kill Jeb, the real killer might try to kill me. He said I'd be safest in the jail."

"How horrible," Myra said. "The most awful things seem to happen to you. You must tell me if you have any idea who this killer might be. I'll see the sheriff arrests him this instant."

"I've thought about it for five years, and I can't imagine who could have killed Jeb."

"You don't have to have hard evidence," Myra insisted. "Just tell me who you suspect. I'll see they stay in jail until the Judge can get back."

"I don't even have any suspicions."

"Does this Trinity Smith have any?"

"No, he's only concerned with finding Chalk."

"That could take days, possibly weeks," Myra said. "You can't mean to stay here all that time."

"I didn't want to stay here even one night, but Trinity said he'd be back in a couple of days. And Trinity always does what he promises."

"You think a lot of this Trinity, don't you?" Myra observed. The suggestion that she might be more than ordinarily interested in Trinity flustered Victoria just enough to cause her to miss the slight change in Myra's tone.

"I suppose it's foolish to be impressed with the man who brings you back to hang, but Trinity is no ordinary man. He promised he'd prove I didn't kill Jeb, and he will."

"Well, I'm overjoyed to hear that," Myra declared. "I've always insisted you couldn't have killed Jeb. You just aren't the kind of person to shoot anybody, much less your husband. Now let me take you home."

"No. I really can't," Victoria insisted. "I'd be a nervous wreck, knowing the Judge still thinks I murdered his son."

"Then come with me to the hotel. I'll rent a room and you can stay with me until this Trinity person gets back with Chalk Gillet."

"Thank you so very much, but I can't."

"Really, Victoria, it's rather bad of you to insist upon remaining in this deplorable place."

"I don't mind, not really."

"Then if you won't think of yourself, at least think of me. How can I endure the shame of knowing my own daughter-in-law is in jail?"

"You endured it before," Victoria said, rather too bluntly for Myra, whose eyes grew hard as agate.

"I always insisted you were innocent."

"I know, and I'll be forever grateful, but I have to stay here. Trinity made me swear."

Myra was clearly furious. Victoria knew she was accustomed to getting her way, even in little things, but she didn't mean to budge. She might have if Kirby hadn't come to the ranch after her. He looked petrified, like he expected some terrible punishment any minute, but Victoria was no longer interested in Myra or her son. She just wanted Trinity to come back and fix everything.

"I trust you know I shall not forgive you for this," Myra stated in her most majestic manner. "It's humiliating."

"I'm sorry. I really am."

"At least let me bring you something decent to eat," Myra said, relenting slightly. "You can't possibly survive on the garbage this man will give you. That way I shall at least *appear* to be concerned about my own family."

"I'd be delighted to let you bring me food," Victoria said, truly grateful for Myra's thoughtfulness. "You wouldn't believe what I've been forced to eat during the last few weeks."

"Don't tell me," Myra said, shuddering eloquently. "You will surely ruin my own appetite. I will send for my cook immediately. I can't eat anything the hotel prepares anyway. Are you absolutely certain you won't come with me?"

"I really can't," Victoria said, hoping Myra wouldn't ask her again. She would dearly love to say yes. The thought of a decent bed, a hot bath, and getting away from the smell of her cell was almost too much for her resolution.

"It is too bad you won't come with me, but I shall see you are made more comfortable," Myra promised. "It will not be said that a member of the Blazer family has to live like a pig. Come with me," she said to the sheriff as she turned to go. "You will do exactly as I say, or tomorrow morning you will be chasing cows through the brush."

"Hello, Kirby," Victoria said to the boy before he could follow his mother from the jail. "You've grown up since I last saw you. I bet the girls are glad when you come to town."

"I think it's rotten you have to stay in jail," he managed to say before he hurried after his mother.

Victoria didn't remember the boy being so bashful. He looked petrified, like he wanted to run and hide. Myra probably kept him tied to her apron strings. She was a managing female. Maybe she would invite him to come visit her and Trinity after she got out of jail. It would give him a chance to get away from his mother and develop a little self-confidence.

Victoria had to smile at herself. Wouldn't Trinity be surprised to know she'd not only decided he was going to marry her and they would live at the Demon D, she was already making a list of people to invite to stay. But she knew he wouldn't mind. Besides, it would help keep his mind off Queenie.

She sat down on the bunk. She ought to be thinking about what she could do to help him get over Queenie and his guilt about his father's death. His father was dead, and nothing would bring him back. He had no idea where Queenie had disappeared to, not that Victoria could see any advantage to learning Queenie's whereabouts. In fact, knowing where she was would be just about the worst thing she could think of for Trinity.

Maybe she would ask Myra. She had had a great deal more experience with men. Maybe she would know what to do. At the least, maybe she could offer some advice on how to begin.

Victoria yawned sleepily when Sheriff Sprague interrupted her afternoon nap. Everyone seemed in league to keep her from catching up on her rest.

"There's a visitor to see you. Says he's a lawyer. Says your uncle hired him."

Victoria stared curiously at the man. He seemed awfully young to be a lawyer, very clean-cut, his dark suit and boots showing no signs of the dust which always choked the streets of Bandera in the summer. Even his white shirt retained its crispness despite the heat.

In his turn, the young man stared at Victoria's cell. It had been completely transformed.

A brass bed piled high with feather mattresses took up almost all the room in the cell. There was only a narrow passage between the bed and a pile of boxes stacked against the opposite wall, each contained a dress Victoria could no longer wear. A thick rug covered the floor, and sheer curtains billowed at the windows. A small table with a lamp, a pitcher and basin, and the dishes with the remains of her last meal stood next to the bed. The sheriff was quick to remove the dishes.

"Sheriff Sprague tells me you insist upon remaining in jail," the man said. "I confess I couldn't understand why until now. This must be what the inside of a Turkish harem looks like."

Victoria chuckled delightedly. "My stepmother-in-law's attempt to salve her conscience." She extended her hand. "I'm Victoria Davidge."

"David Woolridge at your service," he said, executing a courtly bow.

324

"Please sit," Victoria said, chuckling again. "And please, no more bows or remarks about harems. You'll shock the local matrons, not to mention Myra."

Woolridge seated himself in a chair which had been squeezed into the tiny space between the table and a stack of dress boxes.

"How is my uncle? And Buc?" Victoria asked.

"I don't know. He communicated with our office in Austin by telegram. I live in San Antonio, so I was chosen to take on your case."

"What have you done?"

"Very little as yet. I've only been here a few days, but it seemed most important to get a stay of execution. Once we have that, I'll have the leisure to investigate the evidence in the case more closely."

Victoria held her breath. "Did you get it?"

"There are quite a few irregularities involved with this case, not the least of which is the dead man's father acting as the presiding judge."

"Did you get it?" Victoria demanded, impatient with his tedious narration.

"My office informs me the order has been signed."

Victoria felt weak with relief.

"I should be receiving the official papers in a day or two. There's really no reason for you to stay in this cell any longer."

Victoria was overjoyed to find the shadow of the gallows no longer loomed over her head, but half her pleasure was denied because none of the people she most wanted to share the news with—Trinity, Uncle Grant, Buc, and all the men at the ranch—were here. Of course, she would tell Myra, but she wondered whether Myra was more upset or embarrassed by her daughter-in-law being in jail. Oh well, it didn't matter. She could leave now.

But where would she go? She didn't want to go back to the ranch without Trinity. She didn't want to go to the hotel with Myra. She couldn't go to the ranch with the Judge. But she couldn't go anywhere else.

"I think I'll stay here until Trinity gets back."

"There really is no need. You're in no danger."

But Victoria wasn't convinced of that. She didn't know what the killer might do, but she'd be happier letting Trinity worry about that.

"Nevertheless, I'll stay where I am."

Mr. Woolridge looked about him and his eyes crinkled with amusement. "You're probably more comfortable here than I am at the hotel."

"And I don't have to worry about visitors or social engagements."

Woolridge stood. "I understand you had an eventful night. I'll let you get back to your nap. I wish you had let me know you were in the area."

"I didn't know you were *in the area*," Victoria replied. "Besides, I had meant to stay safely out of sight."

"It would have been better."

"Tell that to Kirby."

"I've already met the young man. He seems to be thoroughly abashed at his conduct."

"He ought to be." Victoria couldn't be angry any longer. She was too happy.

"A Pinkerton will be arriving any day now. He'll probably want to talk with you."

"You know where to find me. At the moment, my engagement calendar is entirely empty."

"I'll see what I can do to remedy that in the future."

"I already have."

Mr. Woolridge looked inquiringly at Victoria, but she declined to enlighten him. It was her secret, and she wanted to keep it to herself a little longer.

Kirby rushed past Sheriff Sprague and skidded to a stop in front of Victoria's cell. He stared in stunned surprise through the bars. Victoria lay on the bed, her body racked by convulsions.

"What's wrong with her?" Kirby demanded, staring at her with horror-stricken eyes.

326

"I don't know," Sheriff Sprague replied, abject fear in his voice. "She took sick just a few minutes ago. She's been moaning something awful ever since. Every time I ask her what's wrong, she groans even louder and gets sick all over again. What am I supposed to do? We can't have her making all those terrible sounds. Sounds worse than if the jail was haunted."

"Have you sent for the doctor?"

"He's away."

"I'll get Mother. She'll know what to do."

"I don't know what caused it," the sheriff insisted. "Maybe she's had a heatstroke or something. It's right hot back here in these cells."

"You better hope that's it," Kirby replied. "If she dies, there's going to be hell to pay."

Chapter Twenty-four

Trinity was real irritated at Ward, at Kirby Blazer, at Sheriff Sprague, and at himself. He was particularly irritated with Chalk Gillet. If he could have gotten his hands on that spineless coward just now, Chalk would have had two smashed wrists to complain about.

Because of Chalk Gillet he'd been away too long and Victoria had ended up in the Bandera jail.

Ward's disgust and shame with his own performance had prevented Trinity from working off more than a fraction of his temper on his foreman, but he was spoiling to smash something or anybody who crossed his path.

But it seemed the citizens of Bandera were in league to continue his frustration. The hot afternoon sun had driven them off the dusty streets. Even the benches on the hotel porch and the chairs set out under awnings by merchants were empty.

The town of Bandera had developed in sections. Mexicans shared the southern portion with the saloons and dance halls, frequented mostly by gamblers, cowhands, and people who didn't want their identity or location known. The commercial district lay north of that along the main street. Behind that and along the edge of town were the homes of the merchants, prominent citizens, and some of the cowmen prosperous enough to have a house in town.

The jail straddled the line between the merchants and the saloon keepers.

Trinity was even more irritated when he walked inside and

328

found no one there. Victoria was not to be left unguarded, not even for one second. The sooner Wylie Sprague understood that, the better. Trinity headed to the back of the jail toward the cells.

He almost burst out laughing when he saw the bed piled high with mattresses and pillows and the boxes of clothes, even the door was open. The sheriff was using his head. Giving Victoria the run of the jail as well as every possible luxury was good insurance for later. No one would be able to say he hadn't given an innocent woman every possible consideration.

The cell was empty. Damn, that was going too far. What good was it to put Victoria in jail if she had the run of Bandera? That was no protection. Judge Blazer could have her picked up off the street, and he wouldn't send boys to do it.

On his way out again, Trinity nearly collided with Sheriff Sprague.

"What kind of jackleg sheriff are you, letting your prisoners go gallivanting all over town?" Trinity groused. "Victoria should be here where you can keep an eye on her, not prancing about in some dress shop or visiting friends. Where the hell is she?"

The sheriff's mouth opened, but he uttered nothing more than a few strangled syllables.

"Speak up, man. I've got Gillet's confession and a stay of execution in my pocket. She's a free woman. For the first time in five years she can go anywhere she wants, do anything she likes."

"S-she's at the h-hotel," the sheriff managed to stammer.

"Why did you let her go there? Anything could have happened to her. Some damned fool sheriff you are."

"She's sick. Myra Blazer put her in her own room."

"What's wrong? Did she get a queasy stomach from eating the swill you serve in this place?"

"Myra doesn't know what's wrong."

Trinity had never had any respect for Sheriff Sprague, but the man's near panic finally penetrated his scorn and irritation.

"What happened? What did you feed her?"

"Nothing. She gets her food from the hotel."

Fear such as he had never known seized Trinity's guts and twisted them into an agonizing knot. He grabbed Sprague by the front of his shirt and shook him so hard buttons flew off and seams ripped.

"What's wrong with her? Tell me, you goddamned sniveling coward."

"I don't know. She just took sick about thirty minutes ago."

"What have you done for her?"

"I didn't know what to do. That's why I sent for Kirby."

"Is she okay? Is she better?"

"She's dying. She'll probably be dead by the time you get there."

With a roar of rage and anguish that sounded barely human, Trinity picked the sheriff up and threw him through a window twenty feet into the middle of the street. Then he charged down the street like a man possessed by the demons of hell.

"I don't know what to do," Myra said to Doctor Roundtree, wringing her hands. "She hasn't responded to anything I've done."

Victoria lay on Myra's bed in the hotel; her face pale, her body motionless, her skin hot and dry, her pulse rapid and irregular, her breathing fast and shallow.

"Does she have a history of heart problems? Has she had a similar attack like this before?"

"I don't know," Myra said. "She's my daughter-in-law, but she's been living in Arizona for the past five years. I really know very little of her history. Did she ever mention an illness to you, Kirby?"

Kirby stood like a statue, apparently too deeply shocked to answer his mother.

"I wish the Judge were here," Myra said, nervously twisting the huge emerald-cut diamond on her right hand. "He and her father were longtime friends. He might know something to help."

"I hesitate to treat her without knowing anything about her," Dr. Roundtree said. "I could so easily prescribe the wrong medicine."

"You must do something," Myra insisted. "You can't let her die."

The door slammed open and a dust-covered, wild-eyed stranger burst into the room. Ignoring everyone who stared at him as though he were some sort of apparition, he plunged across the room and fell on his knees beside the bed. He grasped Victoria's limp hand in his and crushed it to his lips. His eyes, wide and frightening, stared at her deathly pallor.

"How dare you force yourself into private rooms," Myra declared furiously. "Release my daughter-in-law's hand and get out."

The man turned blank eyes to the doctor. "What's wrong with her?"

"I don't know," the doctor replied. "No one can tell me what might have caused the attack."

"I demand that you leave at once," Myra repeated, her face rigid with fury, "or I shall call the sheriff."

"What have you done for her?"

"Nothing. I don't know where to begin. No one knows her medical history, and she has been unconscious ever since I got here."

"Kirby, fetch Sheriff Sprague. I want this man removed immediately."

The stranger turned to Myra. The expression of hatred in his eyes was so vivid, so vibrant, it felt like a living, palpable thing.

"Get out," the stranger ordered.

Myra's eyes burned with a fury almost as great as the stranger's. It was clear she was not used to being ordered about, and she had no intention of submitting to such treatment. Most certainly not by a dirty cowhand. "I will not. This is my room and I'll—"

"Leave, or I'll kill you."

Trinity palmed his gun, pointed it at Myra's head, and pulled the hammer back.

"You touch me and—"

The deafening roar of a gun being fired in the close confines of the room startled the occupants. They gaped in disbelief when the coil of ebony hair at the side of Myra's face exploded into tiny fragments which scattered all over the room like a cloud of lint. Myra nearly collapsed with terror, her face dead white under her makeup. She stared at the man, unbelieving, uncomprehending, then fled the room.

Kirby ran after her.

"That was Judge Blazer's wife," the doctor informed him, horrified. "He'll hang you for that."

"What do you do for poison?" the man asked, turning back to Victoria.

"There's no question of bad food. The sheriff says—"

"She was poisoned," he stated. "That's Queenie. She poisoned my father."

The doctor gaped at Trinity.

"She was poisoned. See she doesn't die, or I'll kill you and Queenie both. I'll kill the Judge if I have to."

The doctor swallowed. "I don't know who you are, but you're mistaken about that woman. She's not your Queenie, whoever she might be. She is Myra Winslow Blazer, Judge Blazer's wife. Everybody in town knows she's been trying to take care of this young woman.

"When she refused to leave the jail, she had a bed and many of her things taken over to the jail. She even had the hotel prepare her meals. Good God, man, you can't expect me to believe she would poison her own daughter-in-law."

"Believe it," Trinity said. "Your life depends on it. What are the most common poisons around here?"

"I don't know. I never thought about it."

"Then think of it now."

"I suppose you can buy several kinds of preparations for—"

"No. Plants. Something you can find growing in a garden or along a stream in spring."

"There are lots of those."

"Which ones would produce these symptoms?"

"I can't say for sure. I would have to know the dose,

how long ago it was given—"

"Guess, goddamnit! That's all we've got time for. What would be the most likely?"

"I suppose something like deadly nightshade. Maybe horse nettle or jimsonweed. They're all pretty much the same. They have the same symptoms."

"That's it then."

"If you're wrong . . ."

"She's going to die if you don't do something."

"Yes, I expect she will."

"Go ahead. At least this will give her a chance."

The doctor began to search the inner recesses of his bag. "I still must protest your notion that Mrs. Blazer is in any way responsible for this."

"I don't care what you believe as long as you save Victoria."

"I shall do my best."

"And don't tell Queenie I know who she is."

The doctor started to protest, but the expression on Trinity's face stopped him. "No, I won't tell her."

Five minutes later, someone pounded on the door. When Trinity opened it, an irate Sheriff Sprague tried to barge into the room. Trinity blocked his path.

"Now look here, Smith," the sheriff said, "I know you're upset about this young woman, but you can't go running people like Mrs. Blazer out of her room."

"There are other rooms," Trinity said, slamming the door shut.

There came a furious knocking. Trinity opened the door again.

"But she's Judge Blazer's wife."

Trinity drew his gun and placed the end of the barrel against the patch of skin between Sheriff Sprague's eyes. He drew back the hammer. "Don't bother us again."

The sheriff staggered back against the far wall. Trinity closed the door and locked it.

There were no more knocks.

An hour later, the doctor took Victoria's pulse once again. "It's come down some. It's still terribly elevated, but there's nothing more I can do for her. If it's one of the poisons I mentioned, she has a chance. If not, my treatment has been entirely useless."

"It was poison," Trinity assured him.

The doctor looked unconvinced. "I hope I got here in time." He gathered everything into his bag and put on his coat. "Now we have to wait and see what her own body can do."

"How long?"

"I can't say. If she's alive in the morning, I think she'll pull through. I have other calls to make, but I'll come by as often as I can."

The door opened after a single warning knock. Doctor Roundtree entered and approached the bedside to check Victoria. A young man accompanied him. Trinity didn't look up.

"Will she live?" the young man asked.

"I don't know," the doctor replied.

"Has anyone notified her uncle?"

Trinity shook his head.

"I think you should."

Trinity made no response.

"If you have no objection, I'll send a telegram immediately." Still Trinity didn't respond.

"I'm David Woolridge. Her uncle hired me to defend her." Trinity's gaze remained on Victoria.

"She's about the same," Dr. Roundtree said to Trinity. "I'll come back later in the evening."

Mr. Woolridge looked undecided, then followed the doctor from the room.

"Who's that man with her?" he asked the doctor as soon as they were outside the door.

"I'm told he's a very dangerous gunman named Trinity Smith. He seems quite unbalanced to me. For the good of us all, I hope that young woman survives."

"But what's he doing in there? He's the man the sheriff deputized to bring her back."

"I don't know anything about that. I just know he drove Mrs. Blazer out at the point of a gun."

"I heard. The story's all over town."

"He's positive she's been poisoned."

"Has she?"

"It's quite possible."

The young man looked thoughtful. "Does he have any idea who did it?"

"He says it was Myra Blazer."

Woolridge looked stunned.

"Do you think he's right?"

"I don't see how he can be, but I know his kind. They don't often make mistakes."

After the doctor left, Trinity took Victoria's hand in his once again. Even though she couldn't see him, hear him, or feel his touch, he desperately needed to touch her. It was all that kept him from going crazy and shooting everyone in Bandera. All of them had taken a part in bringing her to this point, and he wanted to kill every one of them.

He especially wanted to kill Queenie.

He didn't know how he managed to conceal his shock when he looked up and saw her. She had altered her appearance, but he would have known her anywhere. The long blond hair, which used to hang from her head in great masses like golden clouds, was changed to black hair dressed atop her head. Her cheap, brightly colored dresses had been replaced by a magnificent silk gown, her gaudy red lips and brightly rouged cheeks had given way to a delicately tinted complexion. Her predatory anxiety had been replaced by complacent acquisitiveness, but he knew her without a doubt.

He would never forget Queenie. Now that he had found her, he meant to see she never harmed anyone again. This time he wouldn't expect anyone to believe him, and he wouldn't attempt to achieve justice by legal means.

He intended to kill Queenie.

He didn't know how she pulled it off, but he was sure Queenie was responsible for Jeb's death. It was inexcusable that she had planned for Victoria to spend the rest of her life as a fugitive from justice. In Trinity's eyes, Queenie signed her own death warrant when she tried poisoning her when the gallows failed.

He looked down at Victoria. She couldn't die now. She had too much to live for. She was free, never again would she have to look over her shoulder and fear what tomorrow would bring.

She could marry, have children, and live to a ripe old age.

She could marry *him*. She could have *his* children. She had to live for a very long time because he wanted to die in her arms. He didn't want to live one minute of his life without her.

Trinity could hardly bear to look at Victoria, yet she was all he wanted to see. He had thought of her nearly every minute since he left for Uvalde. For the first time in thirteen years he had a real purpose for his life, a focus that had nothing to do with hatred or guilt or escape. He knew he would never have to chase down another criminal. He was through with all that.

He had looked forward to asking Victoria to marry him. Never once did he imagine she would refuse. The memory of their one night together remained fresh in his mind.

He had never known such pleasure with a woman, and he didn't believe it stemmed from either the perfection of Victoria's body or his long enforced abstinence. Clearly it owed nothing to her lovemaking skills. The source of his pleasure was Victoria herself.

Even if she had not been so physically desirable, he would still have wanted to take her to bed a dozen times a day. He had experienced real fulfillment for the first time. Certainly he hungered for her, he always would, but he knew his greatest pleasure came from just being with Victoria, being loved by her. Anything else was a bonus.

And now she lay on this bed, her pulse racing as though she had run all the way from Arizona; her life hanging by a thread, and all because of Queenie.

It was all he could do not to kill Queenie right now. It would only take a few minutes. She was still in the hotel, probably just down the hall. He could be back in a minute.

But he couldn't leave Victoria even for a moment. If she

should wake up, he had to be here. If these were her last hours on earth, he had to be here. Now that she was Judge Blazer's wife, Queenie wouldn't leave. She had too much to lose. He could kill her later.

Trinity got up off his knees and sat down on the bed next to Victoria. Gently lifting her from the pillow, he cradled her in his arms. If she had to die, he wanted her to die in the arms of the one person who loved her more than life.

He realized now what he had suspected for years. His love for Queenie was no more than a young man's infatuation: partly with an older and very beautiful woman, partly with the heady sensations of love, and partly with his own emerging manhood. All of these had come together at once with such force he hadn't been able to analyze the feelings which drove him to such wild actions. He had only been able to act.

His father, still sunk in the mire of self-pity and sorrow over his wife's death, couldn't help. Naturally he hadn't listened to the advice of his friends or of the older men who counseled caution. He dismissed them as jealous and of his success; they wanted Queenie for themselves.

And he finally realized something else. He wasn't responsible for his father's death. Queenie hadn't simply lured a grief-stricken man into a disastrous marriage. His father had married Queenie knowing she was the woman his son loved. His father must have known Queenie was more interested in being the wife of a rancher than an impetuous boy. He just didn't know she was willing to commit murder for the sake of money.

But that had been his father's mistake, not his own. And his father had made it nearly impossible for Trinity to bring Queenie to justice. By willing his property to Queenie rather than his son, he had virtually disowned him. It was the same as publicly stating he trusted his wife more than his son. By letting his son go off to Colorado at an age when he should have been at home, he further proclaimed his disaffection. No matter how his father really felt, his actions put public sympathy with Queenie rather than with his son.

It was just as Victoria had tried to tell him: He wasn't responsible for his father's death. And, if he wasn't responsible, he didn't have to avenge his death.

Trinity had never suspected the weight of that burden until it began to lift from his soul. If Victoria hadn't been lying near death in his arms, he'd have performed a song and dance. For the first time in his adult life, he felt free to live his life the way he wanted.

Now that he was free of the need to avenge his father's death, he was also free to admit that killing Queenie would ruin his own life. He had suspected it before, but he had never admitted it. He'd never had a life worth preserving, but now he had a future which included much more than salvation through vengeance.

Now he was free to be Victoria's husband, to build a life together, to raise a family, to build a ranch he could leave to his children. As he faced the fact that Victoria might not live to enjoy that life, Trinity felt the same killing rage all over again. Even as he worked himself free from one of Queenie's cursed legacies, she'd trapped him with another.

Would he ever be free of that woman? He knew she had poisoned Victoria, probably through the food she sent from the hotel. That alone would have been enough to convince him she had been the cause of Jeb's death. Knowing Myra Winslow Blazer was really Queenie removed any doubt whatsoever. Murder was her way of gaining the wealth she craved. He couldn't see her changing now, not when the largest fortune in Texas stood within her grasp.

Again, he didn't know how to prove it, but he knew she would probably try to poison the Judge. Might she not try to blame that on Victoria? As Jeb's widow, Victoria would inherit her husband's estate. Unless the Judge made specific provisions, Victoria might have a claim upon the Judge's estate as well. Queenie wouldn't allow that. She would never invest all this time in a marriage only to see the fortune pass into Victoria's hands.

Now that Trinity knew she had a son, he felt even more certain Queenie planned to murder the Judge, especially if she had convinced him to adopt her son. She probably intended to get the entire estate. She couldn't afford to let Victoria stand in her way. If Victoria didn't die now, she would try again.

Could he afford not to kill Queenie?

He didn't see how.

Four hours in the same position had caused Trinity's arm to go dead. His whole body felt numb, but he didn't move. All through the lonely hours of the night, he held her close to him, sharing his warmth, trying to give her his strength, hoping he could feel the will to live in her.

He spent the long hours reviewing his life, wishing he could have it to live over again, hoping Victoria would be there in the future to make up for the waste of so many years. But no matter how far away his memories carried him, his attention never wavered from its intense awareness of Victoria.

He sensed the crisis moments before her heart stopped beating.

"No! Please, don't!"

Surely it would start any second. It had to. She couldn't die!

But it didn't.

The breath went out of her body. She lay in his arms. Motionless.

Chapter Twenty-five

"Mother of God!" Trinity hissed as he jerked himself into a sitting position, causing Victoria to fall away from him. Not heeding the pain in his deadened limbs, he sat her up, grabbed her by the arms and shook her like a rag doll.

"Breathe, goddamn it! You can't die on me. Not now."

Victoria's head bounced from side to side like her neck would break, but she didn't breathe.

"Please, God, make her breathe." He shook her again, but still nothing happened. "Make her breathe!" He grabbed her under the arms and tried to make her walk, but her lifeless limbs dragged the floor. He dropped her back on the bed and fell down on her body.

A cry of heartrending agony erupted from his throat.

"Why?" he demanded. "Why should she die and that murdering bitch live?"

He brought his fist down upon Victoria's chest.

"Damn it to hell! Breathe! Don't give up now. Don't you let that she-devil beat you."

He struck her chest again, a sob escaping his throat.

"Breathe, for God's sake. Don't leave me here alone. I had to live all those years when I wanted to die. I don't want to die any more. I want to live, but I can't do it without you." He pounded on her chest again and again. "I can't! I just can't!"

Trinity fell upon Victoria's body, his arms wrapped tightly around her, sobs of heartbreaking bitterness and deep anger wrenched from an unwilling throat. Through the swelling tide of his grief, he felt Victoria's body shudder. Instantly he became dead still.

Victoria's heart thumped wildly in her chest, her body shuddered once more, then breath rushed into her lungs.

She breathed once, twice, three times. Gradually some of the color began to return to her white face.

Trinity offered a prayer of thanks.

Victoria felt her eyelids flutter two times before they opened. She didn't recognize the room. She had no idea where she was. At the same moment, she realized she wasn't alone. She turned her face and found herself looking into Trinity's eyes.

"You're back," she said, surprised she didn't remember his return or their coming to this room. Neither did she remember feeling so weak. Her voice sounded like a faint whisper. She couldn't move. Her body felt weighted, tied down to the bed.

"Did you find Chalk Gillet?"

"I not only found him," Trinity said, a smile slowly erasing the lines on his face, "I got a signed deposition from him saying you didn't kill Jeb. I also got a judge to give me a stay of execution in case the sheriff failed to stand up to Judge Blazer."

"I knew you would," Victoria said, happy her faith in Trinity had been justified, "but I wish you'd woken me up when you got in instead of bringing me here so I could wake up in a fancy hotel room. This is the hotel, isn't it?"

Trinity nodded.

"It nearly scared me to death waking up in a strange place. For one horrible instant I thought I'd been carried off by Red Beard."

"What do you remember?"

"I don't remember feeling so weak." She tried to sit up and failed. "Have I been sick?"

"Yes."

"How long?"

"Since yesterday."

"Was I very sick?"

"You nearly died."

Victoria paused to digest the somber expression on Trinity's face, the gravel in his voice. "You don't think I got sick naturally?" Trinity shook his head. "You think somebody made me sick?"

"You were in a coma when I got here. Everybody thought you were going to die. They would have given up on you if I hadn't insisted."

"You always did have a way of making people do what you wanted," Victoria said, thankful for once that Trinity was so overbearing.

"What's the very last thing you can remember?"

"I remember . . ." Victoria paused, puzzled. "I remember eating lunch and lying down for a nap, but I don't remember anything else. I can't even remember what I had for supper."

"That's because you didn't have any supper. You were poisoned, probably at lunch. Myra Blazer is Queenie, the woman who killed my father. I recognized her the moment I saw her."

Victoria gaped at Trinity, her mind unable to equate the elegant, imperious Myra with her vision of a furtive, sinister Queenie. "She can't be. Myra lived in Ohio until her husband died. He was a banker. His name was Winslow. He was Kirby's father."

"I don't know anything about a banker named Winslow, and I have no idea where she got Kirby, but Myra is Queenie. And she poisoned you."

"But she has been so good to me. She tried to persuade me to go to the ranch or at least move into the hotel with her. When I wouldn't, she had a bed moved into my cell and everything she thought I would want brought from the ranch. She even sent for her cook to prepare my meals."

"So she could poison you," Trinity said, certain he was right. "She's Queenie, I tell you. I'd know her anywhere. I'm certain she's responsible for Jeb's death, too. I don't know how she did it, but I'm sure."

"I can't believe that," Victoria said, hearing Trinity's words with skepticism. "She always insisted I didn't kill Jeb."

"Probably because she knew you'd be convicted no matter what she said. I don't know what happened. We probably won't ever know, but promise me you won't have anything to do with her. She's the most dangerous woman you'll ever meet."

"I probably won't see her again except to thank her," Victoria assured Trinity, still unable to believe Myra Blazer could be Queenie.

"If you have to see her, wait until I can be with you. And no matter what you do, don't eat or drink anything she gives you."

Victoria promised, but her promise was given more to make Trinity happy than in a belief Myra posed any real danger to her.

"Did anyone notify Uncle Grant?"

"I believe so," Trinity said, remembering with difficulty. "Some lawyer your uncle hired."

"Mr. Woolridge. Tell him to send another telegram right away. I can't bear the thought of Uncle Grant thinking I'm dead."

Victoria's recovery progressed rapidly. At the end of three days, she was up and moving about for hours at a time. She felt only slightly tired. Agreeing that Victoria should not be disturbed or moved during her recovery, Myra had taken other rooms at the hotel.

Trinity had demanded and was given the room next to Victoria's with the connecting door. Victoria had received no answer to her telegram to her uncle. She could only hope he would arrive quickly.

Victoria received visits from Doctor Roundtree, Myra, a clearly uncomfortable Kirby, the sheriff, and David Woolridge. Trinity never left her alone, not for as much as one second. He personally oversaw the preparation of every bite of food and every drop of medicine. He formed a one-man line of protection for Victoria.

Trinity had apologized to Myra for his rudeness, and Myra had graciously accepted his apology, accepting his explanation that it was the consequences of an overwrought mind. However, Victoria noticed Myra was not happy with her new hairstyle. Knowing Myra, Victoria suspected she would forgive Trinity's rudeness long before she forgave his ruining her hair.

Even though they spent hours in each other's company, Myra never showed any signs of recognizing Trinity. She was angered by Trinity's continual rejection of her offers to help with Victoria's care, but he refused to let anyone help.

"You can't be at my side forever," Victoria said, when she couldn't convince Trinity to relax his vigil. "You're going to have to let me live a normal life someday."

"I've been thinking about that," Trinity said. "You'll never be safe as long as Myra's alive. The Judge will be home any day now. Once he's convinced you didn't kill Jeb, he's going to start looking about for someone else to suspect. And he's bound to think of Myra and Kirby. I don't know if the boy had anything to do with it . . ."

"He couldn't have," Victoria said. "He was too young."

". . . but he looks scared to death of something. I think he suspects his mother has done something, and he's petrified we'll find out."

"Besides, he was inside the house when Jeb was shot."

"That doesn't matter. Obviously your being alive threatens Myra, if not because of Jeb, then for some other reason. Myra will always be a danger to you, and I can't allow that. We'll have to sell the Demon D and go somewhere else."

Victoria didn't know how to respond. She wondered what it would do to Trinity to run away from Myra. Trinity had never run from anything, but now he must, and she was the cause of it. She didn't know if she could let him do that. She didn't want him to be constantly looking over her shoulder, but she didn't want him to feel like a coward.

"Do you have the money to buy a ranch like the Demon D somewhere else?"

"I can sell the herd."

"Without selling the herd or the horses?"

"We can start with a smaller ranch."

Victoria searched his face, but she could find no sign of indecision, no hint of regret.

"You'd do that for me?"

"Nothing is more important than your safety—not the ranch, the cows, or the horses."

"You haven't said anything about Uncle Grant or my money."

"I won't take a penny from your uncle. And your money is your hedge against the future. I wouldn't let you invest it in something as uncertain as a ranch. The cows could die of thirst or the horses could eat milkweed. We could go broke the first year."

"I have faith in you. I'll back you to make a go of anything you set your mind to."

"You would really trust me with your money?"

"I trusted you with my life, didn't I?"

"I don't think I gave you a chance to make an objective decision."

"Well, I'd trust you with it now. My money's much less important."

"Then you don't mind leaving Bandera?"

"Not if you don't feel like you're running away from Queenie. I know how you felt about your father's death."

Trinity sat down next to her. "I finally realized what you'd been telling me was true. I wasn't responsible for my father's decisions, and I wasn't responsible for his death. I still feel like I ought to be able to do something about Queenie's killing him, but your safety is much more important to me. I also realize my being arrested for Queenie's murder won't help anybody. I've just got to learn to live with the knowledge I can't do anything about her."

"Can you?"

"As long as I have you, nothing from the past has the power to bother me."

* * *

"I wish you'd told me you were going to sell them dang cows before I trailed them all the way from New Mexico. I musta swallowed enough dust to make a right good-sized county."

"You should have asked," Victoria pointed out.

"Wouldn't have done no good, ma'am. You done shook him up so much he don't know what he's going to do next himself."

Ben had arrived in Bandera the previous evening. To make up for not being around when she needed him, he'd spent most of the hours since trying to keep Victoria entertained.

"I know the Bible says marriage is a blessed institution, but seems to have done nothing but addle Trinity's brains."

"I'm not married yet."

"You might as well be. You couldn't have stuck closer to her skirt tails if you'd been her nursemaid."

Fortunately for the well-being of Ben's neck, Red chose that moment to burst into the hotel room.

"The clerk downstairs said you nearly died," he blurted out. He plunged across the room to Victoria, ignoring Trinity and Ben.

"Red!" Victoria exclaimed. She jumped up from the chair and gave the boy an enthusiastic hug. "I've been worried sick about you. When did you get here? We would never have left if we hadn't—"

"Doc Mills told me all about those miners. I warned Mr. Davidge that Trinity couldn't take care of you. Now I find out he nearly let you die."

"Trinity had nothing to do with my being sick. In fact, if it hadn't been for him, I would have died."

"Who is this fire-eating bantam?" Ben demanded of Trinity. "And why haven't you shot him for putting his hands on your woman?"

"This is Michael O'Donavan, also known as Red," Trinity said, amusement dancing in his eyes. "He followed us from Texas to make sure I took good care of Victoria."

"Has he been reading about Sir Walter Raleigh, too?"

"I doubt it," Trinity said. "His gallantry comes naturally, not out of a book."

"Well, of all the ungrateful—"

"Come along. Let's allow Red to catch Victoria up on what happened to him."

"I sure didn't expect you to leave that young hot britches alone with your woman," Ben said once they were outside in the hall.

"If I have to worry about Red, I don't deserve Victoria. And stop calling her 'my woman.' She beaned Buc with a pole when he said it."

"You sure you're up to this marriage stuff?" Ben asked. "She's pretty enough to knock the sense out of Solomon, but she seems to be followed by a host of trouble."

"You let me worry about Victoria."

"Okay, but it's never wise to turn your back on a carrot-top, even a little one. Heard something you might be interested in," Ben said, changing the subject.

"What?" Trinity asked.

"About Chalk Gillet."

"What about him?"

"He's dead. He got into a knife fight with some Mexican. The guy slit his throat."

"You think he was set up?" Trinity inquired.

"Don't you?"

"Could be."

"That doesn't upset you?"

"Why should it?"

"Because there's nothing standing between Victoria and the gallows but that piece of paper in your pocket," Ben pointed out.

"What are you saying?"

"You've got to get that to a judge as soon as you can. And I don't mean Judge Blazer."

"The nearest judge is in Austin. You can leave in the morning."

"I'd be happy to take it if I thought I could, but if Chalk was set up, we're talking a whole different kind of scrape. If Queenie has hired herself a gunhand, I won't be in his league,

347

and you know it. I can rope a cow at fifty feet, but I can't hit a tin can at twenty. You're the one who can slip through a war party of Apache without them knowing. I'd end up getting killed, and you'd lose your only chance to clear Victoria."

"Sorry. I've been so worked up over Queenie's being right here in the same hotel I wasn't thinking. I'll go, I'll leave tonight, but you've got to swear you won't let Victoria out of your sight while I'm gone, not for as much as a minute."

A big grin split Ben's face. "Nothing easier. I can look at her just as long as she'll let me." Trinity could tell his smile came as much from relief as pleasure in bedeviling his friend.

"I said look."

"That woman doesn't have eyes for anyone but you. I swear I could lay my heart at her feet and she'd walk over it without noticing. Not that you're any better. I swear you're going to get yourselves killed some day. You'll be so busy gawking at each other you won't see a train or something coming."

"You're just jealous."

"I don't say I would mind having something like Victoria to look at now and again. It's just that I wouldn't enjoy having my wits that addled. I don't have all that many. Not that you seem to have a whole lot to spare. I never saw a sensible man so muddled. A year ago you'd have put a bullet between that black-haired witch's eyes and been done with it. Now you're thinking about selling up and moving away."

"I have a lot of things to consider now besides what I'd like to do."

"That's another thing. Women complicate a man's life something awful. The pretty ones do it worse. I don't think I'm up to it."

"Then it's a good thing Victoria fell in love with me."

"Yeah, safer, too."

"But it's an invitation from the Judge," Victoria told Ben. "He wants to see me, to make amends for some of the unpleasantness over Jeb's death."

"If this judge wants to see you so much, why doesn't he come to town?"

"He's in poor health. He says the trip from Austin exhausted him so he can't leave the house for several days yet."

"What about that Queenie woman?"

"You mean Myra. What can she do to me as long as you're with me?"

"Trinity said I wasn't to let you go near her under any circumstances."

"You won't have to. You can go with me."

"I still don't like it. Why don't you wait until Trinity gets back. He can go with you."

"I'd much rather go without him," Victoria eyed Ben mischievously. "If you won't go, maybe I'll ask Red."

"Don't you try your tricks on me," Ben said. "Trinity might not care that scrawny redhead don't seem to know where to put his hands, but I can tell him so's he'll remember. You ain't going nowhere with him. You take my advice and wait for Trinity."

"You don't understand," Victoria said. "Trinity insists Myra is the Queenie who married his father. He ought to know, but I'm sure he's mistaken somehow. There's a lot of tension when they're together. He doesn't think much of the Judge either."

"I guess not, steering his own daughter-in-law to the gallows."

"You forget it was his only son who was killed."

"No, I don't forget," Ben said, "but a dozen of him weren't worth one of you."

"That's a sweet thing to say, but it doesn't change anything. It's just a short visit. We can leave in the morning and be back before dark. Trinity will never know we've been gone."

"Yes, he will," Ben predicted. "You can swear every person between here and the Oklahoma territory to secrecy, but he'll know before he's been back five minutes."

"Well, it won't matter. We'll be back, and nothing will have happened. There'll be nothing for him to be angry about."

"I ain't so sure of that," Ben said. "I'm going against my instinct to let you go, and I always get in a load of trouble when I do that."

"I don't suppose you will believe me, but I'm very sorry for everything I did," Judge Blazer said to Victoria. "There didn't seem to be any possibility you weren't guilty, and I desperately wanted someone to suffer the way I had."

Victoria could hardly believe how much the Judge had changed. He had stopped actively running the ranch after his accident ten years earlier, but he had always been a proud, outgoing, handsome man.

He had become terribly thin and complained constantly of burning in his throat and stomach. His skin was much darker, as though he'd been spending too much time in the sun, and his face and legs seemed swollen, especially about the ankles and eyes. He seemed to be sweating, but his skin had felt cold and clammy when he embraced Victoria.

Even his personality had changed with his illness. He was querulous, lethargic, and unwilling to leave the house.

"I don't blame you for what you did," Victoria said.

"How can you not?"

"I used to, but I've learned a lot about life and people since then. I realize there's a great deal in everyone's life they can't control. We also make a great number of mistakes."

"I suppose you mean I shouldn't have made you marry Jeb."

"You didn't *make* me marry Jeb any more than my father did. You just wanted me to do what you thought was best for both of us. Unfortunately, Jeb and I weren't at all suited."

"I supposed I spoiled him too much. But after his mother died, I didn't know what else to do."

The Judge went into a spasm of coughing. He had been doing that ever since Victoria arrived. Victoria was unhappy Myra should have chosen this afternoon to go visiting.

"Could I get you something? Do you have any medicine?"

"I have too many, and none of them do any good. I would like a cup of coffee. That always seems to put the fire out for a little while. Would you mind making some?"

"Not in the least," Victoria said. "You stay here and rest."

"I suppose I shouldn't have any," the Judge called to Victoria

350

through the open doorway. "Myra said I was to wait until dinner. The doctors say it's not good for a weak heart, but it's gotten so I can't do without it. I didn't used to drink it much. Before I married Myra it was whiskey. When the doctors took me off alcohol, I started in on coffee. Myra keeps a pot of her own special brand going practically all day. I never saw anybody drink so much coffee."

Victoria couldn't really understand what he was saying, but she let him keep on talking.

It seemed strange to be in the kitchen once again. Almost without thinking she went unerringly to the container with the freshly ground coffee. Just enough for four cups. After she put the pot on to boil, she looked through the cupboards for the extra coffee. She had been brought up to refill a container when she used the last. Their cook had drummed that into her head time and time again.

Victoria wished Myra were here now to take care of her husband or at least tell her what to do. He must have medicine to take. Coffee might make him feel better, but it certainly couldn't do him any real good.

She found the extra coffee behind a tin of lard. More than half of the contents had been used already. She put exactly as much coffee in the coffee container as she had taken out, replaced the rest behind the lard tin, and took down three cups. Even though he had refused to come inside, Ben might like some. At least she could offer him some after he rode so far with her.

"That's good," the Judge said after he'd taken a few swallows. "You'll have to tell Myra what you do. I don't know when I've tasted coffee this good. I want you to come live here with us," the Judge said, changing the subject. "You're my daughter-in-law. Your home should be here."

"Thank you, but I can't."

"Don't say no because of what I did," the Judge pleaded. "I'll do anything I can to make up for that. As Jeb's widow, you have a considerable amount of money coming to you."

"Please, I don't want Jeb's money. If we'd been married longer or had children, it would be different, but Daddy left

351

me more than enough."

"It's yours. Jeb put it in his will."

"I know, but he really didn't like me. It wasn't his fault. We just didn't suit. I wouldn't feel right taking his money."

"What are you going to do, go back to Arizona?"

Victoria felt herself blush. She guessed she felt a little embarrassed talking to the Judge about her happiness when he was so unhappy. "I'm going to get married."

"To your uncle's foreman, the boy who broke you out of jail?"

Victoria felt herself blush even more. "No, to Trinity Smith, the man who brought me back to Bandera."

"Are you crazy?" the Judge nearly shouted. He sat up like he'd been shot. "You can't marry a bounty hunter."

Chapter Twenty-six

"He's not a bounty hunter," Victoria shot back. "He only goes after people because nobody else will." Even as she explained Trinity's reason for his work, she recognized her own accusations in the very words the judge used. How ironic she should have to defend Trinity now.

"I still don't like it," the Judge said. "You realize people won't take to him. You'll never get invited anywhere. And what about your children? You might as well be marrying one of the outlaws he chases."

"I know that," Victoria said, finally realizing the price Trinity had paid for his dedication to his task, "but Trinity is a great man. I'll be only too happy to share his isolation. If people refuse to associate with him, it'll be their loss."

Just as quickly as he got upset, all the steam seemed to go out of the Judge, and he sank back in his chair. "You always were a sensible girl, a sight more sensible than I was. You bring your young man by, and if I like him I'll see what I can do. There aren't many people in Texas who'll stand against me. There's nobody ready to go head-to-head with Myra."

"That's very kind of you, but I don't think Trinity cares much about social acceptance."

"You tell him it's for your children. He can spend all his time with his cows if he likes, but your children will have to make their own way in the world. A few friends along the way will be a great help."

"It's very generous of you . . ."

"No, it's not. After what I did, it's the least I can do." The Judge stopped, like he had just remembered something. "You say your young man believes his stepmother killed his father?"

"Yes, but he has no proof. It happened in Galveston fifteen years ago. He tried to get the sheriff to investigate, but he wasn't interested."

"Shame I didn't know about it. I'd have gotten them on it fast enough. What happened to the woman?"

"She disappeared."

Victoria couldn't bring herself to tell the Judge that Trinity believed his wife was Queenie. She probably should tell him. If Myra really were Queenie, he ought to be warned. But if she weren't and Victoria believed she wasn't, it would cause a tremendous amount of trouble for nothing.

"How's he going to support you?"

"He owns a ranch."

"Where?"

Victoria didn't want to explain why they weren't going to stay on the Demon D. "In New Mexico." She didn't think Ben would mind her appropriating his ranch just this once. "But he intends to buy a larger one."

"I suppose you'll want control of your own money?"

"Yes, I would."

"Does he know he's marrying a very rich woman?"

"Am I rich? No one ever told me how much Daddy left me."

"Over two hundred thousand dollars."

Victoria sat forward in her chair. "Are you sure?"

"Positive."

Victoria felt elated. There was more than enough money for Trinity to buy the biggest ranch he could. And cows. And horses. There would be plenty left over for building a house and having children and doing all kinds of things she had dreamed of while she was locked away in Arizona.

"It's a good bit more than that now," the Judge added. "One investment I made worked out rather nicely."

"You take it."

Enough of his energy returned for the Judge to act hurt by

her suggestion. "Absolutely not! Why should I?"

"For looking after everything for me. You didn't have to."

"Yes, I did. I wanted to see Jeb's murderer hang, but I never wanted to hurt you. Can you understand that?"

Victoria understood it very well.

"I'm glad. I didn't want to dislike you either, but you frightened me. You were so very determined to bring me back. Will you try to find out who did kill Jeb?"

The Judge seemed to wilt again. "I don't know. I just don't care much about anything anymore. I feel so tired all the time. If I didn't have Kirby, I don't know what would become of this place. He's still young, but he does the work of a grown man."

"Kirby's always admired you," Victoria said. "I think he feels like you're the father he never had."

"He's a good boy. I've grown very fond of him. I just wish Myra would give him a little more rein. She's such a strong woman she doesn't realize she's suffocating him. I tried to get her to let me send him away to school, but she wouldn't hear of it."

Victoria felt uncomfortable. She had never liked it when she became involved in any disagreement between the Judge and Myra. She didn't like it any better now. She saw Ben get up from his seat under the trees and head for the house. She latched onto that as an excuse to bring her visit to an end.

"I have to start back," she said, getting to her feet. "It's a long ride back to Bandera."

The Judge started to get up but settled back into his seat. "Come again soon and bring your uncle. You'll always be welcome."

"I will. And you take care of that cough. Have you seen a doctor?"

"Dozens of them, but they all scratch their heads and mumble behind my back. I think they're afraid to tell me I'm dying. If they only knew that I don't care. I don't care at all."

* * *

Ben looked nervously about him. The quietness of his surroundings didn't seem to comfort him. He approached each patch of brush or clump of trees as though he expected an ambush. It didn't take long for his skittishness to communicate itself to Victoria.

"I wish you'd stop jumping about. You're making my horse nervous."

"I don't know why you had to visit that old man today. I've had a bad feeling ever since I got up this morning."

"You just didn't want to get out of bed."

"You're right, I didn't. Trinity told me to stay in that hotel and keep an eye on you, and I was perfectly happy as long as I did just that. But I wasn't content with doing what I was told. I had to let you talk me into coming on this jaunt."

"And it's been perfectly uneventful."

"Except that I got a feeling someone's got dead aim at my back."

"There's nobody here, certainly not anybody who wants to bother us."

Ben sighed resignedly, but he didn't look convinced. "You're probably right. You know, before I took up with that man of yours, I was an easygoing kind of man."

"What do you mean by 'that man of yours'?" Victoria demanded.

"I hustled a few cows, drank a little whiskey, chased a few women, and listened to a lot of trail talk. Never had a worry in the world and slept like a baby at night.

"Since I took up with him I been saddled with a herd of cows I didn't want, and I've taken to looking over my shoulder so often my neck has a permanent crick in it. I been chased by bad men from New Orleans to California, I've slept on the ground so often I've forgotten what a bed feels like, and I'm so nervous I can't eat good. Now I've taken to escorting young women on daylight outings to visit old men."

"From desperados to debutantes. My, you have come down in the world."

"It ain't the coming down I mind. Chaperoning is a nice

356

safe job. For the most part it's quiet and restful. It's the rest of it. Every one of those men he brought in has a bunch of relations that's as sore as a nest of rattlers. No telling when they might decide to even things up a bit. Associating with your young man ain't none too safe. Maybe you ought to reconsider."

"You think I ought to marry someone else?"

"You might think about it." Ben grinned ingratiatingly.

"You have any candidate in mind?"

"It's not for me to say. You'd be doing the marrying."

"I know, but as a friend, you might give me some advice."

"Well, he ought to be an obliging fella, one who won't expect you to rustle up the grub or mess up your hairdo chasing about on horseback."

"You think I would enjoy having a cook and a closed carriage?"

"It's the only way to live. A pretty little thing like you wouldn't be wanting to arrive at parties all rumpled and dusty. People would gossip."

"Maybe I ought to find a husband who would like to live in town, one who wouldn't mind sleeping late, eating too much rich food, and going to parties all night."

"Not many men who can keep up that kind of pace."

"Do you think you could?"

"I might."

"But that would be stealing your best friend's girl!"

"When it comes to a gal like you, ain't no man going to worry his head about a best friend."

Without warning, Ben leaned over and grabbed Victoria, practically pulling her out of the saddle. Furious that he could be so stupid as to take her nonsense seriously, she hit him as hard as she could. Her blow landed on the side of Ben's neck and nearly cut off his air.

"There's somebody on that ridge with a rifle," Ben gasped.

Immediate corroboration came in the sound of a rifle shot and a bullet splitting the air over Victoria's head.

"Ride like hell!" he shouted and brought his hand down on Victoria's mount's rump.

A second rifle shot reinforced his command.

"Whoever they're after, they mean to get both of us. Make for that clump of brush."

"We'll get killed if we try to ride through there."

"We'll get killed if we don't."

Victoria closed her eyes and rode straight for the wall of thorns.

Trinity was thoroughly angry.

He had arrived in Bandera feeling rather pleased with himself. He had handed the affidavit to the judge in Austin. Victoria was free. Now all he had to do was ask Victoria to marry him and decide where to live. He had spent the weary miles on the way back to Bandera going over every part of the country he had seen, considering each for suitability for a ranch. There were hundreds of spots exactly like what he was looking for.

But he had also looked at them from the standpoint of a home for Victoria and their children. That changed everything. He didn't want to end up somewhere in the panhandle of Texas, the wilds of New Mexico, the mountains of Arizona or Colorado, or the plains of Wyoming or Montana. He came to the conclusion that the ideal place was right here at the Demon D, situated between Bandera and San Antonio.

It would be perfect . . . except for Queenie.

He had tried to put Queenie out of his mind, but once more she was forcing him to do something he didn't want to do, to make a decision that was not the best for him and his future family. Hell! He'd be damned if he'd let her do that again!

Okay, so I mean to stay at the Demon D. What can I do about Queenie?

He knew Victoria didn't believe Myra was Queenie. She had never said so, but he knew. He could understand. Myra had changed everything about her, even the smallest details,

358

but Trinity never had any doubt. He'd have known her anywhere, anytime.

He was certain Queenie wouldn't stop until she poisoned Victoria. And if she ever remembered who he was, she'd try to poison him as well.

It went against the grain to run from Queenie. Even worse, it galled him to be chased away from his home. But he also had to be reasonable. Could he always protect Victoria? How about his children? They would be perfect targets for Myra's revenge. Would he always be around to protect them? Was his pride worth a lifelong vigil?

Queenie would never give up.

Trinity hadn't reached any conclusions when he arrived at the hotel, only to be informed Victoria had gone to visit Judge Blazer and wasn't expected back until late afternoon. It would take the clerk about ten years to use all the new words he learned that afternoon.

"Her uncle is due in this afternoon," Red said. He had come to the hotel looking for Victoria. He waved a telegram David Woolridge had given him. "He still thinks she's dead."

"You stay here and wait for him," Trinity said. "You can explain what happened. I'll go bring her back."

Trinity cursed himself for choosing to ride Diablo. He had been riding the stallion a little each day since he returned from Uvalde. He never wore spurs or carried a riding crop. But even though he was very careful never to use his heels, guiding Diablo entirely with the bit and his knees, the horse still fought him.

"If I had the time, I'd take you back," Trinity told Diablo as the stallion circled and bucked and generally took twice as long to cover a hundred yards as he should. "But Victoria said you were as fast as the wind, and I need your speed today."

Diablo apparently wasn't in the mood to give it. He whirled and covered twenty-five yards in the wrong direction before Trinity got him turned around again.

"Damn you. I've never known such a contrary beast in my life."

Fifteen minutes later, Trinity was still trying to convince Diablo to cooperate when he noticed a rider coming from the direction of Bandera at a gallop. When he recognized Kirby Blazer, he pulled up.

"He's going to kill Victoria," Kirby shouted as he shot by without stopping.

Digging his heels sharply into Diablo's side at the same time he brought his open palm down on the stallion's rump, Trinity set him in pursuit of Kirby. Diablo responded with a glorious burst of speed.

He ran Kirby down with the ease of a gazelle chasing a donkey.

"Who's going to kill Victoria?" Trinity shouted, the wind valiantly trying to tear his words from his lips.

"German Lyman."

"Who the hell is German Lyman?"

"He took care of Mother when my father deserted her and left her pregnant. He's been with her ever since."

Diablo tried to savage Kirby's thoroughbred gelding. The gelding was so frightened of the huge stallion he went into a full-out gallop. Diablo kept up effortlessly.

"How do you know this man is going to try to kill Victoria?"

"I saw one of the hands in town. He said German left the ranch this morning several hours before mother went visiting. German would *never* let mother go anywhere without him, not unless he had something more important to do."

"What are you going to do?"

"I've got to make her stop him. I'm sure he killed Jeb. I won't let him kill Victoria, too. It would kill the Judge."

The whole story seemed utterly fantastic to Trinity. He wouldn't have given it a moment's credence if he hadn't known Queenie. Where she was involved, anything was possible.

"What's he going to do?" Trinity asked as he continued to foil Diablo's efforts to attack Kirby's gelding.

"I don't know."

Trinity realized it was useless to question the boy. He was nearly hysterical with fear and worry. He was tempted to use

360

Diablo's greater speed to hurry ahead, but he stayed alongside because he knew Kirby would be better able to guess where an ambush might take place.

Trinity had never felt so helpless . . . or so murderously angry. If Queenie hurt Victoria further, he would kill her. If anything happened to Victoria, it wouldn't matter what they did to him. Not as long as he killed Queenie first.

Diablo pricked his ears. Trinity couldn't hear what had attracted the stallion's attention, but he felt his muscles gather, his pace quicken. They left Kirby behind in a half-dozen strides. Going on instinct, Trinity let Diablo have his head. The great black stallion wasn't fighting him any longer. He had lost interest in Kirby's gelding. Something ahead riveted his interest.

Then Trinity heard it. Faintly at first. But as they rounded the edge of a small rise, it suddenly grew much louder. The sound of gunfire! Diablo screamed with fury and galloped even faster. Trinity had no way of knowing why Diablo hated the sound of gunfire, but this afternoon he was glad. It just might save Victoria's life.

He saw a lone rider first, a rider chasing something in the brush and firing almost as rapidly as he could cock his rifle. Whoever he was chasing had to be in the brush. He hoped it wasn't Victoria. She wouldn't come out alive.

He saw her when she and Ben made a dash from one clump of brush to another. Even at a distance he could tell her clothes were being torn to ribbons. With a howl of rage, he drove Diablo after the rifleman.

Diablo needed no encouragement. The distance between them closed with dramatic swiftness. Trinity drew his gun but didn't fire. He wanted to be closer. He didn't want to kill this man. He wanted to know who sent him after Victoria and why.

The rifleman was so intent upon following Victoria, Diablo was almost upon him before he realized he was being pursued. With a look of fury he whirled about in the saddle, his rifle raised.

Trinity fired, and the man's body jerked, but he didn't drop his rifle. As Diablo drew closer, he raised it again. Trinity shot into him a second time, and still the man retained his hold on the saddle and his rifle.

Diablo reached the flanks of the straining mount. With bared teeth, he bit viciously into the tired horse. The animal screamed in pain and whirled around to defend himself. The sudden motion caused the rifleman to lose his hold and tumble to the ground. . . . Right under Diablo's pounding hooves.

Trinity wrenched the stallion to one side but not before he felt the sickening impact of driving hooves on soft flesh. He leapt from the saddle and ran to the body lying motionless on the dry prairie.

He thought he recognized the man as one who used to hang around Queenie when she sang at the dance hall, but he couldn't be sure. Time had changed him too much. The man's eyes opened, and he stared at Trinity.

"Who are you?" Trinity asked. "Why are you trying to kill Victoria? Who sent you?"

The man said nothing, just continued to stare at Trinity with hate in his eyes.

"You need a doctor. Tell me who paid you to kill Victoria, and I'll take you to Bandera."

Still the man remained silent, motionless.

Kirby came galloping up. He leapt down and bent over the fallen man.

"That's German Lyman."

"So Queenie did send you to kill Victoria."

"He won't say anything," Kirby said. "He'd die before he'd say anything that might hurt Mother."

Trinity thought the hatred in German's eyes grew even more intense when he looked at Kirby. He must consider the boy a traitor.

"Is he going to die?" Kirby asked.

"I don't know. I promised to get him to a doctor if he'd tell me who sent him, but he refuses to talk."

"He won't. You'll never know."

Abruptly Trinity lost interest in German Lyman or anyone else. Victoria and Ben were riding up, and they looked torn to pieces. Victoria tumbled from the saddle into his arms.

There was blood all over her. She looked like she'd been chewed up by a threshing machine. Great rents had been torn in her clothes, pieces of cloth were missing altogether. Her horse appeared to be equally bad.

Ben looked worst of all.

"There wasn't any other way," Ben explained when Trinity gave him a look which had death written all over it. "It was the only way out."

"Ben made me stay behind him," Victoria muttered. "Otherwise I'd have been torn to pieces."

Trinity looked quizzically at his old friend.

"Sir Walter Ralcigh, again. You read too much about those queer birds and you start acting like them."

Trinity heard a whisper of movement behind him and turned just in time to see German Lyman sitting up on his elbow, his rifle aimed straight at Victoria.

The sound of a shot exploded in his eardrums. Trinity expected to see Victoria collapse before his horrified gaze. Instead German slumped to the ground.

He was dead.

Kirby's gun slipped from his limp grasp, and he stared at the body in horror. "He was going to kill Victoria. He had the rifle pointed straight at her."

Trinity felt an overwhelming desire to march up to the ranch and shoot Queenie on the spot. Two things stopped him: Victoria and Kirby.

He had to get Victoria to a doctor. She had been badly mauled by her ride through the brush. He didn't think she had any serious injury, but he wouldn't know until he got her back to the hotel. She was more important than Queenie. She always would be.

Also, if he rode up to the ranch now, Kirby would follow him. And no matter how angry he was, no matter how much she deserved it, he couldn't shoot Queenie right before her son's eyes.

The boy was barely hanging on to his sanity as it was. And Trinity remembered too well how he felt after his father's death. Not even his awful rage would cause him to do that to someone else.

But he would find Queenie some day, and he would kill her. He had no other choice.

"Oowwww!" Victoria moaned as Trinity pulled out the last thorn embedded in her shoulder. "You don't have to pull it out sideways."

"It would serve you right if I left it in," Trinity said as he discarded the thorn and cleaned the wound. "You wouldn't have had to ride through the brush if you had stayed here like I told you."

"I've already admitted it was my fault. I've said I'm sorry until I'm sick of apologizing. I can't even look Ben in the eye. That's punishment enough. You don't have to keep piling it on."

Ben and the horses had been turned over to Ward and Doctor Roundtree. Trinity had reserved the pleasure of taking care of Victoria.

"He shouldn't be attending you at all," Grant Davidge protested. He and Red had been waiting at the hotel when Victoria returned. From being overjoyed to learn his niece was alive, Grant had progressed to outrage when he learned that she and Trinity practically shared the same room. He was furious when she arrived looking bloody and tattered. His sense of propriety was further offended when Trinity, rather than a doctor, attended her wounds. "Why won't you let Dr. Roundtree do that?" he asked Victoria for the third time.

"I'm going to marry Trinity," Victoria explained wearily. "I'd prefer him to see me half naked than some doctor."

"But it's not proper for even your fiance to see you like this."

"Then you do it."

But Grant drew the line at doing it himself. "I'm not sure I

364

approve of this engagement. I could hardly believe it when Red told me."

"He should have left that to me."

"He was too shocked to think straight, poor kid."

"Then he should have stayed in Mountain Valley where you can take care of him," Victoria snapped. Trinity was pouring raw spirits on her wounds, and the pain was terrible.

"I don't understand why you're acting this way, Victoria. It's almost like you're trying to shock me."

"Compared to what has happened to me during the last few weeks, this is nothing. Now stop buzzing about like an angry wasp and tell me about Buc."

Grant looked unhappy, but he was obviously at a loss to understand how his niece could have changed so much in such a short time.

"Buc's wound will heal, but he's leaving Mountain Valley. Going to California. He said he couldn't stay. Everything reminds him of you."

Victoria wanted to curse. It was just like Buc to try to make her feel guilty. "There's no need for him to do that. I'm not going back."

"He couldn't know."

"Then send him a wire."

"He won't get it."

Victoria lost patience. "I think you ought to see that lawyer as soon as you can. There's no telling what he's started and you'll have to stop. And then there's the Pinkerton. Trinity will have me all bandaged up and looking proper again by the time you return," she said when her uncle hesitated. "Then he'll go away, and we can have a long talk."

"You don't have to do that."

"You deserve the chance to give your niece the benefit of your advice," Trinity said. "I want to marry her more than anything else in the world, but I can understand your reservations. I've gotten her in quite a bit of trouble."

"You seem to have gotten her out of it, and a bit more besides," Grant admitted.

"I didn't have much choice, did I?" Trinity said with the puckish grin Victoria liked so much. "Not with Red breathing down my neck."

"You know he's never going to approve of you."

"I don't know of anybody who does . . . except Victoria."

"You're sure?" Grant asked his niece.

"More sure than I've ever been in my life."

Chapter Twenty-seven

"You don't believe Myra is Queenie," Trinity said. Victoria's uncle had gone, and they were alone. "Don't deny it, I know you don't. I wouldn't mind if she weren't so dangerous. You have to admit somebody paid to have you killed. Who else could it be but Queenie? And who else would be hiring their killers from the Tumbling T hands but Myra?"

"I admit I was wrong. Just seeing Kirby after he killed that man was all the convincing I needed. Do you think he'll be all right?" She was sincerely concerned.

"It'll take a little while. He's obviously not a killer, but he'll get over it. It all depends on Queenie."

"What do you think she'll do?"

"I don't know, but whatever it is, she won't do it tonight. Now take off that robe. I want to check your wounds."

"They can't have gotten infected already."

"You never know."

"Oh, all right. Inspect away," Victoria said, willing to indulge Trinity. "Are you done?" she asked when he had checked the last scratch.

"Yes."

"Do you mind if I get some clothes on?"

"I mind very much."

"Trinity, you can't mean to . . ."

"Yes, I do."

"But I'm covered with scratches."

"I love your scratches."

"It'll be like making love to a hospital patient."

"I love hospital patients."

"You don't know a thing about hospital patients."

"I'm willing to learn."

Victoria gave up any notion she had of teaching Trinity propriety. Clearly the man was besotted; a desperate case; putting him out of his misery was the only humane thing to do.

"I hope you don't think I'm going to make a habit of this."

"You don't have to. I will."

"You're hopeless. And shameless."

"You're right."

"And you don't care."

"I care passionately."

"Balderdash."

"I care passionately about being shameless with you every-day of my life."

Victoria surrendered. It was so much more wonderful to let herself be carried along on the tide of their mutual passion. She didn't think she would ever get tired of Trinity's need to make love to her. She loved his gentleness when he kissed her and held her close. She loved his strength when he overpowered her and drove his tongue deep into her mouth. She loved his impatience when he wanted her so much he couldn't wait.

But most of all she loved it when he made love to *her.*

Everything else was merely a prelude, an overture before the main act. She relaxed and let him make slow love. But as he touched her arm or brushed her shoulders with his lips, she thought of the riotous sensations those same lips would cause to erupt when they suckled her nipples. When his fingertips feathered across her lips or traced maddening arabesques on her abdomen, she remembered the exquisite agony they called forth from her loins.

When his hands cupped her breasts or gently massaged her thighs or stomach, she anticipated the desperate need she would feel when they parted her thighs. When his tongue darted deep into her mouth, searching out the sweetness in every far corner, she longed for him to sink his manhood deep into her, searching for the kernel of need which would never be fully satisfied.

"Love me," she groaned, too desperate to wait any longer. "You're driving me crazy."

But not as crazy as when he circled her nipples with his hot tongue, or as frantic as when he nipped at her swollen nipple with his teeth, or as frenzied as when he suckled her nipple.

"Hurry!"

But Trinity didn't hurry. He continued to torture her breasts while one hand slowly ventured down her ribs, over her hip, and tantalizingly low across her abdomen before returning to cup her breast.

Victoria writhed. "Stop torturing me," Victoria pleaded.

Trinity moved inside her and Victoria groaned. Throwing herself against his hand, she tried to draw him deep inside. He found the tender nub of her pleasure and gently massaged it with the roughness of his fingertip.

Victoria thought she would explode.

She helped him out of the last of his clothes, ripping and tearing in her haste. She wrapped herself around him, capturing his body and drawing him inside her. She didn't know what pleased him most, but at this moment she didn't care. He would quench the fire in her loins even if she had to become the aggressor.

Trinity had dropped all restraint. He wanted Victoria as much as she wanted him. They came together in a tremendous release of energy. Once released, there was no restraining their drive to fulfillment. Trinity's thrusts into her body were controlled and measured, but there was no advance and retreat, no attempt to prolong the tension. Each move was a steady drive toward consummation.

Wave after wave of pulsating hunger washed over Victoria, each more exquisite and more agonizing than the one before. Again and again she called out to Trinity to ease her agony, to release her, but he rode the bronco of his own yearning. He heard nothing but the call of his loins driving him on to utter exhaustion.

After one final thrust, and one deep breath, Victoria let go.

She felt all the need melt away within her as she floated away on a cloud of utter content.

Victoria woke with a premonition of disaster. Then she remembered Trinity's making love to her the night before and her foreboding fled. Her first movement made her acutely aware of pain and stiffness in her arms and shoulders. She inspected her wounds. Some of them looked rather nasty. He had loved her passionately even though she looked liked she had spent a whole afternoon being dragged naked through a rose garden.

Never again would she worry about Trinity not wanting to touch her. Any man who could love her the way she looked now would love her for the rest of his life.

She laughed to herself with pure happiness. There was so much about these last days she wanted to remember, to enjoy until she had drunk all the sweetness. Life was wonderful, people were wonderful, and Trinity was the most wonderful of all. She could hardly believe that while being cloistered at a ranch in a remote region of Arizona she had had the good fortune to run into anyone like him. The odds were incredible. She felt tremendously fortunate.

Her years of unhappiness and misfortune seemed to be less than nothing now, only a moment in a sea of happiness. She thought she might even go back home to Alabama one day. She wouldn't mind letting her imperious aunts get a look at Trinity. Certainly their colorless, perfectly behaved daughters hadn't found a husband even remotely as exciting and handsome as Trinity.

That made her laugh. Her aunts would have fainted, all in a row, if any one of their daughters had brought home a Trinity. She didn't know what they feared a man like Trinity would do, but she had the pleasure of knowing it couldn't hold a candle to what had actually happened to her.

She also had the pleasure of knowing she had survived every bit of it in perfect order. Okay, so she had a few dozen scratches, but they would heal.

She turned over, thought about getting up, but changed her mind. Trinity had dressed and gone. He probably wanted to check on Ben and the horses. He'd come back soon and they'd have breakfast together.

She enjoyed breakfasting alone with Trinity. Even when they were on the trail and she hated him and felt horrible, there was a kind of magic about being alone with him.

She chuckled to herself. That horrible trip from Arizona would probably become a much-too-often-retold piece of folklore in future Smith households. In all likelihood it would be romanticized until it bore no resemblance to the truth. Already she remembered only the good things. All the danger and fear and discomfort were forgotten. Only the excitement and wonder remained.

She hoped, when she approached the end of her days, she would be able to look back on her life in just that way. She knew living with Trinity would mean acknowledging his stubbornness, but she didn't care about that. As long as no one came out of his past to disturb their happiness, she didn't care how stubborn he might be.

His guns were gone!

Victoria sat up in the bed, clutching the sheet to her breasts. She hadn't noticed that at first, but if he was just going to see Ben, why would he need his guns? Her earlier uneasy feeling returned. She tried to tell herself she was just imagining things, but it didn't work.

Something was wrong, and she knew it.

Victoria jumped out of bed, wrapped a robe around her, and opened the door to the hall. No one was in sight. She scampered along the hall until she reached the door to Ben's room. A drowsy voice invited her to take the first bucking bronco to hell. She went in anyway.

"You're feeling mighty unfriendly this morning. God, you look awful!" she exclaimed the moment she got a look at Ben. "Are you all right?"

Ben's neck, shoulders and upper body were practically covered in bandages. His face was swollen and discolored from the numerous thorn wounds.

"I'm perfectly fine," he mumbled, moving his lips as little as possible. "I enjoyed it so much as soon as I get out of these bandages I'm going to go out and do it again."

Victoria felt a wave of guilt. Ben had done everything he could to keep her from going to see Judge Blazer, and then he had sacrificed his own body to protect her from her foolishness.

"You shouldn't have ridden in front just to protect me."

"Oh yes I should. I might look like hell now, but all this mess will heal. If I'd let you come out of that briar patch looking like this, Trinity would have killed me."

"You know he wouldn't."

"Now you look here," Ben said, moving so quickly he winced in pain, "there are a few things about Trinity you don't seem to understand too well, and one of them is how he feels about you. If any man on earth had let you go first into that pincushion from hell, he'd have killed him. Period."

The ominous words reminded Victoria of her reason for coming to Ben's room in a near state of undress.

"Trinity's gone. Do you know where he went?"

"He didn't say anything, just checked to make sure I was still alive. But if you ask me, he's gone to fix that Queenie bitch. I'm surprised he didn't do it before. After yesterday, I'm surprised he waited until today."

Victoria ran back to her room as fast as she could. Heedless of the pain of her own wounds, she threw off her robe and put on the first clothes she came to, her torn and tattered clothes from yesterday. Dashing into the hall, she nearly ran over Ben who, driven by the fear of Trinity's restitution if he didn't stop Victoria, had risen from his bed.

"You can't go chasing after Trinity. I didn't say he went to kill Queenie. I just said I thought he had."

"That's the same as knowing. You're both crazy the same way."

"Well, if that's appreciation, I sure don't recognize it."

"I haven't got time to be nice," Victoria said. "I don't care about Queenie. I care about Trinity. If he kills Queenie, he'll ruin his life. And mine, too."

Impervious to astonished stares, Victoria raced through the hotel lobby and down the street until she came to the livery stable. "Did Trinity Smith ride out of here this morning?" she asked a man sitting by the barn door.

"Yes'um."

"When?"

"About half an hour ago."

"Did he head up or down the street?"

"Down."

He had gone in the direction of the Tumbling T.

"Saddle Diablo."

"That horse don't like being saddled," the man mumbled. "He's likely to maul me if I try." He made no move to get up.

Victoria knocked the chair out from under him. "Saddle him, or I'll maul you worse than Diablo."

The man hauled himself to his feet and, after giving Victoria an injured look, led the way to Diablo's stall. Victoria put the bridle on Diablo and held his head while the man saddled him.

"He was out yesterday," the man complained as he adjusted the saddle and tightened the cinch on the fretting stallion. "He's probably worn to a nubbin."

"He's still the fastest horse in Bandera."

Victoria flung herself into the saddle. Diablo didn't buck once. He exploded through the livery stable door at a full gallop.

"He is fast," the man muttered as he righted his chair, settled in, and leaned against the door.

Victoria didn't need to urge Diablo to his utmost speed. He stretched out his legs and ran for the sheer joy of running. Even though fear for Trinity filled her mind, Victoria marveled at the speed, power and stamina of this remarkable stallion. If he could pass it on to his offspring, he would make Trinity a rich man.

But would Trinity be around to become a rich man?

If he killed Queenie, he'd hang.

She couldn't let that happen. No matter what Queenie had

done, no matter what she might do in the future, nothing was worth Trinity's life.

And her life as well.

He couldn't throw everything away, not without talking to her first. He had no right. He had said he loved her, that he wanted to marry her, that he wanted them to live together for the rest of their lives. That meant his life belonged to her as much as it did to him, and she had no intention of letting him squander it.

The ride seemed endless. She wouldn't let herself consider the possibility that she might arrive too late. She tried to think of what she would say to convince him to leave Queenie alone, but as she drew closer to the ranch, her fear of arriving too late increased. If Trinity had decided to kill Queenie, he would succeed.

She almost sobbed with relief when she rounded a clump of willows and saw Trinity's buckskin in the distance. He was trotting. She could tell he still hadn't made up his mind about what he was going to do. When Trinity rode with a purpose, he rode at a gallop. He pulled up when he recognized her.

"What are you doing here?" he demanded when she drew rein at his side.

"What a charming way to greet your fiancee. I hope you improve on it after we're married."

"I don't have time for teasing. Why did you come?"

"To stop you from killing Queenie."

"I'll kill Ben," Trinity swore.

"Nobody told me what you were going to do. Nobody had to. I know you, Trinity. After yesterday, there was only one thing you could do. I just didn't expect you to go after her so soon. I won't let you do it," she said when he didn't answer her. "I know how you feel, but our future together is more important than Queenie."

"If Queenie has her way, we won't have any future."

"Then find another way to stop her."

"I have."

Now she understood the trot. He had been thinking, working out the angles. "What is it?"

"What's the most important thing in the world to Queenie?"

"I don't know. Money, I guess."

"Being married to Judge Blazer. Money comes with that, but as Judge Blazer's wife she's somebody important. No matter where she goes, people fall over themselves trying to please her. Take away her position and what does she have?"

"Can you take it away?"

"I think so. After she stole my father's ranch, I think she worked her way through the West fleecing anyone she could."

"Can you prove it?"

"Not yet, but I have a strong notion that a lot of people still remember Queenie. Anyway, I know enough to put a good scare in her."

"So you're going to offer to keep quiet about her past if she'll swear to leave us alone?"

"That's about it. Not very much like me, is it?"

She could tell he was unhappy with himself. He may have decided he had to compromise, but he hadn't learned to like it.

"No. It's much too sensible. Do you think she'll accept it?"

"Queenie hates to lose anything, but she's got just about everything she wants now. Why take a chance on losing it just for revenge? She's a young woman. If the Judge divorces her, she faces a long life of disgrace."

Victoria felt the muscles in her neck and shoulders relax. She didn't know if Trinity's idea would work, but it was a chance that they could have their life together without more killing.

As they drew near the Tumbling T, Victoria was surprised to see several horses in the yard. There was also an unusually large number of men gathered around the house.

Something was wrong.

"What happened?" Trinity asked one of the hands as they dismounted.

"The Judge's wife's dead."

"What!" Victoria exclaimed.

"When did it happen? How?"

"I don't know. Ain't nobody told us nothing."

Victoria and Trinity hurried up to the house. No one met them at the door. They found everyone gathered in the parlor: the Judge, Kirby, Sheriff Sprague, Doctor Roundtree.

Victoria went straight to Kirby and enfolded the stunned boy in her arms. The grief he had held back in the presence of men found release in Victoria's touch, and he sobbed out his heartbreak in her arms.

"What happened?" Trinity asked the sheriff.

"Nobody knows. The maid found her like this when she came in to tidy up. No sign of a struggle. No wound I can see."

"What killed her?" he asked the doctor.

"I don't know. Could have been heart failure. She seems to have had a seizure or something before she died. See, she knocked over her coffee cup."

Trinity looked at the dropped cup. He picked up a coffeepot sitting on the table next to Myra's chair and swirled it around. There was still a little coffee inside.

"Have this checked. I think she was poisoned."

"That's absurd," Sheriff Sprague said. "Who would do that?"

"I don't know, but test it anyway."

The doctor handed the pot to a maid and directed her to put the contents into a clean jar. "I'll have the results by tonight. You think it's the same poison?"

"You can tell that better than I can. Are they the same symptoms?"

"No. If it's poison, they're more consistent with arsenic."

"But how would rat poison get in the coffee?" the Judge asked.

"I have no idea. Has anyone else been ill recently?"

"I've been ill for years," the Judge said, and began a detailed recital of his symptoms.

"I would like to examine you," Dr. Roundtree said.

"I have my own doctors in San Antonio and Austin," Judge Blazer replied, surprised a strange doctor would make such a request.

"Nevertheless, if your wife has been poisoned, you might have been as well."

"Oh all right. We can use my study, but I can't give you very long."

"I'll only take a few minutes," the doctor assured them.

"It might be a good idea to tell the men outside what's happened," Trinity suggested to the sheriff. "Better than their making up their own version."

The sheriff nodded agreement and left.

Kirby's sobs had dwindled into hiccups.

"I should have told the sheriff, but I couldn't. After all she was my mother."

"Told him what?" Trinity asked.

"She was poisoning the Judge. I didn't find out until last night. We had a tremendous fight after I brought Lyman's body back. I told her I knew she was trying to kill Victoria, that if she didn't stop, I'd tell the Judge. That's when she told me what she'd been doing. It wouldn't do any good, she said. She had already poisoned the Judge, she said. He would die any day now. There was nothing I could do to stop it. I must have looked horrified. Anyway she got even more furious. She started to taunt me about being a coward, saying I didn't have the guts to do what it took to get ahead in life. How did I think she'd been able to get out of the miserable shack where she was born? I ought to get on my knees in thanks that she hadn't abandoned me when my father deserted her.

"That's when she told me about the men she had cheated and killed. It was horrible. It made me sick to my stomach, but that only made her madder. That's when she told me she killed Jeb. She had Lyman do it. He'd been shadowing Jeb for weeks just waiting for the perfect opportunity."

"Why was she poisoning the Judge?"

"She *hated* him. How could she, especially after he's been so good to me! Sometimes he treated me better than he treated Jeb. Sometimes he treated me better than my own mother did."

"I'm sure your mother loved you," Victoria said.

"No, she didn't. She told me so. She only wanted me because the Judge is leaving everything to me."

"Not your mother?"

377

"No, but she would be my guardian until I'm eighteen. She had to kill the Judge before my birthday if she was to control the money."

"And once the money was safely yours, you knew she might poison you because she would then inherit everything," Trinity suggested.

Kirby hung his head.

"Good God, Trinity, she wouldn't do anything like that!" Victoria exclaimed. "Not to her own son."

"My father was a cattle buyer from Chicago," Kirby explained. "He promised to marry Mother and take her back with him. She hated me because I represented the man who'd deserted her."

"How was she poisoning the Judge?" Victoria asked.

"She put arsenic in his coffee."

"But she drank the same coffee," Victoria said.

"She kept a special tin for him. Said it was better for his heart. She kept it behind the lard tin and forbade anyone to touch it. I found it last night and threw it out."

Victoria blanched.

"I put some coffee from that tin in the coffee container yesterday. I'd used all there was in the container to make some for the Judge and myself."

All three hurried to the kitchen. The container was empty.

"She drank the Judge's coffee," Victoria said, shock and horror reducing her voice to a barely audible thread. "I poisoned her."

Victoria fainted.

"The Judge will make a full recovery," Doctor Roundtree told Trinity and Victoria a few days later. "Apparently she had been giving him small doses over a long period of time."

"How much of this is going to come out?" Trinity inquired. The doctor looked to Victoria.

"Nothing," Victoria said. "Don't frown at me. You were ready to make a compromise a few days ago. Well, everyone else is ready now. The Judge doesn't want a scandal about Jeb or his wife. There's also Kirby to consider."

"Don't try to convince me. Just tell me what you've decided to do."

"I discussed it with the Judge and Kirby," Victoria said, making sure he knew it wasn't her doing alone, "and they agreed everyone will be told Myra died of heart trouble, probably from shock that one of the Tumbling T hands had attempted to kill me."

"And that's all?"

"That's all."

"I feel sorry for the judge, but you know, I feel sorriest for Kirby. He has nowhere to go."

"Not exactly."

Trinity's eyebrows went up. "I gather you've been busier than I thought."

"No, I just suggested the obvious."

"Apparently I'm not clever enough to see the obvious. Enlighten me."

"Kirby idolizes the Judge. He always has. And the Judge depends heavily on Kirby. He's said time and time again he doesn't know what he'd do without him."

"So you told the Judge to marry Kirby."

Victoria threw a pillow at Trinity. "I suggested he legally adopt Kirby. Kirby has been a Blazer in name; now he'll be one in his heart." Trinity just stared at her. "They're both without a family. They've lived together for eight years. They've grown to be very fond of each other. It only makes sense."

"You think it'll work?"

"Don't you?"

"Yes. It sounds like the perfect solution."

Victoria landed in his lap to collect her kiss of congratulations. She collected several more for good measure.

"Now what plans do you have for me?" Trinity gleefully asked.

"I suggest you marry me as quickly as you can. The Judge has agreed to officiate, and Uncle Grant will give me away."

"You little . . ."

Victoria put her finger to his lips. "Be careful what you say. I'll remember it forever."

". . . darling," Trinity finished. "Would this afternoon be soon enough?"

"Perfect. The hotel parlor is just the right size, and the Judge can be here any time after noon."

"Any more orders?"

"I think Ben ought to be your best man, and you ought to wear black. It makes you look so mysterious."

"It's also the death of my freedom."

Victoria gave him several mock scratches on the face and a very real punch to the middle. "You are a horrible man. You deserve to be married to a managing female."

"What are you going to wear? It's impossible to get a dress made by this afternoon."

Victoria giggled. "I'm going to wear that awful skirt and blouse I wore for the first week on the trail. You kidnapped me in it. Now you can marry me in it."

Chapter Twenty-eight

"Sydney!"

"Sydney Carlin Attmore," Trinity said.

"Sydney," Victoria repeated in accents of loathing. "You can't seriously expect me to call you by that sickening name."

"My mother did."

"I don't care. I couldn't do it and keep a straight face."

"You should try being named Sydney."

"You're no more a *Sydney* than I'm a *Petunia*," Victoria declared. "What would our sons think? Trinity at least has character. But Sydney!"

"Then call me Trinity."

"But it's not your name!"

"I don't care. You can call me George, Frank, even Attmore. I won't care as long as you call me something."

Victoria laughed. "I'll call you Trinity. You might be used to being called Tom, Dick, or Harry, but I can't think of you as anyone but Trinity. What were some of your other names?"

"Tom, Dick, and Harry."

"I'm serious. I want to know."

"Maybe I'll tell you someday, but not now."

"Why?"

"Because I want to forget that part of my life. There's not much there to be proud of."

"I think there is. There are probably a lot of things you don't want to remember just now, but they won't bother you so much a few years from now."

"Probably not."

"Anyway, I don't want you to wait until you forget too much."

"Why?"

"I'm not sure. I guess it's because there's a little bit of you in each of those names. I want to know everything about you. Maybe someday I'll go to all the places you've been and collect the bits."

"Some of the bits aren't very pleasant."

"I didn't expect they would be, but I don't want to miss a single one."

"The only bits that count are here, right now. The others belong to somebody I tried to be but never was."

"Are you sure?"

"Absolutely."

"Hmmmm. Sounds like a man trying to hide his secrets. I wonder if I should talk to Ben. I'll bet he knows some real juicy bits."

"You're the only juicy bit I have any interest in." Trinity picked her up and deposited her on the bed.

"Trinity you can't mean to . . ."

"I certainly do."

"But we're getting married in less than an hour."

"What better way to celebrate our union."

"People usually wait until *after* the ceremony for this celebration."

"Before and after is better."

Victoria gave up. She didn't mind letting him have things his way . . . as long as his way was her way as well.

PASSION BLAZES IN A ZEBRA HEARTFIRE!

COLORADO MOONFIRE (3730, $4.25/$5.50)
by Charlotte Hubbard

Lila O'Riley left Ireland, determined to make her own way in America. Finding work and saving pennies presented no problem for the independent lass; locating love was another story. Then one hot night, Lila meets Marshal Barry Thompson. Sparks fly between the fiery beauty and the lawman. Lila learns that America is the promised land, indeed!

MIDNIGHT LOVESTORM (3705, $4.25/$5.50)
by Linda Windsor

Dr. Catalina McCulloch was eager to begin her practice in Los Reyes, California. On her trip from East Texas, the train is robbed by the notorious, masked bandit known as Archangel. Before making his escape, the thief grabs Cat, kisses her fervently, and steals her heart. Even at the risk of losing her standing in the community, Cat must find her mysterious lover once again. No matter what the future might bring . . .

MOUNTAIN ECSTASY (3729, $4.25/$5.50)
by Linda Sandifer

As a divorced woman, Hattie Longmore knew that she faced prejudice. Hoping to escape wagging tongues, she traveled to her brother's Idaho ranch, only to learn of his murder from long, lean Jim Rider. Hattie seeks comfort in Rider's powerful arms, but she soon discovers that this strong cowboy has one weakness . . . marriage. Trying to lasso this wandering man's heart is a challenge that Hattie enthusiastically undertakes.

RENEGADE BRIDE (3813, $4.25/$5.50)
by Barbara Ankrum

In her heart, Mariah Parsons always believed that she would marry the man who had given her her first kiss at age sixteen. Four years later, she is actually on her way West to begin her life with him . . . and she meets Creed Deveraux. Creed is a rough-and-tumble bounty hunter with a masculine swagger and a powerful magnetism. Mariah finds herself drawn to this bold wilderness man, and their passion is as unbridled as the Montana landscape.

ROYAL ECSTASY (3861, $4.25/$5.50)
by Robin Gideon

The name Princess Jade Crosse has become hated throughout the kingdom. After her husband's death, her "advisors" have punished and taxed the commoners with relentless glee. Sir Lyon Beauchane has sworn to stop this evil tyrant and her cruel ways. Scaling the castle wall, he meets this "wicked" woman face to face . . . and is overpowered by love. Beauchane learns the truth behind Jade's imprisonment. Together they struggle to free Jade from her jailors and from her inhibitions.

Available wherever paperbacks are sold, or order direct from the Publisher. Send cover price plus 50¢ per copy for mailing and handling to Zebra Books, Dept. 4173, 475 Park Avenue South, New York, N.Y. 10016. Residents of New York and Tennessee must include sales tax. DO NOT SEND CASH. For a free Zebra/ Pinnacle catalog please write to the above address.